Libby Morgan: Reunion

For Judy
Enjoy!
Remember to Speak life!
Leah Zieber 2017

Leah A. Zieber

Libby Morgan: Reunion **By Leah A. Zieber**

Books may be purchased in quantity by contacting the publisher directly at
Zieber Quilts, Inc.
30290 Tradewater Ct
Temecula, California 92591
www.zieberquilts.com
email zieberquilts@gmail.com

Author: Leah A. Zieber http://zieberquilts.com
Cover Design: Jennifer Quinlan http://historicaleditorial.blogspot.com
Editor: Jennifer Quinlan http://historicaleditorial.blogspot.com
Interior Design: Create Space

ISBN-13: 9780990481607

ISBN-10: 0990481603

This book is dedicated to the man who told me my story was worth publishing without even reading it – I love you Gary!

To my kids, my family and friends – it took a great deal of your encouragement and support to write and publish this story. You were my sounding boards, mentors, readers and critics. Thank you from the bottom of my heart.

I met an exceptional person during this indie-undertaking and she became the editor who made me a better writer. Jennifer Quinlan, you rock!

Finally, Praise to God, who planted in me a desire to speak light and not compromise my story with darkness.

Main Characters

Elizabeth Jane Morgan (Libby) – b. 1842, Boston, Mass.

Mary Jane Abbot Morgan – b. 1822, England. Libby's mother, a seamstress and daughter of Captain Gerald and Caroline Abbott.

Thomas Alexander Morgan – b. 1822, Boston, Mass. Libby's father, a tailor and son of Margaret and Edward A. Montclief Morgan.

Margaret Jane Hammond Morgan (Mother Morgan) – b. 1800, England. Libby's paternal grandmother, wife (widow) of Edward A. Montclief Morgan. Renowned seamstress in London and Boston.

Edward Alexander Montclief Morgan – b. 1796, England, died in America. Libby's paternal grandfather; nephew and sole heir to Baron Montclief.

Captain Gerald Cephas Abbott – b. 1796, England. Libby's maternal grandfather, an English merchant ship captain; school friend of Edward A. Montclief Morgan.

Caroline Abbott – b. 1797, England. Libby's maternal grandmother, wife of Captain Abbott.

Ellen Morgan Randal (Aunt Ellen) – b. 1824, Boston, Mass. Widow of Albert Randal, daughter of Margaret Morgan, sister to Thomas Morgan, and mother of Albert and James Randal.

Albert Morgan Randal and James Alexander Randal – b. 1848, Boston, Mass. Twin first cousins to Libby and sons of Ellen Morgan Randal.

Baron Montclief – b. 1760, England, deceased. Uncle to Edward Alexander Montclief Morgan.

Baroness Montclief – b. 1779, England, deceased. Wife of Baron Montclief.

Finnian McAlister – b. 1840, America. Stow-away boy Libby meets on steamship.

Gertrude Tredwell – b. 1841, New York. Friend Libby meets on steamship during Atlantic Crossing.

Chapter 1

1855

Jostling along the deeply rutted road to Ashford was beginning to wear on Libby Morgan, and her irritation was starting to show itself on her young face. It had been a long coach ride from Boston, and though she was nearing her destination, she was quite tired of having her teeth rattled from the bumpy ride. She shifted in her seat, adjusted her skirt for the tenth time in as many minutes, and looked across the coach at her mother. She did not ask the question that tried to push itself from her lips because she had already asked it too many times in the past few hours. Instead, she let out a longer than acceptable sigh of boredom. Her mother, Mary Jane, flashed a disapproving look that Libby felt penetrate her skin despite being turned toward the window. Knowing she was pushing at the boundaries of her mother's patience, she tried shifting yet again in hopes of finding a more comfortable position turned even farther away from her mother's sharp stare.

Libby's grandfather, Captain Abbott, had graciously paid for a private coach to take the family to Connecticut for a visit with Aunt Ellen on Grandmother Morgan's farm, and the small coach was a more pleasant way to travel than by public coaches or by wagon. But the rainy spring had taken its toll on the roads, and the jarring ride was proving longer than Libby had expected. It had already taken nearly three full days and two sleep-disturbed nights to reach the outskirts of Ashford.

Now, tired, cranky and more than ready to make her destination, Libby glanced back at her mother and then over at Grandfather Abbott and gazed in amazement at how the two seemed undaunted by the long, uncomfortable ride.

Her mother spent the many hours in the coach patiently sewing on her patchwork, never missing a stitch as she pieced her bits of fabric together. Her grandfather had passed the time poring over the logs from his cargo ship, the *Arianna*, or sleeping, as he was just now. Libby could not fathom sleeping in such conditions; every time she relaxed enough to doze, a lurch of the coach would launch her from her seat, nearly throwing her to the floor. She marveled at her grandfather, fast asleep in the seat opposite, and surmised that his life as a sailor had honed his ability to roll with the motion and sleep soundly in difficult circumstances.

Bored from just watching the scenery pass the coach window, Libby had tried reading during this last leg of her trip, but the jarring of the coach made it impossible to hold her book still enough to read. She glanced back out the window. "Trees, trees, trees. Mother, there are so many trees!" Libby sighed. "How much longer do you suppose till we arrive in Ashford?" She couldn't help herself as the question slipped out.

"Elizabeth Jane," her mother rarely used her full name, and on this occasion Libby could tell that she had pushed her mother's patience to the end, "you really must learn to have some patience. I told you it was going to be a long journey." Handing Libby her tin with the fabric pieces, Mother added, "Why don't you sort my patches? It won't be much longer."

Libby's mother had spent the long ride sewing bits of fabric together into small units called blocks. Marveling at her skill, Libby had watched her fingers move quickly and tirelessly. It appeared to be an endless task, and Libby wondered how there would ever be enough of the small pieces to cover an entire bed. "I'm glad of our arrival today," announced her mother. "I am excited to show Ellen and Mother Morgan how many patches I have pieced. Perhaps we may have time to put the quilt top together while we visit." A new bed covering was a real treasure for the family, especially one made with the help of Mother Morgan, Libby's grandmother on her father's side.

Taking the tin grudgingly from her mother, Libby thought to herself, "Patience! How can I have so much patience? I've only lived twelve years, well, nearly thirteen, truth be told, and this journey requires much more patience than I could possibly muster in so short a number of years!" Libby kept her thoughts to herself as she looked at each of the patches her mother had made. She turned them over and admired the fine stitches and the selection of colors and fabrics. She was not skilled at sewing like her mother, and she was a bit disappointed with herself for not making more of an effort to learn.

Born in Boston, Libby was the daughter of a well-positioned tailor and fine seamstress. She was also the granddaughter of a merchant captain and had received the education suited to her status. Libby proved an excellent student in mathematics and literature but had not sought to develop the finer arts of the needle like most girls her age. She could mend a stocking or torn garment when needed, but turning bits of leftover fabric into a beautiful bed covering, or making a silk dress with pearl beading—well, that was more than simple sewing, and she couldn't even imagine the patience it would take to make something of that caliber.

"Your stitches are so tiny, Mother, how do you manage on such a bumpy road?" Libby glanced up to see her mother smile back. As she continued to examine the fine workmanship of her mother's sewing, she contemplated her parents' trade. Perhaps this visit to Mother Morgan's farm would provide the opportunity she needed to improve upon her underdeveloped sewing skills.

It was late in the afternoon on the third day when they finally arrived. As the coach rounded the corner and headed up the main road to the house, Libby could see the large red barn with cows in a nearby pasture. She waved excitedly in return to one offered by a farmhand. "Are you sure this is the right place, Mother?" Libby questioned. "I don't remember the house being so big." She thought the house seemed larger than the one in her memory, but it had been more than four years since her last visit, and her recollection was a bit hazy from so much time passing. A covered porch ran along one entire side of the house, and Libby had a flash of memory from her last visit, when she sat upon that very porch, fascinated by the fireflies in the early evening hours. "Yes, I remember now, this is the place!"

As the coach pulled into the yard, Mother Morgan emerged from the front door waving to the occupants of the coach, and Libby felt a tug at her heart with the sight of her. She was exactly as Libby remembered with her fading auburn hair pulled back tightly and her dress and apron impeccably clean and orderly. Her face, though wrinkled with age, was lovely, and her eyes were gentle and kind. Until just this moment, Libby had forgotten how much she loved her grandmother and missed her company in Boston. The coach slowed to a stop just as her two young cousins came bursting from the house, and Libby giggled to hear her Aunt Ellen shouting for the boys to get back from the horses as she followed on their heels.

She was quite disheveled from being confined to the coach for so long; with her dress front stained from lunch and her bonnet askew, Libby stepped out of the coach and nearly fell onto the coachman. Grandfather was stiff from the long ride but managed to straighten himself and place his hat squarely upon his head as he stepped out of the coach. Mother, though, had somehow managed to arrive as attractive as ever. Her beautiful chestnut hair was still arranged nicely, and her clothes were as fresh and crisp as the day they were washed. Libby looked admiringly at her mother then down at her own dress front. She was a bit embarrassed by the comparison and thought perhaps she should make more of an effort to stay neater. "I am, after all, nearly a grown woman!" she thought as she remembered her upcoming birthday.

The family was excited to see Libby and her mother and her grandfather. "The boys are so big!" was Libby's first thought. Her cousins, twin boys named James and Albert, had been babes toddling around in dresses when Libby had seen them last. They had nearly doubled in size, were full-fledged little boys, and talked nonstop. James reluctantly hugged Libby, but Albert exuberantly threw his arms around her and squeezed tightly. Libby croaked a bit from the tight squeeze but giggled as she hugged him back just as tightly and nearly lifted him off the ground.

"These boys have been so excited for your visit, Libby, dear!" Aunt Ellen explained as she hugged her niece. "They have asked repeatedly this past week just exactly when you and your grandfather would arrive." Libby glanced at her cousins to see them wrapped in her grandfather's arms. She was heartened to see the love they had for each other. Though he was not their grandfather, she could see that they loved him as if he were.

The family reacquainted themselves and caught up on the latest news from Boston and England as they enjoyed a tasty meal of Friar's Chicken, fresh biscuits, and a cup of cool, farm-fresh milk. As the exhaustion of her long journey began to set in, Libby found herself desperately trying to keep her eyes open. She tapped her mother's foot under the table to get her attention, then covered her mouth as she let out a rather long yawn. Mary, quick with the hint, excused herself and Libby to unpack, but before they left the room, Albert jumped from up from his seat, babbling on about how Libby simply must see the new calf before she retired for the night.

"Please, please do come, Coz," Albert begged. "Our calf is the most beautiful in Ashford, and twice as smart as any other."

"I guess a nice walk to the barn would be just fine," replied Libby politely. She didn't wish to disappoint her young cousins so early in her visit. She looked questioningly at her mother. "May I go? I'm sure it will feel good to walk some after sitting for three days in that dusty coach."

"All right, then," responded Mother with a smile.

"Take my paisley shawl, dear," said Mother Morgan, gesturing toward the peg by the back door. "I feel a chill this eve."

The sun was just low enough in the sky to cast long shadows, and the air was cool but not yet crisp. Albert guided Libby to the barn at the bottom of the hill with James bashfully trailing along behind. He chattered on about the new calf's long lashes and soft nose and how the family had tried to find a name that suited the new beast. He told how James had insisted she be named "Rose" after the beautiful flowers in Mother Morgan's garden. As they approached the barn, the smell of hay was sweet and new to Libby's senses. She was more accustomed to the salty smell of sea air and the sooty smoke from the city rooftops of Boston.

Rose was a beautiful dun-brown calf with long eyelashes and a soft, dark nose just as Albert had described. "Rose seems a proper name for her," Libby told James after first inspection. James smiled with pride. She scratched the young calf behind the ears and patted her neck while the mother cow sniffed her dress and sized up the visitors. Touching the calf's soft nose and feeling the tickle of her whiskers gave Libby a feeling of anxiety coupled with familiarity. She had not had much contact with large farm animals, and it brought out a bit of the same fear she felt when standing near carriage horses; but the soft calf with long whiskers made her think of her own pet left with her father back in Boston.

Princess was Libby's very own and very fluffy white cat. Grandfather had brought the kitten home from the docks one rainy spring evening when Libby was eight years old. He told them how he had nearly stepped on it while getting into his coach and how the poor creature was drenched and shivering from the rain, and obviously starving. The kitten was all skin and bones with extra long whiskers and large eyes full of curiosity. Libby's mother had protested at first, but Grandfather insisted that Libby have some sort of playmate since she didn't have any siblings. Libby's father thought the cat would help to keep the mice out of his shop. And so Princess came to be Libby's playmate and dear companion.

Libby noticed the wide eyes of the mother cow standing just a few feet away and could see her concern building as Albert bounced around her calf and grabbed the poor creature's tail. She thought it wise to leave the beasts to their evening meal and so she asked if she could see the garden. James was first to respond this time. "Oh yes, Coz, do come and see. It is a most beautiful place." As he started out the door ahead of the others, Albert commented to Libby that the garden was James's favorite place on the farm.

"He knows many of the plant names by heart," Albert said. "And he loves to help Mother Morgan tend the vegetable garden. Mother says that he is sure to be a farmer, but I would much rather be a sailor like Grandfather Abbott and sail on the ocean in a big boat!"

At this, Libby chuckled a bit, "They are called ships, Albert. Boats are much smaller vessels." She spoke with authority as she addressed him.

"Boats, ships, they are all the same to me. As long as I get to be out on the ocean with nothing but water as far as the eye can see. Just imagine, not seeing land for days and days, meeting pirates and scoundrels. It sounds so exciting!" Albert looked dreamy and began to whistle a tune, but James just rolled his eyes.

Libby reflected on the ocean, thinking about her home in Boston not far from the waterfront. She would often look out to sea and wonder where Grandfather might be sailing. She wondered about pirates, too, and if they might harm him. To Libby, a sailor's life was more frightening than exciting. "The ocean is a dangerous place, Albert, and one which demands respect." She spoke firmly but knew her words fell upon deaf ears as Albert sang his sailor shanty and danced his best jig.

As they made their way to the garden on the other side of the house, Libby could smell the sweet scent of the blossoms before she could see them. It was mid-May, and many spring flowers were blooming already. The lilacs were thick and aromatic. They hung over the garden fence in large purple clusters exploding with fragrance. She could see the daffodils on the far side of the garden lined up under the crab apple tree. They looked like little yellow soldiers guarding a budding green giant. The roses were just getting ready to bloom, but a few early blossoms had already appeared, and Libby felt the silky petals as she walked past. They did feel just as soft as the calf's nose.

She listened to James point to and name each of the flowers and plants as he passed them. "Impressive!" she said to Albert as James chattered on about what each plant was used for in the kitchen or what medicinal purpose it held. Libby could see James come alive in the garden and thought he seemed a different boy altogether. She smiled and acknowledged him with each comment while Albert looked on impatiently and rolled his eyes when James tried to pronounce a particularly difficult plant name. Nearing the back gate, Libby noticed a nest in the crab apple tree. Two birds were hopping in and out of the nest and chirping frantically. She stopped to watch the crazed little pair when she noticed a striped orange tail twitching behind a bush at the base of the fence. "Oh, Albert!" She pointed to the bush and cried, "Don't let it eat the chicks."

Albert quickly leapt to grab the cat just as it was ready to jump into the tree. "Ginger, you mean ol' gal!" Albert scolded. "You leave those birdies alone now!" Clutching the ginger cat close to his chest, Albert made his way out of the back garden gate and headed toward the house.

Libby followed close behind with James, now returned to his quiet, bashful self. Looking back at the garden, Libby could see the birds getting back to the business of mending their nest now that the predator had been removed from the premises. The sun had set below the horizon, and the sky was turning lovely shades of pink and orange. She slowly took a deep breath, and her senses were inundated with the smells of fresh grasses and trees and a slight undercurrent of barn animals. As she let out her breath, she became aware of just how tired her body was feeling from the three-day journey, yet her mind was so excited to be in Connecticut she seemed to notice every detail of her new surroundings.

Back at the house, the table had been cleared and the dishes washed. Grandfather had retired to his room while Mother Morgan had moved to the parlor to finish the binding on her most recent quilt. Libby knew very little of her grandmother's life, but what she did know was that Mother Morgan was renowned for her sewing skill throughout Windham County. Libby's father had told her how Mother Morgan had grown up in England, where she and her sisters had learned to use a needle by the age of five. As young women, they had mastered their skills making fine garments and bed hangings for a prosperous family. While Mother Morgan had excelled at making clothing, her real passion was making decorative bed coverings and curtains. Without the limitations of fashionable clothing styles, Mother Morgan could set her imagination free to make her counterpanes, and the results were quite handsome.

Using the leftover pieces from bed curtains and clothing she was hired to make, Mother Morgan had made several special quilts of her own. One of her quilts was made in the chintz-cutout style. Arranged like the expensive palampores from India, the counterpane was

9

comprised of birds and flowers, branches, and other foliage cut from their original fabrics and sewn to a plain piece of white fabric forming a large tree in the center. The borders around three sides were more cut-out images of the same fabrics with an intertwining vine. Each image was meticulously embellished with fine embroidery stitches. Mother Morgan called it her "tree of life," and she only used it for special family members. As the only granddaughter in the family, Libby felt sure this counterpane would be on the bed she and her mother would share during their visit.

Two other quilts Mother Morgan had made were the ones she called her lovely "framed angels." These two nearly identical quilts had chintz panel centers of beautiful flower bouquets that were surrounded by many different patchwork borders. They were both finished with lapis-blue chintz borders. Libby's mother had once explained that these quilts held special meaning for Mother Morgan. Her first two children had been girls—twins that had died shortly after their birth. Mother Morgan had made the two quilts within the first year after the death of her daughters—it was her way of keeping busy and dealing with her grief. When she had finished the quilts, it gave Mother Morgan something tangible to see and touch, something special to hold and to help her remember the two beautiful little angel girls.

But the most prized quilt made by Mother Morgan was her mosaic garden spread. Libby had seen this treasure only once before because it was always put away in the blanket chest. Mother had told Libby that it was a bed cover fit for a king and that Mother Morgan only brought it out for her most special visitors. From what Libby could remember, the quilt was made from small hexagonal pieces of block-printed French and English cotton fabrics that had been meticulously cut for their unique designs and then sewn together in rings of colors that looked like flowers. The flower units were set apart from one another with plain white linen hexagons that created a path among the flowers, just like in a garden. Libby wanted to see the beautiful mosaic quilt again, and she secretly hoped Grandfather Abbott would be the royal guest for whom Mother Morgan saved her most prized possession.

Ready to retire, Libby and her Mother went to the far end of the house where they would share a room during their visit, and to Libby's surprise, it was Mother Morgan's own room they would share. Her grandmother had moved some things to Aunt Ellen's bedroom, and Grandfather had taken the boys' bedroom. Albert and James would sleep on pallets in the kitchen near the fireplace.

When she approached the room, Libby stopped short in the doorway as the sight on the bed took her breath away. There was the beautiful hexagon mosaic quilt she had seen only one other time. She stood frozen, staring in amazement at the beauty of the quilt; it looked so like the garden she had just visited with its vivid hues and brightly colored flowers. She hugged herself and laughed out loud. "What is it, dear?" Mother asked. "Why so pleased?"

"I'm royalty!" Libby announced with a wide grin. "I simply must be because Mother Morgan was saving her best quilt for only the most special visitors. You said so yourself. And here it is, on *my* bed!"

"It is a rare treat indeed," Libby's mother replied, "and an invitation of sorts. I'm sure Mother Morgan would love to teach you to make your own quilt, if you were interested in learning." Libby's mother offered her an encouraging smile, and Libby paused a moment to consider making such a bed covering. She though about the time necessary to make something so intricate and wondered if she had the patience it would take to complete such an undertaking. Her rudimentary sewing skills would certainly need to be improved upon, and the thought of it was making her even more tired. She quickly decided her considerations would have to wait until tomorrow; the day had finally caught up with Libby, and her heavy eyes were finding it difficult to focus on the quilt. She let out a wide-mouthed yawn, which she forgot to cover, and found her mother's eyes upon her as she turned, mouth agape, to get her nightdress from the trunk. She quickly averted her face but did not utter an apology; tonight she was just too tired to care about manners.

Mother and daughter silently readied themselves for sleep, both looking forward to the comfort of a quiet home and a cozy bed covered in the magnificence of Mother Morgan's garden spread!

Chapter 2

*L*ibby woke to the sound of chirping birds, and for a few moments, she lay quietly in Grandmother's bed listening to the peeps, squeaks, and squawks just outside the bedroom window. Back home in Boston, the hustle and bustle of the city streets and yelling from the nearby docks would have drowned out the morning birds, but here in Connecticut, their ruckus could be heard quite clearly. As she lay listening to the unfamiliar sounds of the farm, the luxury of her grandmother's soft, cozy bed begged Libby to tarry longer, but the clattering of dishes emanating from the other side of the house prompted her to get up and get moving. The kitchen was bustling with the business of breakfast when she finally arrived, and Libby felt a bit guilty for lounging so long.

In Boston, she was responsible for getting up first and starting the kettle. Mother had showed her how to bank the fire each evening so that the embers were still hot in the morning. With just a few pieces of dry kindling and a gentle blow, the fire would crackle and pop to life again. Libby would get the fire going and put the water kettle on for tea before anyone in the house was awake. This morning, however, she was the last to arrive in the kitchen. Mother Morgan was setting the kettle on for tea, Aunt Ellen was up to her elbows in flour and dough, and Mother had put the pieces of pork on to fry. The warm kitchen smelled wonderful, and Libby could feel her stomach rumble in anticipation of her morning meal.

"Libby, darling, you're up at last," said Aunt Ellen with a kind smile. "Did you sleep well?"

Libby flushed slightly at the thought of being the last out of bed. "Delightfully," she replied, rolling up her sleeves. "Is there something I can be of help with, Auntie?"

"Do be a good girl and help the twins fetch the eggs," Aunt Ellen replied. "I fear they have run off without the basket. It's just there, by the back door."

Libby snatched up the egg basket and set out the door in search of Albert and James. The morning was warmer than she expected, and she realized at once that she would not need the shawl. She set it on the porch, and with basket in hand she headed for the barn. Albert was just getting ready to drop from the hayloft onto an unsuspecting James when Libby entered through the large barn door. "Look out, James!" called Libby, and James moved just as Albert let go.

Albert hit the floor and rolled through some muck from the animals. James and Libby both burst into laughter, but Albert just scowled at his brother. He stood and tried to brush the muck from his breeches, but it only made the spot worse. "Mother Morgan is going to tan my hide if she sees my breeches, they were just washed fresh yesterday," moaned Libby's young cousin.

"Why don't you run down to the creek and get them wet?" suggested James with a wry smile. "She'll think you fell in and feel sorry for you."

"No she won't!" Albert hollered back. "She'll just tan my hide harder for being down at the creek! You know we're not supposed to be down there alone. You're just trying to get me into trouble, James!" Libby considered James's smug expression and wondered why he wasn't more upset at Albert for trying to jump on him from the hayloft. As an only child, Libby often pondered what it would be like to have a brother or sister around, and from the looks of things, she could see it must surely be fun and maddening at the same time.

"We had better gather the eggs," Libby suggested as a diversion from the situation. "Your breeches aren't that soiled. Perhaps if we don't say anything, no one will notice. But they will notice if we take too much longer getting the eggs."

James mentioned that the hens' new favorite place to lay eggs was on the back side of the barn near the sheep pen, so Libby suggested they start there first. They headed in the direction of the bleating sheep, and within a few moments, they had found a gold mine of fresh, brown eggs. Not pleased to find their morning's work taken right out from underneath them, the hens flapped and clucked as the children reached for the eggs. One even pecked Albert's hand as he reached beneath to take her clutch, and Albert swatted the hen on its backside. "Shoo!" he shouted and swiped at her as she tried to protect her eggs. Libby could see his mood had been darkened by the muck on his breeches and thought to chide him for the way he treated the innocent creature, but she decided it was best to leave the situation alone.

Their basket brimming with freshly laid eggs, Libby and the twins headed back to the kitchen. "There you are!" scolded Aunt Ellen as they entered through the back door. She scrutinized the boys up and down and added, "I hope you haven't gotten dirty; Reverend Masterson is stopping by after the morning meal." Libby saw Albert scamper out of the kitchen at the mention of the word "dirty." James maintained his smug expression as he brought more wood for the fire.

Grandfather entered the kitchen, teapot in hand, in search of more tea. "Let me get that for you, Captain," said Mother Morgan as she reached for the kettle.

"Nonsense, Margaret, I am completely capable of filling a teapot. On ship, I often make my own tea. Truth be told, I much prefer it to the watered down version made by my cabin boy." But Mother Morgan would have no man in her kitchen. She took the teapot from the captain with a smile and handed him a basket of warm biscuits for the table. With a full teapot, the warm biscuits, some jam, and a platter of fried pork, Libby and her family settled in to a delightful breakfast.

"So Libby, darling, I heard from a little birdie you're having a birthday tomorrow." Mother Morgan smiled as she continued, "Were you hoping for something special?"

Libby blushed slightly at the question. Of course she was hoping for something special; she had spent the entire year dreaming of a quill and ink and paper all her own, but should she be so bold as to speak it? She thought for just a moment and decided it best to keep her wish to herself. "Why, Mother Morgan, I thought you had already given me my birthday gift," Libby responded with an honest smile. "You have allowed me to be your royal guest and sleep in your own bed beneath your most prized treasure. I was certain that must be my gift."

Mother Morgan straightened and smiled broadly. "I'm pleased you noticed, child. My garden spread is truly a treasure, and I am glad to share it with you. I was hoping to get you started on a treasure of your own this visit."

"Do we get to have a celebration in honor of Cousin Libby?" interrupted Albert as he rubbed his tummy and licked his lips. "Will we have a cake?" Libby laughed knowing her birthday cake would bring her cousin great joy.

"How old will you be, Coz?" inquired James.

"I am to be thirteen," Libby responded proudly.

"Thirteen years old!" exclaimed Mother Morgan. "My goodness, Libby, you are nearly grown. It's high time you learned the finer crafts of the needle, child."

"Oh, Niece, you will love learning to sew from Mother Morgan," Aunt Ellen interjected. "She is a superior teacher and very patient indeed." Libby noticed her grandfather nodding his head with Aunt Ellen's statement.

"She is also the most skilled seamstress on the whole of the Eastern Seaboard," Grandfather announced. Mother Morgan seemed to flush at the compliment, and she fanned herself with her napkin, "Oh, Captain Abbott, you are too kind."

"I simply state the facts," said Grandfather to Libby, then he looked at Mother Morgan and said, "There are none as skilled when it comes to sewing. Your reputation and talents are known on both continents, Margaret."

"Libby, dear," her mother asked tentatively, "are you interested in learning to sew?" Her mother and father had both grown up in families that excelled in the art of sewing, and it was, in fact, their family's trade, but neither wanted to force their interests on their only daughter. Although they knew that every girl must learn the basics of mending and sewing for a family, they had also encouraged Libby in reading, writing, and mathematics from an early age. They wanted to give her every opportunity to find her own way in life.

Libby glanced around the table at her family as she contemplated the question. Her eyes came to rest on Mother Morgan. "Can you teach me to make a beautiful garden spread like the one on my bed?" she asked of her grandmother.

"But of course, child," responded Mother Morgan. "And we will start right after your birthday celebration tomorrow. Today, however, we will enjoy a visit from the Reverend Masterson and his new family. They shall be here shortly, and we really must tidy up."

"What business brings the reverend today? He rarely visits without some sort of business venture to suggest," Libby's mother asked. Libby found herself trying to imagine this "reverend" character with his many business proposals for the family to consider. His name seemed familiar, but she could not put a face to it.

"He has a trade proposition for Captain Abbott, I believe," replied Mother Morgan. "He was quite excited to hear that the captain was visiting this May. And he is bringing his new wife, Letticia, and her girls as well as his younger brother, John." Mother Morgan gave Aunt Ellen a smile with the mention of John Masterson, and Aunt Ellen turned crimson and began busying herself with clearing the table. Libby noticed the exchange and wondered what it was all about.

It had been six years since Aunt Ellen had been widowed. Her husband, Albert Senior, had been lost at sea when his ship got caught in a hurricane and he fell overboard. After two years of praying he would return to her and her twin babies, Ellen and Mother Morgan relocated to the small farm in Ashford, hoping the change of scenery would improve Ellen's disposition. Though they were not wealthy, the two women were secure enough in their fortunes to hire the overseer and hands needed to work the farm.

Libby couldn't remember seeing Aunt Ellen so out of sorts before. She seemed to be excited and uncomfortable all at the same time, and a funny smile lingered on her lips. Libby had a notion that today's visit from the Mastersons would likely be very revealing.

After breakfast and following the morning chores, the family retired to the parlor to await the expected guests.

Libby was seated in a chair near the door reading the book she had brought from Boston. Her attention was directed away from her book when she noticed the largest pair of shoes she had ever seen walk in through the door. "That man has the biggest feet I've ever seen!" Libby thought to herself and very nearly spoke it aloud when Reverend Masterson entered the room. He was so tall he had to duck when he entered through the parlor door, and when he took off his hat, his jet-black hair stuck out in all directions. His wrinkled jacket and unkempt hair seemed to contrast greatly with the picture of perfection seen in the woman and girls who followed on his heels. The young ladies looked like fresh spring flowers with their beautiful silk dresses, tidy, coiffed hair, and bonnets decorated with colorful ribbons and bows. Libby watched as the girls curtsied to Grandfather Abbott, as did Mrs. Masterson, and he bowed graciously in return then shook Reverend Masterson's hand. "Good morning, sir," the Reverend greeted eagerly. "It is good to see you in such fine health. I had hoped to meet with you in Boston last summer, but alas, I was otherwise engaged." He smiled to his wife and continued, "As you can see, I have newly married and acquired a family in one fell swoop."

"A fine family it is, sir. I was otherwise engaged last summer as well, Mr. Masterson. I spent several months in Glasgow visiting relations and bringing my son current on the affairs of an old business venture we are reviving."

Mother Morgan greeted the ladies and invited them to the lawn for some refreshments so the gentlemen could speak privately in the parlor. "Letticia, dear," Mother Morgan began as she led the ladies to the lawn, "I'm sure you remember my daughter-in-law, Mary Morgan. I believe you became acquainted several summers ago when she visited us here in Ashford. And this is her daughter, Elizabeth Jane." Libby curtsied politely to the guests and offered her best smile.

"I'm so very pleased to see you again, Mary. And what a handsome dress, such fine craftsmanship, to be certain," Letticia replied in a formal tone more fitting that of an aristocrat than a country parishioner's wife. "And may I introduce my daughters, Sophie—" here she paused and gestured first to her eldest, then to her youngest, "—and Catherine." The introductions were exceedingly more formal than Libby was accustomed to.

With the niceties behind them, the ladies were free to talk about the latest news and fashion from Boston and New York. Sophie

Masterson was quite attentive to the conversation, especially after she heard Libby's mother was a seamstress for some of the wealthier Bostonian families. Libby could tell at once that Sophie was a bit of a socialite and not at all interested in the conversations a thirteen-year-old girl had to offer, so she decided to turn her attentions to Catherine. From the looks of all the fidgeting and rearranging of her skirt, Libby thought perhaps Catherine was as uninterested in the conversation about fashion as she was, so she asked Catherine to join her for a walk in the garden.

"Oh yes, that would be just lovely," Catherine said loud enough for the others to hear and then whispered quietly to Libby, "I simply must get away from this silly conversation." They excused themselves politely and headed across the lawn.

On the way to the garden, Catherine begged Libby's pardon and offered in explanation that her sister was simply consumed with talk of the new dresses she wanted, or how the latest bonnets from London were so much prettier than their simple ones from New York. "It is the dullest conversation, to be sure," proclaimed Catherine. Libby felt that Catherine was more sensible than her older sister. She had an easy, friendly manner that made dialogue simple and straightforward. She liked her immediately.

When they reached the garden gate, Libby saw a rider approaching on horseback. "That will be Uncle John," Catherine commented. She wore a knowing smile and giggled, "Did you know he is in love with your Aunt Ellen?"

The question took Libby aback at first, then, remembering what had transpired in the kitchen that morning, she absentmindedly said, "I thought something was different about her, I just didn't know it was love," Libby's comment was more a spoken thought than a response to Catherine's question.

"Then she returns the affection?" Catherine prodded.

Caught off guard and realizing she had spoken her thoughts aloud, Libby stuttered, "Um, well, she didn't actually *say* she loved John Masterson, but she does walk around all day with a silly expression on her face." This made Catherine laugh out loud. Libby's inexperience with courtship was evident from her comments, and she felt for a moment that Catherine's laugh was directed at her immaturity.

"He is coming this day to ask for her hand," Catherine informed with a cunning smile. "Will she say yes, do you suppose?" she added more casually but still intent on the answer.

Quick to see that Catherine's questions were a fishing expedition of sorts, Libby did not reply immediately. The idea of Aunt Ellen being married to anyone other than Uncle Albert was strange. She thought about her uncle and tried to remember the time when he was still alive. He was a handsome man, with a reddish beard and sea-green eyes, she remembered that much. And he was a happy man—of that she was sure, for she still remembered the tune he whistled at night by the fire. Aunt Ellen and Uncle Albert had lived just two streets over from Libby's home in Boston. The families spent a great deal of time together—particularly when Uncle Albert was away at sea with Grandfather Abbott. Libby remembered how much in love Aunt Ellen and Uncle Albert had been. Though she'd been very young, she could recognize their happiness together, just as she knew the happiness and love her own parents shared. She thought about how hard it must be to lose a husband so dearly loved. And now, with this latest news of John Masterson, she wondered if Aunt Ellen had forgotten Uncle Albert.

Catherine cleared her throat and shuffled her dress loud enough to draw Libby from her own thoughts. "I guess we shall see," was all Libby could think to say in a pinch. She did not intend to be impolite, but she was confused about the situation and wasn't sure about her Aunt Ellen's feeling for John Masterson.

However, one thing was quite clear to Libby: Catherine was obviously digging for information. Her own ignorance had already provided the girl with gossip, so she made a mental note to be more discreet around her new friend. In an effort to change the conversation, she suggested, "Perhaps we should join the others."

Chapter 3

Handsome was the best description for John Masterson. He was not as tall as his older brother, but his hair was the same jet-black and his eyes were crystal blue. He tipped his hat to the girls in the garden as he passed on his way to the front of the house. Catherine smiled broadly and waved in reply; Libby simply stood and looked at him. Her feelings about this stranger were mixed. It was certain John Masterson would ask for Aunt Ellen's hand, and for that Libby was excited. Yet she could not help but feel that she and Aunt Ellen had somehow betrayed Uncle Albert.

The girls left the garden and joined the rest of the family. Albert and James were standing on either side of John Masterson's dapple-gray gelding, holding the reins and looking up at him with awe and respect. Libby thought they seemed quite happy to see Mr. Masterson, and she found it a little unsettling to see them so comfortable with this stranger. He was a commanding figure of a man, but when he greeted Libby, she sensed a gentleness of character and immediately felt at ease. "You must be the Libby I have heard so much about." Mr. Masterson bowed graciously toward Libby and smiled broadly. "Pleased to meet you, sir." Libby curtsied in response and then went to stand next to her mother, feeling shier than normal with this guest who seemed already a part of the family.

Aunt Ellen came out of the house smiling such as Libby had not seen before today. John Masterson removed his hat and bowed before Ellen.

He took her hand and kissed it softly as Aunt Ellen curtsied deeply and blushed. Libby was embarrassed by the exchange of affection. She watched as Aunt Ellen smiled and touched her hand to her own lips when he released it. "You look lovely, Ellen," John greeted. "How have you been these past weeks?"

Ellen and John spoke together quietly before the rest of the adults joined them. Grandfather Abbott and Reverend Masterson had brought more chairs out to the lawn for the adults while the young girls spread a blanket out to sit upon. Everyone was together under the shade of the red maple tree enjoying tea when John Masterson turned to Mother Morgan and asked the much-anticipated question. "Mrs. Morgan." He cleared his throat and Libby thought his once-commanding personality seemed so ill at ease at this moment. He continued, "I have come this day to ask for your Ellen's hand in marriage. I have hoped these past months that she would consent to becoming my wife, and as she has newly agreed, I would ask now for your blessing."

Libby watched as her grandmother studied John Masterson without reply or expression. Her tone was not harsh nor was it overly accommodating; she simply turned to Ellen and asked, "Do you return the affections of this gentleman, Ellen?" Her question was direct and unmistakable. She would not give her blessing for a loveless marriage. The exchange seemed overly formal to Libby.

"It is with a joyful heart that I say I do, Mother," Ellen responded with a look of affection toward John Masterson. But that didn't seem to be enough for Mother Morgan to give an immediate blessing, and Libby wondered why she paused so long before asking her next question.

"And are you prepared, sir, to take on *full* responsibility for this family?" Mother Morgan looked toward the twins sitting on the blanket, their faces intent upon the outcome of the question. She narrowed her eyes and observed his response sharply. Libby had not even considered the implications of the twins, and she barely had time to think about it before he answered.

"I can assure you, Madam," he responded with an honest smile at James and Albert, "that I shall give this family more than just my name and my fortune. I shall give each of them all of my love and affection until the end of my days."

With his statement, James and Albert sat up taller than usual and grinned at one another.

"And what of the farm, sir?" Mother Morgan asked this next question for more than the obvious reason. "I am informed that you take residence in Hartford with your parents. Will you continue to do so?" Libby was again taken aback; there were so many circumstances she had not even contemplated with regard to her aunt's proposal.

Mr. Masterson was ready for this question. He offered his gentle smile and responded sincerely, "We would live as *you* desire, Mrs. Morgan, for Ellen could not bear to leave her beloved mother, and I should not ask you to leave your home. Here in Ashford or there in Hartford, there is no difference to me as long as I am not parted from Ellen again." Ellen gave him an encouraging smile and addressed her mother.

"I do not wish to be parted from you, Mother, for you have been my rock these past six years. We would stay here with you, if you choose not to leave Ashford. No matter the place, we both want you with us."

Mother Morgan flushed at the outpouring of love, and Libby saw her countenance immediately soften. "I do give my blessing with a joyful heart. Here or Hartford, it matters not to me, as long as we are together."

Libby's mother was the first to offer her congratulations. She hugged Ellen closely and whispered, "Dear Sister, I have dreamed of the day I would see you smile in love again. I can see he is a good man who loves you dearly."

Grandfather Abbott was shaking hands with John and expressing his congratulations while Letticia Masterson was offering her opinions for a June wedding, and everyone was smiling and hugging and chattering on about the upcoming nuptials. Everyone, that is, except Libby. She sat alone on the blanket under the tree, scratching the ears of the ginger cat, who had wandered into her lap. She again remembered her Uncle Albert.

Aunt Ellen joined Libby on the blanket. "That old Ginger is sweet, isn't she?" prompted Ellen.

"When she's not eating little birdies, she is," responded Libby with a slight smile and a gentle rub under the cat's chin.

"Is there something bothering you, Niece? You seem preoccupied with your thoughts."

Libby looked at Aunt Ellen's face. She could see the happiness reflected in her eyes. There was no denying the fact that Ellen loved John. "I'm just confused, Auntie…" was all she could croak out without crying, "…but all is well." She didn't want to put a damper on the joyous occasion, and so decided not to continue.

Aunt Ellen took hold of Libby's hand and asked, "What is it, dear? What troubles you?"

Tears were beginning to form in Libby's eyes. She remembered the happy times Aunt Ellen and Uncle Albert had spent with her family. She had seen her aunt's great grief when Albert was lost at sea; Aunt Ellen had lived for weeks with Libby's family until Mother Morgan came to take care of her and the babies. She could not reconcile how Aunt Ellen could now be so happy and in love with another man.

"It's a funny thing about your heart," Aunt Ellen spoke as though she knew Libby's thoughts. "When it comes to love, there is always room for more."

Libby gave her a confused look and asked, "What do you mean?"

26

"Think of a mother, Libby, who has a child she loves dearly. She is certain she couldn't possibly love another as much as she loves this child. And for a few years, she is happy and full of love for the babe as it grows. But illness strikes, and the child is lost; the mother is heartbroken." At this, Aunt Ellen looked off into the field and paused for a sad moment. Then she continued, "She is certain she will never love another. But fate has other ideas, and soon she has another child. To her surprise, she finds that there is indeed more love in her heart for her new child, and she is happy again."

"Has she forgotten the first child?" asked Libby, referring more to Uncle Albert than the fictitious child in the story.

"Never in a million years," replied Ellen with a knowing smile. "She could never forget her first child and the love she shared with him. And yet, here is her new child, so different and yet so similar to the other. She loves the new child in a way she thought she never would love again. And she is happy again, too. The mother thinks on her first child with fond memories, and honors those memories by living her life to the fullest and not pining away for the love she lost."

"I *am* happy for your new love with Mr. Masterson, Aunt Ellen," said Libby sorrowfully. "It's just that I never want to forget Uncle Albert, and I am afraid that I will now that Mr. Masterson has become your new love."

"I can't see how you could ever forget him, Niece," Ellen said with a tear in her eye. "Simply cast your eyes upon Albert Junior and you will see your uncle. For I have never seen a son more the likeness of his own father as young Albert. He is the incarnation of your Uncle Albert, body and spirit." Libby looked toward Albert Junior and realized the truth in Aunt Ellen's words. His ruddy complexion and dancing green eyes were that of his father's. Then she remembered her conversation with Albert Junior in the garden the evening before and how he longed to sail upon the ocean. *A sailor's heart, just like his father,* she thought. He was wild and happy and full of life. And when he cocked his head and glanced back at Libby, a shudder ran through her body, for she felt sure it was Uncle Albert who had just smiled at her. She seemed to understand now how a person could love more than just once in their lifetime, and she felt sure that Uncle Albert would not be forgotten—he would live on through his sons.

Chapter 4

*L*ibby was not the last to enter the kitchen the next day. She was, in fact, the first. She rose before the dawn, too anxious to remain in bed a moment longer. Today was her birthday, her favorite day of the year. Throughout the year, she looked forward to this day with great anticipation. And each year, she arose earlier than the year before. From the looks of the sky outside, Libby figured it must be around five o'clock. The birds were just beginning to rise and forage for an early breakfast, and as she looked out the back door she heard the unfamiliar screech of a barn owl on its return from a night of hunting. She saw the large silhouette of the bird make its way inside the roof of the barn, and she told herself she must remember to ask James about it later for she was certain he would know about the creature.

Libby stirred the embers, got a nice fire going, and was just filling the kettle when Mother Morgan walked into the kitchen. She was still wearing her nightdress and robe, blinking and yawning and trying to wake up when she noticed Libby with the kettle in hand. "My goodness!" she exclaimed. "You're up rather early this morning. What wakes you, child?"

"I like mornings, Mother Morgan. It's a quiet and peaceful time of day. It's my job at home to get the fire going and start the kettle. And I like to watch the sun rise over the ocean and count the gulls as they make their way to the ships to forage for their breakfasts." Libby set the kettle on the stove then moved to the table where Mother Morgan was sitting.

"With all the excitement of the wedding proposal and guests yesterday, I hope you have not forgotten about today." Mother Morgan smiled and patted Libby's head as she had done when she was a very small child. The familiarity of the gesture comforted Libby, and she was happy to be in the company of her grandmother again.

Libby glanced rather sheepishly at her grandmother. "I was hoping *everyone else* didn't forget," she said honestly.

"I can assure you child, I am as excited for your special day as you must be. I have longed to have a young lady around with which to share my gifts. Your cousins are about as interested in sewing as they are in learning to read and write." She gave Libby a wry smile and continued, "We will have a wonderful time this summer teaching you to sew." She reached for the tea safe and began filling the pot. "But before we begin our day, I must offer you my most heartfelt blessings on your birthday." She turned to Libby and gave her an honest hug and a kiss on the cheek. "I have been wondering what type of cake you would like for your birthday?" she added.

Libby gave the question great regard. Deciding upon a birthday cake only happened once a year, and she didn't want to rush her choice. She thought about her favorites; honey cake was one of the best, but gingerbread—ooh, gingerbread, now that was good. She remembered how the cake was sweet and spicy at the same time. She had had gingerbread for five of her birthday cakes. She thought about asking for the honey, but remembering how delicious the gingerbread smelled when it baked, she asked, "Mother Morgan, do you have what is needed to make a gingerbread cake?"

"Well, let's see, shall we?" Mother Morgan replied as she reached for her book of recipes. She began speaking out loud, "Flour, butter, a grated nutmeg, ginger, sugar, three small spoons of pearl ash dissolved in milk, and four eggs. Yes, I think we can manage that. Would you like to press the top? I have some lovely presses." Mother Morgan moved to the corner cupboard in the kitchen. From the bottom drawer, she pulled out a rather large wooden box.

Libby was immediately curious about what was inside. She scooted closer to Mother Morgan and looked around the side to see the contents. Among the folds of a cotton cloth were presses of every shape and size. There were many smaller stamps for adding decorations to the top of butter. These were carved of wood and were circular in shape. As Mother Morgan emptied the box, she handed each press to Libby and watched her expressions.

Libby took time to notice each of the molds and stamps, turning them over in her hand to see all sides. Some of the images were wonderful and unique—her favorite butter mold was the one with two acorns and oak leaves. She knew the acorn was a symbol of luck, and she imagined how all her butter could be lucky with this stamp and never spoil. As they got to the bottom of the box, Mother Morgan pulled out a larger mold and kept it turned facedown in her lap, saving it for Libby to see last. When all the molds had been considered and commented upon, Mother Morgan revealed her treasure, and Libby knew immediately that this was the image she wanted on her birthday cake.

The wooden mold was about twelve inches long and six inches wide with a recessed carving of two beautiful horses pulling an ornate coach. There were two coachmen, one in front and one in the rear of the coach, and each was finely dressed with their tricorn hats and plaited hair. The image on the mold reminded Libby of her long journey to the farm in Connecticut and her time spent sorting her mother's patches and looking out the window at the passing trees. She felt as if she could step into the mold and find herself inside the coach. It was the perfect choice for the cake.

Libby felt Mother Morgan's eyes upon her as she turned the mold this way and that, looking at all of the intricate details of the coach. "This one is perfect," she said with a smile.

Mother Morgan took the mold and set it on the table then put away the other presses and molds. "I knew you would like this one, that's why I saved it for last."

Together they began the preparations for the gingerbread birthday cake. Libby followed the directions given by Mother Morgan with great care and accuracy; she measured the ingredients and stirred the mixture exactly as instructed. "My, my, child!" exclaimed Mother Morgan. "You do pay attention to the details. Work habits such as these will come in quite handy when we begin our sewing lessons."

Libby looked up at her grandmother and replied, "I only hope I can be as skilled as you one day."

"Well, my dear," Mother Morgan patted Libby's shoulder and remarked with a look of sincerity, "just remember that practice makes perfect."

Early morning passed quickly, and the rest of the family joined the birthday girl for breakfast. Everyone remembered, and each greeted Libby with a hug and a wish for many happy returns of the day. Once the smell of gingerbread filled the house, Albert was single-mindedly focused on the party to come.

"Mother Morgan," Albert questioned, "when may we give Libby her gifts?"

"Shouldn't we wait for the celebration?" Libby watched as Mother Morgan responded to Albert's prodding with a kind expression and she knew her grandmother was trying to teach Albert how to be patient by example, but her efforts were in vain. Libby had discovered that no matter what Albert wanted, he wanted it in totality and immediately.

"Tell me again, please, when will we have the party?" Albert pushed.

"After supper, Albert. Now run along and fetch me some apricot preserves from the pantry. And send James, I need him to fetch some herbs from the garden."

"Yes, ma'am," Albert responded dutifully.

Libby was going to watch the morning milking, but she didn't want to leave without asking if Mother Morgan needed any help with the meal preparations.

"No thank you, my dear. I am only waiting on James for the herbs and all will be ready for our roasted lamb with potatoes. And where are you headed?"

"I thought I would go to the barn and watch the milking. I've not seen it before and have always wondered exactly how one gets the milk from the cow. Is it all right to watch?" Libby asked.

"Just stand back and don't get in the way of the hands, they have much work to do before the day is done. It's hard enough for them to complete all their tasks with Albert and James getting under foot. There is a platter of food and some ale in the cupboard for their lunch. I'm quite sure you would be welcomed if you brought it with you when you visited."

"Yes, ma'am," Libby returned. "I'll try not to be a bother," she added. She retrieved the wooden platter of bread, cheese, and sliced pork, as well as the pitcher of ale and cups from the cupboard, and headed for the milking shed.

The day was in full bloom now, and Libby was happy to be outside. The sun shined warmly on her shoulders. Her favorite blue delaine dress was probably warmer than she needed, but it was so beautiful, and since it was her birthday, she felt inclined to wear it for no other reason than to feel special. She would suffer the heat in order to feel pretty on her special day.

At the milking shed, two young men were just dumping the buckets of fresh milk into the barrel that was to be delivered to the Old Oak Inn at Ashford town center. Libby had learned that they purchased all of their milk from the Morgan farm, and some of their corn as well. The two young brothers, Matthew and Michael Bigalow, were hired hands responsible for the milking and tending of the livestock on the farm. It was a hefty job as the Morgan farm held more than a dozen milking cows, a hundred head of sheep for wool, and about half as many goats for both milk and meat. There were oxen used in the fields and half a dozen pigs, plus two teams of horses for the buggy, wagon, and coach. The brothers performed the morning's milking after all the livestock had been fed, watered, and rotated in their grazing pastures.

Libby's arrival was welcomed with a smile from Michael. "Who do we have here?" he asked as he rescued the pitcher of ale from its precarious position in the crook of Libby's arm. "It looks as though she's come bearing gifts, Brother Matthew." His thick English accent reminded Libby of Grandfather Abbott's, and she greeted the young men with a smile.

"Well hello, miss. Many thanks for the food and drink." Matthew bowed as though greeting a queen.

Libby curtsied and introduced herself, "Hello, good sirs. My name is Elizabeth Morgan, but everyone calls me Libby. Mother Morgan asked me to bring along your lunch." She set the platter of food on a nearby barrel.

"We are the Brothers Bigalow. This is Matthew, and I'm Michael. A pleasure to meet you." Libby smiled at Michael's formal greeting. "Many thanks for the refreshments; we were just about finished here, and something to fill our bellies is most welcome."

"Have you finished milking *all* the cows?" Libby asked disappointedly.

"We have but the one left," Matthew replied, indicating toward the large brown cow in a round pen near the milking shed. She was bleating with anticipation of the relief to come and seemed to pace in front of the door as though she was anxious to get things moving. Libby was happy to hear there was still one cow left to milk.

"Mother Morgan said I may watch if I am careful to stay out of your way." She looked with anticipation toward the cow and could see the bag under the cow's belly was full and swollen. She knew the milk was there, but she couldn't fathom how it was to come out. Michael smiled at Libby's curiosity and asked if she had ever milked a cow before. "Not ever!" Libby replied with exuberance.

"How about if you finish the milking for us so we may have our lunch?" Michael suggested. "It's none too difficult; many a farmhand learns to milk at an early age, much younger than you, you know."

Libby was more than excited to help with the milking, even though she still had no idea how she would get the milk out of the cow. The men were wearing long white aprons that covered most of the front of their clothing, and each was smeared with some muck from the animals. Not wanting to soil her best dress, she asked Michael for an apron. He kindly removed his own and handed it to Libby. It was clearly too large for her to wear properly, so she tied the top part around her chest and tucked the long front into the waistband of her skirt. It covered her dress better than she had hoped.

Michael was kind in his instruction and didn't laugh when Libby took the milking stool and went to the rear end of the cow looking for a place to put it down. "Here, lass, the stool goes here, next to her side." Libby blushed slightly but wasn't dismayed by her mistake. She sat upon the milking stool and waited for the next instruction. Michael showed her where to place the bucket under the milk bag. He showed her how to nudge the bag with her fist gently, to encourage the cow to let down the milk. "Just like the calf would do with his nose before he suckles,"

Michael explained. He showed her how to grasp the teat between her thumb and forefinger, how to squeeze gently at the top to stop the milk from going back into the bag, then how to close her hand in just the right manner to get the milk from the teat. "Notice how you don't pull down on the teats. Everyone always thinks you tug on them to get the milk out," Matthew said through a mouthful of bread and cheese. "But that just stretches them out and gives you an empty bucket." Michael chuckled as he showed Libby how to aim at the ginger cat's mouth and give a squeeze. "She is here every morning, just waiting for a mouthful of milk for her breakfast."

Libby laughed each time the cat was sprayed with the milk. Ginger opened her mouth and licked like crazy as soon as it splashed on her nose. Then she would use her paws to clean her face of the heavy drops of warm, fresh milk. Once clean, she would meow for the next mouthful. It was the most entertaining thing Libby had seen since her arrival on the farm, and it made her wonder if her Princess would like to have her morning milk in such a manner. But after a few more sprays into Ginger's mouth, she concluded that Princess was too much a "city cat" to allow milk to be sprayed into her face. Princess much preferred her saucer set before the warm fire each morning where she could gently lap up the liquid without making a mess. Princess was a very clean cat.

After a few more corrections to her milking maneuvers, Libby was soon double-handedly filling the bucket of milk. It was fun at first, but after some time, she realized how much work milking a cow could be. She was glad that Mother Morgan hired out and didn't expect the children to do the work on the farm. Tired as her hands and back were getting, she continued to work diligently until her bucket was full of milk and the Bigalow brothers were full of lunch. Matthew helped Libby pour the bucket into the large barrel. He also poured some of the milk into another plain white pitcher

36

that was on the table. This would be brought back to the kitchen for household use.

"Many thanks for the short respite from our work, Mistress Libby. It was kind of you to deliver our lunch and help with our chores." Michael bowed as he took the apron from Libby and handed her the empty platter and jug. He was so formal when he addressed her that she really was starting to feel like royalty.

"The pleasure was entirely mine," Libby returned with a large smile. "For now I can tell Papa that I milked my first cow on my thirteenth birthday. It is turning out to be a day to remember."

"Many happy returns of the day!" the brothers said in unison then looked at each other and laughed at the coincidence of their salutation. Libby laughed, too.

She curtsied to the hired hands as best she could with her hands full, turned, and headed to the back door of the kitchen. She again felt the warmth of the sun on her shoulders. She noticed how different this inland weather was from the weather on the coastline. Back in Boston, she would not have seen the sun until much later in the day because of the coastal fog, but here in Ashford, the morning mist burned off much earlier. She was really enjoying her visit to the country, especially now that she had milked her first cow.

Libby's hands felt sticky from the milking, and her clothing smelled of the barn despite her precautions with the apron. She decided a quick wash was in order, so after depositing the platter and pitcher in the kitchen, she headed to the bedroom to wash up.

As she walked through the bedroom door, she again noticed the mosaic quilt on the bed. Not wanting to soil such a treasure, she took the time to properly clean her hands and brush the remains of the barn from her clothing. Only then did she return to the quilt on the bed, but to sit upon such beauty was something Libby could not bring herself to do. She pulled the footstool close to the bed and took a seat.

For a moment, she just sat gazing at the quilt. The sheer number of different fabrics found in the patchwork struck her. Never before had she seen so many different prints in a single bed covering. Her own bed quilt was a simple design of Turkey red and indigo blue baskets that had been constructed of leftover pieces of clothing her mother had made for patrons. The blocks were set with muslin sashing and red and blue stars as cornerstones. The outer border was a blue resist print that had come from one of her mother's older dresses no longer in fashion. Though the quilt was not as stunning as Mother Morgan's mosaic garden spread with its endless array of colors and prints, it reflected the fine craftsmanship and design elegance of a skilled seamstress.

As she sat next to the bed and looked over the expanse of the mattress, Libby felt as if her eyes had fallen upon a beautiful field of wildflowers, full of deep blues, rich reds, and bright yellows and pinks. Thrown in here and there were the bright oranges, greens, and purples that attracted the eye, and in just about every flower there was the anchor of the rich browns from the many different glazed chintz prints.

Libby picked up the corner of the quilt that hung over the side of the bed and admired the quality of the workmanship—since both her parents were skilled with the needle, she could easily recognize superior stitching. This piece was the best she had ever seen. The stitching was so tiny it seemed as if little faeries must have put the hexagons together. As she contemplated the hours Mother Morgan must have spent on her treasure, Libby walked her fingers along the white linen hexagon path that separated the flower units and pretended that she was in a garden. She was lost in her own thoughts when she was startled back to reality by a polite cough coming from the direction of the door.

"Oh!" Libby startled. "Hello, Grandfather."

"Hello, child," Grandfather replied kindly as he entered the room. "Admiring the quality of your grandmother's work, I see. She is the best, you know, and not just in America—there are families in England that still ask after her skills."

"Her stitches are so tiny. I was just thinking it looked like faeries put the pieces together." Libby smiled and looked up at Grandfather. He was wearing his good coat and shirt in preparation for the party. She wondered what gift he had for her this year. His gifts were always very exotic and wonderful.

Last year, he had given her a lovely string of beads that came all the way from Africa. The beads, carved from the nuts of a palm tree, each showed a different face—some were those of animals and some of people. Grandfather explained that the necklace told a story of how a young boy had wandered from his village and was lost for several years. As he told the story, he pointed to each of the beads and explained their significance in the tale—how the monkeys had helped the boy find food, how the elephant had helped him find shelter, and how the birds had warned whenever the jackals were near. He told how the boy was able to find his way home at last with the help of a migrating gazelle that often grazed near the villages. It was a lovely tale, and Libby cherished the necklace. She often took it out of the silk bag it came in and told the tale to her cat—just so she wouldn't forget the details of the story.

"Grandfather," inquired Libby, "I wonder why Mother Morgan left England, if she was so sought after for her skills?"

"Life is funny, Libby," he replied with a sad expression as though remembering some tragic event. "Things don't always turn out like we want them to, and sometimes people behave badly. Mother Morgan will tell you her story when she thinks you are ready. Until then, be content to know that she is a wonderfully gifted woman who wants to share her gift with you. Be a good student." He kissed the top of Libby's head and made his way out of the room.

The smell of Grandfather's tobacco lingered in Libby's nose as she reflected on what he had said, and she wondered if it was Mother Morgan who had behaved badly or someone else. She looked back at the quilt on the bed. She couldn't help but stare at its beauty; it seemed to whisper to her heart. She had never really given much thought to sewing before, but now she found herself excited to begin lessons. To think that she could one day create something so fine looking had sparked a small fire in her soul, and it was exciting to know that soon she would start her first quilt. It was certainly turning out to be a birthday of "firsts."

Chapter 5

The afternoon passed in a slower than usual fashion. It seemed as if every ten minutes one of the twins was asking if it was "time yet" to start the party. Libby could see that her Aunt Ellen was trying hard to be patient with her boys, but after having been asked the same question so often over the course of the morning, she was nearly at her wit's end. So Libby and her mother came up with the idea that the boys could walk with Libby into Ashford town center and pick up a newspaper from Boston. Libby knew her mother was missing Father, and some news from her hometown would ease her homesickness.

The boys were practically bouncing off the furniture when they heard they would get to walk into town under the authority of their cousin Libby, and they were given strict instructions to mind her every word. Even James with his quiet manners was excited to go on the outing. He asked Mother Morgan if he could inquire about any new or unusual seeds from the apothecary shoppe, but Mother Morgan strictly forbade him from entering that store without her standing next to him and told Libby as such—evidently the proprietor was somewhat of an eccentric. James seemed a bit downtrodden as he looked at his cousin but brightened when he was given a copper penny to get a piece of hard candy from the mercantile store. Albert stuck out his lower lip and pouted, but only for the moment before he was also given a copper for candy. Libby had money and a note that had some words and numbers written on it that didn't make much sense, so she asked what it meant.

"I'm having you purchase the fabric we shall need for your first sewing project," Mother Morgan explained. "You may also buy the newspaper and a sweet with the change. Now keep the money safe in your pocket and don't show it around. I would hate to see you robbed on your birthday."

Libby was a little nervous about this last statement, but the excitement emanating from the boys far outweighed her own trepidations of being robbed. With their money pushed far into the depths of their pockets, the three set off up the road toward Ashford Township just as the sun was reaching mid-sky.

It was a quarter of a mile from the farm to reach the main road, and then another mile to reach the outskirts of Ashford. By the time they reached the mercantile store, Libby felt like she had walked to Boston and back. Her boots were dusty, and her jacket had been removed because she was heated from the exertion of trying to keep up with the twins. The boys, on the other hand, were still full of the energy they had started with despite the fact that they took every opportunity to lag behind while they looked at a toad, or to run ahead to see over the next rise in the road. She was certain it would take more than a walk to town to wear those two out.

Before she entered the store, Libby dusted her boots and put her jacket back on properly. She checked her reflection in the window and adjusted her straw hat. All things considered, she didn't look too worse for the wear.

As they entered the shop, the bell on the door announced their arrival. A large black dog sleeping near the back door looked up and gave a low "woof" to confirm that someone had come inside. From the back room, a lady's voice called out, "Be right with you."

James and Albert made straight for the jars of candy that were lined up on the counter and began to banter back and forth about which one was best and why. Libby strolled slowly through the shop and looked at all the goods on display. She ended at the counter that held the cabinet of cotton spools, needles, and scissors. Inside a glass case, she saw a small silver thimble with a tiny carved thistle on one side. Beautiful didn't begin to describe this thimble; it was a masterpiece of workmanship that looked like a tiny silver faerie's cup turned upside down. She had never really considered a thimble before and certainly never thought of them as beautiful. They were just another of the tools that her parents used in their trade. But this thimble was something more than just a tool—it was a treasure. As she gazed upon the silver treasure, she could hear the escalation in the twins' voices as they debated lemon drops over spice drops. Libby turned and gave them a loud "SHH!" just as the shopkeeper entered from the back room.

"Well now, who do we have here?" the shopkeeper asked with a welcoming smile. "The Randal twins, aren't you?" she added with a look of discernment.

"Yes, ma'am, that's us," Albert said, returning her smile. "And this is our cousin, Libby Morgan . . . well, her proper name is Elizabeth, but we call her Libby."

Libby smiled to the woman behind the counter and gave a half-curtsy. She noticed that James was trying his best to be invisible by staying behind his brother and keeping his eyes on the ground. She had not known that he was so shy with new people. Albert was quite the opposite. He was rambling on to the woman behind the counter about the candy and why it was unfair they should be sold by weight since the hard lemon drops were so much heavier than the gummy spice drops. He insisted it would be impossible to get an equal amount of lemon drops and spice drops for the same price.

The shopkeeper was doing her best to explain to Albert that a penny per pound was equal regardless of whether it was a pound of lemon drops or a pound of licorice pieces, but Albert was just not buying into the idea. Libby thought that it was probably a good time to give the woman the list from Mother Morgan, so she tapped Albert on the shoulder and said, "I really must interrupt." Handing the list to the shopkeeper, she continued, "Please, ma'am, here is the list from my grandmother for some items she would like me to purchase."

With a look of relief at being rescued from the monotonous conversation, the woman took the small scrap of paper from Libby and read the two items that were written down. "Here is the latest word from Boston." She handed Libby a copy of the *Boston Atlas* that appeared to have been read at least once already. "Well, it looks as if someone will be making something very special; I see that Mrs. Morgan has asked for our finest white goods." The woman smiled at Libby and continued, "Why don't you come with me, Libby, and leave the boys to decide on the sweets they would like." She headed to the large counter at the back of the store where the fabric bolts could be seen on the back wall shelves. She reached below the counter and pulled out a snowy white bolt of cotton yard goods. The fabric was of the finest quality, tightly woven and very smooth. Libby ran her hand over the white cotton that felt as soft as silk and tried to imagine how it would look in her own quilt. She had read the note on her walk into town and knew she would only be purchasing the white fabric for the quilt, but she just couldn't figure out where Mother Morgan intended to get the printed fabrics.

The shopkeeper measured out the length indicated by the note, pulled out a pair of rather large scissors, and cut the white fabric away from the remains of the bolt. She neatly folded the cut piece and then wrapped it in some brown paper and tied it with a string. "Remember to wash your hands, child, before you begin to stitch. That way your whites will stay white." She gave Libby an encouraging smile and handed her the package. Libby accepted the package but not before she noticed the fair amount of dirt that had accumulated on her hands during her walk into town. She must remember to wash as soon as she returned.

Libby picked out a piece of caramel for her sweet because she knew it was a long walk home and it would give her something delicious to last the whole way. The boys were having a terrible time coming to a decision about their own sweets, so Libby suggested that they each get something different, that way they could share it on the walk home. Before she left the shop, Libby went over to the glass case that held the silver thimble. She gazed at it for a few moments, trying to etch the memory of the engraved thistle in her mind. She wanted to remember it exactly the way it was, shiny and beautiful, so that when she got back to the farm she could describe it to her mother.

As the three children headed out of the town of Ashford, the church bell rang out two chimes. "Let's not dawdle on our way home, boys. It's already nearly supper time, and we have a lot of things to do today." Libby tried to sound authoritative but also kind in her encouragement.

"Yeah!" Albert said with a wink to Libby. "After all, somebody's got a party to get to!" he added with a laugh. Then he grabbed James by the arm and started to trot back up the road toward the farm.

Chapter 6

$\mathcal{T}$he children arrived back at the farm in high spirits, full of sweets and ready for a party. Libby was excited, but she was sure that Albert was even more excited because he rushed into the kitchen to again ask, "How much longer?"

"Albert Morgan Randal! If you ask me that question one more time, I shall send you to the milking shed to help the Bigalow brothers with the afternoon milking. Then you won't have to ask 'How much longer?' because you will have missed the party entirely." Albert had pushed too far and Aunt Ellen scolded him for his impatience. He skulked into the back corner of the kitchen and sat on the floor near the wood pile. As usual, though, he didn't let the scolding put a damper on his mood; he quickly picked up a stick, pulled out his pocketknife, and began to whittle as he whistled a lively tune.

Libby observed the exchange between mother and son with an awkward silence. She had always fantasized about having lots of children, but time with her cousins was making her rethink that dream. She wasn't sure she would ever have enough patience to deal with more than one child, especially if they were as high spirited as Albert. Remembering she had not given the paper to her mother yet, she scooted out of the kitchen and headed to the parlor, where she handed the package of fabric to her grandmother and the newspaper to her mother. Libby's mother took the paper and sat herself near the window where the afternoon light poured in through the panes of glass. As she opened the paper, Libby could read the word "Boston" from across the room, and her heart sank a bit. This would be her first birthday without her father, and it made her sad to know he would not be here for the celebration.

She turned to observe her grandmother untie the package string and put it into her apron pocket. She took off the brown paper wrapper and called for James. She gave him the paper with instructions to put it in the top drawer of the corner cupboard in the kitchen. Then she took the muslin fabric and put it on a chair in the parlor. Mother Morgan was so methodical in every action, and it amazed Libby how organized she was. Secretly, she hoped some of her grandmother's attributes had been passed down to her, but alas, none had yet to surface. Libby was neither tidy nor organized.

"Libby, dear, would you like to help me get the table set for supper?" Grandmother inquired.

"Yes, ma'am," Libby responded with a smile.

They made their way into the large dining room. "I thought we would hold our celebration in here, Libby, with the special china and silver. Here, child, help me get the dishes down from the cupboard." Libby's grin broadened to think that her birthday warranted the use of the "special china" dishes.

Mother Morgan handed Libby a lace tablecloth and asked her to spread it across the table. As Libby reached for the beautiful white lace cloth, she was reminded of her dirty hands, and she quickly pulled them back without taking the cloth. Making her excuse to wash before handling something so precious, she made her way to the basin in the kitchen.

With clean hands and face, she returned to help her grandmother with the table setting. Libby was handed a stack of handsome red china plates, and as she put the plates on the table one by one, she looked at the pattern on the dishes. The closer she looked at the plate, the more of the details in the scene she could discern. There was a lovely little stream beside some trees and a wonderful castle in the background. She closed her eyes for a moment and imagined herself standing in the grassy meadow having a charming picnic with friends.

She was startled back to reality when Mother Morgan tapped her shoulder and tried to hand her the bread plates. In her surprise, Libby dropped one of the china dinner plates on the table with a loud crash. The plate did not break entirely, but it did suffer a rather large crack through the center and a chip on one edge. "Oh, Grandmother, I'm so terribly sorry." Libby cringed, on the verge of tears, and truly, she was sorry, for she wanted nothing to spoil the mood of the day—it had been so wonderful up to this point.

"Don't fret, child." Mother Morgan wrapped her arms around Libby's shoulders and held her close. "You mustn't get upset. It's not as if you intended to break the dish. I have never seen the necessity in getting upset over accidents. Here, let's get another plate for that place." Libby was struck by the calm manner in which her grandmother dealt with the accident. Her own mother would surely have scolded her for her clumsiness. "These are just dishes, child, and accidents happen. It is important you learn the difference between *things* and *people*. People are so much more precious than any material thing in this world. If I had chosen to get angry over a broken dish, it would have spoiled our celebration, and you may have only remembered your birthday as one of anger and harsh words. Instead, we must accept that accidents happen and *things* get broken. It's reasonable for me to be disappointed at the loss of a dish, but anger is simply not warranted. Now, put your smile back on, and let's finish setting our table!"

Mother Morgan finished setting the silver around the plates while Libby wiped her eyes on her kerchief. She was handed the linen napkins to fold and put at each place. As she was putting the last of the cups on the table, James came in from the garden with a beautiful bouquet of spring flowers for the table.

"For you, Coz," James said with a crooked smile. "I know we were supposed to wait to give you your gifts until after the meal," he looked at Mother Morgan apologetically, "but my flowers couldn't wait another moment; they were starting to droop." And so they were, Libby noticed. She took the bouquet from James and kissed his cheek sweetly. Albert snickered at seeing his brother kissed; James blushed a deep crimson.

"Thank you kindly, James, they are so wonderful," Libby said sincerely.

Libby asked Mother Morgan if there was a pitcher she could put the flowers in for the table, so the three headed to the kitchen to see what could be found for a vase.

With the table set and the meal ready, Aunt Ellen announced that it was time for the birthday celebration. Everyone joined Libby and James in the dining room, and they all stood holding hands around the table. It was a lovely sight with the good china dishes, the silver, and the colorful bouquet of flowers that adorned the center of the table. Grandfather offered the blessing, gave thanks for the food and for the hands that prepared it, and then he asked God for a special blessing on the Birthday Girl. Libby flushed at the mention, and her mother and Aunt Ellen both squeezed her hands when they all said, "Amen."

Chapter 7

The meal was delicious, though Libby didn't know how Albert would have known, for he gulped down his food faster than anyone at the table. His mother asked him several times to slow down so as not to choke, but he just couldn't control his exuberance. The sooner everyone finished, the sooner he could give Libby her gifts. And better than that, the sooner he would get some of that gingerbread cake.

With the meal finished and the dishes cleared to the kitchen, Grandmother set the gingerbread cake out with dessert plates and a small dish of something rather interesting. Mother Morgan had made a spicy, sugary syrup to be poured on the cake. Albert had, several times, put his finger into the dish to taste the sweet, sticky goodness. Luckily for him, no one except Libby noticed his ill manners, but try as she may, she was unable to stifle her giggles. Hearing Libby's chortling and noticing the direction of her gaze, Mother Morgan shot Albert a sharp look. He immediately put his hands in his pockets and sat still as a stone. The group then stood together around the table, raised their glasses, and gave three cheers for Libby, "Hip, Hip, Hurrah! Hip, Hip, Hurrah! Hip, Hip, Hurrah!" Libby was again embarrassed at being the center of attention and blushed various shades of red, from bright pink on her nose to deep crimson at her ears.

"It's time, it's finally time!" shouted Albert as he leaped from his place to get his gift for Libby. Aunt Ellen threw up her arms, exasperated at Albert's behavior, but Grandfather Abbott just chuckled and said, "Boys will be boys, Ellen. Don't fret, he is with his family. As long as he minds himself in the company of others, you needn't worry."

Albert rushed to the woodpile in the kitchen and fetched a small paper package from behind a log. Grandfather Abbott excused himself to the bedroom and produced a rather large painted box. Mother Morgan pulled from her pocket a smallish package that was wrapped in a beautiful piece of toile fabric and tied with a ribbon of silk. Aunt Ellen and James brought out their gifts and set them on the table, and Libby's mother returned from the back bedroom with two packages: one big and bulky and one small and shaped like a book.

James politely asked if he could give his gift first. Mother Morgan nodded, so he stood and wished Libby "happy returns of the day" and handed her two very small seed bags. "These are some of the flower seeds from the fall garden last year. I know that you live in the city, but perhaps you can plant them in a box and set them by your window to grow."

Libby looked closely at the two little seed bags with their drawstring closures. Each was only about three inches long, two inches wide, and was made from printed cotton fabric. One was a tiny bud print in soft pink, and the other was a bright madder red-and-orange striped print. "James, how sweet it is for you to think of such a gift. I *will* plant them and put them in the window in our kitchen. They will remind me of you and my birthday celebration." Libby hugged her cousin, kissed his cheek, and thanked him again. Embarrassed by the affection, James dropped his eyes to the table and just smiled in satisfaction.

Albert was simply bursting from his chair, so Mother Morgan said he could give his gift next. He handed Libby the package and said proudly, "I made it myself! I hope you like it." Libby opened the small paper package to find a piece of carved bone with a simple design on one side of a sailing ship on the sea, and a whale with water coming from its blowhole on the other. "I've been practicing my carving so that when I'm a sailor, I can carve my designs on the ivory of the beasts I kill. I think it's pretty good, don't you?" There was no humility in Albert, but it didn't bother Libby. She loved her gift because it reminded her of Uncle Albert. She hugged the carved bone to her chest and told him that she would treasure it always. He, too, was kissed upon the cheek in thanks, but instead of being embarrassed, he quickly wiped it away and said, "Yuck!" rather loudly.

Mother Morgan handed Libby her next gift. The package was so beautiful that Libby almost didn't want to open it, but her curiosity was too much, so she untied the soft piece of pink silk ribbon and folded back the red toile fabric to find a rather unusual gift—a plain brown *huswif*. The stark contrast between the bright red wrapping fabric with the old and somewhat faded brown huswif prompted Libby to stop for the briefest of moments and glance at Mother Morgan with a confused look.

Mother Morgan offered an explanation. "Child, I have mentioned often enough that I am looking forward to teaching you to sew. And as I have thought about your birthday these past few weeks and pondered what to give you, it dawned on me that you have no tools for sewing. How could you learn to be a skilled seamstress without the necessaries? So I have given you my very own roll-up filled with the tools you will need to learn the craft. Open it," she encouraged Libby with a soft smile and gentle eyes.

Libby could see that the sewing roll-up *was* full to the point of bursting and that the tie barely made it around the piece. As she untied the string intended to keep the roll-up closed, she was struck by the contrast in the plain brown fabric that was on the outside and the bright, vivid colors found on the prints inside the roll-up. There were five different, vibrantly colored pieces that made up the pockets inside the huswif, and the entire edge was bound in a delicate brown-and-blue striped woven tape.

Each of the pockets contained items that Libby would need for her sewing project. She found a wonderfully carved ivory needle case that held a variety of needles in several sizes. She found several different shaped thread holders that had different colored threads wrapped around them. In the bottom pocket of the huswif, Libby found a small piece of cotton that had something hard inside, and as she unwrapped the cotton fabric, her heart pounded with anticipation. As her eyes fell upon the small silver thimble, she very much wished that it was the one from the mercantile store, and the closer she looked, the more her dream became a reality. There on the side of the silver thimble was the tiny carved thistle she had looked at so longingly through the glass case. But the closer she looked, the more she realized that this thimble was different from the one she saw earlier that day. It had the tiny thistle on one side, but she also noticed the carved braiding that wrapped the opening and the two tiny birds sitting on a branch on the opposite side. It was all she had wanted and more.

"Mother Morgan, it is so wonderful. Such a perfect gift and so much like the one I saw in the shop today. How did you know I wanted one like this?" Libby asked her grandmother.

"These tools were mine, child, when I was a little girl. My mother helped me make the roll-up to keep my necessaries in. I have kept them these many years for just such an occasion. I'm pleased that you like them," Mother Morgan replied.

"Try on the thimble, Libby," Her mother instructed. "Put it there, on your middle finger. How does it fit?"

"Perfectly!" announced Libby, proudly holding up her hand to show the group.

"Open the next one!" encouraged Albert, anxious to get to the gingerbread cake with spiced syrup.

"Here you go," said Aunt Ellen, handing Libby a flat wrapped package.

Libby carefully put the items back into the huswif and set it on the table. She removed the string and paper from Aunt Ellen's gift to find a small stack of *Godey's Lady's Books* from several years past. "I have been saving these copies for you because I knew one day you would learn how to sew. And these have the best patterns. I know that the fashions are a bit dated, but you will find some patchwork patterns—and there are some wonderful stories in them as well. I hope you enjoy them as much as I did."

Libby reached over and gave her Aunt Ellen a hug. "Thank you for these, I know they will be useful for many projects, and you know how much I love to read. I will enjoy the stories, I'm sure." Libby gave her aunt a sweet smile.

Grandfather Abbott was next to give Libby a gift. He placed upon the table a large, round, pantry-style box that was painted deep red with images of flowers and leaves. Libby's eyes lit up when she saw the box. "Oh, Grandfather!" she exclaimed. "It's lovely."

"Open it, dear, and see what's inside."

"There's something inside?" Libby asked. "But surely the box is enough, it's so grand."

"Open it," he encouraged with a smile.

Libby lifted the box off the table and set it in her lap; it was rather heavy, and she wondered what on earth could be contained inside. As she removed the lid, her eyes brightened and her smile grew to cover her face. Inside the box, Libby found stacks and stacks of small cuttings of fabric. Each piece measured about five inches square. The box must have held hundreds of them. "Oh, my goodness!" Libby's mother exclaimed. "What a wonderful treasure, Father, however did you think of it?"

"Well, to be honest, your Thomas told me how nice it would be to have some bits of fabric for Libby to learn her sewing, and since my ship is usually carrying quite a lot of it from England, I though it might not be missed if I took a small swatch from time to time. Your mother also sent me along with some from her hidey-hole in the sewing parlor. We have been anticipating Libby's desire to sew for some time." He smiled at Libby affectionately. "It seemed the perfect gift for her birthday. Do you like it, Libby?"

She was so absorbed in sorting through the different bits of fabric swatches that she completely missed his question. "Libby, dear, Grandfather has asked you a question," remarked Mother, somewhat embarrassed by her daughter's lack of attention.

"What?" Libby asked with an honest questioning expression. "I'm sorry, this box is so wonderful. Each piece is a treasure and so different from the next. I wasn't listening, I'm very sorry." Libby looked apologetically at her grandfather.

"You have already answered my question, dear. I can tell that you like the gift."

"Like it? I simply love it," Libby said with sincerity.

"Well, my darling, I guess this is the last gift. It is from Father and me. He is sad to have missed your celebration, but be assured that he wishes you many happy returns of the day." Mother got up from her chair and hugged Libby tightly, and then she kissed her forehead. "I was under the strictest instruction to give you the hug and kiss first. So that was from your father, and these are from both of us." She gave Libby a large, lumpy package that was wrapped in paper and tied with string.

She untied the string and laid it on the table, slowly opening the paper wrapping to reveal some smaller wrapped packages. The first contained the steel nib pen she had wanted so much. In the other packages, she found a brilliant cut-glass jar full of writing ink, some extra nibs for her new pen, and a stack of blank paper that was wrapped with a red ribbon. There was a stick of green sealing wax and a brass stamp for sealing the letters. The stamp was even monogrammed with *her* initials. With each package, Libby's eyes got bigger and bigger.

The final gift was a bit confusing to Libby. Her mother handed her a package that Libby thought was a book, but when unwrapped, she found a large stack of old letters that were tied with a red ribbon. "These are for templates when you make your bed covering," Mother explained. "You may cut them up into the shapes you will need."

Libby looked at the stack of letters and could tell that some were very old. Her curiosity could not be contained. "How old are the letters, Mother?"

"Older than you." Mother smiled. "They are some family letters from many years past. But the paper will be fine for you to cut up for your templates," she explained. "I expect that they are pretty old. Your father has been saving them since before you were born. Most are from before we were married. But since paper is so dear, it's a good idea for you to use them for your patchwork templates instead of the blank writing paper." Libby nodded in understanding and tucked the letters into the box of fabric from her grandfather, making a mental note to come back to them later, after the celebration.

The gifts were more than she had ever dreamed of, and yet here they were right in front of her in the center of the table. Individually, each was superb, but collectively they were spectacular! It was most certainly an extraordinary birthday.

"Hurray!" Albert shouted. "It's cake time!"

Everyone at the table laughed at Albert's delight. The cake was cut and passed around with the biggest piece placed in front of Libby, much to Albert's dismay. Seeing the look on his face, Libby graciously traded pieces with her cousin. "You have waited so long, Albert, and have been so patient. You certainly deserve the biggest piece."

Chapter 8

The celebration was over, but everyone's fine mood continued for the remainder of the evening. Libby gathered up her gifts and made her way into the bedroom where she and Mother slept. There was a comfy chair in the corner near the window, so she set her gifts on the floor, and, taking the box of fabric, snuggled into the chair as the afternoon light began to change into the softer hues of evening.

She was intrigued by the pieces of printed cotton that her grandfather and grandmother had given her. Taking them out of the box one by one, she took time with each piece, examining them front and back. Before too long, she found herself sorting the pieces according to their overall color. She thought this was the best way to keep track of them since there were so many. It was impossible to sort them by the prints or the scale of the prints because they ranged from very tiny dots to very large floral chintzes and *Toiles de Jouy*.

She examined the piles after she reached the bottom of the box and noticed there were far more browns, reds, and blues than any of the other colors. She had the fewest in the purple and yellow stacks, but the green and pink piles were sufficient. She began to notice that sometimes the same print had been done in several different color backgrounds, or that different prints often had some of the same design elements but in a smaller or larger scale. It was fun to notice the differences and similarities between the fabrics, and she got excited when she would find something that she hadn't noticed the first time she looked at a piece. It was almost like being on a treasure hunt.

After a time, Libby started to put pieces that looked good together into separate piles. She tried to find colors that complemented one another, or images that could be cut out that would look good in the center of a hexagon shape—like her grandmother had done on the mosaic garden quilt. Before too long, she had spread fabric pieces all over the floor of the bedroom.

Libby missed the soft tap at the bedroom door as Mother Morgan entered, but as the glow of the candle that Mother Morgan carried brightened the room, it was clear to her that someone had entered. She startled a bit and knocked over a small stack of fabrics.

"Enjoying yourself?" Mother Morgan asked with a wry smile. Libby had been so absorbed in her fabric sorting that she hadn't noticed the light in the room was fading quickly and that she would soon be sitting in the dark.

"Oh! Grandmother! You startled me. I didn't notice you standing there. I'm sorry." Libby realized the entire floor of the bedroom was scattered with fabric stacks. "I really should pick these up, I'm sorry for the mess."

"Nonsense, child," her grandmother replied with the wave of her hand. "Leave it. This is part of the fun of making a patchwork. So tell me, how have you sorted your pieces?" Libby watched her grandmother consider the floor, but she opted for sitting in the chair instead.

Libby got up from the floor and reached for the candlestick on the bedside table. She lit it with the flame from Grandmother's candle and set it such that it illuminated a particular group of fabric stacks. From the stack, she pulled several pieces and placed them on her grandmother's lap. "Look at these, aren't they wonderful? I started sorting by color, but then I got distracted with the designs and decided I would start picking some pieces that looked good together. You know, just like in your mosaic spread, the way you made the rings with the pretty centers." Libby's enthusiasm shined brightly in her eyes.

"Well, my dear. It looks like you are on the right track. These look lovely together. I particularly like the purple with the green. It will make a lovely block. Do you think you are ready to learn how to make the patches?" Mother Morgan asked.

"I think so. I know how to mend my socks and sew on a button. And Father has showed me how to do a nice running stitch. But I'm sure there must be other stitches I'll need to learn. Should I get my huswif?" She was anxious to get started.

"No, no, child," Mother Morgan patted Libby's hand, "candlelight is not the best by which to learn. How about we start first thing in the morning, when the light is at its finest? The sun shines brightly on the porch in the early hours, and the air has been warm these past few days; it should be a nice place to begin your lessons. What do you say?" Mother Morgan gave Libby a smile. "We both love the mornings, so a nice, early start is best, I think. Don't you?"

"Yes, I agree, Grandmother." Libby smiled back and was suddenly caught off guard as a large yawn escaped from her face. She barely had time to cover her mouth with her hand. "Goodness, please forgive my manners. I guess the excitement of the day has made me more tired than I realized."

Grandmother giggled out loud, and Libby laughed in response, knowing she'd found a kindred spirit in her grandmother. They hugged and then together picked up the pieces of printed cotton and placed them back in the wonderful painted box.

Libby could barely keep her eyes open as she changed into nightclothes, washed up, and braided her hair for bedtime. Mother Morgan had retired to bed and now that Libby was alone, she realized the excitement of the day had overtaken her almost completely. Then she remembered the stack of letters her mother had given her to use as templates in her patchwork. She had forgotten to look at them after the celebration, and now, though tired, she was curious as to their content.

She opened the painted box and started to straighten the fabric swatches that had been hastily put away when she remembered why she had opened the box in the first place. Laughing to herself about how easily she was distracted by the beautiful fabric, Libby returned to her purpose. Finding the letters at the bottom, she gently removed them from the box and sat in the chair with the stack of letters on her lap. She took great care to remove the red ribbon and set it on the table—she wanted to keep it with the letters just as her mother had given them to her.

The very top letter was the most recent; she could tell because she recognized her mother's handwriting. With a quick glance through the stack, Libby noticed that someone had organized the letters chronologically, with the earlier ones at the bottom. She picked up each letter, turning it over and looking at both sides of the folded pieces of paper. Once or twice, Libby noticed that a letter was inside an envelope, but mostly they were simply folded and sealed with wax. Some of the letters even had writing on the outside, as if the writers had run out of room inside the letters and simply continued their sentiments on the backs of the folded pieces of paper. The seals had long been broken open, but on some of the letters there were bits of wax still clinging to the paper. The two most recent letters had pink and green wax seals that were completely intact, so Libby squinted in the candlelight to make out the design on the seals.

One was a monogram, "TM"—for Thomas Morgan, she thought as she looked at the handwriting on the front of the letter with the green seal. Another was harder to identify as it was scrolled together, but with careful squinting and close examination, she figured it to be "MAJ." Libby reasoned that the center letter was for the Abbott, and the "M" and "J" were for her mother's name, Mary Jane.

Looking over the stack of letters, Libby gently stroked the green wax seal with her fingers and reflected on her father's face. She was sad that he had not been with her on this wonderful day, but she knew he was thinking of her—probably at this very moment when she would normally be kissing him good night. A smile crossed her lips as she raised her fingers, kissed them, and touched the seal.

"Saying good night to Father?" her mother asked from the doorway.

"How did you know?" responded Libby with surprise.

"Mother's intuition," she said with her sweet, motherly smile.

"Is this Father's?" Libby asked, pointing to the squashed green wax seal with the initials "TM."

"It is," she assured Libby as she moved close to the chair and placed a hand on her shoulder. "He has always used green wax to seal his letters. Mine were sealed in pink or red, as you will see if you read them. Will you read them, do you think?" her mother asked. "Before you use them for your patchwork, I mean. I think it would surely be a waste *not* to cut them up for templates—paper is so costly these days."

"Do you mind if I read them?" Libby asked apprehensively. "I won't, if you'd rather I didn't," she added quickly, "but if you wouldn't mind, I shall like very much to read them before I cut them to bits."

"I think it would be fine for you to read them." Her mother touched Libby's cheek and continued, "It is good to know one's family history. I don't know if you will understand what the letters talk about. Most of these letters are from before you were born, so you may be unfamiliar with some of the names—it's been so long since they were spoken in our home. But ask if you have questions, and I will try to answer as best I am able. Mother Morgan or Grandfather may also be of some help, though I fear your questions may stir some memories they would rather leave in the past."

Libby thought about this last statement for a moment and then asked, "What sort of memories?" She figured that since her mother had brought it up, her question would be tolerated.

"Well . . ." Mother dragged the statement out longer than normal and worried the handkerchief in her hands. "I guess memories about life—life and choices—hard choices that no one should have to make." She appeared to be talking more to herself. "Funny, now, being on the other side of the circumstances—it all seemed to work out for the best, even though much was lost." Libby shifted in her chair, and her mother returned to the present conversation. "When you read them, start at the bottom of the stack. I've put the letters in order with the oldest on the bottom so that they make a little more sense. The first is from a distant relative named Baroness Montclief. She was your father's great-aunt. The letter is addressed to your Grandfather Morgan." She paused and her countenance changed ever so slightly as though she were sad. "It was written when he was a young man, not long after he married your grandmother."

"We have a baroness in our family?" Libby blurted out without thinking, and her comment immediately brought her mother's attention back to the current situation.

"Well, I guess we do, though we hold no claim to her title. Now don't go getting any high ideas," she said, seeing the excitement growing on her daughter's face, "we are far from being nobility." Libby's mother chided her gently, but her expression was one of mirth.

"How exciting that we have English nobility in our family," Libby considered out loud. Her brain was racing with the thought of it. She had so many questions. Who were these English relatives? Why did her family no longer have ties to them? She was trying to picture these new relatives with their English title. In her own small social circle in Boston, she had no friends with ties to English nobility. Most of the girls from her school were from families with similar financial backgrounds: merchants and other middle class families with enough income to afford a proper education for their children, but not so much as to be classified as "wealthy." Libby's eyes glazed over just a bit as she recalled a story she read recently where a child was taken from poverty into the house of a wealthy woman. As she recalled, the story was quite tragic. She had a feeling her own family's story with these noble English relatives was going to be tragic, too.

"Well, child, I think you will find that we are about as far from aristocracy as one can be. Particularly now!" Her mother placed a hand on top of the stack of letters Libby was holding and with an uncompromising tone said, "Let us put these away for tonight; there has been enough excitement and questions for one day."

"Yes, Mother," Libby responded obediently. She rewrapped the ribbon around the letters and placed them back in the painted box. Mother Morgan and Aunt Ellen appeared at the door to offer their final good wishes for Libby's birthday. They each hugged Libby in turn and wished her sweet dreams then left her alone to get into the big bed with the beautiful hexagon quilt.

As she drifted off to sleep, she reflected on the conversation with her mother and began to wonder exactly what was meant by the exclamation, "Particularly now!" She understood this statement to mean that *something* had happened to disconnect the family from its noble ties to the Baroness Montclief. Despite efforts to stay awake until her mother came to bed, for she fully intended to ask more questions, exhaustion from the day's excitement overtook Libby, and she found herself dreaming about sailing ships full of printed cotton fabrics on their way to Boston.

Chapter 9

The morning sun was not yet up when Libby opened her eyes and blinked her dark room into view. It took a few moments to reconcile her brain to her exact location, for she had slept quite hard. As she lay in her bed in the hour before dawn, she recounted her plan for the day. She would begin her first patchwork, and she knew Mother Morgan was excited to teach her how to make the hexagon quilt. Then she remembered that she was going to be cutting up the letters for templates, and that brought to mind a frightening thought: Libby had yet to read any of the letters. Cutting them to bits before she could read them gave her a sick feeling inside that she knew she must rectify, so she extracted herself from the bed as quietly and as quickly as she could. Trying hard not to wake her mother, she stealthily grabbed the box of fabric, her huswif, and the letters then closed the bedroom door quietly before she headed out to the kitchen.

Keeping her eyes on the floor so as not to trip in the dark, Libby crept wide-eyed down the dark hall in her stocking feet quietly as a mouse. Just as she rounded the corner in front of the other bedrooms, she ran smack into Mother Morgan, who was slipping stealthily out of Aunt Ellen's room. They both startled at the collision but quickly hugged in relief when they recognized one another.

In the kitchen, Mother Morgan lit a candle and Libby stoked the fire—together they silently padded around the kitchen, putting on the kettle to boil and fetching the teacups from the cupboard. Mother

Morgan poured the water into the brown-and-white china teapot, and they sat at the small table waiting for the tea to steep. Neither spoke a word until the tea was poured into the china cups and Mother Morgan had passed the honey to Libby.

"Child, why in heaven's name are you up so early today? I would have thought that with all the excitement of yesterday you would have slept until noonday."

"Goodness, no, Grandmother. How on earth can I sleep with so much to be done? I wanted to make sure my chores were finished before we began our lessons on the porch this morning and well . . . honestly . . . I wanted to read the first of the letters before we cut them to bits." Libby was unsure how her grandmother would feel about her reading these letters. She looked into the bottom of her cup and said somewhat defensively, "Mother said it would be fine to read them. She said there is a bit of family history in those letters and that it is important for one to know her own history. So I thought I would do my chores and get ready for my lesson and still have enough time to read one or two."

"Sounds like a fine idea to me!" Mother Morgan said matter-of-factly as she took her last sip from her cup.

Libby looked up with a smile and blurted out excitedly, "You don't mind, then?"

"Mind what, child? That you read the letters that tell my story and the story of your mother and father and the rest of the family? Heavens, no! Here, give me those letters." Mother Morgan reached across the table and took the stack of tied letters.

"Mother said she organized them with the oldest letters on the bottom and the most recent on top," Libby informed while she watched intently as Mother Morgan untied the string and took the first letter from the bottom of the stack.

"Goodness, me!" Mother Morgan whispered as she read the address on the front of the letter. "This is from Baroness Montclief. I haven't seen this letter in years." Libby saw her expression change as she looked the letter over front and back. She touched the remnants of the crimson seal, and a shadow fell across her face. "May I?" she asked Libby, indicating that she would like to open the letter.

"Of course," Libby responded, not knowing what to think. Her grandmother's somber expression made her question her curiosity with the letters. Libby continued to observe Mother Morgan as she carefully opened the letter and started to read, though she did not read out loud. Sitting quietly and a little uncomfortably, with her empty cup of tea in her hands, Libby looked between her cup and her grandmother's face to note the expressions. As each page was read and placed behind the next, Libby noted how lost in the moment Mother Morgan seemed. Occasionally, the older woman winced as though the words on the page physically hurt her in some way. As she turned to the last page, a tear escaped her eye and she gently wiped it away with her napkin. Quietly, she folded the letter and placed it back in its place in the stack.

Libby was uncomfortable with the sorrowful expression that seemed to linger on her grandmother's face; she felt awkward and unsure of what she should say or do to lighten the mood.

Mother Morgan looked at her empty teacup and then at her granddaughter's concerned expression. "Another cup, child?" she asked in a voice that was almost normal.

"Only if you are having one, please," Libby responded, surprised at her quick return from distress.

"I think, my dear, that if you are to read these letters, you should have some background on the subject. Otherwise it may not make much sense. We will start at the beginning—the beginning for me at least."

Mother Morgan poured them each another cup of tea, and Libby scooted her chair closer to the table and sat up straighter with an eager expression.

"You already know that I was a seamstress in London." Libby nodded her head as her grandmother continued, "My entire family worked for the Montcliefs. The Baron Montclief and his wife were very wealthy, with a large estate just outside London called Braidsmuir, and they had several smaller homes in London proper and in Scotland. They employed many people, some as servants inside the house and some to work the fields, gardens, and stables. My father was the head groom at Braidsmuir, and my mother, sisters, and I sewed all the clothes and household goods. I'm being modest when I say we were good at our trade. My own mother was much sought after by the social classes for her skill with the needle. It just happened that the Baron Montclief was willing to hire my father as well as my mother, sisters, and I. You see, Mother and Father were very committed to one another and would not live apart, so any position they took would have to include us all.

"I am the eldest child in my family. My sister Jeanine is two years younger, and Louisa is five years younger than I. We were but small girls when we first started working for the Baroness, and as I think back on it now, she *was* kind in the beginning, likely because she very much wanted my mother to sew her fashions. But by the time the Baroness was through with my family, no household in England would employ my mother or my sisters. She was the ruin of my family." The last statement was filled with so much melancholy that Mother Morgan was quiet for a moment longer than normal in order to regain her composure. She stared out the kitchen window with an expression that almost broke Libby's heart. Libby wondered if she should stop the conversation, but before she could speak up, Mother Morgan began again, only this time her countenance was brighter.

"I was eleven the summer we moved to Braidsmuir. My mother and father were very excited to be in the Montcliefs' employ because the salary was enough to put some money aside for a small farm in the country, and they thought perhaps we girls could be educated while we lived in such a fine household in London. My family had our own apartment in the south wing of the estate, but we always sewed in a suite near the west wing kitchen, just a few doors down from the main dining room. The Baroness insisted we work in the main part of the house because she liked to stop in and check our progress while we were making some new fashion or bed hanging.

"Truly, I admit, I was always uncomfortable working in the 'sewing suite,' as we came to call the room where we worked, because the Baroness frequently popped in unannounced to scrutinize our stitches. As I think on it now, she never complimented our work much; she only made the odd expression or grunt if she was pleased. She was quite particular about her things—so much so that she never allowed us little girls to even put basting stitches in her undergarments, though we *were* fine seamstresses in our own right. It was fine for Jeanine, Louisa, and I to make the linens, towels, and bed curtains for the rest of the household, and even some of the servants' costumes, but only Mother could handle the personal items for Baroness Montclief.

"As I said, Baroness Montclief was kinder to us girls in the early years. She gave Mother the leftover bits of silks and ribbons to do with as she pleased—I think because she knew my mother liked to make patchwork, and she used the bits of fine fabrics to teach us girls how to stitch properly without snagging the silks. While we were still small, she would comment on our auburn curls and long eyelashes. From anyone else, the comments would have been compliments, but from the Baroness, they were simply facts that were often said with a foul tone and a wrinkled nose. She made sure mother dressed us in pretty calicos with white starched aprons because she didn't like her servants to look shabby. But as we got older, she seemed to find us objectionable at every opportunity, and in particular her contempt was directed at me.

"I didn't understand it back then, for we were model children. We never spoke back, were always clean and tidy in our appearance, and we responded with the utmost manners—Mother always insisted upon good manners. Nonetheless, the Baroness grew to dislike us, and she was not discreet about her disdain. She even began asking our mother to keep us out of sight of the guests and visitors to Braidsmuir. The older we got, the more hateful she became. Compliments totally disappeared, and her words became critical, her tone malicious."

Libby had been keenly observing her grandmother as she told the story, and now, as she relayed the next bit, Mother Morgan absentmindedly reached up and touched her own cheek as if remembering something painful. "When I was but fifteen, she slapped my face for speaking out of turn. I remember it as though it happened just yesterday. She had been ranting at the servants throughout the day because someone important in her social circle was coming for dinner, and she insisted on everything being perfect. Louisa had been very ill the week before, and she was not yet feeling her best, so Mother made sure she was not working on any of the finer linens. She was just finishing a monogram on one of the servants' towels when the Baroness entered and asked us to go back to our rooms as the guests would be arriving soon. Just as she finished speaking, Louisa yawned without covering her mouth, and it seemed to annoy Her Ladyship. She walked over and snatched the towel from Louisa's hands, and, tapping her foot, she scrutinized the stitching while she made a *tsk-tsk* sound with her mouth. Then she barked at Louisa, 'I have told you, I do NOT like it when the stitches look so uneven! Now remove them and do it correctly!'"

Mother Morgan mocked the voice of the Baroness with an expression of nastiness Libby had never seen before in her grandmother, and it almost frightened her. Then her grandmother continued in her own voice, "But before that woman had finished her sentence, I was across the room and had grabbed the towel from her hands to examine the stitches for myself. 'Her stitches are fine!' I said in defiance and looked at my mother. You see, Elizabeth," Mother Morgan paused here and smiled a wicked little smile, "I was growing very weary of *The Lady* Montclief's manners, and it was increasingly difficult for my young mouth to remain closed when she treated my baby sister with such hatefulness."

Mother Morgan's face seemed to reflect the defiance that was relayed in the story, and a grin grew across Libby's face as she thought how glad she was that Mother Morgan had stood up to the mean Baroness. Then her grandmother continued, "Baroness Montclief took the towel from my hands and threw it at my mother. Spinning on me, she slapped my face hard with her open hand. Then she stood very close to me, lowered her voice, and in a superior tone that made my blood boil she said, 'Your impertinence has cost your family one month's wages. I suggest you remember your position in the future.'

"That slap was the beginning of the end of my time at Braidsmuir. Having cost my family a month's wages, I felt sure I was a disappointment to Mother and Father, but they did not scold me for defending Louisa. My mother understood my anger and simply let the matter pass without punishment. But I could not forget the slap, nor could I forget the condescension that flowed so easily from the Baroness when she addressed me. You must understand, Elizabeth, I was quite innocent to worldly situations, and I could think of no reason why she should dislike me so. But it was only a matter of time before her reasons, though quite unjustified, were clear to me." Libby watched as Mother Morgan paused and took a sip of her tea and looked into the cup as though thinking what next to say.

"In the summer of my sixteenth year, a young man came to visit Braidsmuir." Mother Morgan's eyes brightened as she spoke of this young man. Libby was intrigued by the comment and listened more intently. She could not take her eyes off her grandmother as the story being told came to life in her own mind. "My sisters and I would catch glimpses of him through the window as he rode his horse out the side gate each morning." Here she paused for just a moment and smiled a youthful smile. "He was very handsome. We eventually found out from one of the kitchen maids that he was Baron Montclief's nephew, Edward Alexander Montclief Morgan."

Libby gasped when she heard the name, for she was again shocked that her own grandfather was nephew to a baron. "I can't believe Grandfather Morgan was nephew to Baron Montclief!" She sat with her mouth agape, and Mother Morgan chuckled at her expression.

"Goodness, child! It's as though you've just found out you were a princess! It means nothing, I assure you. We have no claim to the Baron, his lands, his monies, or his title! *I* made sure of that!" Mother Morgan laughed right out loud with a laugh that had no regrets, but Libby thought it rather disappointing to have "no claim" to the Baron's title.

Libby's mother and Aunt Ellen had been quietly standing in the doorway listening to the exchange between grandmother and granddaughter when Grandfather Abbott tapped them both on the shoulders and whispered loudly, "What is it we are listening to?" Startled by the unexpected taps, they jumped and squealed as Mother Morgan and Libby looked over their shoulders to see what the commotion was all about.

"Goodness, me!" Mother Morgan exclaimed. "How late is it?" she asked no one in particular as she glanced at the light pouring in from the window. She sprang from her chair and proceeded to pull the frying pan to the front of the stove "Libby, quickly, put on some fresh water to boil. We really must start the food for breakfast." Libby couldn't hide her disappointment at the idea of stopping the storytelling, and Mother Morgan added, "Don't worry, child, we shall finish the story while we eat."

Libby's mood brightened as she fetched the water for a fresh pot of tea and stoked the fire a bit to help the water boil faster. She hurriedly got the butter from the pantry and brought out yesterday's bread for slicing and toasting near the fire. Mother Morgan and Aunt Ellen were finishing the cooking while Libby's mother fetched the boys to gather the eggs and some fresh milk from the Bigalow brothers.

Grandfather Abbott set out the dishes and finished making the pot of tea. One by one the ladies finished preparing their parts of the breakfast and brought them to the table. The boys returned from the barn with the milk and eggs for the day, quickly deposited them in the pantry, and then they made their way to the table. Once all were seated, the blessing was said and the meal was served all around.

"Grandmother," Libby began as she swallowed the bite of sausage she had chewed longer than necessary, "I have been wondering, why do you suppose the Baroness would be so nice to you girls while you were little and so mean as you got older? I don't understand; did you do something terrible?" Before Mother Morgan could respond, Libby corrected her sentence, "I mean, not terrible, really, but naughty, perhaps?"

"Truly not, child, I assure you. We were all good girls. And when my own mother finally understood why the Baroness disliked us so, she was quite ready to find employment elsewhere, for it was a petty reason. You see . . ." Mother Morgan looked at Libby and her mother, and then smiling at Grandfather Abbott, she stuttered, "It's just that . . ."

"Oh, for heaven's sake, Margaret, just say it!" Libby noted the irritation in Grandfather's voice and looked at Mother Morgan, but despite his tone, her grandmother remained silent.

"Libby, your grandmother is far too modest to say why that beast of a woman disliked her, but I am not. When your grandmother was young, she was stunningly beautiful. So beautiful, it fact, that the Baroness Montclief couldn't stand it. Mostly because *she* was not! In fact, she was a homely woman. And since I have seen her on many occasions, I can say with certainty that she was *ugly*—inside and out! She was also aware of how the men in her household looked at Margaret and her younger sisters, for they were all striking. I believe jealousy consumed her, and she simply couldn't stand the attention the girls were given." Grandfather looked at Mother Morgan apologetically and added in an honest tone, "Margaret, it was not my intention to say that your beauty was reserved for your youth, for you are *still* stunning." He winked at Mother Morgan and smiled broadly at the others at the table.

"Captain, your chivalry is not lost on my vanity, I assure you." Mother Morgan blushed.

Libby continued to over chew her food as she thought about the circumstances of her grandmother's childhood at Braidsmuir. She looked at the woman, now weathered with age, and could see that she was still beautiful despite her fading auburn hair and bright blue eyes turning to gray. How tragic it must have been for her and her sisters to be hated for something they could not control. They could no more change their appearance than they could the weather, and to hate a child for such a thing was utterly despicable. Her imagination allowed a vision of the Baroness to come to mind, and it was an ugly vision, to be sure.

She heard her name for what she was sure was a second time before surfacing from the thoughts of her grandmother's youth. Embarrassed by her lack of attention to the others at the table, Libby smiled and tried to fit back into a conversation of which she was clueless. Her mother stood and began to clear the table of the dishes and smiled at her daughter. "I said, Elizabeth, that if you and Mother Morgan would like to get started on your patchwork, you really should get ready for the day. Go wash and dress, then gather your things and meet your grandmother on the porch for your lessons."

Libby rose from her place and started to pick up her dish, but her mother shook her head and pointed to the door. "I'll take care of these for you today—consider it an extra birthday gift." She smiled at her daughter and continued to clear the table. Libby clapped her hands in excitement, smiled broadly, and scooted out of the room.

Chapter 10

fter hastily washing her hands, Libby thought about the coolness of the morning in the kitchen with her grandmother. The chill crept up her limbs from the carpeted floor, so she decided to wear her brown and green delaine, as it was warmer than her blue cotton, but not as hot as her wool dress. She was trying, ever so ineffectively, to get her hair coiffed as she had seen on the young Masterson girl, but it was no use. Each time she got the left side up, the right side fell. Mother Morgan entered and stood behind Libby, facing both of their reflections in the looking glass, "Here, child, allow me."

She gently took Libby's hair and proceeded to twist and braid the back section and wrap it around the back part of Libby's head, pinning it in place. She then took the front sections and, with wet hands, made ringlets that fell on either side of Libby's face. With the natural curl to her hair, Libby's dark auburn ringlets held. As she gazed at her own reflection, Libby smiled then noticed her grandmother's expression of satisfaction. "You are a beautiful girl, Libby, dear." Mother Morgan patted Libby's shoulder and turned to leave the room. Noting the sad expression on her grandmother's face as she left the room caused Libby to wonder if dredging up her grandmother's childhood memories was really a good idea.

Just then, her mother walked into the room and stopped short when she saw her daughter. "My goodness, aren't you lovely!" She walked all the way around Libby, examining every side of her hairstyle. "Did you get your hair up all by yourself?" she asked with an approving look.

"Goodness, no! Grandmother helped me," Libby began and then paused as if she didn't know how to proceed. "Mother . . . I think . . . it's just that . . . well, she just seems so sad. Perhaps we shouldn't read those letters after all. I don't want to upset Mother Morgan, and it seems the more she talks about her childhood, the more melancholy she becomes."

"Well, Libby, it was a sad situation and one that I'm sure is difficult for Mother Morgan to recount. But I also believe that if she didn't want to tell you her stories or have you read her letters, she would say so. She is a direct woman with a mind of her own, and if she doesn't like something, she'll let you know—politely, of course, but directly, I can assure you. So don't let it worry you any further. Now, get your sewing things and get out to the porch—she's waiting for you."

Libby got her huswif and the box of fabric and letters then headed to the front porch where Mother Morgan was waiting for her. She saw two chairs facing one another, and to the left was a table that Libby recognized from the parlor. All were set in a sunny location, and Mother Morgan was seated with her head leaned back on her chair, her face turned toward the sun. As Libby approached, she said without opening her eyes, "It's warming to have some sunshine on these old bones."

"It does feel good to be outside in the sunshine," Libby replied with a smile as she seated herself in front of her grandmother. "So, how do we begin?" she added as an afterthought.

"I think we should reread that first letter from the Baroness Montclief. Then we will have some paper to cut into templates. Besides, it will give me great pleasure to put *that* letter to scissors." Mother Morgan lifted her head as she made this last statement and winked at her granddaughter.

Libby chortled a little to herself and pulled the ribbon from the stack of letters. She retrieved the first letter and tried handing it over to her grandmother, but Mother Morgan shook her head, waved away the letter, and said, "Reading it this morning was enough for me, child; you may read it this time, if you don't mind."

Feeling self-conscious of her reading aloud skills, she fumbled opening the letter and paused. "I'm not sure I can pronounce all the names correctly." But Mother Morgan simply motioned with her hand for Libby to continue. "I'll help, don't worry, child. Just read on."

"Grandmother, are you sure you want to do this?" Libby blurted out, at last free of her bottled up question, and the pressure she felt from not asking for so long.

"Do what, child?" Mother Morgan asked in a perplexed tone of voice.

"Are you sure you want to read these letters again and dredge up all these memories? They seem painful." Libby was quite direct in her question, and Mother Morgan was a bit taken aback.

"Your directness reminds me of someone, Libby, dear." She smiled at her granddaughter and added, "It's fine, do not over worry yourself. Sometimes it's good to remember unpleasant things. It makes you appreciate happier times even more. Now read me that first letter, and I'll help you understand why she wrote it."

Libby took the first letter from her lap and unfolded it at the seal— which she noticed was a red script "JM" that was crumbling ever so slightly. She began:

> *To my nephew, Edward,*
> *Your uncle sends his fondest regards and asks that you reply to his last letter at your earliest convenience. He is worried you have stayed too long away from Braidsmuir and begs for your return as soon as you are able. While I can assure you*

he is in fine health, he is given to bouts of dark moods since your hasty departure, and the longer you remain absent, the darker his moods rage. It is his mental health that concerns me now, for he has taken to shutting himself up in the library for hours during the day. He neglects his duties to his tenants and no longer rides out for the hunt.

I relay this information to you, Edward, not in an effort to alarm you, but to beg you to come back to Braidsmuir, back to your uncle's estate so that reconciliation may be made between us.

I am saddened that you would take the word of a servant over your own relation, but I pray circumstances will reveal the truth behind that wretched girl's false accusations toward me. I have always treated her with great kindness and can see no reason for her to turn you against us except to better her own situation.

Please do not allow this harlot to come between you and your last remaining family. I implore you to return to your home and seek the wise counsel of your uncle, for I am sure he will guide you in what is right for your future. Do not act in haste and find yourself beguiled by the lure of feminine charm and beauty—for hers is a beauty that is sure to fade, and her charms will last only until a more prosperous situation comes along. She is not worth all that you have to lose, Edward. This I can assure you!

Make haste with your return, for you are sorely missed.

Your Aunt,
Baroness Montclief of Braidsmuir

Libby refolded the letter and placed it on top of the stack. She was very uncomfortable at reading the words aloud, for she knew the "harlot" called out in the letter was her grandmother. She sat quite still, waiting for a response of some sort, but Mother Morgan remained quiet for what seemed an eternity. Finally, she spoke, "Where was the story when we left off in the kitchen? Did I explain about Edward and I?"

"You did say that Edward Alexander Montclief Morgan was visiting the estate and that he was quite handsome." Libby remembered her grandmother's expression when she mentioned young Edward. "But you did not say how you two met." Noting Mother Morgan's smile, Libby was pleased the storytelling would begin at a happy place.

"Edward had come to live at Braidsmuir in the summer of his twentieth year. I was only sixteen, but I was mature for my age, and my features made me seem older still. I had glimpsed him through the window on several occasions as he was leaving to ride out; sometimes he would go with his uncle on matters of the estate or to tend to the tenants. He was learning the business of being a baron, I guess, for he was to inherit the entire estate and all its holdings. You see, Libby, Baron and Baroness Montclief had no children of their own, and Baron Montclief had but the one sister, Franchesca Montclief Morgan—Edward's mother. Since Edward was an only child, there was no one to challenge him for the estate. The Baroness would have liked it very much if her own family could have benefitted from the estate, so she was intent upon making a match for Edward from one of her many nieces and cousins. But Edward was a man who knew his own mind, and he would *not* be persuaded to marry someone as a matter of property. He greatly loved his uncle—his own father had died fighting in France when Edward was just ten years old—so his uncle filled the gap left by grief and loss. Montclief was a natural father with wonderful instincts for raising a boy properly.

"Edward often spoke of his uncle with the greatest regard, for he considered the Baron more than just his uncle and fill-in father—he was a dear friend. This letter you have read mentions the distress the Baron felt upon Edward's departure from the estate, and I can tell you that Edward, too, was deeply distressed by leaving. Understand that the difficulty was never leaving behind the money or estate—these were mere things to Edward, and they held no place in his heart. Edward was only ever saddened by the loss of his friendship with his uncle. It is unfortunate that they could not have reconciled before it was too late."

Mother Morgan paused for a moment, and Libby was glad to see her melancholy expression replaced with one of love. "But enough of that, I was to tell you how Edward and I met. Let me think now, I was just sixteen the first time I actually met Edward, and as I said, he was so very handsome. He needed some new clothes for an upcoming ball, so the Baroness instructed my mother to send young William to take Edward's measurements—she would never have allowed me to do it. William was my mother's servant, and no sillier boy has there ever been. He paid little heed to the house rules and was often found exploring in places he didn't belong. Being cuffed on the ear was an event that William came to accept with a foolish grin because it occurred so frequently he was practically immune to the pain. The Baroness Montclief liked to bash him about the head, particularly when I was about, because she couldn't take her anger out on me. William was an orphan and had no one looking out for his well-being. I, on the other hand, had my mother—and since Her Ladyship desired the skills my mother possessed, she rarely struck me or my sisters.

"William was on his way to Edward's apartment when we passed in the hall. He had the measuring tape about his shoulders, the paper in his hand, and the pencil was tucked behind his ear. He was talking to himself as he looked at the pictures hanging in the corridor, and I remember thinking how silly he was to speak aloud his thoughts, for it usually got him into trouble." She looked at Libby and said in a thick and haughty British accent with her nose in the air, "Servants are to be quiet unless spoken to!"

Libby chuckled at her grandmother's wrinkled-up expression of disgust. "That must be what the Baroness Montclief said?"

Mother Morgan nodded her head and continued in her normal voice, "I asked William where he was headed, and he told me he was going 'to visit the King of England to get his measurements for a new ermine robe!' He was being rather amusing, acting sillier than usual, dancing about with his tape measure, pretending to measure the invisible king, when the head butler rounded the corner and saw his foolishness. He barked at William to stop acting like an idiot and went to smack him on the back of the head, but just as he did, William turned and took the blow straight in the face. The butler hit harder than expected, and William's nose burst forth with blood that dripped down the front of his white shirt, bold and visible for all to see. Crying and bloodied, William begged me to take care of his task so that he could clean up before the Baroness saw him in such a state and found out that he had been in trouble yet again. I was so sorry for young William that I agreed to get the measurements needed for the clothes and to meet him outside the back kitchen so he could return to my mother, his task completed with none the wiser of his misfortune. You see, Libby, he had been in so much trouble of late that I was worried he would lose his position as my mother's assistant, and if he did, there would be nothing left for him but the workhouse."

Pausing from her story, Mother Morgan reached for her pencil and the tin template that was sitting on the table. She handed them to Libby and said, "While I finish my story, I would like you to trace this hexagon shape on the letter. Fit as many as you can on the paper. If you finish before my story is done, you may begin to carefully cut out the shapes; the scissors are on the table."

Libby took the tin shape from Mother Morgan and looked at the paper. She set the template down at one corner then flipped it across the page to see how many she could fit. On the second row she aligned the shapes so that the edge of one was the edge of another. Cutting once yielded a cut for two pieces, so there would be little waste using this method. Once she was satisfied with the way she could lay the template down to get the maximum number of pieces on the page, she picked up the pencil and started to trace the shape.

While Mother Morgan continued her story, Libby worked on her templates, taking care not to make any mistakes. "I went directly to Edward's apartment so that I could complete William's task and return the measurements to him as soon as possible. I gently tapped on the open door to announce my presence, and I observed Edward's profile as he stood in front of the window. When he turned, his expression gave away his mind—he was shocked to see me standing in the doorway with pencil and paper in hand; clearly *I* was not the expected servant. As he walked toward me, he was looking at my eyes so intently that he tripped on the carpet, bumped into the table, and fell cursing onto the settee." Mother Morgan glanced at Libby and laughed out loud. Her smile lightened Libby's thoughts—perhaps these weren't such bad memories after all.

"I could tell that he was embarrassed by the redness that moved up his neck and onto his face, so I tried to dispel his awkwardness by looking at the floor instead of his eyes, but this was difficult for me because his eyes were so captivatingly blue. He stood, cleared his throat, and said in a completely recovered tone, 'How do you do, I'm Edward Morgan.' He spoke to me as though I were an equal. It was rather unusual, for I had never been addressed so formally before, particularly from a Montclief, so I curtsied and said that I was there to take his measurements for his new clothes. But before I could finish my explanation, he interrupted, 'You did not introduce yourself. What is your name?' His words were spoken slowly and with purpose, and as he spoke, he looked directly into my eyes. I remember thinking that this must be what it felt like to swoon—for my stomach did flip-flops, and I felt weak in the knees standing before him with our eyes locked. I awkwardly curtsied again, all the while trying desperately to look at anything except his eyes, and I begged his pardon for such bad manners. I introduced myself as Margaret Jane Hammond, the seamstress's daughter, and stated that I was there to get his measurements for the new clothes."

Libby's tracings got an approving nod from her grandmother. "It was difficult for me to stand so close to Edward, difficult and unnerving, for I had to touch his shoulders and measure his legs. All the while, I fumbled with the tape measure and the pencil; I had to do most of the measurements twice because I had forgotten them before I could write them down. He was clearly aware of my unease at being so close. As he stood before me with his arms outstretched to the sides like a scarecrow, I quickly slipped my arms around him so I could grasp the tape and get his waist measurement. Before I could get my arm back to the front he slipped his arm around me as well. He was smiling and muttering something about being close enough to dance, and he even tried to take a step or two with his arms around me. I think he was trying to make light of our awkward situation, and despite his rather foolish expression and clumsy dance steps, his gesture had quite the opposite affect. We both stood frozen for a few moments, arm in arm, looking into each other's eyes. When we realized our situation, we quickly pulled apart.

"Feeling completely out of sorts, for I had never been so close to any man except my own father, I gathered my implements and scooted out of the apartment as quickly as I could without drawing too much attention. I had to stop at the nearest alcove to catch my breath, for my heart was pounding so hard I felt sure it would burst from my chest. I waited until my heartbeat was normal and my cheeks no longer felt flushed before I tried to find William; I wanted to be sure I showed no sign of discomfiture before I met anyone, particularly my mother, for she would surely see through any lie I could muster regarding my anxiety. I found William, gave him the measurements—some of which I had to make up, and without any discussion I quickly returned myself to our own apartment to recompose before dinner."

Libby interrupted at this point and said enthusiastically, "It was love at first sight, wasn't it, Grandmother?"

"Well," she grinned coyly, "if I were to make a wager on such a thing, then I would say yes, it was love at first sight for me. For every time I looked at that man, my knees would wobble and I would feel lightheaded. And it remained so for many years—particularly whenever we locked eyes."

"And was it so for him as well?" Libby asked without looking up from her tracing.

"I believe his actions speak for themselves. He pursued me with great regularity—always trying to catch me in the hall when I was on my way to our apartment or the kitchen or some other place. He was relentless in his desire to see me, and I was solely interested in making it easier and easier for him. I was the first to volunteer to run any errand or make any delivery of towels or linens to various places in the house. Anything I could do to be seen by him was worth the extra work I endured. I would have to say that, yes, we were *both* love struck!"

Libby set the template on the table and picked up the scissors, but before she cut the letter, she looked up at her grandmother for affirmation. With a look of assurance and a nod, Mother Morgan said, "Cut away, my dear, for that is one letter I will enjoy seeing cut to bits!" So cut Libby did, and when she was finished, she had a lap full of small paper hexagons, and Mother Morgan had a look of complete satisfaction on her face.

"Now that you have your templates, I want you to pick out some of the fabrics that you like so we can make your patchwork flowers." Libby pulled some of the swatches she had begun to pair up the night before from the box.

Getting pins from Libby's huswif, Mother Morgan showed her granddaughter how to pin each of the paper templates onto the wrong side of the fabric, making sure to leave enough space between templates for the seam allowances. She instructed Libby to place the templates in a specific location on the fabric in order to get a design in the very center of each template, and she explained that when those pieces were sewn together, they would create a special secondary design. Once the fabric was cut around each of the papers, always leaving enough seam allowance to turn the edge down, she showed Libby how to use the needle and thread to baste the fabric onto the template so that the edges were tacked down to the wrong side and there was a smooth, finished edge all the way around the piece.

She then explained how Libby would need a center hexagon in one fabric color and six "petal" hexagons in another fabric to create one of the flowers. Once these were all basted, Mother Morgan showed Libby how to use a whip stitch to join the hexagons, starting with the center and attaching each of the six petals to create the flower units. She explained how important it was to leave the papers in the hexagons until all of the six sides of each hexagon were attached to other hexagons—this prevented the edges from fraying. She said that sometimes people left all the papers in the spread until the top was completed, then they would take them out prior to quilting; others left them in the quilt for added warmth and never took them out, however this did make quilting the top difficult.

Libby tried very hard to remember her grandmother's words; she wanted to prove herself a good student, and it mattered what her grandmother thought of her sewing skills. The swatches of fabric her grandfather had given her were not very large cuts, so there was little room for error if she was to get six petal pieces from one of the swatches. She was careful to lay the templates on the swatch just right to get the maximum pieces from each cut. The many swatches of chintz and calicos were a treasure to

Libby and she did not want to waste a single inch. In some cases, she would only be able to get three hexagons from the fabrics, for they were smaller swatches, but Mother Morgan explained that she could use three from one fabric and three from another to also get a lovely design.

The sun was reaching mid-sky by the time Libby had completed one whole flower. She found it took more time than she thought to baste all the pieces and then whip stitch them together, especially with her inexperienced fingers, but she was "coming along nicely" according to Mother Morgan. Her grandmother, on the other hand, had completed five flowers for Libby's quilt. Not only was she quick in her stitching but her accuracy and the quality of her stitches was undeniably the best Libby had ever seen.

"Mother Morgan," Libby began, "do you think I will ever sew as well as you? You seem to achieve perfection without any thought for what you are doing. How is it you can do it so quickly and still keep your stitches so uniform and tiny?"

"When you have been sewing every day for as long as I have, child, then you will understand. My fingers know the motions without my having to think about it. Just as you now know how to write your name and numbers without effort, and your letters are uniform and even, so, too, will stitching become for you, if you do it every day. Sewing is an art that is only learned through practice." Mother Morgan glanced back at the front door to see Libby's mother coming out with a tray. "How nice, your mother is bringing us lunch." Libby looked toward her mother then down at the single completed flower in her lap and suddenly felt a surge of embarrassment for how little she had actually accomplished for a full morning's effort. As her mother approached, Libby quickly stuffed her patchwork into the box of other fabrics and began clearing the table so her mother could set down the tray. "Here, Mother, let me take that from you," she said too hastily.

"I've got this, dear, why don't you run inside and bring out another chair so I may join you?"

Libby went to get the chair. As she was walking back, she saw the look her grandmother gave to her mother, a look of approval for the work Libby had completed. "Mother Morgan says you are coming along nicely, may I see your progress?" she asked her daughter.

"I haven't done nearly as many as Mother Morgan, but I do like the combination I put together. I think it looks like a lovely flower." Libby opened the box of fabric and took out her patchwork flower. She handed it to her mother then asked, "Shall I pour the tea, Mother Morgan?"

"That would be fine, child." As Libby poured three cups of tea, Mother Morgan and her mother commented on the finer aspects of Libby's patchwork. "She does have lovely stitches," said her grand-mother. "They are very even in both length and spacing. I'm quite impressed. You and Thomas have taught her the rudimentary skills quite well."

"It is Thomas you have to thank, for I do not have the patience to teach, especially when the pupil isn't particularly interested." Libby got a sidelong glance from her mother and then a smile. "It's nice to see her so intent upon this project. I knew that you would be able to pique her interest. I think Thomas is a good teacher, but your instruction is much more interesting." She glanced back to her daughter. "Isn't it Libby?"

Excitement overtook Libby and she blurted out, "Mother, did you know that Father's father was the heir to the Baron Montclief's *entire* fortune? And he threw it all away for the love of Mother Morgan. It's so romantic! And that mean old Baroness, I just know she did something terrible. She tried to make herself out to be innocent in the letter and blamed the servants, but I just know she was the bad one. What exactly did she do?" Her question was innocent and without regard for the answer that it would bring, but her mother and grandmother easily forgave her ignorance.

Mother Morgan looked off toward the barn, and there was an awkward silence, so Libby's mother interjected, "How about we finish our nice lunch before we have any more stories? Grandfather was kind enough to make us some of his famous ham and cheese with pickle chutney. I think we need to enjoy our meal—the stories can wait awhile yet."

Libby was again disappointed that the stories must stop for a bit, but she was mature enough to recognize her grandmother's altered expression and somehow knew that the next part of the story was going to be sad. She quickly thought of a change in subject. "How soon will Aunt Ellen marry John Masterson? Do you think we will come back for the wedding, Mother?"

The new subject pulled Mother Morgan back from the edge of sorrow and restored her countenance to its normal, relaxed happiness. She smiled at her granddaughter as she wiped away the beginnings of a tear and took a healthy bite of Grandfather's pickle chutney. When she finished chewing she said, "I hope that you will stay long enough for us to have the wedding before you go home. I was speaking with Ellen last night, and she feels that a wedding while you are still visiting would save you a trip this fall. She thinks it wouldn't take much to get things ready and has asked if we would make her gown. Little does she know, I started the lace months ago in expectation of John's proposal." Mother Morgan winked at Libby and gave a toothy grin.

The three sat for another hour chattering over their lunch and planning the upcoming nuptials. Libby continued to baste her templates to the pieces of fabric until she had enough for another two flowers. She would sew more on her patchwork later that evening by the fire, for it was time to help with the afternoon chores.

Chapter 11

My Dearest Daughter Margaret,

    I pray this letter finds your health much restored, though I fear it will take more than letters to restore your spirit after such tragedy as you have endured these past months. My heart breaks for you and Dear Edward at the loss of your sweet babes. I pray you seek the comfort of your Savior—His grace is sufficient to heal your soul. I sorely miss you, my sweet. Not a day goes by that I do not think upon you and pray that you will allow yourself to be healed of the pain from the loss of your girls. God will surely bless you with more children, and when your wounds are not so fresh, you can rejoice in knowing that you will be restored unto your sweet girls in the Kingdom of Heaven.

    I know there is a special suffering set aside for the Baroness, a particular anguish that awaits her in a wretched place where she will atone for the terrible deed she has done those innocent children—God will not allow her wickedness to go unpunished in this life or the next.

    I write to give you news of our new home and the adventure we have begun since our dismissal from the Montclief Estate. Your father's frugality and the generosity of Franchesca Morgan allowed us to find comfortable accommodation in Renfrewshire near Glasgow. Your father takes work where he may find it. There are several well-made families that require his skills with the young horses, so we are nicely settled with plenty of coal for heat and food to eat. Do not fret after us; God's will be done in our lives and we trust Him with our future—thankfully we require only the simplest of accommodations.

We have begun to make fashions for the women in the district and have acquired a small shop in which we sell our wares. They were sufficiently lacking in experienced seam-stresses despite this being a textile town, so we were quite welcomed by the community. We advertised our trade in the papers and have received more than adequate orders to keep us busy the entire winter through. I have made some connections with several of the young girls that work in the mill, and we have taken to trading bits of fabric. It's delightful to see the many lovely prints that are being produced here locally, and though they do not have the same opulence as those we get from France, they do give my spreads character. I recently sold one of my spreads to a merchant's wife; so pleased was she with the quality of my work that she promised to bring her sister along to purchase another when next she comes to Glasgow. I have set the extra income aside as it will be of great help to settle your sisters.

My heart is glad that you have found a new home in Boston and are settled nicely. Edward is lucky to find such good employ in the Americas, and Captain Abbott's assistance was greatly appreciated, I'm sure. I have included some patch-es of the cotton chintzes that Captain Abbott sends our way. He is a most generous young man, and we are thankful you and Edward have such a devoted friend—indeed, that we all have such a great friend as he. I am sure with your fine skills and Captain Abbott's connections, you will be making high fashions for the gentle folk of Boston before you know it.

Your father sends his fondest regards and inquires after the weather. We hear that Boston has much more snow in winter than London, and so we wonder how you are faring with such cold.

Louisa asks me to say she misses you desperately and begs a visit as soon as traveling becomes possible. Jeanine has included some snippets of a dark green check and a cream print of tiny flowers. They are from a recent day dress she made, and she wonders if you would approve of how she has trimmed the delicate print in the dark green check. She says it is sure to become all the rage in "country attire," and I don't doubt it for a moment—the dress is quite smart.

I will close this letter for now and write again soon. Give Edward our fondest regards and ask him to write your father on the matter they discussed prior to your leaving. Father is anxious to begin the task for Edward. What plans are they scheming together, I wonder?

I pray you lean on your Heavenly Father for the comfort you seek in this most mournful hour. Sent with all my love and fondest regards for my beautiful daughter,

Your most loving Mother

Libby set the letter on the table next to the candle and picked up her handkerchief. As she wiped away her tears, she noticed that all the ladies in the room were also wiping away their tears, and Grandfather Abbott was staring at his hands in his lap.

"A tragic time indeed!" Grandfather broke the silence that enshrouded the room. "That was surely a sad time in our lives."

"Mother Morgan," began Libby's mother, "are you sure you would like to discuss this tonight?"

"Of course, Mary," Mother Morgan said with a forced smile. "It was a very difficult and sad time in all our lives," she directed this part at Grandfather Abbott, "but we should not let the evil in this world stop us from remembering the goodness. And my babes were pure goodness, if only for a few short weeks."

Libby shifted in her seat uncomfortably. She was glad that Albert and James had retired for the evening on their pallet in the kitchen. She didn't think Albert's exuberance was the right mood for the conversation at hand.

"I guess you must be wondering about this letter, Libby. And I shall tell you all that there is to know; only first we must go back to where we left off earlier today. What is the last part you remember?" she asked Libby.

"We talked about how you and Grandfather Morgan loved one another so much." Libby blushed as she said this and looked at her patchwork in her lap. "You said it was love at first sight." She smiled at her grandmother as though she had just revealed a secret.

"In love we certainly were," replied mother Morgan. "We were in love and it was all that we could manage to 'accidentally' bump into one another during the day. I often made excuses as to why I needed to step out of our apartment in the evenings, just so I could see Edward." Mother Morgan paused and Libby looked up from her patchwork to see Mother Morgan smile at Grandfather Abbott. "We even had our accomplices from time to time." She gave Grandfather Abbott a nod before she recounted the next part of the story.

"Most days we were lucky enough to have some time alone, for the house was large enough to find a quiet place out of sight of servants or staff that might make trouble for us. We would sit and hold hands and talk about our lives growing up. Edward loved his father and mother and often talked about how he thought he had wanted to be a soldier just like his father. But his mother had begged him to go to school and find a profession that was not so dangerous—she could not bear to lose her son as she had lost her husband. So Edward studied the law, more specifically the law as it relates to international import and export of goods. He was quite respected for the time he spent at school and was planning to go abroad to study further in India, and then America. The Baron Montclief was helping him with his overseas contacts. Edward was scheduled to leave for India late in the fall, and though we had only known each other a few short months, I did not want him to go. Every moment we were together brought us closer and more at ease with one another.

"In early June, Edward had to travel to Glasgow for a few weeks, and it was torture to have him away. I wandered the halls like a ghost looking for my lost love, always wearing a despondent look on my face. We knew it was unsafe to write one another for fear of our relationship being discovered by a servant or the Baron, so we had no contact during his absence. I spent a great deal of time standing in front of the window, waiting for him to ride up on his horse. When he did finally return, we were careless with our meeting—you see, we both missed each other so desperately that we had little care if someone found us out. And they did!" She looked at Grandfather Abbott and said, "You were the first Captain; remember when you found us in the garden holding hands?"

"I remember quite well, Margaret. You were so surprised when I rounded the corner and caught the two of you hand in hand. You blushed so crimson you shamed the roses." He laughed and continued, "Edward knew me well enough to know that I would not reveal your secret. I feel strongly that people should love where they may find it. And I had seen Edward with other young ladies; I could tell that he was feeling something he had never felt before. It was clear he was in love with you."

"You were our dear confidant, Captain. Someone we could trust with our secrets." She paused here and reached to pat Captain Abbott's hand, then she turned to Libby and continued, "And did we have a secret to keep!" She smiled a broad smile and looked at her granddaughter. "We got married," here she leaned toward Libby and whispered, "secretly." She gave a youthful giggle then continued, "And only Captain Abbott, Edward's mother, and my parents knew about the ceremony. In late July, my parents and I traveled to Southampton under the guise of visiting a sick relative, and Edward made an excuse to visit Captain Abbott on some business matters. We met up at a small parish on the outskirts of town and had a quiet ceremony in the evening—the parish clergyman was quite willing to perform the service since we both were of consensual age and both of our parents were present. The rather large sum of money Edward put in the poor box helped to buy the clergyman's silence. We all agreed to keep the marriage a secret until such time as Edward could meet with the Baron privately—you see, at the time, the Baron was infirmed from a rather nasty bout of the ague, and Edward didn't want to make the situation worse with news of our elopement. It was more than two months before he was well enough for Edward to talk with him privately, and by then I was with child. So we thought it best to keep our secret a little longer.

"As the time drew near for Edward to leave for India, he was desperate to find a reason why he should not go—a reason that he could share with his uncle. He finally insisted that his trip be postponed until the spring, arguing that the Baron was not fully recovered enough to carry out all of the duties on the estate. He maintained that he would stay and help, at least until he felt certain his uncle was fully recovered. Over the next few months, Edward was able to convince Baron Montclief that there was still much for him to learn at the estate, so it was agreed that his trip should be postponed indefinitely for the time being." Mother Morgan sat back in her seat, and Libby looked up from her sewing to see the shadow that had fallen across her grandmother's face, so she braced herself for what would be revealed. She knew the twins had died, but she did not know the details.

"We had quite a time hiding my condition from the Baroness. In the early months, it wasn't too difficult because I wasn't showing, and I never suffered from sickness in the mornings. I was just more tired than usual, often dozing off in the middle of the day, but Mother was ever watchful for the Baroness or the housekeeper's staff. She was my savior on many an occasion when someone would enter the sewing suite without knocking. Then, as I began to show, Mother made sure my dresses fit so that it was difficult to see my belly. No one suspected anything as wild as a pregnancy, mostly because we were such well-behaved girls and we were never seen out of the company of my mother."

"But wait! What about Edward?" Libby interrupted. "Did you get to see him very much?" She was sitting at the edge of her seat, hanging on her grandmother's every word and ignoring her patchwork. She was trying to imagine living with such a huge secret—a secret that would clearly be visible to everyone before too long.

"My Edward was quite a resourceful young man, Libby," her grandmother continued. "He paid close attention to the staff's comings and goings and was always able to sneak into our apartment for a visit. Though we could not live together, we did see one another almost every day. Toward the end of my time, Mother made every excuse she could think of for my absence from the sewing suite. You see, I was quite large by the end of the pregnancy. We didn't know it, but I was carrying twins."

Mother Morgan paused and looked off into the fire. The silence was awkward, so Aunt Ellen told the next bit. "Mother Morgan had two little girls." She offered her niece a bittersweet smile and said, "Their names were Franchesca, after Edward's mother, and Louisa, after her own sister."

Libby thought back to the two medallion quilts that her grandmother called her "framed angels." She tried to bring them to mind but could only remember that they were nearly identical, with chintz flower bouquets in the center of each. Knowing the quilts were linked to the story made Libby want to see them up close; she wanted to touch them and lie under them. She was beginning to understand the feelings that went into the making of those quilts, and she knew now why they were so treasured by her grandmother.

Mother Morgan was recovered enough to continue, "They were perfect in every way; small, but perfect!" She held her hands apart to show Libby how small the babies were. Libby didn't know much about newborn babies, being an only child, but she was sure that most babies were certainly bigger than what her grandmother was showing her. "The delivery was pretty easy for me," Mother Morgan said matter-of-factly. "I guess God knew that I needed to be quiet about it, so he made my angels small. My sisters both knew of the situation, and they were careful not to speak of it when out of our apartment. They were such dears, each held one of my hands and quietly encouraged me through the pain of the birth while mother did the necessaries for the delivery. It didn't take long, and there were no complications, thank goodness, because Mother was called to see the Baroness not long after they were born."

Grandfather Abbott interjected here, and Libby turned her attention to him. "I had been with Edward all that day." He gave Mother Morgan a comforting smile as he told his part of the story. "He was so anxious about his beloved Margaret's labor and he longed to be nearby during the delivery, but that was impossible. In our ignorance, we felt sure no one knew of the situation; indeed, we were certain of it—but we were wrong." Grandfather Abbott's gaze moved to the fire as the tone of his voice changed to loathing. "It was very early in the morning, and we were in the library, pacing in front of the fire, trying to decide if we should chance a visit to the apartment, as we had no news of the delivery yet. Baroness Montclief came in wearing a smug expression that gave away the secret she *thought* she knew. She looked at me with such disdain and contempt, for she thought *I* was the reason her servant was with child. She railed on and on about how disgusting it was for a man of my caliber to have a relationship with a member of her staff and 'how dare I embarrass the Montclief Estate with my behavior.' She was relentless, but I did not utter a word. She began to attack Margaret's character, calling her terrible names."

Grandfather Abbott looked apologetically at Mother Morgan. "Finally, Edward could take no more of her ranting. He grabbed her by the wrist and jerked her toward him, telling her to shut up. She was taken aback by his actions, and the shock of it was enough to make her stop talking long enough for Edward to yell at her again, 'The child is MINE! And I will not stand by and listen to you insult my WIFE in such a manner. I'll thank you to shut your filthy mouth!' I thought the Baroness was going to fall over when he let her go." Grandfather Abbott chuckled and said, "I had never seen that woman at a loss for words, but Edward's confession had certainly shut her up.

"The relief Edward felt from exposing the truth was enough to cause his collapse into a nearby chair, but only for a moment. Realizing his secret was out, he quickly decided the best place for him to be was by his beloved's side, so he bolted from the library and headed for the apartment. I was left to contend with Baroness Montclief and her recent shock."

"You poor dear," Mother Morgan sympathized. "That must have been just dreadful."

"It wasn't as bad as that," Grandfather Abbott continued. "She was recomposed from the shock of Edward's outburst by the time he left the library. She simply screwed her face into a makeshift smile and asked me who else knew of the situation. Had I but known what she was planning, Margaret, I would have told her that *everyone* knew." He looked at Mother Morgan so guiltily and forlornly that Libby was herself saddened by the exchange. "Instead, I told her no one knew." Libby tried to offer her grandfather a comforting smile, but he did not look up from his lap.

"You could not have known, Gerald. I in no way hold you responsible for *her* evil actions. Surely you know that by now. You must believe you are not to blame." Grandfather Abbott just stared into his lap and shrugged his shoulders.

Libby was growing impatient; she was the only person in the room who didn't know what had happened to the babies. She was anxious to keep the story moving but didn't know how to prompt them along without sounding ill-mannered and inconsiderate of her grandmother's feelings. Her face must have given away her desire to hear more of the story because Mother Morgan began telling the story again.

"It seems, Libby, that the Baroness grew suspicious of me when she was told by another of the staff that I was staying confined to our quarters more than usual. She never let on that she knew something was awry. Her desire for fashionable attire was stronger than her disdain for me, especially since she did not suspect that it was Edward's child. It was not until the night of the delivery that she learned the entire truth about my condition.

"Late in the morning, after the birth, the Baroness called my mother to her private office and instructed her to tell no one of the babes—not that she was planning to anyway, but the Baroness was quite threatening about the situation, stating that she would ruin any chances of employment for anyone in our family if we told that the babes were Edward's. So we all kept quiet while Edward tried to convince his uncle that he loved me and wanted to make his life with our children and me.

"In the days just after the birth, the babes were thriving, eating often and doing quite well, though they were small. I was slowly coming to terms with knowing that I would have to face the Baron and his wife when I was recovered from the delivery. The Baroness insisted that my mother and sisters return to their duties immediately so that the household would not be disturbed by the event. Mother didn't like it, but what choice did she have? To do otherwise would surely result in our dismissal. So I was often alone with the babes in our apartment during the daytime. We did not have visitors, not even the other staff and servants—I don't believe anyone knew much about what was going on with me. It seems the Baroness told them I was suffering from some sort of contagious illness, so they stayed away from our apartment as well as from my mother and sisters.

"Edward, evidently, spent a great deal of time those first few days in counsel with his uncle. He visited us a bit but could not stay any length of time, as his uncle was so distraught by the events that he had taken to his sickbed. On the eighth day after the delivery, the Baroness insisted that Edward attend to some business regarding tenants at the outermost edge of the estate. It seems there was a dispute between two of the tenants regarding some livestock, and since the Baron was too ill to travel, Edward would have to handle the matter. Edward rode out in the early morning, intent upon resolving the situation quickly and returning that same evening."

Mother Morgan again broke from her story and looked sorrowfully into the fire. Libby was acutely aware of how quiet the room was. Only the fire and the flicker of the candles could be heard. Mother Morgan began again at almost a whisper, "I fell asleep in the chair next to the fire." Her voice sounded so childlike and sad—so terribly sad that Libby could not look upon her grandmother's face. She felt awkward and uncomfortable as her grandmother spoke the words of the terrible deed done to her innocent children. "The babes were sleeping in the cradle next to my bed. I was so exhausted I didn't hear the door open. My sweet girls didn't make a sound as they were taken from my room." She paused again and this time released a long, sad sigh, as though resigning herself yet again to the realization that her babes were really gone.

"I don't know how long I slept . . . too long, though! I was startled awake by a popping in the fire and sat for a while longer thinking how good the girls were to allow me such rest. I knew the babes needed to eat, so I arose and walked to the cradle. At first I didn't understand why they weren't there in the cradle, so I quickly looked around the room, thinking perhaps Mother had come in and moved them. I began to panic and started screaming for help, and as I threw open our apartment door, my father was there coming up the hall, begging me to tell him what was the matter. I was hysterical, crying and begging him to find my babes when my mother came running with my sisters. Mother was able to calm me down enough so that I could explain that the babes had been taken from my room. She went straight to the Baroness; Father took a horse and rode out to find Edward. My sisters cradled me in their arms, cooing and trying to reassure me that the girls would be fine. Together the three of us waited for any news."

Exhausted from retelling such a traumatic event, Mother Morgan stopped talking and sipped her tea. Libby let out the breath she had been holding as quietly as possible, but given the silence in the room, it was impossible not to be heard. She didn't think that was the end of the story, but she could see quite clearly that her grandmother was not able to continue just yet. Her grandfather spoke up, "Edward was fetched back to the estate, though many hours passed before he arrived. There was a great deal of yelling and threatening as staff and servants were brought into the library for Edward to question. Margaret's father even insisted that the London police be brought in to question the staff, but Baron Montclief forbid anyone in the household from talking with authorities and insisted that he would find out who was behind the kidnapping. Meanwhile, Margaret and her family stayed alone in their apartment—shattered by their loss. They did not leave one another's side, for they felt at odds with everyone in the household except Edward and I, and they worried for Margaret's safety as well. Someone who could kidnap newborn babes from their mother would surely have no qualms about harming a young lady, so Edward insisted she not be left alone, both for her safety and for her emotional well-being."

Mother Morgan placed her hand on Grandfather Abbott's and smiled. She was ready to convey the next part of the story. "It had been two days since the babes were taken from me. They were the longest days of my life, for I did not know where my girls could be, or if they were even alive! It was so horrible; I cannot begin to explain the heart-ache—I only pray you never have to feel the hurt of it.

"On the evening of the second day, there was a quiet knock at our apartment door. I remember that Edward had been sitting near the fire talking quietly with Father, and he froze in mid-sentence, eyes turned toward the sound. We were all afraid of the news that was waiting on the other side of the door—terrible news waiting to come in and tear our world further apart. Father opened the door, and there stood one of the washer women whom we knew as Dwyn, her eyes red and swollen as though she had been crying for days. She was particularly dirty and smelled like she had been sleeping with animals. I remember how Louisa removed herself to the far back corner of the room with a handkerchief covering her nose and mouth—Louisa always did have a weak stomach for things that smelled badly. Dwyn was clutching something in her hand that looked like a scrap of fabric, and as she looked into my eyes from across the room, tears began rolling down her face.

"'I do so beg of your forgiveness, my dear,' she pleaded with me over and over as she wailed into the cloth in her hands. My father put his arm around her shoulder and guided her to his chair by the fire. His compassion shocked me, for I knew she was in some way responsible for my missing babes and I wanted to tear her to pieces. But then I heard him say 'Speak, woman,' his angry yet very controlled tone was one I had never heard before, 'and hold nothing back, for God's wrath will surely feel like feathers falling on your head compared to what I will do if you do not tell all that has been done.'

"The washer woman continued to shed large tears as she told of how Baroness Montclief had paid her five gold pieces to take the babes from the house and leave them at an address in London, just north of Great Ormond Street. Dwyn spoke of how reluctant she was to come back to the apartment to collect the babes for fear of being discovered, but the Baroness insisted she would get Edward away from the estate, and she would make sure no one was in the apartment except me. Dwyn looked apologetically at me when she uttered the next part, 'The Baroness told me to take the babes without incident if possible, but if necessary, I was to use force.' She continued to clutch the piece of fabric as she recounted her instructions for leaving the babes at the door of the building located at the address on the paper she was given; she was told to leave nothing with the babes except the swaddling clothes, and she was instructed to burn the paper with the address after she left. When she was finished with her task, she would be given another five gold pieces and new employment at an estate closer to her hometown in Wales.

"Her tears poured out like rain as she made excuses about missing her own children greatly and that the only reason she did the task was so she could go home. When I begged her to tell us where in London she had taken the babes, she paused long before answering. 'I took them to Bloomsbury Fields, Mum!' she whispered with downcast eyes, and my own mother let out a cry of shock. I felt sick to my stomach, though I didn't understand the implications of the name, so I asked Mother, who clearly knew the place, what it meant. She said in a voice I will never forget, 'It is where unwanted babes are left by mothers who cannot care for them.' She had left my babes at the Foundling Hospital.

"'My conscience would not allow me to leave them unidentifiable,' Dwyn said at last. 'I left them with bits of this fabric, and though I cannot write so as to have left them with a note, I told the nurse that their mother

would collect them as soon as she was able and to please keep them safe.'
She held out to me a piece of printed cotton and said that I could collect the
babes as long as I had this piece of fabric. Snatching the piece of cotton from
her hand, I glanced at Edward, stood, and headed for the door. Father and
Mother were close behind. Edward knew my intentions and was yelling at
the staff to fetch a coach immediately. Before too long, we were driving the
horses hard for the Foundling Hospital."

The room was very quiet; no one stirred or made any sound.
Mother Morgan wore a haggard expression. With sad eyes, Aunt Ellen
looked at Libby and finished where Mother Morgan could not, "They
were too late." Her voice seemed small and forlorn. "The babes had
taken ill, developed a fever, and could not nurse. Louisa had passed
away the day before, and the nurses had buried her near the chapel wall.
Franchesca died in Mother Morgan's arms."

Libby sniffed and used her handkerchief to wipe her eyes. She hadn't
even realized she had been crying throughout the last of the story. Her
lap was wet from her tears and her hands were shaking. What tragedy!
Her mind reeled from the thought of someone willing to steal a babe
from its mother—and yet this woman had taken two.

"I think you can understand the last letter a little better now, Libby,
can't you?" Mother Morgan asked with downcast eyes.

Libby nodded and sniffled and wiped her eyes again. "So you left
and came to America?" she asked as she remembered the details from
the letter and her mind put all the pieces together.

"We left," Mother Morgan sighed, "and we have never gone back."

The stillness of the room reflected the mood of its occupants.
Sadness seemed to drip from the candles as they burned. Libby, too,
was downcast, though she didn't really understand why. It all happened so long ago, and she had played no part in the story, but the
impact of the great loss was etched in her grandmother's eyes, and
bitter anger could still be seen in Grandfather Abbott's expression.

She felt their pain and their anger. The words of the letter rolled around in her head, and she understood her grandmother's disdain for Baroness Montclief.

Libby's Mother was stirring in the corner, loading up the tray with the teacups and teapot. Mother Morgan broke from her mournful trance and offered a genuine, though slight, smile to her granddaughter. "I'm afraid I haven't given you very pleasant thoughts for your bedtime dreams. But I promise tomorrow's stories won't be so dark."

Libby quickly arose and crossed the room to her grandmother's side. She knelt and placed her forehead on her grandmother's hands and said, "I'm so sorry for your loss, Grandmother." Then she looked up with an expression that conveyed her hatred. "The Baroness is a terrible woman, and I hope what your mother wrote in the letter comes true—I hope there is a special suffering set aside just for that dreadful woman."

"Libby, dear, let's not be dramatic." Mother Morgan patted Libby's hands and gave a resigned smile. "Life does go on, and for those of us who know Christ as our Savior, we are called to forgive others as Christ forgives us. I was so sad for a time, and very angry, and I wanted nothing more than to hurt Baroness Montclief for what she had taken from me. It took a long time, but I think I have forgiven her. And Mother was right—God blessed me with more children." She gestured to Aunt Ellen. "And grandchildren!" She turned her smile back on Libby. "Learning to forgive such a grievous crime pulled me from a dark pit of hatred and brought me into the light of God's grace and mercy. I came to feel sorry for the Baroness; she was so intent upon status and wealth, so shallow and weak in character. Her life was sad, child, don't you see? Though I did have some great sadness, I have also had great happiness— something I'm sure Baroness Montclief never experienced."

Libby rose and embraced her grandmother. "Thank you for sharing your story with me."

"Thank you, my dear, for allowing me."

Chapter 12

*L*ibby had a restless night of sleep in the big bed next to her mother. Her fretful dreams of crying babies that could not be found in the dark streets of a strange city awakened her before light, and she could not go back to sleep, so she decided to slip out to the kitchen to work on some patchwork before the rest of the household awoke.

Quietly as possible, she got the fire blazing in the stove and put the tea kettle on; she put her candle on the table and lit an extra one for added light, got out her box of patchwork, and began stitching together some of the pieces she had basted the night before, not noticing Mother Morgan standing in the doorway silently observing her.

"Good morning, child." Mother Morgan greeted Libby with a smile and pat on the head. "I see you are diligently working on your patches."

"I just thought I would get in an hour of sewing before everyone else awoke. Did you rest well last night, Grandmother?"

"As well as can be expected after such storytelling, I guess. And you?"

"Not so well, that's why I'm up," Libby responded uncomfortably. She felt guilty confessing that the stories she had wanted so badly to hear had upset her. She set down her patchwork and started to get up, but Mother Morgan interrupted her.

"Sit, child. Work on your sewing. I will get the tea started for us."

"Thank you," Libby replied as she returned to her patchwork. "I'm coming along with my flowers. In fact, after this one, I'll be ready for more templates."

Mother Morgan looked over Libby's shoulder. "I'm quite impressed with your work, Libby. I like the color combinations and lovely patterns you have put together." She picked up a particularly striking patchwork flower made with a vivid yellow-and-orange ombre print and turned it over to examine the stitching. "Lovely, just lovely," Mother Morgan complimented as she put the patchwork flower back on the table. "Your cuts are all uniform and straight. I'm impressed with your precision despite your inexperience. Yours will be a spread to rival my own."

Libby beamed at the compliments and sat just a bit taller for having them. She couldn't seem to stop grinning as she continued to sew the last seven hexagons together. Grandmother brought the tea to the table along with some slices of raisin bread that had been made the day before. She sat at the table with Libby and watched her affectionately as she finished sewing the last of the basted pieces together.

"Well, it appears we need another letter," said Mother Morgan.

Libby put her thimble and needle away in her huswif and picked up the stack of letters. She took the next in the stack and examined it front and back. There was no seal remaining on the letter, though she could see that the wax had been a dark green. The handwriting was different from the last two letters she had read; it was not nearly as fanciful as the first from the Baroness, and it wasn't as delicate as the letter from Great-Grandmother Hammond.

"I wonder who wrote this letter." Libby glanced inquisitively at her grandmother as she turned the letter over and began to open it.

"Well, pass it over and we shall see," replied her grandmother with an outstretched hand.

Libby finished opening the letter, noted the salutation, and handed the letter over to Mother Morgan. "It is addressed to you and Edward," Libby added as she passed the letter. "Oh, excuse me, I mean you and *Grandfather Morgan*." Libby blushed at her use of her grandfather's Christian name; she was not accustomed to using such familiar terms when referring to adults. The closeness she was beginning to feel with her grandmother was crossing the boundaries of adult and child; she was finding a friend in her grandmother.

"So it is!" exclaimed Mother Morgan with a smile. "And it's from Gerald—that would be *Grandfather Abbott* to you." She winked at Libby. As she read the first part of the letter, she said, "I haven't seen this letter in years. I remember now . . . he sent us this letter after we had lived in Boston about five years. We were pretty well settled by then; I was working in a shop in Beacon Hill, and Edward was working for a cotton exporter, reviewing their contracts with the European countries. It was a somber time for us both. You see, I missed my mother terribly, and I wasn't really over losing my babes. And Edward, well, he missed his country. He was so sad to leave England; the idea that he was immigrating to the United States and would no longer belong to England troubled him deeply. Captain Abbott was our dearest friend, and we had few other connections to England, save for my family and his mother, so we wrote often.

"My mosaic garden spread was constructed using so many of those wonderful letters. I remember piecing the flowers and touching their handwriting; just to hold the papers in my lap as I assembled the spread made me feel wrapped in their arms. That spread took many months to put together, and it was filled with bits of fabrics your Grandfather Abbott would send to me from his voyages. He sent me swatches just like he collected and put in your box. It was always a treat to get a letter from him." Mother Morgan turned the letter over a few times and looked at each page with a perplexed expression. "I wonder why I saved this particular letter?" she pondered out loud.

Libby sipped her tea and ate a few bites from the raisin bread. She snickered to herself then said, "Why not read it and find out?"

"Cheeky girl," Mother Morgan giggled in return. She turned to the page with the salutation and began reading.

To my Fondest Friends Edward and Margaret,

I send to you our most heartfelt congratulations on the recent news you have written concerning your upcoming addition to the family. I pray that all goes according to God's will and you are able to grow your family as you have long desired. I have news of my own to share concerning a similar matter. My own family is expecting a new addition, as Caroline is now with child. Such amazing fate befalls us that we shall both expect our children in the same month. The wonders of God never cease to amaze and delight; we both find ourselves very blessed indeed!

Dearest Margaret, Caroline sends her fond regards and asks me to convey the message that she would love to hear of the news of Boston as soon as you are able. She has begged for a trip to visit you this year, but given our new circumstance, I think such a journey is out of the question for the time being; perhaps next year we shall find ourselves in the Americas.

My letter is more than just the congratulations I offer on your upcoming addition. You will be happy to know that although the Baroness blocked my petition to speak with your uncle, I learned that after his weekly meetings with tenants, he spends Saturday evenings enjoying a pint of spirits at the Lost Lamb near Chelsea. I was fortunate enough to come upon him one Saturday while I was enjoying a pint of ale with my first mate, Jacobsen. Your uncle was rather surprised to see me seated in the corner of the public house, and I lifted my glass toward him as he walked to his seat. He tipped his hat and returned the smile, though it was troubled and not particularly inviting; however, I chose to take it as an invitation, regardless of its true meaning. I reached his table, and as he rose, I offered my hand. We shook and I could feel the weight of his troubles in his grip. After polite conversation about my recent appointment to the Ariana, the Baron looked at me with an expression of surrender and asked, "And what news of Edward?"

Though I was eager to tell him of your position with the Boston and Springfield Company, and to tell him of your wonderful news of the new babe on the way, I did not run headlong into the conversation. I felt the best way to play my hand was to make him want to hear about you even more than he already did. I smiled at him politely and said you were well then quickly changed the topic to his recent investments in cotton printing in Scotland. He was clearly eager to talk with me about you, but I didn't feel he was hungry enough to hear all that I had to say, so I drained my drink and made excuses for my hasty departure, but not before explaining that I would be visiting the Lost Lamb on the following Saturday evening and would enjoy partaking in some bitters with him were he to find himself available.

It was a risky bet to think he would come back, but he did, and we were able to talk over several hours and many pints. He informed me that his wife was on an extended visit to some family member in the border regions near eastern Scotland, and I must say, he seemed quite pleased about her absence. He spoke candidly of his displeasure over her actions and said he had deliberately sent her away from the estate and the lifestyle she loved so dearly. I will add that society gossip regarding the Baroness is not favorable, and all here have snubbed her invitations or requests for visits. I'm sure she suffers over it, though it is not suffering enough for the ills she has caused you.

Your uncle was heartened to hear that you were well settled in a good firm in Boston. He was concerned you had not the experience necessary to be well placed, but I explained that America was still a young country and welcomed fresh ideas

from young men willing to work hard—a very different place
than our stodgy, old England.

The Baron was also quite frank about his feelings of
abandonment by you, and no matter how many times I tried
to explain that the Baroness left you no other options, as she
would not acknowledge your marriage to Margaret, he stilled
banged down his mug and shouted that you had left him without an heir. We talked long into the evening and he begged
me write you that he is so very sorry about your daughters.
He confessed that he did not know anything about his wife's
schemes, but if he had, he would have stopped them before any
harm could come to your wife or children.

Edward, I believe him. He was genuine in both speech and
gesture. I hope you can forgive him for the great ignorance he so
clearly displayed in this circumstance and move to rebuild your
relationship. He loves you and I believe he wants the best for
you. I promised to pass along his regards, and with that done,
I will end my conversation about the Baron with one final comment. Your reconciliation with the Baron is foundational to any
hope we have of bringing our import plans to fruition.

I have more news of the Hammonds in Glasgow. Margaret
will be happy to hear that her cherished sisters, Louisa and
Jeanine, have both found themselves suitors. I was in Glasgow
for a visit to bring some chintzes and Indiennes I had picked up
on a recent trip to France. Shortly after I arrived, Louisa threw
her arms around me and exuberantly informed me that she was
in love, and that I would have the pleasure of meeting her beau
that very afternoon. I'm pleased to report that the gentleman
with whom she is enamored is simply perfect for her in every way.
He practically falls over himself to accommodate her every whim
and deepest desire. He brought with him that afternoon an older

cousin who was recently returned from Ireland, and I will say that he was captivated by Jeanine. We spent many hours in pleasant conversation and played some games around the table. The next day, the whole family picnicked at a nearby stream, and the two couples were inseparable. I hope I'm not jumping to conclusions, but I wouldn't be surprised if upcoming nuptials were in at least one couple's future. I will close my letter with this pleasant prediction for a happy future concerning Louisa and do ensure you will be first to know if it turns out otherwise.

I look forward to your letter and of hearing how you have written your uncle; he is anxious, Edward, and desires reconciliation. I pray you act quickly.

Ever Your Most Faithful Friend and Servant,
Captain Gerald Cephus Abbott
The Ariana

Libby looked up at her grandmother and smiled as she refolded the letter from Grandfather Abbott and placed it back on the stack of the other letters. "He writes quite eloquently, don't you think Grandmother? I could just picture them in my mind's eye, picnicking in a field near a stream, enjoying slices of fresh peaches while they gazed lovingly at one another. It's a pretty picture indeed." Libby smiled as she looked at her grandmother.

"It's a lovely memory, to be sure. I understand now why I kept this letter all this time. I feel close to my sisters even now as I read this letter so many years later." Mother Morgan looked at the cup she was holding and then looked at Libby and smiled. "Well, child . . . it seems rather self-explanatory. Do you have any questions about the letter before we cut it to bits?"

Libby gasped and quickly grabbed the letter and clutched it to her chest. "Surely you wouldn't cut this letter up, Grandmother?" Libby was taken aback by the ease at which Mother Morgan offered the letter up for sacrifice.

"Nonsense. There is no longer any need to keep this letter. Louisa and Jeanine write to me often, and Gerald and Caroline spend a great deal of time with me, particularly lately. I do not feel as if I will lose any precious memories by using this letter in your quilt. In fact, it will give the letter added meaning to know that it has made its way into your quilt and thus passed to future generations in the family."

Libby looked at the letter in her hands then at her grandmother. She thought for a moment about the words in the letter that had piqued her interest. What exactly had Grandfather Abbott said about "reconciliation" and bringing "plans to fruition"? She opened the letter quickly and began to reread until she found the part she was looking for. "It says here," Libby pointed at the lines in the letter, "that Grandfather wanted a reconciliation between the Baron and Grandfather Morgan if they were to bring their 'plan to fruition.' Was there? Reconciliation, I mean." Libby asked her grandmother.

Mother Morgan looked down sadly at her teacup. She looked back at Libby and shook her head slowly. "Unfortunately, there was not. Edward did write him a letter to say he was returning to England on a very important matter, but the Baron passed away before he could see him again. Edward's passage was booked for just after Thomas was due to be born. Sadly, we received a letter from solicitors just one week before the ship's sailing date that told of the Baron's passing. Edward was heartbroken, to be sure."

Libby felt sad as she thought of her poor grandfather's broken heart. She presumed that without reconciliation, there was certainly no hope of inheritance. She looked at the letter then asked, "What 'plan' was Grandfather talking about?"

"Plan?" Mother Morgan asked. "Show me?"

Libby pointed to the line in the letter and read it aloud, "*Your reconciliation with the Baron is foundational to any hope we have of bringing our import plans to fruition.*"

"Hmm," Mother Morgan scratched her head and replied, "I can't imagine what those two were scheming. I think this is a question you will have to ask your grandfather. He should be up any time now, perhaps at breakfast we can inquire as to this mysterious plan of his."

Libby looked out the window to see the sun inching its way over the horizon. She could hear the bleating of the cows as they were being guided into the milking barn, and she surmised that the ginger cat would be following close behind. She remembered how the cat lapped up the milk that was squirted at her face, and a smile spread across her own with the memory of her morning spent milking cows with the Bigalow brothers.

Chapter 13

*R*eluctant to interrupt the breakfast conversation, Libby slowly chewed her bacon beyond necessity. She was eager to ask her questions of Grandfather Abbott concerning the mysterious "plan" that was mentioned in the most recent letter she had read, but her mother and aunt were monopolizing the conversation with talk of wedding plans and how the dress should be fashioned. Albert and James were casting wearisome glances at one another. Failed efforts to get his mother's attention were wearing on Albert's patience, so he reached over and began tapping her repeatedly on the arm. He blurted out rather rudely, "Excuse me, please, ma'am, but we need to ask you a question and your conversation is dragging on so, I fear we will not have an opportunity to leave the table before dark."

Libby was particularly quiet because she knew this situation wasn't going to end well. She could see the irritation growing on her aunt's face as Albert unsuspectingly continued to tap her arm. He tapped and tapped with an annoyed look on his face until he glanced up and his eyes met his mother's.

Her expression was severe. "Have you forgotten yourself, Albert?" She glanced at the other adults at the table and begged their forgiveness for her son's impertinence then returned her stern gaze to Albert. "Young man, you have been reminded often enough that you should not interrupt adult conversation. It is disrespectful to speak to me in such a manner. Apologize, please!" she insisted

"I'm sorry, Mother, it's just that all this talk of dresses is simply dreadful to my ears, and James and I had hoped to go to the creek with Grandfather to catch something for our supper, but we really must get our chores finished if we hope to go before the day is too warm for fishing." Albert offered his most angelic smile and batted his long eyelashes lovingly at his mother as he now softly stroked her arm.

"That is no excuse for bad behavior!" She spoke harshly at first, but try as she might to maintain the authority in her voice, she was soon conquered by his sweet, familiar charm that was so like his father's. "Next time, wait until there is a lull in conversation before you try to gain my attention, and for heaven's sake, stop tapping my arm repeatedly. A single tap is sufficient to let me know I am needed. Now run along, you little charmer, and don't let me catch you swimming in the creek without Grandfather there to watch, or I will have reason to get my yardstick and tan your hide."

Successful in his task to get what he wanted without getting thrashed, he turned his attention to his cousin, "Would you like to come with us, Coz?" Albert asked Libby as he grabbed the last piece of toast and pushed the entire piece in his mouth, much to his mother's horrified expression.

"I do have some questions I would like to ask Grandfather," Libby started, and then she looked at her mother. "Would it be all right if I went with them? I could take along the last letter and trace my templates while I ask Grandfather my questions."

Her mother looked at Mother Morgan, and Libby noticed an unspoken conversation occur between them; she then looked back at Libby and said, "Yes, dear, that will be fine. But when you have finished, come find your grandmother and I—we have some things we would like to discuss with you."

Intrigued by her mother's comment but undaunted from her quest to find out what the "plan" was that her grandfathers had been scheming,

Libby excused herself from the table and went about the business of clearing the dishes. She quickly stepped through her other chores and completed the morning's ritual of her toilet. She was getting better at putting up her own hair into a style similar to what she had seen on Catherine Masterson, though she could not make her ringlets look quite the same as her grandmother had done. With her coolest day dress on—for the day would be hot—Libby gathered her sewing implements, her template, and the most recent letter, put them in a basket she had brought from the kitchen for that purpose, and headed to find her cousins.

The boys were standing in the kitchen near the stack of wood next to the stove, and Libby could tell they were having a disagreement. They both held something in their hands, and as she drew closer, she noticed that Albert held a small tin cup filled with dirt, and James held some wriggling worms. James said, "But it's so cruel, Al! Don't you think the worms will feel it when the hook goes through their bellies? Can't we just use some bacon?"

Albert shook his head and pushed the tin cup at James. "This is how *real* sailors fish, James. Now stop being such a sissy and put the worms in the cup." Albert had very little patience for his ever-so-slightly younger brother. "The worms eat the dirt! The fish eat the worms! We eat the fish!" Albert chanted. "That's how it works."

James took the cup and gently placed the worms in one by one. Then he took the cup and put it in his jacket pocket.

Libby saw Albert cast an exasperated look at James, who was mumbling something about the worms being a sacrificial offering to appease the fish gods, then she watched James sulk out to the porch to fetch the fishing poles, all the while grumbling about how silly it was to use worms when bacon was just as effective, and the worms were of better use in the garden soil than on the end of a hook.

"I sure hope he doesn't ever try to be a real sailor!" Albert stated as he looked at his cousin. Libby smiled and didn't engage in conversation with Albert because she knew it was pointless to explain to a single-minded boy that there were other things in the world besides sailors and fish and the sea.

"Where is Grandfather?" Libby diverted Albert's attention to something other than his sibling. "I hope he is still going with us."

"You bet I am," came her grandfather's booming voice from behind. Libby turned to see her grandfather coming through the kitchen door, and she couldn't help but stare. His breeches were clean, his white shirt starched and bright—but the entire outfit was seriously lacking the usual formality with which her grandfather dressed. Gone were his tie and starched collar; no longer did he don his double-breasted coat. He was so casual in these new clothes that Libby though he looked the part of farmhand, not merchant ship's captain. "I wouldn't miss a morning of fishing with my three favorite people for any amount of begging by your grandmother. She wants me to hold her yarn while she knits a new pair of stockings. What say ye, First Mate Albert? Are we ready to pull anchor?" He patted Albert on the back as he spoke and Albert beamed.

"Ready to set sail, Captain Abbott! Shall I hoist the mainsail?"

Libby was amused at how much Albert loved to speak nautical terms with his grandfather; she thought it must make him feel like a true sailor talking with a real ship's captain.

"Not before the entire crew has been accounted for," Grandfather replied. "Where is James?" Grandfather Abbott was looking around as James came back through the kitchen door still mumbling to himself about the worms. "Ah, there you are. Are you ready to catch your supper, young man?" Grandfather Abbott inquired of James, who hadn't noticed that everyone was looking at him.

"Huh? What? Excuse me, sir. Were you speaking to me?"

Libby recognized James's guilty and confused expression as he quickly put the can of worms behind his back in an effort to hide it, though he was more obvious than inconspicuous.

"Let's get going," Albert begged without paying any attention to James. "The sun is on the rise, and if it gets too hot, the fish take naps." He was pulling Libby's arm as he moved toward the door.

The three children and their grandfather headed out through the back door and followed the path past the barn and down toward the stream. Being late in the spring, coupled with a dryer than normal month of May, the stream had slowed its pace past the back of the barn, and it now drifted slowly off toward the south. There were many spots along the stream where the water had cut back on itself during the rainy season, leaving sandbars and large pools. These were just the places where the trout liked to hole up, and Albert was quite familiar with them. He plodded through the brush ahead of the others, all the while ignoring the calls from Libby to wait for them.

At one point, Albert got too close to the steep bank, and his foot started to slide out from under him just as Grandfather caught his arm and pulled him back away from the edge. "Now there, sailor, steady as she goes!"

Albert grinned up at his grandfather as he regained his footing and said, "Thanks, mate! I just about capsized there!"

Libby scolded, "You need to take more care, Albert! And for goodness' sake, slow down!" She was getting tired of hollering at him to wait.

After a few moments, the path opened into a lovely sloping bank that lead to the stream's edge. The sandy shore cut back far into the bank to reveal a dark, deep pool that was shaded by a willow tree. "This is the place." Albert smiled as he headed to the sandbar that had been created by the cut back of the stream. "James, where are the worms?"

Looking down at his shoes, James did not make eye contact with his brother; he simply handed over the tin cup that contained the fish bait. Grandfather was getting the pole line ready. Remembering

James's guilty face back at the house, Libby paid close attention to the boys because she presumed there was something amiss with the bait.

"Hey! Where are all the worms?" Albert hollered at his brother as he dug his fingers through the tin cup that was full of dirt but no worms. Albert's face was turning bright red in anger as he dumped the dirt onto the ground and spread it out to find no fish bait in the cup. "What did you do, James?" Albert barked.

"I couldn't do it!" James looked at his grandfather with eyes that begged for mercy. "I just couldn't let those good worms be wasted on the end of a hook. Please don't be angry, Albert. Look, here," he retrieved from his pocket a greasy handkerchief that was folded into a neat little package and tried to hand it to Albert, "I brought you some bacon. I bet it works just as well as worms."

Ignoring the package that James held out, Albert was tossing his hands in the air, walking in circles around his wormless dirt pile, and ranting on and on about how he should never have entrusted the worms to James.

Trying to diffuse the situation, Grandfather Abbott grabbed a fishing pole and said, "Well, there is nothing to be done about it now, Albert. Best we get to fishing with what we have before it's too late." He took the greasy rag from James with a kind and understanding smile.

Albert and Grandfather headed to the sandy spot near the pool and began baiting their hooks. They spoke in quiet tones about how the biggest fish would by lying just near the edge of the bank, in the darkest and deepest spots. Albert was quite efficient at casting his bacon-baited hook in the exact place pointed out by Grandfather.

James and Libby found a comfortable patch of grass under a nearby tree and sat down together. Looking more despondent than normal, James did not initiate any conversation, so Libby just sat quietly with him and patted his back. Finally, she broke the silence, "Fear not, James, you are not alone. I do understand your reasoning." Her voice was compassionate and her touch sympathetic. "Worms *are* more useful in a garden. Anyone can see that it is so. They are good and faithful servants to the farmer, helping to make the soil fertile and fruitful. But to the fisherman, they are simply a sacrifice that may *or may not* end up providing a meal. Albert will forgive you, do not fret."

James smiled at Libby's kind words, but before he could reply, he heard Albert holler, "Got one!" They jumped up and headed to the sandy spot where the fishermen were wrestling the recent catch to the shore. The catch was a large brown trout that flopped frantically on the sandy bank. Albert wrestled the hook from its mouth, and just as he was putting the fish in the basket, Grandfather hooked himself another. Albert's excitement at actually catching fish shone on his face. No longer could Libby see his irritation toward his twin, in fact, he hollered for James to bring him "more of the *magic* fish bait he called bacon." James beamed with pride as he handed his brother a slice that was the same size as a worm. "They are biting like crazy, James. They seem to love your bacon," Albert said with an exuberant smile.

Grandfather Abbott gave Libby the fishing pole, and it didn't take long for her to hook a small brown trout. "Grandfather!" she hollered. "I've got one! I've caught my first fish!" Together they brought the fish up onto the sandbar and looked it over, but decided that it was too small, and it would be best to throw it back in the water. They had caught so many fish by this time that throwing back a small one didn't seem to matter much.

After a time, James was given Grandfather's fishing pole, and he and his brother were contentedly sitting together waiting for the next fish to bite, talking quietly about what other type of fish bait they might try.

Grandfather and Libby were seated in the grassy spot under the shade tree looking at the letter she had brought with her. "Mother Morgan explained most of the letter to me already," Libby began, "but she couldn't remember anything about the 'plan' you mention just here." She pointed to the particular lines in the letter.

"Hmm." Grandfather scratched his chin. "Now let me think a moment. This letter was written just after I found out we were going to have a baby. Do you know who that baby was?" he asked his granddaughter with a smile.

"Well, since my mother and father were both born in the same month, I figured it must have been my mother. Was it?" she replied.

"Yes, that's correct, it was your mother. We were so excited to be having another baby. Your mother was a welcome joy to our small family. We had just received a letter from your grandmother informing us that she was expecting, and it was glad news as it had been several years since losing the twins. I had feared she may not have more children. We were trying desperately to get Edward back to England so that he could meet with his uncle and resolve the issue of his disinheritance. You see, Libby, Baron Montclief had no heir except Edward. There were no male children to inherit the estate, and though the Baroness would have loved for one of her own brothers to be the heir, it simply would not happen. Many years before Edward was born, legal papers had been drawn up indicating that the estate *must* pass to an heir in the line of the Montclief family—specifically, a male heir—and it forbade the passing of the estate to someone outside the Montclief family. The Baron's own father had had the papers drawn up just after his son was married because he didn't care much for his son's choice in women. He recognized her greed and took measures to make sure she would never be able to inherit the estate. If his son had no children, then the estate would pass to his daughter's sons or grandsons. A nephew or grand-nephew was also acceptable if no direct heir was living. And since the Baron had no children, his nephew, Edward, was the last legal heir.

"Your Grandfather Edward and I knew that with the Baron's failing health it was imperative that the two be reconciled as soon as possible. Our *plan* was to get Edward back to England for a visit with his uncle under the guise of securing a financial investment in a textile printing mill in Thornliebank near Glasgow, Scotland. A friend from school, Alexander Crum, had developed a new way to print indigo, and we were quite interested in exporting the goods from Glasgow to America, but we needed a financial backer for the mill's export company. Since I knew the Baron was anxious to see his nephew, I felt sure that a meeting over business was the perfect way to break the ice and get the two talking again. And if they were talking, they could reconcile their differences and Edward would be reinstated as the heir to the Montclief Estate. Not that Edward gave a hoot for the estate or the money and title. He had given that up with the loss of his daughters— he had chosen a new life in America and did not see himself returning permanently. But he did love his uncle and desired deeply to mend the broken relationship."

"Mother Morgan said that they never did reconcile," Libby stated forlornly as she fondled the letter.

"Sadly, that is true." Grandfather looked back at the letter. "It was unfortunate to learn of the Baron's death. When I went to pay my respects at the funeral, the Baroness asked many, many questions—none of which I answered. She was quite anxious to learn any news of Edward and Margaret. You see, the Baron had been willing to allow her to return to Braidsmuir, but he was quite unwilling to ever speak to her again. He was so angry at the deed she had done your grandparents; also, I think he knew that she did not regret her actions, and they were self-centered actions, to be sure. She had a greedy soul and wanted desperately to see the money go to someone in her family. So Baron Montclief did not give her the satisfaction of knowing whether or not he had reconciled with Edward. In fact, he would take all knowledge of the estate's future to the grave, and the estate has remained in trust these many years.

"The Baroness was allowed to live at Braidsmuir and was given a small stipend each month for household expenses; however, she did not have control over the fortune—that was left for the solicitors to handle.

I have only recently learned of some new legal documents that surfaced following the Baroness's death. You know, that wicked woman lived to be quite old, Libby. She was nearly ninety when she died." He looked off down the creek, and a contradictory expression crossed his weathered face. "I heard it was quite a painful death." Libby thought she could see a slight smile on her grandfather's face. "My wife's maidservant had family that worked as Braidsmuir's kitchen staff, and they spoke of her final days as being agonizing. She had suffered an apoplexy and lived, though she was unable to walk or talk. It took nearly five years for her death to finally come."

"It was not painful enough, if you ask me," said Libby with a tone of hatred.

"Now, now, child." Grandfather wagged his finger at Libby and shook his head. "Let no evil fill your heart for the likes of her. God's plan is such that we may never understand why people so evil are granted so many years on earth. Regardless of our understanding, she was part of His plan of glory, and it is for glory's sake that we do not hate—not even her."

Grandfather had not been mean about his scolding of her attitude; it was simple and straightforward. So Libby took the chiding in stride and allowed him to continue his story without pouting.

"I have asked the Reverend Masterson to collect my correspondence from Boston and bring it by the farm on his return to Hartford. I am expecting a letter of great importance." With this last statement he looked at the boys, who had begun to argue over the final bit of bacon, and remarked that it was about time for them to head back to the house. "Supper is long overdue, don't you think?" He smiled at his granddaughter and patted her hand. As he rose from his seat in the grass, he stretched and groaned like an old dog. "My goodness, these old bones are not used to sitting on the ground for so long. Shall we go, my dear?" He extended his hand to Libby, and she smiled as he hoisted her to her feet as though she weighed nothing. "Collect your things, child, and I'll bring the boys along."

As she picked up her things, Libby contemplated her grandfather's comments. He was expecting a letter "of great importance." What could that mean? If the Baroness was now dead and the estate was still without an heir, could it make any difference to her family? It seemed doubtful; after all, Mother Morgan did say she had "made sure" that she would never inherit any of the Montclief estate. As these questions and speculations rolled around in her head, Libby absentmindedly picked up her basket and followed the boys and her grandfather along the path toward the barn. Her young mind was reeling from the thought of her family being heir to a fortune in England.

They boys chattered on about how many fish they'd caught, and James reminded Albert that bacon really was the best bait—better than any old worm. Albert happily agreed as he held up his string of trout and insisted that next time they try ham chunks to see if they would work just as well. "They will probably stay on the hook better than the bacon, don't you think, Grandpa?" Albert asked with a backward glance at Grandfather Abbott.

"Sailors often use salt pork, Albert, when they are desperate to catch something. It doesn't work well with the saltwater fish, but these freshwater types really seem to go for the bacon, so I say give it a try."

As the group tromped up the path to the back of the house, Mother Morgan gestured to Libby from her chair under the tree. "Libby, dear, can you join me for a moment please?"

The boys ran to Mother Morgan and held up the string of trout. "Can you believe it, Grandmother?" Albert burst forth. "Look at how many we caught."

"Pure abundance, Albert! How lucky you were to catch so many," Mother Morgan replied with a reluctant smile as she recoiled from Albert's swinging string of fish.

"It wasn't luck," said Albert as he patted James on the back. "It was pure genius on the part of James. He pitched the worms back in the garden and brought bacon instead. I never thought it would work, but it did. He deserves the credit."

James stood taller with the compliments and added, "It took some skill to catch them, too, Albert, and that was all you."

Libby was heartened to see the exchange between her cousins.

"Well, they are lovely trout. Go ahead and take them into the kitchen so that your mother can prepare them for supper. I would like to speak with Libby privately." She smiled at her grandsons then added, "And please remember to wash up before you tromp through the house. Leave your boots outside; you brought quite a bit of the riverbank home with you."

As the boys headed back to the house, Libby knelt beside her grandmother's chair. She could see that Mother Morgan was working on some lace and asked, "Is that for Aunt Ellen's wedding?"

"Yes, isn't it lovely? It is some Chantilly that your grandfather brought me from France—a birthday gift some years past. I thought your auntie would like it for her veil. What do you think?"

"It's quite lovely. I'm sure she will adore it." Libby reached to touch the cream-colored lace and then remembered what the shopkeeper had told her about washing her hands before handling her white fabric. She glanced at her hand then withdrew it to her lap and smiled apologetically at her grandmother.

"Your mother and I thought you might like to help make your auntie's wedding trousseau. I believe you have a nice hand with your needle, and Aunt Ellen will require several handkerchiefs. I was thinking it would be an excellent project for one as talented as you. What do you say? Would you like to help with the trousseau?" Mother Morgan asked.

"Do you really think I'm talented?" Libby asked with honesty, for she did not feel that her skills were at all a "talent."

"Quite! You have taken to sewing like a duck to water. Even your father was not so determined when he began. I think your abilities are more than sufficient for the kerchiefs your aunt will require. I have some finer white goods for the kerchiefs. Your mother will show you how to put the monogram in the corner. You may decorate them as you like—as long as it is tasteful. Perhaps you can sleuth out Aunt Ellen's favorite flower and add that to an opposite corner or as an edge trim." Mother Morgan smiled at her granddaughter and patted her head. "Now tell me, did Grandfather answer your questions?"

"Questions?" Libby looked confused for a moment. "Oh, I almost forgot. Yes, he did. He explained about an investment opportunity they were planning with a mill in a place called Thornliebank near Glasgow, Scotland. AND . . ." this part she said with such enthusiasm it made Mother Morgan stop her stitching and look up, ". . . he told me he was waiting for news from England—news about the Montclief Estate. He said something about new legal papers that surfaced after the Baroness's death. Did you know she had died?" Libby added the last bit as an afterthought.

"He did mention it to me upon his arrival." Mother Morgan patted her granddaughter's hand. "Though he didn't elaborate much about the subject. He is careful not to speak often of her because he believes it upsets me." She gave her granddaughter a sideways look. "I can assure you," she remarked unconvincingly, "I don't give that woman a second thought!" She flung her sewing into the basket on the other side of the chair and began to get up.

"Aren't you a little curious about the legal papers?" Libby asked hesitantly.

"If they pertain to me, I guess I will find out soon enough," she remarked as she picked up her basket of sewing. "But I am sure it is not likely that it has any thing to do with me. Now let's head in. I suddenly find myself in need of a cup of tea."

Chapter 14

*L*ibby spent the next several days working on her patchwork and her aunt's wedding handkerchiefs. The stack of *Godey's Lady's Books* her aunt had given her as a birthday gift proved most useful. She found a pattern for lovely handkerchiefs that even provided instructions on how to monogram. Between the *Godey's* and her mother's assistance, Libby had succeeded in creating several lovely and delicate additions to Aunt Ellen's wedding trousseau. Her amateur needlework impressed all the ladies of the house, and Libby was quite proud of her accomplishments.

She had also read several more of the letters, which were, for the most part, uneventful. A few were from her Great-Grandmother Hammond, who wrote the details of Jeanine's and Louisa's engagements and weddings. Grandfather Abbott had been right in his assumption that the girls would be married before too long. Libby was heartened to learn that her great-aunts had found true love and lived happily, each having babies of their own. She asked Mother Morgan if she wanted to keep the letters by which to remember her sisters, but as before, she was encouraged to cut them up and use them for her templates.

There was one letter in particular that was a bit puzzling to Libby. It was written by a Mr. John James Basset III of Cornwall—a name she had never heard mentioned before. His one-page note provided a simple greeting and a single question. He asked, "How long must I await your reply?" The letter was dated about two years before she was born, and it was addressed to Mary Abbott, her mother, at an address she recognized as Grandfather Abbott's home in England. The letter was signed "Your most *affectionate* servant," and Libby found the closing line perplexing because it expressed a great deal of sentiment despite its briefness. She decided that since it was addressed to her mother, she would take her questions directly to the source.

Libby found her mother sitting in the parlor with a copy of *The Daily Atlas.* She was commenting on an article regarding a new clipper ship called the *Flying Cloud.* "It was built by one of our patrons," she said to Aunt Ellen. "A Mr. Donald McKay." She followed up with a rather wicked comment, "His wife is a lovely woman who doesn't seem to understand that yellow silk, no matter how costly, does terrible things to a redhead's complexion, particularly in the daylight." Her mother tossed her head in the same manner that Libby recalled seeing Mrs. McKay do when she was in the shop looking over fabrics. Her mother gave a sheepish smirk and Aunt Ellen laughed out loud, but upon seeing her niece standing quietly in the doorway, Aunt Ellen stifled her laugh with a cough. "Goodness, Libby, you snuck in here like a little mouse." She glanced at Libby's mother and tried to cover a guilty smile.

"I beg your pardon, Auntie. I needed to ask Mother a question, and I didn't want to interrupt." Libby's tone was ever so slightly condescending for having caught the ladies in the act of mockery, and as a result, her mother turned a bright shade of crimson.

Libby stepped through the doorframe and entered the room. She sat on the footstool and produced the letter from her apron pocket. "I wonder, Mother, if you can help me to understand this letter, please?"

Libby handed her mother the letter, which she looked at for a few moments before she started to giggle like a young schoolgirl and handed the letter over to Aunt Ellen. Confused, Libby frowned and slumped back on the stool with a pout. She'd been sure she had discovered a dark secret that her mother had been keeping and half expected her to be shocked by the appearance of the strange letter. Aunt Ellen looked curiously at the letter, opened it, and then burst out laughing, but this time she didn't try to cover it up. "Oh my," she guffawed, "I had forgotten all about HIM!" Aunt Ellen handed the letter back to Libby's mother as she tried to curtail her chuckles.

"Who is he?" Libby asked, somewhat irritated at the joke that seemed to accompany the letter, and to which she was not privy to appreciate.

"Well . . ." her mother began hesitantly, "his name was John."

"I can see that," Libby prodded. "But *who* is he, or, rather, what is his relationship to the family?" She glanced back and forth between her mother and aunt. She could see the way the two women silently communicated. Then she saw Aunt Ellen nod her head, and she realized they had reached a decision to include Libby in the conversation without even speaking a single word.

"He was a young man I knew in London, Libby," her mother began.

"A rather *wealthy* young man!" Aunt Ellen added with a teasing tone and smirk.

"Now Ellen, you know very well it was his father's money," Libby's mother replied.

"True enough, but it did naught to limit his spending it!" Ellen stated mater-of-factly.

"But who is he, Mother?" Libby beseeched—her patience was wearing thin at being left out of the knowing.

"We met at a poetry reading and . . . I guess you could say we . . ." her mother paused and looked again at Aunt Ellen for support, ". . . courted."

Libby was hanging on her mother's words, leaning forward in expectation, but when "courted" came out, she was so caught off guard that she reeled backward and fell off the footstool with a bump.

Looking up from her resting place on the floor, Libby mumbled, "Courted?" She was trying to wrap her mind around the fact that her mother had courted someone other than her father. "But how is that possible?" she asked looking between her mother and aunt confusingly. Then, remembering what the note said, she asked disapprovingly, "You weren't going to marry him, were you?"

"Well, he did ask me," was all her mother could say.

"Of course she wasn't going to marry him, silly girl." Aunt Ellen gave a disregarding wave at the letter and added, "She was in love with Thomas from the first time they met as children. They were destined to be together, and no silly, rich boy from London was going to change that fact."

"Goodness, Mother, will you please tell me the story of this John person?" Libby's exasperated tone was just short of rude.

"As I said," her mother's voice was calming, "he was a young man I knew in London, someone with whom I shared an interest in poetry. He was a year younger than I, and he knew no one in town because he had just come back to England after a long stay in India, where his father had been conducting some sort of business. He was like a lost, little puppy, so I befriended him. We often sat together and discussed the poems and literature we enjoyed—it was quite harmless." Libby thought she sounded a little defensive.

"Your auntie is correct, though. I was in love with your father from the moment we met. You see, your grandfather had allowed me to accompany him in my fourteenth summer to visit the Morgans in Boston. I got to meet Thomas and Ellen firsthand, though we knew one another quite well by then through our correspondence. We had been writing to each other ever since I was old enough to make my letters; Father had decided that we would all benefit from a penned relationship, me learning of the Americas and them learning of England. So we wrote often and became dear friends. The summer I visited, we were

129

together every day! It was such a fun visit, do you remember, Ellen?" She returned her sister-in-law's smile, and Libby scooted closer to hear the story, no longer feeling annoyed, only curious.

"Thomas and I had so much in common—we loved all the same books and enjoyed the same foods. We often sat and talked for hours about nothing at all. It was like I had found my other half." Libby thought about her mother's dreamy expression as she talked about her father. It made her feel good to know there was so much love between them.

"But then I had to leave him and go home to England." She noticed the slight change in her mother's voice. "Over the next few years we wrote to each other frequently. Our friendship grew and we became closer, but I never imagined we would get married. The great ocean that lay between us had drowned any hopes I had for that dream. I believed we would always be friends, but I thought marriage would have to come with someone else. Then I met John, and he liked me. He was someone I could talk with, and not just through one-sided letters. He was a tangible person whom I could look in the eyes and see smile when I said something amusing. It was a very different relationship than what I shared with your father, who lived so very far away.

"And yes, John came from a very wealthy family like your auntie said; I, on the other hand, was the daughter of a merchant captain, and though I was not a social pariah, John and I did not travel in the same circles. I'm sure you can imagine how people talked when they saw us together. Some of the more 'elegant' girls said he lowered his sights when he turned them on me." Libby's mother paused then continued more matter-of-factly, "I guess you could say we courted," she shrugged, adding, "unofficially, though, because his family didn't really know about me. In fact, when he did ask me to marry him, I don't think he had consulted his family for their permission; he was quite secretive about the whole thing.

"It was the spring of my eighteenth year, and John still had another year of studies at his university, but I had finished my schooling and was going to travel a bit with my mother and older sister. I would be leaving when summer came, and poor John was quite distraught with the idea that he may never see me again. As I think on it now, it was such a sweet gesture, his asking for my hand. He was so very innocent and shy. We were sitting under a tree in the park. I remember we had been sitting for almost an hour comparing Dickens to Lever and debating which one was a better storyteller. I began to get distracted from our conversation because I couldn't stop thinking about how hard the bench felt and how my bottom was beginning to go numb from sitting on the stone for so very long. I was shifting about, trying to find a comfortable position for my skirts in hopes of adding some cushion to the seat." Libby grinned with the picture of her dainty mother squirming around on the bench trying to act ladylike.

"Much to my surprise, John fell to the ground on one knee, grasped me by the hand, and began confessing his deepest love for me. At first, I thought I had knocked him off the bench with my wiggling, but as I listened to his words, I began to realize what was happening. He insisted that I not leave and that we get married immediately. In thinking about it now, he looked so childish when he begged me to accept his proposal. But at the time, it startled me so that I practically knocked him over as I jumped to my feet. I must say that I was totally caught off guard, for though I knew John quite liked me as a friend, not once did I consider that he could love me so much he would ask for my hand." Libby noticed her mother's gaze shift to the letter she was holding. "This letter is the only proof that he ever asked me to marry him."

"Well," Aunt Ellen interjected, "that letter *and* all the people at your wedding who heard him plead with you not to marry Thomas."

"He showed up at your wedding?" Libby's mouth was agape. The story was getting more shocking as it went along.

"It really was the sweetest gesture." Her mother glanced again at the letter in her hand. "And it certainly livened up the ceremony."

"What happened? Tell me all the details, please!" Libby begged.

"Well, after his unexpected proposal, I regained my composure as any lady would and explained that I needed time to consider. He was embarrassed by his own haste and said he understood. Then he insisted that I take all the time I needed to come to a decision, and he again expressed that his love was forever and that he would do whatever he could to win my heart. I was quite flattered, for he was such a sweet boy, so very innocent and kind. I'm sure I was his first love. So I wrote to Ellen and Thomas and told them of the proposal and all that had transpired. I asked for their advice and assured them that I would not marry John until I received word from them that it was the right decision. I didn't tell anyone else, not even my mother and father."

"Oh, my goodness!" Libby blurted out. "That must have been such a long time for poor John to wait for an answer. Letters take ever so long to cross the Atlantic; you had to send one and then wait for one to come back. It must have taken forever."

"I never got a letter back." Her mother spoke flatly and without emotion.

Libby was again dumbfounded. "Whatever do you mean? Surely they wrote you, for you did not marry him."

"They did not write me back . . ." she dragged out this part of the story," . . . they came to England, to 'rescue me,' as Thomas put it." She grinned at Libby.

"We certainly did!" exclaimed Aunt Ellen. "How on earth could we ever let you marry that silly boy? He was kind indeed, but he was no match for our Mary." Aunt Ellen directed this last part at Libby. "She would have been bored to tears living with him and his family in Cornwall, with all that money and nothing to do from one day to the next. Surely you must agree, Mary? And besides, they were not the type of people who would have allowed you to continue a relationship with us uncouth Americans. Indeed, we would have lost our Mary forever, so we decided she would not marry Mr. Bassett if we could at all prevent it. We convinced our father to take us to England and talk some sense into her. Thomas and I stayed in London with the Abbotts while Father continued to Glasgow to meet with some business associates."

Libby was quite interested to hear the details of her mother's youth—to know that a very wealthy young man from Cornwall courted her was the most fascinating thing she had heard since finding out her Aunt Ellen had a new suitor in John Masterson. Her mother had never spoken much about her days in London, and Libby had no idea there were ever any beaus before her father. Oddly, the more Libby looked at her mother's appearance, the less surprised she was to know there were suitors other than her father; she was a very attractive woman, with her lovely auburn hair, porcelain complexion, and dancing green eyes that seemed engaging over even the most dreary conversation. Libby found it quite natural that men would see her mother as attractive, though she had never thought much about it before today.

"You should have seen your face when you opened the door to see us standing there. The confusion mixed with happiness was written upon your brow as though with pen and ink." Libby brought her attention back to the conversation and saw Aunt Ellen smile affectionately at her mother. "We had come just in the nick of time—you were quite torn about what to do with Mr. Bassett, and you had begun to talk yourself into accepting his proposal. Fortunately, we showed you the error of your ways." Aunt Ellen went on to explain to Libby that Thomas had really been the key to changing her mother's mind. Her father knew from the beginning he wanted to marry Libby's mother, but they were too young at first, and he could not yet support a family. So he completed his studies and worked diligently, getting himself situated in the shop in Boston. He needed naught but his wife and the connection his father had made for him in Glasgow to begin his new life. "Your father spent many hours in private conversation with your mother. He did everything to convince her of his love for her. But with little money, the convincing had to come in the form of words; gifts were out of the question."

"That is not altogether true," Libby's mother said in her husband's defense. "Thomas did give me a gift to convince me of his love, and of his desire for me to be his wife."

"He did?" Libby's eyes widened at the mention of a gift. "What was it?"

Libby's mother reached into her pocket and retrieved the handkerchief Libby had known her to carry as long as she could remember. Her mother handed it across to her and said, "He gave me this handkerchief, made by his own hand."

Libby took the handkerchief from her mother as though it were a baby bird. She cradled it in her hand and tenderly examined it on both sides. Everything about the gift reflected the love her father had for her mother. The linen was of the finest quality, and the workmanship was exquisite. Even the design was that of true love; in one corner were two linked hearts worked in white silk thread, and in the hearts were the initials "T" and "M" done in the finest satin stitch Libby had ever seen. The opposite corner of the handkerchief had red-and-white stitched satin roses to symbolize his eternal love and the sense of unity he felt for his beloved. The edge of the handkerchief was trimmed in a tiny tatted lace that appeared as though it had been made by faeries. Reflecting on the handkerchiefs she had recently made for her aunt's trousseau, Libby felt a flash of embarrassment for her own clunky stitching.

"Thomas knew my heart, and he knew my desires for life. We had shared many deep, personal thoughts in our letters, and in the short time we had spent together, my suspicions of him were confirmed. I loved him! And though ours was a love that had developed through letters sent across an ocean, it was a deep and unending love that was true. I knew I had to refuse poor John, but letting him down proved difficult."

"Oh my, that is an understatement!" Aunt Ellen interjected. "That boy was so determined to win her love. Do you know, Libby, he sent your mother so many gifts it reached the point of being ridiculous. Every note of refusal she sent trying to explain in some new fashion why she could not marry him was returned to her, resealed with his signet and accompanied by a gift of some sort. He sent everything from flowers to jewelry. Why, he even sent her a carriage and team of horses so she could 'escape the clutches of the wicked Americans,' as he put it. I guess he had never been told no before, and it seemed he was even more determined to win her love after each refusal."

Libby's mother continued with a changed countenance, "It was sad, really, because I had to hurt him, and I never wanted it to be like that. But he would not accept my refusal, or should I say *refusals*, for I had refused him at least six times that I can recall and each more harshly than the last. Finally, I had your Grandfather Abbott speak with his father, and upon his return to the house, he informed me that John was being sent back to India on the first available ship." Her mother gave a half-hearted smile and a shrug. "He didn't stay in India long, though."

"I'll say, just long enough to hop on the next ship back to England. Your sister said he went mad when he found out you had left with us for Boston." Aunt Ellen turned to Libby and said, "Your mother came immediately back to Boston with us, and her parents came shortly thereafter because the wedding was planned for August. It seemed that young John Bassett had found out that Captain Abbott planned to be in Boston for his daughter's wedding." Aunt Ellen winked at Libby and added, "Money will buy you plenty of information on the docks of London, and if there is one thing young John had, it was money."

"And it seems he liked to spend it!" Libby blurted out without thinking. They all laughed at her proclamation.

"Indeed!" Libby's mother replied. "On the day of the wedding, John came to the church."

"During the ceremony?" Libby interrupted.

"Yes, during the ceremony," Aunt Ellen affirmed with an eager nod.

"He burst through the door just as I was asked if I would take Thomas to be my husband. John was a sight to be seen with his hat cocked to one side and dirt on his nice clothes—quite a disheveled mess, to be sure. The church erupted in shock, but as John made his way to the front, everyone quickly fell silent in order to hear what he would say."

"What did Father do?" Libby couldn't wait for the story; she was interrupting with every question that popped into her brain.

"I'll get to that, just be patient." Her mother patted her hand and continued where she had left off. "As John reached the front of the church where Thomas and I stood before the rector, I could see that he had recently been in a fight. His eye was blackened and his nose was bloodied, and there were small drops of blood on the front of his jacket. Thomas stepped between John and I, but I put my hand on his shoulder to let him know it was going to be fine, and so he moved back. As John approached, he dropped to his knees and grasped my feet in his trembling hands. I remember his voice was just a whisper when he said, 'I have traveled halfway across the world to reach you. I could not believe it was you who sent the letters of refusal unless I looked in your own eyes and heard your sweet voice say the words. So if you truly love this man with whom you now stand at the altar of marriage, a simple phrase is all that is needed to tear the very heart that I have offered you from my being and send it into a pit of everlasting pain.'"

Libby found herself holding her breath as her mother recounted the story.

"I stood for a moment, and then I knelt down and took John by the hands. I bid him stand with me, and as he did, I released his hands and reached back to pull Thomas close beside me. Then, with the man I loved at my side, I looked John in the eye and said quite simply, 'I do.' I swear I could hear his heart break as he backed away from the altar. He tipped his hat so eloquently and smiled at Thomas then bid us good day, turned, and left the church. That was the last I ever heard from John James Bassett III of Cornwall." Libby's mother released a great sigh and slumped back into her chair.

"Captain Abbott did recount to us that John was married within the year. Someone his mother selected for him, no doubt. Now Mary, don't fret yourself. He was just a young boy in puppy love, and his behavior was quite ridiculous." Aunt Ellen seemed to be trying to brighten the mood Libby's mother was falling into by making light of the situation. "He even has five children now!" she added.

"Are you sad that you did not marry John Bassett?" Libby asked because she was feeling confused by her mother's onset of melancholy.

"Heavens, no, child!" Libby's mother sounded revived a bit. "It's just that I didn't like to hurt him so. I guess that is why I kept the letter all these years. It served as a reminder of sorts."

"A reminder of what?" Libby asked

"A reminder of just how fragile a man can be when he loves a woman."

Chapter 15

*C*ountry days seemed to pass more slowly than city days despite the fact that Libby felt busy from morning to evening; she was constantly helping with the household chores, baking, sewing, or working in the garden. And her young cousins and their continuous antics always entertained her, especially Albert, who was relentlessly trying to irritate James.

One morning, after an unseasonably rainy two days, James was sitting on the floor in the parlor with Libby reading from the *Farmer's Almanac*; she was helping him with the pronunciations of the bigger words, and they were so engulfed in the pages they did not notice that Albert had slipped quietly into the room and was standing behind them. Libby was pointing at a word and prompting James with the beginning sound, "Cah . . . Cah . . ." when she caught a whiff of something foul. Wrinkling her nose at the noxious scent, she turned to see Albert hovering above them with a wicked grin on his face, covered in dirt from head to toe, and still as a mouse holding something cupped in his hands. She quickly crawled to the other side of the room and covered her nose and mouth with her hand. "Alberrrrt . . . whaattt is dat awful smeeell?" she moaned from behind her hand.

By this time, James had clued in that Albert was up to something, and quick as a wink he scampered across the room and jumped behind the big chair. As he poked his head out, he caught wind of the fetid odor and began to sputter and cough. "Golly, Albert, what have you been doing?"

Albert's plan had been spoiled by Libby's quick reaction, for it seemed he'd had every intention of putting the foul smelling thing he was holding down his brother's shirt. But, found out, he played innocent. "Look what I got!" he said with an innocuous smile; he paid no attention to the fact that he smelled so badly. He pushed his hands forward and opened them to reveal a very small black-and-white animal that was obviously dead. "I found it in the barn!" he said, rather proud of himself. "I think Ginger must have killed it, there were six of them dead behind the hay bales, and Ginger was sitting in the loft cleaning her face. The whole place stinks of skunk. Isn't it the neatest thing you ever—"

"WHAT IS THAT STENCH?" Aunt Ellen inquired loudly as she walked past the parlor door. She stopped dead in her tracks and looked in to see her dirty child standing with a dead baby skunk cradled in his hands. "Albert Morgan Randal! What in heaven's name have you gotten into?" Aunt Ellen stepped back as Albert turned and shoved his cupped hands in her direction. "LOOK!" he said innocently.

Libby remained frozen in place and tried hard not to laugh aloud as Aunt Ellen quickly pinched her nose closed so she couldn't smell the stench that was emanating from her son. She reached in with her other hand and gingerly grasped Albert by the ear and proceeded to drag him from the room. Before she had gone two steps, she began scolding, "I *cannot* believe that you would think for one minute you would be allowed in this house with that much dirt on you. And why on earth are you carrying around that poor dead creature? Sometimes I wonder where your brain has gotten to, young man! Do you ever stop to think about your actions? Don't give me that look of innocence, you know better than to bring dead things into the house!" Aunt Ellen could be heard scolding Albert all the way back down to the barn.

Libby and James didn't move for several minutes after the others left the room; they just stayed put and listened to poor Albert get a tongue lashing until they could no longer contain the smiles that were erupting on their faces. Soon, they were both rolling around on the carpet, laughing hysterically.

"Is it always this entertaining having a brother around?" Libby asked her cousin.

"It is with Albert," James stated bluntly. "He is forever getting into trouble, and most of the time he manages to include me. But not this time!"

"Nope, not this time!" Libby said with a chuckle. "What do you think he was going to do with that skunk?" Libby asked.

"Who knows? I can hardly believe he picked it up and brought it in the house. I wouldn't touch it, that's for sure," James said. "It sure did stink!"

"Poor little creatures! That Ginger sure is a hunter. I just wish she wouldn't go after such innocent little babies like those birdies and now the baby skunks. But I guess she is good for keeping the rats and mice out of the barn."

"She is a great hunter. Before Ginger, we had Tabby Tom. He was a giant of a cat and the best hunter—even better than Ginger." Libby listened with interest as James spoke about his last cat. "He wasn't as friendly, though, mostly because he was a tomcat, and they aren't very cuddly. But he always brought us home part of his kill; he would leave it on the back porch, half-eaten. Mother Morgan said he was giving us a gift to thank us for the milk he got each morning. Sometimes, the animals he killed were as big as him. Once he got a pheasant, and it was a pretty big one, and he only ate the head and one leg. He left the best part of it on the front porch that time. Mother Morgan said it was a special harvest gift." James gazed out the window and fell silent and somewhat melancholy, so Libby waited a moment before she spoke.

"What happened to Tabby Tom?" she asked hesitantly.

"Well, a couple of times he came home pretty beat up, and he let my mom doctor up his wounds. In fact, once he slept for two whole days in the pantry cupboard. Mom said he hurt his paw pretty bad that time. And then, one day, there were no gifts on the porch, and Tabby Tom didn't come home." James's tone was somber as he recounted the story. "I looked for him for two whole weeks. I called and called and called, but he didn't come home. Mother even let me leave out a saucer with milk, but nothing worked. We never saw him again."

"I'm sorry." Libby could tell that James was overly sad at the loss of his pet. "He sounded like a really great cat." Libby patted her cousin's shoulder affectionately.

"He was. Mother Morgan says that cats have adventurers' souls, and we should never get too attached to them. She said they like to wander far from home and get into trouble wherever they can find it. I guess it's true—Ginger is always getting into trouble of one sort or another. But she doesn't wander too far. Mother Morgan says it's because she's a girl, and she won't go too far from her babies. Do you think it's true?" he asked his cousin with a quizzical expression.

"It sounds right to me," said Libby with a comforting smile. "After all, what mother would leave her babies to go exploring?"

"I guess," James said rather sadly. "I just wish no one had an adventurer's soul."

"What makes you say that?" Libby could see he wanted to talk about something, so she turned her face to him and listened intently.

"I don't know, I guess I think of Tabby Tom like I do my father. They both had adventurers' souls, and they are both dead and gone." His face was so forlorn it practically broke Libby's heart. "I know that Albert has the same spirit. He is forever getting into trouble for going too far from the barn, or going into the creek when he has been told not to go without a grown-up. He doesn't seem to mind going off the trail to look at a toad or to chase a rabbit. I just know that one day he is going to get on a sailing ship and never come back . . ." James squeezed his eyes as if to stop tears from coming, ". . . just like my father."

Libby was silent for a long time, mostly because she didn't know what to say. She decided that truth was better than anything she could make up to help him feel better, so she said, "You're right." The statement was so blunt it made James look up in surprise. Libby continued, "He is probably going to be a sailor, James. But that doesn't mean he will be lost at sea like your father. Just look at Grandfather. He has been a sea captain for most of his life, and he has never been lost. I think he has an adventurer's spirit, don't you? I mean, you practically have to have one if you are a sea captain. So it's possible to have an adventuresome spirit and not die from it. And *that* is what we will hope for Albert! We will hope and pray that he can be just like Grandfather Abbott—sailing around the world on his ship but always coming home to his family."

James gave Libby a thankful nod and wiped away a tear. "Yes, that is what we will do."

"Now, I was thinking that since we can't go outside to the garden, perhaps you would like to see how far I have gotten on my garden spread?" She stood and held a hand out to help her cousin up from the floor. "Wait here, I'll be right back."

James nodded, picked up the *Farmer's Almanac*, and sat himself down in the big chair beside the window. Libby scurried out the parlor door and was back in a flash with her patchwork pieces. "Let's go to the table and lay them out; I want to see how big it is getting."

They began to lay the pieced hexagon flowers on the table, and Libby showed James how to leave enough space between them for the plain muslin hexagons to fit. Soon the entire table was covered in her patchwork. She didn't have enough muslin pieces basted yet to fill all the spaces between the flowers, but she had pieced more than forty hexagon flowers, and she could see that her spread was going to be very similar to her grandmother's beautiful mosaic quilt.

"Oh my, how lovely!" said her grandmother as she came into the parlor and saw the progress Libby had made on her patchwork. "You have been busy. I had no idea you had so many flower units completed."

"Well," Libby responded with a smile, "you did help with a lot of them. I don't think I would be so far along were it not for your quick fingers. How many do you think I will need to start assembling the top?"

Mother Morgan scratched her chin and asked, "How big would you like it to be?"

"Well, I think yours is ever so grand, to be sure, but something that size would take the rest of my childhood to finish," Libby answered, feeling a bit overwhelmed.

Mother Morgan replied, "Then how about it we make it half the size of mine, that way you won't feel so burdened. Perhaps then we can get to quilting it while you are still here for your visit. I would guess that between your mother, your aunt, you with your own little, fast fingers, and my own hands, we could have it finished in no time. I think you will need about half again as many blocks. Your mother and I will work on the white pieces for you, and you can focus on the blocks. Aunt Ellen has her hands full trying to get the smell of skunk off Albert. He seems to have found himself some trouble this morning." She winked at James and continued, "Ellen said as he will be sleeping in the woodshed if she can't get the stench off him." That made Libby and James giggle.

Mother Morgan retrieved the book she had been looking for and headed out to the porch to sit in the sunlight that was beginning to poke its head through the clouds.

An idea came to Libby as she was gathering up her patchwork pieces. She remembered the tiny seed bags her cousin James had given her for her birthday, so she asked the question she had been wondering. "James, those lovely seed bags you gave me for my birthday, did you make them?"

"I did!" He smiled in response and asked, "Why do you ask?"

"Well, I had the idea that if you made those little bags all by yourself, perhaps you would like to make some of the flower blocks for my spread. You have a nice hand with the needle; those bags were very well made, even Mother said so." Libby's invitation made James perk up with pride. "I was thinking since our chores are complete, and we can't go outside just yet, *and* we won't be bothered by Albert, maybe together we could finish the rest of the blocks I need. I could really use your help, and it's not difficult, I can show you what to do." She was overselling her idea; she assumed that James wouldn't really want to sew because it was "ladies' work," as Albert liked to put it.

But James seemed eager to help with the first mention of it.

"Really? You would let me help make your patchwork? Mother Morgan rarely allows me into her sewing things; mostly I have to practice reading or doing sums. Want to know a secret?" he whispered.

Libby moved in closely and whispered back inquiringly, "Sure."

In a low whisper he revealed, "I really love to sew." He cast his eyes down when he said the words.

"Silly!" Libby said out loud. "Why is that a secret?"

"'Cause it's *women's work*!" James said, sounding just like Albert.

"I think my father would take offense to that!" responded Libby with and an ever-so-slight tone of resentment. "He sews almost every day, and there is nothing womanly about him."

James scratched his head with a perplexed look on his face, then his expression changed to one of horror, "I'm sorry, Libby. I didn't mean to imply that your father was womanly. I just meant that Albert says girls should sew, and boys should carve or throw rocks or other manly things."

Libby laughed. "It's all right, James. I'm not upset. And you should know that a lot of men sew. In fact, my father told me that the President of the United States and the King of England both have men tailors. It is a very honorable profession for a man with the talent. If you like to do it, you should tell Mother Morgan. I'm sure she would teach you more if she thought you liked it. She even told me she wished you were interested in learning."

"She did?" James's eyes were big with disbelief.

"She did," Libby affirmed, "in a roundabout way," she added after remembering the early morning conversation with Mother Morgan. "So how about I show you how to baste the hexagons and make the flower units, then you can show Mother Morgan your work and ask her to teach you something else?"

Libby was heartened by James's willingness; he smiled a big toothy grin and asked, "When can we start?"

"Right now!" Libby patted her cousin's shoulder and guided him to the table.

Together they spent the morning and better part of the afternoon working on the patches Libby needed for her spread. Partly because they were so quiet and kept to themselves and partly because the rest of the household was trying to figure out how to de-skunk Albert, Libby and James were undisturbed and able to complete many blocks together. James was quite handy with his needle and quickly matched her pace. Libby made a mental note to mention James's accomplishment to her mother—perhaps one day he would make a good apprentice in her father's shop.

Chapter 16

*S*everal more days passed before the preparations for the wedding were completed and the dress had its final fitting. Libby's mother and grandmother had fashioned an elegant gown for Aunt Ellen that was trimmed in the most delicate silk flowers. The veil, made from the Chantilly lace that Mother Morgan provided, turned out more beautiful than Libby could have imagined. The fine details her grandmother added to the lace gave the veil an air of elegance that could only be found in the most costly garments. The ladies had worked hard to complete Aunt Ellen's wedding trousseau, and now that it was finished, a sigh of relief could be had by all. Libby had received several complimentary remarks regarding the handkerchiefs she had made for her aunt.

Trying now to finish up her patchwork, Libby watched through the window as her restless grandfather paced back and forth across the porch for much of the morning. She knew he was anxious for his correspondence, especially for his letter from London concerning the Montclief Estate settlement. Whenever he paused to look at the road, she jumped to her feet and did the same, hoping to see the handsome John Masterson and his lanky brother, the reverend, riding up on horseback. Each time, she was disappointed. She had almost given up on the idea that the Mastersons would come this day when she noticed her grandfather had stopped his pacing and was just standing with a hand on his hip and his cup in hand. When she looked this time, her efforts were rewarded with the sound of hoof beats and the image of two men cantering toward the house. Libby hollered in a most unladylike fashion, "They're here, Aunt Ellen! The Mr. Mastersons have returned!" Then she scooted out the door to join her grandfather on the porch.

Libby thought the reverend and his brother looked quite disheveled and parched from riding in the heat. She glanced back at the door and wondered what was keeping the others; then, thinking perhaps they hadn't heard her shouts, she started to head back in to find them when Aunt Ellen appeared at the door. "Your mother is fetching the gentlemen something cool to drink, Libby. Can you please get us some extra chairs for the porch?" Libby thought her aunt looked especially flushed with excitement.

"Of course," Libby said and quickly collected some chairs for the men to sit upon while they enjoyed a refreshing bit of cider.

Grandfather Abbott greeted Reverend Masterson with a handshake and hollered to James to fetch one of the Bigalow brothers to help with the horses. Aunt Ellen ran to greet John as he handed off his horse to Albert, who stood ready to take the reins. Embracing, John kissed Ellen's cheek, then gazed into her eyes and kissed her on the lips, long and slow. Albert looked at his mother and blushed slightly at the exchange, then seeing his brother coming, he said in a cocky voice, "I get to hold the horse!"

James stuck his tongue out at Albert and then ran to squeeze between the lovers. John stepped back and allowed the boy in, giving him a hug in the process, and James looked back smugly at his brother.

Once the animals were attended to, the men retired to the front porch where the afternoon sun was not searing down on their heads. The men found a comfortable place to sit as the ladies slipped back into the house—Aunt Ellen to freshen her appearance and Mother Morgan to help with the refreshments. Libby sat quietly in a chair and listened to the conversation while she pretended to be interested in what her cousins were doing on the front lawn. She didn't wish to appear to eavesdrop, but she was quite interested in what news the Mastersons had brought with them.

"I am indeed indebted to you gentlemen for collecting my correspondence in Boston," Captain Abbott began. "I have been awaiting word of my next commission."

"Ah, yes, the letters," John said. "Let me fetch them." He excused himself to get the correspondence and, Libby suspected, to sneak another kiss from his beloved should he be so lucky to encounter her along the way.

"All the arrangements have been made for the wedding, Reverend. I believe the final detail is to arrange for the rector. I wonder, will you be conducting the ceremony for your brother and Ellen?" Grandfather Abbott asked.

"It was not my intention, sir, though if the rector from Hartford is unavailable, then of course I will be glad of it. My wife is intent upon having me at her side during the ceremony; she is not the sort of lady who likes to find herself alone during festivities. Were I to conduct the ceremony, I would prove too absent for her liking. She requires a good bit of attention, you see, Captain, and when given, she is a delight. Withhold it, and one finds himself with a price to pay." Reverend Masterson winked at Captain Abbott and they both chuckled.

"I do, sir, understand the situation. I shall inform Mrs. Morgan and have word dispatched to Hartford immediately." Captain Abbott smiled at Mother Morgan and Libby's mother as they returned with mugs of cool cider and a platter of cheese, cold meat, and leftover biscuits from breakfast—the fruit having been completely devoured by the boys.

John and Aunt Ellen joined the group on the porch, John clutching a small pouch and Aunt Ellen wearing a smile that gave away the secret kisses she had recently received. Libby moved herself to the steps of the porch, leaving the chairs for the adults, and before long, the twins joined her.

With John and Aunt Ellen completely enthralled in quiet conversation at the far end of the porch and the Reverend dozing off after his pint of hard cider, Grandfather Abbott opened the small pouch that contained his correspondence—four letters—and began to examine the seals on each.

Libby watched her grandfather with interest and half hoped that her father had included a letter in response to the several she had written him over the past month. Grandfather's first choice was the letter from his ship's company office. "Ah, my new commission," he announced. "I'm to captain the *Argile* between Liverpool and Boston." He refolded the letter with a pleased expression and put it at the back of the stack. Libby waited anxiously to see what he opened next.

The next letter had a deep crimson seal and a red silk ribbon, and Libby knew immediately it was not her father's. Breaking the seal, her grandfather unfolded the paper to find a brief note. "Not exactly what I expected," he grumbled aloud.

He refolded the paper and placed it at the back of the stack. Libby's eyes lit up as he selected and opened the next letter with the familiar green wax sealed "TM" that she knew to belong to her father. But he did not offer to read it aloud. Instead, he handed the letter and the included page he had not opened to Libby's mother, who was looking at him eagerly. She accepted the letter and was immediately consumed with its contents. Libby was disappointed when she was not given a letter directly, but then she heard her name, "Libby, come here, please."

Grandfather Abbott placed his correspondence in his lap and opened his arms to his granddaughter. Libby rose quickly with a smile, went to him, and was immediately swallowed by his enormous frame. He hugged her and tenderly kissed her on the top of the head, then released her and said with a smile, "*That* was from your father."

Libby grinned so big all her teeth showed. She then blushed a little from the attention, straightened her dress, and went to stand next to her mother's chair. She looked over her mother's shoulder at the letter from her father and read the line about giving "a kiss to Libby." Her arms yearned for the arms of her father, but she thought of how comforting it was to have her grandfather so close. He was an excellent substitute.

Grandfather picked up his last letter and turned it over several times before opening the seal. "Ah!" he said aloud.

"All is well, Captain?" Mother Morgan asked.

"Quite!" Grandfather Abbott replied. "You will remember Alexander Crum, Margaret? He was acquainted with your Edward at school. We worked together on some import business ventures in Glasgow prior to Edward's passing."

"I do recall, Captain. And how is the good sir?" Mother Morgan asked. "I remember Edward said he was quite an ambitious man and much renowned for his textile dying and printing skills in Glasgow."

"He is indeed," replied Grandfather Abbott. "Well, let's see what he is up to, shall we?" He shuffled the papers back to the opening page and began to read the letter. "It seems," he interjected, "that Mr. Crum has an acquaintance who is also quite ambitious, and they would like to discuss another business venture . . . it appears they have some new ideas concerning ready-made clothing, and they are looking for qualified tailors and seamstresses to open shops in Boston. Well, well . . . now isn't that interesting." Captain Abbott continued to read the letter to himself while Mother Morgan engaged the now awakened Reverend Masterson, who seemed somewhat out of sorts for having missed much of the conversation at hand.

Libby and her mother spoke quietly about her father and what troubles he was getting into all alone in Boston and whether or not Princess missed Libby as much as Libby missed her. Then abruptly she asked the question that was ever present in her heart, "Mother, how much longer do you think we will stay in Ashford?"

"Well, dear," her mother responded in a hushed tone, "that depends upon how soon we can get the rector from Hartford to come out for the wedding."

"Why don't we just go to Hartford ourselves?" Libby asked in her innocence, her voice louder than her mother would have liked. "Why must we wait on the rector coming here?"

Aunt Ellen and John looked at one another and smiled. "Elizabeth Jane Morgan, that is a fabulous idea, I don't know why we didn't think of it!" Aunt Ellen exclaimed. "What do you think, Mother? It's only a few hours to Hartford by coach; why, we could be there and back in a day. All the preparations are completed for the wedding, and it's just a matter of the ceremony."

John was nodding his head in agreement and interjected, "My brother and I could ride out this evening and make the final preparations for the church. You all could follow on the morn, and it could be all wrapped up by this time tomorrow. You may all stay at my family's home on Grand Street, and I shall stay with my brother until after the ceremony."

Libby quietly watched the exchange of comments she had triggered with her mention of going to Hartford and could see that everyone was agreeing with her point of view. Her excitement grew!

"Well . . ." began Mother Morgan, "I don't see why not! Do you all have any objections?" She directed her question at the other adults, glancing between Grandfather Abbott, Libby's mother, and the reverend.

"I think the timing is perfect," said Grandfather. "I have a pressing matter to attend to in London, and the sooner I am on the road, the sooner things can be resolved."

Libby saw her mother and Reverend Masterson both nodding in approval. The idea that the wedding could be tomorrow was too much for Libby to keep inside, so she jumped up, clapped her hands, and squealed, "Yippee, we are having a wedding *tomorrow!*" Albert and James looked confused at their cousin's excitement—they had not been paying attention to the adult conversation, being too distracted by a nearby toad to know what was going on; nonetheless, they could see that Libby was excited over something special, so they joined her in the revelry and clapped despite not knowing why.

The party on the porch took on a fresh air of excitement with the new plans for an immediate exodus to Hartford and an impromptu wedding. Libby's mother jumped to her feet and shooed the boys off to the barn to inform the Bigalow brothers of the gentlemen's hasty departure and the need to get their horses ready. Aunt Ellen and John embraced briefly and gave reassuring smiles to one another before hurriedly going in opposite directions to prepare for the trip. Libby's mother took her by the hand and exclaimed, "We have a lot to do, child. Let's get busy!" They left the porch and headed for their bedroom and their awaiting trunks.

"Margaret, I have a question for you. One that I pray you will say yes to."

Alone on the porch with Captain Abbott, Mother Morgan was clutching her handkerchief and putting on a false smile.

"What is it, Gerald?" She tried to sound innocent, though she had been anticipating his question and had been mulling over what she knew would be asked of her at some point.

"I'm sure you have guessed that I received a letter today from the Montclief solicitors; but what you may not know is that Thomas has also received the same letter. We have both been asked to London, and we have been told to bring legal representation."

"Interesting, to be sure, but why should that concern me?" Mother Morgan was still playing coy, however unconvincingly.

"You and I have both known this day would come. There is naught to be done save go. And as your dear friend, and now only father to our Thomas, I am asking you, please go with us. Thomas does not have an understanding of these people, and I fear your pain has tainted his opinion—though I believe it was unintentional on your part. Nor does he possess the personal knowledge that you and I do regarding the history behind this delicate situation. And while I know that this journey will be quite painful for you, I feel certain there will be an element of healing as well." He reached over the table and took hold of her hand. She glanced at his face, tears forming in the corners of her eyes.

Struggling to regain her composure, she replied in a tone that came out harsher than intended, "I am quite certain that the business in London could be expertly carried out by my Thomas; he is a very capable man. And, yes, it would be a very painful trip for me despite the passing of these many years. London is not a place to which I ever intended to return. But I do understand your point and will give it my utmost attention over the next day. I shall inform you of my decision following the ceremony." She abruptly stood to leave, stopped, then turned to Captain Abbott and said quite tenderly, for she knew she had been overly harsh, "Gerald, you are my dearest friend, and there are none left on this earth who understand my pain more apart from you and my Lord and Savior. You must know that this journey would require more from me than I fear I have to give. But I shall pray on the matter and give it over to the One who has carried me thus far. And if He puts it upon my heart to go, then go I shall, for I should not like to think myself a *Jonah!*" She offered an apologetic smile, turned, and left the porch to ready herself for Hartford.

Chapter 17

The coach journey to Hartford seemed faster than the blink of an eye; in fact, Libby had just settled into the trip when they were already making their destination. She reckoned the apparent speediness to be due in part to her recent, very long journey from Boston—for it had taken several days and many long hours of sitting before they had reached Ashford.

The twins had kept Libby entertained to the point of distraction on this trip; she had even mentioned to her mother early in the journey that she wished the boys could accompany them home to Boston because they were quite amusing and made the time pass quickly. They seemed to notice every miniscule detail about the inside of the coach and talked or argued incessantly about most of them. The scenery was an exciting topic for them as well—from repeatedly citing the names of the different trees that James observed to the *"Wow what a great fishing spot!"* phrase that Albert squeaked out at every pond, creak, or riverbed they passed. Needless to say, it didn't take long for Libby to find she was growing wearisome of the boys.

"Mother," Libby leaned over and whispered softly, "never mind about what I said earlier. I don't think I could take three days in the coach with the boys." She looked at her mother, rolled her eyes, and smiled just as James declared, "Oh, look, there is another grove of maple trees!" for the fifth time in as many minutes.

Libby's mother winked at her and whispered in return, "They do go on, don't they?"

"Indeed!" replied Libby with an arched brow.

"I believe it's just the confinement of the coach that makes it so tiresome, dear, and look, here we are coming into Hartford; we shall only be a few more minutes." Libby gave a relieved smile to her mother and looked out the coach window at the passing buildings and homes. She felt the familiarity of city life creeping back into her consciousness as she noticed how the large buildings and close-set houses reminded her of the outskirts of Boston. The city spurred a profound longing for her return home. She missed her own bed and the soft purr of her Princess. She craved the smell of the salty sea air. And she wanted her father. His absence was beginning to leave a large void that even her all-consuming patchwork had a difficult time filling. She had already used her new pen and paper to write him several letters; however, the one-sided conversations were simply not enough to suppress the desire to hear his voice and feel his warm good-night hug.

But more than any of that, what she was feeling was a need for that which seemed normal—and having been away in the country, she had been unaware of its absence until now. She had not noticed before how the hustle and bustle of city life made her feel alive and real; how the comings and goings of other people—even strangers—had planted in her a sense of being a part of something bigger—something more than just her little life. She felt like a part of the big machine, just a tiny piece of the puzzle that was, despite her insignificance, incomplete without her. And without the city, she, too, felt incomplete.

As the coach drew to a stop outside the Masterson house, Libby felt a sense of familiarity. The experience left her a little confused, for this was not her home, and she could not ever remember coming to Hartford. "Mother, have we ever been here before?"

"No, you've never been to Hartford. But you will find, Libby, that all cities have the same essence about them. And when you have been away in the country for as long as we have been, any city makes you feel like you are home." Her mother gave her a reassuring smile and gestured for her to exit the coach.

The family would reside at the home of John Masterson's parents while he stayed with the reverend and his wife until after the wedding. The Masterson row house was quite lovely and a good deal larger than Mother Morgan's home in Ashford. The luxury of it struck Libby as less than ostentatious but still quite formal compared to their simple home in Boston or the farm in Ashford. There was a household staff that included a housekeeper, a cook, several maids to attend to the ladies, and a valet who normally attended John Masterson but who would stay at the house and attend to Grandfather Abbott's needs instead.

Wide-eyed, Libby entered the house and found herself curtsied to by the female staff members, and Grandfather's valet bowed deeply when she passed by. Unaccustomed to servants, Libby just smiled and stayed close to her mother, who placed a hand on her arm reassuringly and guided her through the greetings. Recognizing the need to be on her best manners, Libby maintained her most formal pretense. Mother Morgan greeted the staff with a casual, kind smile, and Libby surmised that her grandmother's occupation as a young girl would have given her a different perspective of household staff—a perspective of equality, not superiority or, as in her own case, trepidation.

Aunt Ellen made her way into the house at last, the twins trailing her with their hands in their pockets and their faces bright with curiosity. It was clear to Libby that they had been sternly instructed to keep their hands off of anything that wasn't located inside their pockets. As the valet bowed to the boys, Albert stood taller than normal and bowed in return, mimicking the servant, much to his mother's dismay. Libby knew that he, too, had never been exposed to staff before, and his obvious lack of etiquette embarrassed his mother to the point of blushing.

"Albert," Grandfather Abbott called to the boy, "it is not necessary to bow to the gentleman. A simple nod of your head is proper when addressing the people whom your new father employs." His correction was simply to educate, and Libby could see that Albert took it as such when he turned to the valet and nodded his head. The valet smiled, bowed again to Albert, and then turned and bowed to James, who turned beet red, nodded his head quickly, then scooted over to his mother's side and took her hand—James was not fond of strangers.

The family was quickly settled into their rooms and allowed a few moments to freshen up and change out of their traveling clothes. They then gathered in the dining room for a lovely spread of cold ham sandwiches and refreshing cider. When all had eaten their fill, they reassembled in the nearby parlor and awaited the arrival of John Masterson and his brother. The ladies brought with them their sewing baskets and continued to stitch on their patchwork.

Albert and James were entertaining themselves with *The Youth's Companion,* which had been specially ordered for the boys by Mr. Masterson and had arrived from Boston that very morning. Standing at a corner table, quietly pointing at the image of a gray squirrel that was in the newspaper, James was trying to make out what the story said and was having great difficulty pronouncing most of the larger words. Libby was intrigued and decided they could use some help, so she set aside her patchwork, rose from her seat near the window, and hovered over the backs of the boys to see the paper.

Just then, John Masterson made his entrance into the parlor with his usual grace and elegance. Libby looked up and noticed the handsome features of the man she had seen only twice on the farm in Ashford; she had previously paid little attention to his attire and was now quite impressed with the formality of his clothing. He looked splendid in his twill waistcoat with his high-collared, starched white shirt and hunter-green plaid breeches. His shoes were shined to perfection, and his jet-black hair was combed off to one side and swept away from his face. He did not sport any facial hair as did many of the men of his time; instead, he was clean shaven, and she found that she much preferred it to the usual beard and mustache. With her father and grandfather sporting full beards, she had a difficult time discerning their dispositions. Often she wondered what they might look like without their facial hair; however, she would probably never find out since Grandfather Abbott had sworn to take his beard to his grave, and her own father pledged that until he had another child, he would not shave his face. John Masterson, on the other hand, could be read quite easily with his wide grin unhindered by whiskers.

As he swept into the room, his eyes were only for Aunt Ellen. He greeted her first with a lovely bow and a kiss upon her cheek. By the expression on Aunt Ellen's face, it was clear she too liked the clean-shaven face of her betrothed. He next greeted Mother Morgan and gave Captain Abbott a hearty handshake. Libby had moved closer to her mother as John bowed to her. He turned and extended his hand to Libby, and as she reached her hand toward his, he took it, gingerly kissed it, and said, "Greetings to you, my soon-to-be niece; how was your journey from Ashford?"

"Quite lovely," she responded in her most formal tone. Then she looked at her mother, who smiled approvingly in return.

"And where are my boys?" John said as he scanned the room. The twins had quickly hidden in the first available hiding spot—behind the sofa—the moment John had entered the room.

"Here we are!" shouted Albert and James as they popped up from behind the sofa. John opened his arms, and the boys ran to him and hugged him. "Today is the day!" Albert beamed.

"It is indeed!" John replied with a smile and a glance at Aunt Ellen. "I have had the papers all drafted up, and after the ceremony, we will have the official reading so that you boys may understand your adoption and what it all means."

"It means you will be our real father!" squeaked Albert with enthusiasm and a second hug for John.

"It also means that you are my heirs, and all that I have is yours." John glanced at Mother Morgan and smiled. "We really should be heading to the church soon." He turned and looked at Aunt Ellen. "Say, an hour, my love, is that time enough to prepare?"

"It won't take an hour," she smiled and looked at Libby's mother. "Shall we?"

"We'll be ready in a snap." Libby's mother turned to her and said, "Will you please gather our patchwork and join us upstairs? I'm going to help Ellen into her dress."

"Yes, Mother." Libby headed across the room to gather the sewing baskets that had been set aside. The exchange between John Masterson and her young cousins affirmed in Libby the knowledge that Albert and James would have a father at long last, and she felt happy knowing he was a good and loving man.

Aunt Ellen turned at the door and asked of her mother, "Will you please help the boys get changed? I've laid out their clothes in their bedroom."

"Gladly, dear. Now off you go! I'll be in to help with your hair as soon as I've polished up these two and set them in a cupboard to stay clean." She winked at Libby and grabbed Albert and James by the hands and marched them out the door behind Libby's mother and Ellen. Libby fell in as the caboose and followed the rest of the train up the stairs.

Captain Abbott and John were alone in the study. "How goes it, young man? Are you feeling nervous about this hasty ceremony?" Captain Abbott inquired with a lighthearted tone that had undercurrents of sincerity.

"Not in the slightest!" he reassured. "I am only sorry we could not have had the ceremony weeks ago. But at the time, I was uncertain as to whether Mother Morgan would give her blessing. She has been quite distracted and seemingly troubled over much these past months, and though I wanted to ask for Ellen's hand months ago, I felt it best to wait until Mother Morgan seemed more at ease. Your visit has greatly improved her state of mind, and I am quite glad of it as it gave me my opportunity. And a hasty ceremony makes me all the happier as I am quite anxious to start our lives together."

"Well, you should know that I have asked Mother Morgan to accompany me on a trip back to Boston and on to England. I pray she will join me; you see, it is quite important for her son, Thomas. There is a great deal at stake, and her presence would most certainly help the situation. But the journey is one she does not wish to make. So I would be indebted to you if you could reassure her that you will take good care of her daughter and the boys. Knowing they are well settled may help my cause." Captain Abbott shrugged, and shaking his head, he added, "Though if she does not wish to join me, there is not much to be done of it. Margaret is a tenacious woman."

"I see a bit of that in her daughter as well." John grinned and poured the captain a glass of whiskey. Handing it to him, he said, "And I see it in young Libby—she seems older than her years."

"Libby is a wonderful girl; she has certainly managed to steal my heart," Captain Abbott chuckled. "I look forward to the day I can bring her to London."

"Perhaps she could be Mother Morgan's companion on your upcoming trip," John suggested.

A wily expression surfaced on Captain Abbott's face as he remembered how Libby had been so direct in her questions about the family letters. And then it hit him. *Libby should come to England!* He beamed a wide, mischievous grin in John's direction. "Sir, I believe you may have solved my problem!" he exclaimed. "I will simply ask Mary if Libby can join Thomas and I on our trip to London. It will be a wonderful opportunity for Libby to get to know her cousins and aunties in England. It's a perfect educational trip for the young girl!" Captain Abbott rattled on the details as if working them out as he went. "Mary will be unable to join us—both she and Thomas cannot be gone from the shop at the same time—and I know she would never allow Libby to travel without female companionship. Mother Morgan will be the logical choice, especially now that Ellen is settled and will be on her honeymoon." He looked at John with a hopeful smile and added, "An excellent idea! Now all I have to do is sell it to my daughter!"

Chapter 18

*A*unt Ellen and John stood before the rector hand in hand, eyes locked upon each other. Their love was visible for everyone to see, and it warmed Libby's heart to know her aunt had found love again after the loss of her first husband, for she was still so young. How tragic it would have been for her to raise her boys alone. As the two lovers said their vows, they spoke clearly and with great sincerity of devotion. All the ladies dabbed their eyes as the couple kissed and were then presented to the onlookers sitting in the pews.

Libby reflected upon the story of her own mother's ceremony and the interruption of young Mr. Bassett of Cornwall. She glanced at her mother and tried to imagine her standing before the minister with Mr. Bassett on his knees at her feet and Father standing close by her side. She thought Mr. Bassett quite audacious for coming all the way to America for the woman he loved, only to be sent away brokenhearted. "What is it about love that makes people behave so . . ." she couldn't put a word to it—well, actually there were so many words that could be put into her sentence, "brave . . . silly . . . reckless." Her words were not uttered, but they seemed to hang in the quiet, still air of the church.

She reflected on the stories told by her grandmother of her own "love at first sight." And she thought of her parents' love, growing over time through letters sent across an ocean. She cast a dreamy look in the direction of the couple before the altar and wondered how her own love story would play out. Would it be love at first sight? And would she be courageous in love or simply silly and fickle as she had seen some of her classmates in Boston behave? Boys had yet to really pique her interest, partly because the ones she had been exposed to were either too old or too young to be of any real attraction for her, but mostly because the ones of her own age were far too interested in kissing the popular girls to even glance in her direction. "Love," thought Libby, "will just have to wait."

Following the ceremony, an intimate gathering of those in attendance was held at Reverend Masterson's house. Letticia's daughters rode in the coach with Libby, her mother, her grandfather, and Mother Morgan. It was a tight squeeze with six in the coach, especially with the extravagant dresses worn by Catherine and Sophia Masterson. Their mother had purchased new dresses just for the wedding, and the added flounces on each of the dresses seemed to swallow the occupants of the coach. Libby sat nearest the door and practically fell out when the coachman opened it. She was followed closely by her mother and grandmother, who both gulped in the fresh air as they exited the coach and tried to cover their giggles by straightening their dresses. They had both been holding their breath for the majority of the journey. It was pungently clear that young Sophia had adorned far more perfume than was acceptable for such close quarters. Mary discreetly whispered to Libby the importance of "less is more" when it comes to a lady's scent. As the remaining guests exited their coaches and approached the front door, Letticia and Reverend Masterson were standing just inside waiting to greet them.

Aunt Ellen and John arrived with the boys in a separate coach. The boys were given strictest instructions to again keep their hands limited to the things inside their pockets, and Libby was told quietly by her mother to be on her best behavior. John and Aunt Ellen were first inside the door with hugs, kisses, and congratulations all around.

The party was slightly more formal than Libby was accustomed to, though she quite enjoyed the poetry reading performed by Catherine Masterson. Her selected pieces were by Elizabeth Barrett Browning, and they all spoke of true love. Her recitation was rather good, and her ability to speak with intense feeling about something which she was obviously too young to have experienced was quite remarkable. Even the boys were captivated by Catherine's voice as she recited "Sonnet 43"—it was, in fact, the only time all night when Ellen didn't have to shush the boys when someone else was speaking, singing, or playing the piano.

Letticia Masterson's cook made a delicious meal for the wedding party, and when everyone had eaten their fill, they were reminded that a special wedding cake and tea would be served in the parlor. Upon John's special request to the hostess, the children were allowed to dine with the adults in celebration of the wedding, though Letticia was not at all fond of having meals with children. Much to her horror, the boys squealed with delight and clapped their hands when they heard there was to be cake, each donning a smile that was exceedingly larger than normal and wiggling in their chairs excitedly.

Libby tried to maintain an air of maturity, but Mrs. Masterson's expression caused her to laugh, which she tried to cover with a cough. Libby knew she was old enough to have better manners than the little boys, and her mother insisted on them, but try as she might, she couldn't wipe the grin off her face.

Everyone departed to the parlor and glasses were poured all around for a special toast to the newlywed couple—even the children were given glasses of cider. Albert was completely fixated on the wedding cake and nearly dropped the glass the maid was trying to hand him. Grandfather Abbott and Mother Morgan stood together and lifted their glasses to the newlyweds. "Here is to a happy and long life together," Grandfather said.

"And may you be blessed with many more children to bring you the same great joy that you have given to me," Mother Morgan added with a loving smile to her daughter.

Raising their glasses, they all cheered for the newlyweds then sipped their drinks. Everyone, that is, save Albert. He gulped down the cider, slammed his glass promptly on the tray of the maid standing to his right, and turned to his mother with a big smile. "Can we have cake now? Can we please, Mother, can we?" Aunt Ellen placed her hand over her brow and shook her head at her son's ill manners. Libby almost choked on her drink—Albert was so exuberant, and it made her laugh to think of the changes that were in store for her young cousin. Manners were the first thing he would have to change if he were to reside happily in his new surroundings. But she was heartened to hear the kind and patient response from Albert's new father.

"Yes, lad, you *may* have cake now," John answered in Aunt Ellen's stead, and he guided the young boy over to the table. His correction was done lovingly but firmly. "You and James *may* even have the first pieces!" Libby watched as the smile on Albert's face grew, if that was even possible, and he clapped his hands and beckoned his brother to come closer.

Libby caught sight of Grandfather Abbott taking the opportunity to move closer to the corner where her mother and Mother Morgan had positioned themselves on a settee. He sat himself down in the chair nearest them and began to engage in a quiet conversation. Libby tried ever so inconspicuously to listen in on the adult conversation, but Catherine Masterson found her and began to chatter on about the literature she had selected to read this evening. Much to Libby's annoyance, she found it impossible to hear what her grandparents and mother were talking about.

"Mary, I have a question for you to consider," Captain Abbott began quietly, "but before you give your answer, I beg you to contemplate my request until you return to Boston and have an opportunity to discuss it with Thomas. Do not be hasty in your decision, for it is a rather large request and I would like to think that you gave it your utmost attention."

Out of the corner of his eye, he noticed Mother Morgan turn her attention away from the rest of the group to listen intently to their conversation.

"Yes, Father?" Mary asked with a quizzical expression and a hushed voice. "What is it?"

Rather than dance around the subject, he simply asked, "I would like you to allow Thomas to bring young Libby with him and myself to London." He paused and then quickly added, "Now before you close your mind to the idea, take some time to consider that she is certainly old enough to make the journey. You were far younger the first time you made your trip, and it would be lovely for your mother to see her granddaughter. It has been several years, and Libby has quite grown up since your mother last visited Boston. She would get to know some of her cousins, and it would be a grand adventure for her to write about in her journals. Thomas will be there if anything were to go awry, and your sister has hired a tyrant of a governess for her own children, so she would not be without supervision or schoolwork, I assure you." He looked at the expression Mary now wore, one of contemplation shaded by hesitation, so he added quickly, "Now do not be hasty in your decision, Daughter. Give my request some thought and talk it over with Thomas. You may let me know your answer when we get back to Boston. We can easily book another passage as soon as you decide." He never once looked at Mother Morgan, but in his peripheral vision, he could see her face begin to screw up into an annoyed expression.

"Have you asked the child if she is interested in making such a journey, Gerald?" Mother Morgan interjected.

"I have not, Margaret. I didn't feel it was right to get her hopes up if her parents decided she was not to go." He smiled sweetly back at Mother Morgan, but she just wrinkled her nose at him and shook her head.

Grandfather Abbott offered Mother Morgan his most cunning smile and said, "May I get you ladies some cake?"

Chapter 19

*L*ibby had paid close attention to her mother throughout the rest of the evening. She'd seen the distraction in her mother's eyes and knew that the conversation she had missed out on was to blame. Later, after the family had returned to John Masterson's house, Libby and her mother were preparing for bed, and she was aware of the overly close attention her mother paid to helping her get ready.

She offered to brush Libby's hair, something she had not done in a long time, and feeling it was somehow important to her mother, Libby allowed this moment of extra attention and sat herself at the dressing table. She watched their reflection as her mother lovingly removed the braids from her hair; she saw her mother's thought-filled eyes and watched as she brushed the dark copper strands. It was as if she were longing for the days when Libby was still a small child—when she was not nearly grown as she was now.

Libby had nearly worked up the courage to ask what was affecting such a mood in her mother when there was a knock at the door. Her mother stepped over and opened it.

"Mary, dear, I was just coming to say good night." Mother Morgan stepped inside the door and glanced about the room. "Ah, Libby, I wonder, could you run down and fetch me some milk?" she asked rather abruptly.

"Of course," Libby replied obediently.

She put on her robe and slippers then stepped through the door and headed down to the kitchen, wondering why Mother Morgan wanted milk so late at night.

Mother Morgan let out a sigh of relief. She hadn't expected Libby to still be awake. Turning, she looked at Mary and in a hushed tone added, "I would like very much to speak with you privately."

"Of course, but why the secrecy?" Mary whispered.

"I don't wish to have your father know of our conversation."

"Indeed," Mary responded with a quizzical expression then walked to the door and quietly closed it, but not before checking the hall to be sure they were alone. "What is it? What is troubling you?"

Mother Morgan began, "This request of your father's, to invite Libby on his trip to London . . . well, it is just plain ridiculous. He knows that Libby must have a companion for the trip. She is far too young to travel without adult female supervision." Mother Morgan paused and was just about to explain that Captain Abbott's invitation was simply a ploy to get her to come to London when Mary excitedly interjected.

"I was thinking about that very thing all evening. I have been trying to figure out how I will leave the shop and accompany her, and there is just no possible way I can go if Thomas is to go as well. And with Ellen newly wed, I don't feel inclined to ask her to accompany Libby, or to oversee the shop for the duration of the trip. I was just about to give up on the idea when you appeared at my door, and then I had the most wonderful thought." Mary grasped her mother-in-law's hands, offered her the sweetest smile, and asked, "Why don't you go with Libby to London? She loves you so, and I know with you she would be safe. You could continue your sewing lessons while on the journey."

Mary's expression was sincere, and Mother Morgan could tell she had not been put up to making the offer. She had come to the conclusion on her own. She sat quietly for a moment looking at Mary's face and then said quite plainly, "London is the last place I want to go. Even after all these years, the memories there are more than I could bear. I feel certain it would be too much for me." Her statement was resolute.

Mary's face was downcast, but she offered an understanding smile, "It's all right, I do understand." She released Mother Morgan's hands and said, "Anyway, Libby hasn't even been told of the trip. She will be none the wiser, and so there will be no disappointment. Please do not over trouble yourself, Mother Morgan. I really do understand. Perhaps next summer we can arrange a trip for her with Grandfather Abbott, and I will be able to accompany her then."

Mother Morgan could tell that Mary was let down despite the pleasant smile she now offered. There was an overly long pause of silence in the room, and in a moment of guilt-filled haste, Mother Morgan blurted out in annoyance, "Blast that man! I'll go! I'll make the trip with Libby!"

Mary gasped at the language that erupted from her mother-in-law's mouth. "You'll do it?" she asked excitedly. "You'll be Libby's companion? But what has changed your mind?"

"Well, I'm not sure. It may have been your disappointment or it may have been the challenge put forth by that salty-old-son-of-a-sea-dog you have for a father. Either way, Libby should see the homeland, and since the one reason I had for staying away is now dead," here Mother Morgan's mouth turned up slightly, "I guess it won't be too terrible of a trip. And I do so want to continue Libby's lessons. Besides, Ellen and John will be in need of some time alone as they start their lives together; there will be plenty of time for us all to get comfortable with the new living conditions when I return."

"Are you sure?" Mary asked.

"Quite!" Mother Morgan exclaimed decidedly. "And while you give the exciting news to Libby, I'll just go have a few words with your father."

"I believe he is in the south parlor enjoying some tobacco newly come from the Carolinas," Mary said as Libby tapped at the door. She was returning with the milk Mother Morgan had asked her to fetch.

"Hello, child. That was very kind of you." Libby tried to hand Mother Morgan the milk, but she ignored the glass. "And now you should set yourself down, for your mother has some exciting news to relay." Mother Morgan gestured to Mary then kissed Libby on the cheek and made a determined march out the door in search of Captain Abbott.

Libby set down the glass and plate of biscuits she had brought along, sat in the chair near the hearth, and gave her mother a perplexed grin, "Goodness, I can hardly tell, is she happy or upset?" She asked, referring to her grandmother's mood. "What exciting news have you, Mother?"

"Well now, I have a question for you that until just this moment I wasn't sure I was going to be able to ask, but since your grandmother has graciously said yes, I will ask it now." Libby watched her mother prolong the excitement by nibbling on one of the biscuits she had brought back with the milk.

Unable to stand the suspense, Libby blurted out, "What is it, Mother?" She sat at the very edge of her seat and leaned close to her mother. "Please, do ask!"

Mary took a long, slow drink of milk as the excitement grew on Libby's face. She dusted the crumbs from her lap and straightened her skirt. Libby had no patience left. "Mother!" she said, exasperated. "Please! Tell me the news!"

"Well . . ." her mother began slowly, "it seems your grandfather has made a rather generous offer."

"Yes, what is it?" Libby was beside herself with anticipation and kept wringing her hands in her lap and bouncing her knees.

"It seems that he would like to have *you* accompany him and your father to London."

The words resonated in Libby's ears, and she wasn't quite sure she had heard her mother correctly. "Did you say he wants *me* to come to London?" Libby asked just to be sure she had heard things right.

"Yes, that's right. Would you like to go to London next week?"

Again Libby repeated her mother. "Would *I* like to go to London?"

"Yes, that is the question. Would *you* like to go to London? Provided your father agrees, of course."

Before she answered, Libby gave the question some thought, though briefly. "Will you be going?" she asked in a rather serious tone and with a furrowed brow.

"I will not," she replied, then, as if to reassure her daughter, she added, "but Mother Morgan will be your companion."

Libby looked confused, for she understood from the many conversations of late that Mother Morgan had no desire to ever go back to London.

"It seems that Mother Morgan has had a change of heart." Her mother seemed to read Libby's thoughts. "Now that the Baroness is dead, it appears that your grandmother is able to travel to her homeland, and she would like very much to accompany you on the trip. So what do you say? Do you want to go to London?"

Libby continued with her serious expression for only a moment longer, then, unable to contain her excitement she exclaimed, "Oh, Mother, I do! I so very much want to go to LONDON!" She jumped up and threw her arms around her mother's neck, then she paused and pulled back to look at her mother. "Though truth be told, I'm sorry you will not be going." Her joy had quickly turned to sadness as she pondered the reality that her mother would be staying behind.

"Honestly, child, you shan't miss me for a moment. You will have so very many distractions, and your father will be with you. Grandmother Abbott will keep you busy once you get to London, and Mother Morgan will continue with your sewing lessons. The time will fly." She stood and wrapped her arms around Libby and gave her a warm hug. When she let go, Libby jumped upon the bed. "London! How very exciting! I'm going to London!" She fell face-first into the pillows on the bed and giggled wildly.

In the south parlor, Captain Abbott and Reverend Masterson were commenting upon the fine draw of their new tobacco when Mother Morgan entered the room with a loud bang of the door. She stopped in front of the captain, and with her hands on her hips, she shook her head, then she pointed a finger at Captain Abbott and growled, "You may have won this battle, Gerald, but the war has only just started!"

She turned on her heel and headed back out the door in a huff as Captain Abbott chortled, "Ah, Margaret, it seems you have decided to come to London after all."

Mother Morgan stopped at the door, "Good night, Reverend," she said politely with a curtsy. Ignoring Captain Abbott all together, she turned up her nose, turned on her heel, and left the room with a slam of the door. Before she got two steps down the hall, she heard Captain Abbott's laugh ring loudly and felt her own blood boil.

Chapter 20

The day following the wedding, Libby, her mother, Grandfather Abbott, and Mother Morgan returned to the farm in Ashford. Their days were spent packing for their return trip to Boston and getting Mother Morgan's things prepared for the trip to London. Aunt Ellen and the boys remained in Hartford to prepare for their family honeymoon trip to New York. They would return to the farm to say their good-byes just before the family was to leave.

Over the next few days, Mother Morgan and Grandfather Abbott spent many long hours consulting with the farm overseer, Richard Sykes, regarding the farm management. Mother Morgan had always maintained the books and payroll for her property and had allowed Sykes to manage the hands and day laborers needed when the crops were ready for harvest, but in her absence, Sykes would handle everything regarding the farm. Spring planting had already occurred, so the majority of work left to do was in managing the daily activities and accounts, to get things ready for the harvest, and to handle any emergencies that might arise.

Packed and ready to leave, Libby had naught to do except say her good-byes. She had sat most of the late morning on the porch working on her patchwork flowers and waiting for her cousins to return. Having run out of extra fancy fabrics, she was using up some of the duller brown pieces, but just to add something interesting, she included a center piece of bright chrome orange. She liked the look of it and made a mental note to show her grandmother. She had been waiting patiently for the coach that carried Aunt Ellen and the boys, but it seemed to be taking them far longer to arrive than Libby expected, so she decided to head down to the barn to say her good-byes to the Bigalow brothers, Rose the cow, and Ginger the cat, if she could find her. They were leaving extra early the next day, and she would not have time for good-byes in the morning.

She put away her patchwork in the painted box and headed in the direction of the bellowing cows waiting to be milked. As she was nearly to the barn, she looked back to see the coach arrive, and she waved to the occupants, but no one waved in return. She stopped to watch as the coachman climbed over the outside of the moving coach to be ready with the door as they came to a stop, and she giggled as the two boys came cascading out of the coach, squealing with laughter. James dashed into the house and Albert started to go, but remembering his instructions, he stopped suddenly, turned, and stood in front of the coachman. He then gave a nod of his head and graciously, said, "Thank you, good sir," in a contrived adult voice before scampering off to the house. Libby was proud that he was trying so hard to behave as he had been instructed.

Having not been seen by the boys, Libby continued toward the barn again, and with mixed emotions, she pondered her time on the Ashford farm. There had been so many "firsts" for her on this visit— she had milked her first cow with the Bigalow brothers, caught her first fish with Grandfather Abbott, started her first patchwork quilt with Mother Morgan, and made her first trousseau handkerchiefs for her aunt's wedding. It had been an exciting and fun visit and she would be sorry to see it end, but the idea that she was heading back to Boston filled her with anticipation. She couldn't wait to see her father and her soft Princess kitty. The thought that she would see them before the week was out gave her reason to be excited despite knowing it would take three days in a coach before they would arrive. Then she remembered her patchwork and thought of how lucky she would be to have something to occupy her time on the journey home. It would certainly be different than the long, boring ride coming to Ashford with nothing but some reading and the scenery to pass her time.

Libby's mind was elsewhere when she walked through the barn doors, but the bleating of the cows brought her back to reality just in time to see Ginger speed past a loose cow, leap onto a stall gate, and then right up into the hayloft in a practically effortless motion. The cows in the pen outside were bleating loudly and milling around anxiously as the loose cow ran out the back door and past the corral. As Libby came farther into the barn, she noticed both Bigalow brothers flat on their backs, looking up at the hayloft, laughing uncontrollably. Upon seen Libby, they both regained their composure and quickly got to their feet, but the laughter did not stop.

"I seem to have missed the cause of the ruckus, though by the looks of her guilty expression," Libby gestured toward the cat sitting in the hayloft, "I expect Ginger had something to do with it?"

Matthew Bigalow began to dust off his clothes, and Michael picked up the stool and sat back down, all the while rubbing the side of his head. "It seems," Matthew said, "that Ginger was unwilling to wait for her milk this morning. Michael was just getting settled on the stool when Ginger walked under the cow and began to take her milk without being offered. Imagine the cow's surprise to find a mouth full of sharp teeth suckling at her teat. As you can see, she didn't take it well—she kicked Michael off the stool and broke the lead where she was tied. I tried to catch her, but she knocked me down as well. Ginger was lucky to be away with her skull intact—one kick from that cow and it would have been lights out for that kitty."

"Tell me about it!" Michael said as he rubbed his head once more.

"Ginger, you crazy girl, come down here this instant!" Libby called to the cat but was met with a simple expression of "Who, me?" Then, ignoring Libby completely, she continued to lick her paw and clean her face.

"Sometimes I think that cat is more trouble than she is worth," Michael stated rather harshly. "If she wasn't such a good mouser, I wouldn't like her at all."

"Ah, but she is, Brother, and a brave one to boot. She even kills the snakes before they can get to the eggs. She's worth her weight in gold on this farm. I'll get you another cow to milk while you nurse your wounds. Sit tight," he said with a grin to Libby and then turned to fetch another cow.

"So, Miss Elizabeth, news is you will be going to London soon." Libby accepted Michael's earnest smile. "I hear you will be leaving tomorrow and heading to London with your grandparents early next week. You must be very excited for such a journey."

"I am!" she exclaimed. "That is why I have come to the barn. I don't think I will have time tomorrow to say farewell, and I didn't want to leave without saying thank you."

"Thank you? To what do we owe your thanks?" Matthew said as he was returning with the new cow.

"I wanted you both to know that you made my birthday very special, and I am grateful for you allowing me the experience of milking a cow. It was a first for me, and one I will never forget." Her gratitude was heartfelt.

"It was our pleasure indeed," said Michael.

By this time, Ginger had made her way down from the hayloft and was perched upon the milking stool. Libby walked over and gave her head a gentle rub and said, "Good-bye, Ginger, you silly gal. Happy hunting those snakes, but please," here Libby leaned over and looked the cat square in the eyes, "do leave those birdies and cows alone!"

Ginger gave Libby a "ppprrrrooowww" in response and jumped off the stool and headed for the cow again.

"Seems some animals don't learn their lessons the first time," said Michael with a smile, and he shooed the cat away from the nervous, bleating cow.

Libby curtsied to the brothers, said good-bye one last time, and headed back to the house to spend her last night with the family she was going to miss.

Chapter 21

*T*he sun had yet to peek its head over the horizon when Libby was awakened by the sound of the coach pulling into the yard. The family hurried through their morning preparations and began their good-byes, which were filled with hugs and tears. Libby was truly sad to leave her aunt and cousins, but her feelings were a bittersweet mixture of sad farewells and the excitement of going home.

She was especially sad to say good-bye to James, and he, too, returned her emotion. He hugged her several times, and when she looked in his eyes, he quickly looked away, likely trying to hide his tears, Libby thought. She would miss him sorely, for they had become fond friends despite their age difference. "I'll send you something special from London," she said reassuringly, "and you can write to me and tell me all about your adventures with your new father." She gave James one last hug then turned to Albert, who was smiling broadly and jabbering about how lucky she was to be leaving. Libby was sure that Albert's exuberance regarding her departure was centered solely on the fact that she would get to travel on a steamship across the Atlantic. She did not take his outward happiness at her departure as anything more than what it was, sheer delight that someone, anyone, was going to sea. After many one-last-hugs from her Aunt Ellen and her new Uncle John, she stepped into the coach and situated herself for the long journey back to Boston.

Libby commented to her mother that Grandfather's generosity knew no boundaries; the coach he hired for the return trip was nearly twice the size of the one in which they had arrived, and the seats were well cushioned. Her mother informed her that Grandfather wanted to be certain Mother Morgan was especially comfortable, and then she remembered the night before, when she had overheard her grandfather ask her mother if there were any other anxieties that the long journey created for a woman. He'd said, "It is of the utmost importance that she be most contented, well fed, and well rested on this trip." Libby felt that perhaps he was being a tad bit overly solicitous to Mother Morgan, but she chose to keep that thought to herself.

The trip back to Boston actually took longer—in fact, an entire day longer—than expected because they stopped more frequently to allow Mother Morgan and Grandfather time outside of the coach. Despite the added day, Libby felt that the hours moved quickly, and she was never lacking in something to pass the time. She worked on her patchwork most of the trip, and with the help of Mother Morgan's speedy fingers, she had all the flower units completed as well as most of the white muslin pieces that went between. Just a few miles outside of Boston, Libby announced that she was almost ready to assemble the top. Mother Morgan said that they would begin the assembly as soon as their ship left port. She told Libby that it was likely they would have the top finished and ready for quilting long before they made it to England.

"Perhaps Grandmother Abbott has a lovely piece of chintz you can use on the back," Mother Morgan said to Libby, and Grandfather replied with a roll of his eyes.

"Of that you can be sure! She has more fabric than a merchant. Seems like every trip to France she has me bring her back something new, and frankly, I'm not really sure what she does with it all." Libby looked at her grandfather with a curious smile and tried to imagine yards and yards of colorful chintzes all stacked in a back bedroom closet at her grandmother's house. What a treasure that would be to find.

As the coach got closer to home, Libby began to recognize her surroundings. The landmarks became more familiar, and the buildings began to look like places she remembered. It was surprising to her how much she had forgotten about Boston during her visit to the farm, and as the smell of the salty air blew in from the open window, she leaned her face closer to drink it in. Fish and sea, smoke and industry, all the smells of a busy metropolis came rushing back to her senses, and she remembered why she loved Boston so. Busy people rushing to their destinations, coaches pulled by teams of horses, and laborers with their handcarts all dashing about the streets made Libby feel alive. Here in the city, she found a pace to match her own spirit—a pace of excitement and energy.

With every turn of the coach, Libby's anticipation grew, for she now knew exactly where she was in the city, and it was only blocks from her home. "Mother, do you think Father will be waiting for us?" she asked with anticipation.

"I don't think so, dear. He is probably still at the shop; it's rather early for him to close up. But I'm sure Princess is waiting just inside the door for you." Libby cast her eyes down when she heard her father would not be standing on the porch waving as she had envisioned. "But he will be along shortly, don't fret. See how the sun is low in the west, it won't be too long before he comes home, and we will be there to surprise him with hugs and kisses and a warm supper," her mother added.

"Something I'm sure he has been lacking these past weeks!" Mother Morgan added. "I will wager Thomas is looking forward to our arrival for a good many reasons—home-cooked meals being just one of them!" Libby smiled at Mother Morgan, and she said to her granddaughter, "I'm certain he has missed his true love as much as she has missed him!"

As the coach pulled to a stop in front of the family residence, Libby blurted out, "Home again, home again, jiggety-jig!" This nursery rhyme was one that Libby and her father said to one another each time they returned home from market—it was a game they played to see who would remember and say it first. Libby usually won.

"You sound just like your father, Libby," her mother said with a grin. Then her face lit up as she looked at the front door. "And speaking of your father . . ." she gestured for Libby to look, "see who is standing on the stoop?"

Libby looked out the window in the direction of her home, and there was her father, standing on the stoop holding her Princess in his arms and waving the kitty's paw at the occupants inside the coach. She giggled and waved back while she anxiously waited for the coachman to open the door. Excitedly, she sprang from the coach and ran to greet him. As she found herself engulfed in his hug, the familiar scent of his tobacco filled her nostrils; she inhaled deeply and sighed contentedly to be home. Until this very moment, she had been unaware of exactly how much she missed her father, but now, as she stood hugging him tightly, the realization was more than she could contain, and she began to tear up.

"Here now, why the tears?" her father asked earnestly.

"They are happy tears, Father. Happy-to-be-home tears!" she sniffled with a smile.

"I am glad you are home, too, my dear!" He was looking eagerly past her at the coach.

"We've so much to share with you, so many new things to tell you about," Libby said excitedly as she stepped back from her father and scooped up her meowing kitty. She stroked the cat's soft fur and glanced back to see the rest of the family exiting the coach. When she looked up at her father, it was love she saw in his eyes as he watched her mother get out of the coach and walk toward the house. He stepped off the porch and ran to greet her with open arms. He hugged her tightly and kissed her lips, then, stepping back, he looked her up and down and hugged her again. In that moment, Libby saw true love on the faces of both her parents, and it planted a seed in her heart. She knew what real love looked like, and she knew that real love was what she wanted for her own life.

Chapter 22

*T*he family gathered inside and told Libby's father all the news from the farm and the wedding. After an unexpectedly good bowl of bean soup and cornbread, something her father had prepared prior to their arrival home, Libby sat by the fire with Princess on her lap, kneading her leg and purring loudly. Undisturbed by her younger cousins and their constant conversations, and without her patchwork that begged to be worked upon, she found herself at peace and contented by the familiar smell of her own home and the lulling conversation of the adults. Her eyes were drooping and she wanted to retire, but knowing she would not be sleeping in her own bed did not motivate her to rise. She had been very much looking forward to sleeping under her indigo basket quilt without the companionship of her mother, but with Mother Morgan now staying until they departed for England, she would have to give up her sleeping quarters and find her rest on a pallet made near the fireplace in the kitchen. But it didn't completely dampen her spirits, for she knew that Princess would be there to keep her company.

The next few days in Libby's home were filled with the many preparations that go into securing a trip on one of the packet ships to England. Libby's father and grandfather wrote the letters necessary to secure transportation from New York harbor, as it was too late in the summer for the family to depart from Boston. Her grandfather also purchased train passage from Boston to New York—she guessed he had had enough of coaches to last him awhile, and so had she—so they would take the New York and Albany Express Train on the Boston and Worcester Railroad Line to New York harbor.

Libby and her mother spent the entire day before her departure deciding what to bring, packing and repacking Libby's trunk. She was getting tired of her mother constantly quizzing what she should do in this situation or that, and after a particularly long lecture about how dangerous the docks could be for a young lady, Libby questioned rather bluntly, "Weren't you a good deal younger when you made your first crossing?"

"That is not the point!" her mother replied defensively.

"I think Grandfather knows the New York harbor pretty well, and Father could certainly handle any sailor who may get out of line with me. For goodness' sake, Mother Morgan won't let me out of her sight, I can assure you of that! Please, Mother, I'm going to be just fine!" Libby's exasperated expression begged her mother to stop worrying.

Evening finally came, her last evening at home for what Libby surmised would be a few months, and her mother and father retired earlier than usual. Libby was left to sit with her grandmother as the evening closed, so she sat with Princess near the cozy fire and comforted her childhood playmate. "Now, Princess," Libby said in soft tones as she stroked the cat's fur, "you mustn't forget me, Pretty Girl! I know I have been gone a lot these past months, and I will be leaving again on the morrow, but I promise you I will return, and if at all possible, I shall bring you home something special." Libby thought of how Princess would enjoy a nice large ship rat, but the thought of catching one made her skin crawl. Perhaps she could think of something less revolting to bring home as a gift to her kitty.

She glanced at Mother Morgan sitting quietly at the table writing a letter, and upon seeing her with a pen and paper, she was reminded that she had not finished reading the letters she had received for her birthday, so she lifted Princess from her lap and gently placed her back in the chair. She turned and said softly, "I'll be right back, Grandmother; I just want to get something from my room."

Mother Morgan did not look up from her letter but nodded her head in acknowledgement. Libby slipped out and then quietly returned to the room with her letters in hand. She saw her grandmother, faced covered by her hands, and couldn't help but wonder if she was thinking about her babies in England. Should she ask, she wondered? As she sat down across the table and set the stack of letters down, Mother Morgan pulled her hands away from her face and looked up. She offered Libby a tired smile, and Libby decided in that moment she would ask.

"You look troubled, Grandmother."

"Just remembering the last time I was in Liverpool."

"When you came to America?"

"Yes. It was a sad day indeed!" Libby Looked at her grandmother and offered an encouraging expression indicating she wanted to hear more. Mother Morgan continued, "I had been crying most of that day at the thought of leaving my family, but I could no longer stay in England. There was no place in London or in the surrounding countryside where Edward and I could live as equals; too many people knew of his title, and even more knew of mine—the Baroness Montclief had spread such awful gossip that I couldn't even walk into a shop without people whispering and pointing. It was only two months after the babes were buried that Edward suggested we leave, and America seemed the logical place. Captain Abbott was our lifeline; he had many contacts and allowed us passage at no cost. My mother was heartbroken at losing me, but she knew that I would recover faster were I away from all the reminders of my loss."

Libby watched as her grandmother looked into the fire, and her eyes filled with tears. "I can still see their tiny graves, close to the churchyard wall of the chapel. We left them with only a small stone carved with interlocking hearts, their names, and the two dates, only weeks apart." Mother Morgan paused as if deciding to continue or not, and Libby dabbed her eyes with her hankie. "The poor little dear." Mother Morgan recounted the death of her babe in a sad and quiet voice that made Libby sorry she had encouraged the story. "She did not appear to suffer, she just mewled quietly like a tiny kitten, and then a soft coo escaped with her last breath. The finality of that sound haunts me today." She looked at her granddaughter; Libby was upset but tried to cover it with a fake cough, so Mother Morgan added more brightly, "I'm lucky, you know."

"Lucky?" Libby choked out. "How is that lucky?"

"I never lost another child!" Mother Morgan exclaimed with an encouraging smile.

"I don't see how that is lucky." Libby was too young to know the truth about childbirth and raising children. She was an only child and had not experienced death much.

"It's true, I was lucky. Many women lose babes every year in child-birth or from disease. And many more don't live to see their children grow to adults as I have. My Thomas and Ellen are healthy and happy and have families of their own. And though I have lost two, I also have two! And my two have gone on to give me even more children with whom I can share my life." She gestured toward Libby and asked, "Do you see, child, how lucky I am?"

Libby sat quietly while her grandmother wiped away her own tears, and she pondered the question. Luck, it seemed to Libby, was all a mat-ter of perspective! "I guess what you mean is that it just depends upon how you look at something, and in this case, you chose to look at what you have gained, instead of what you lost?"

"That's right, dear. That's exactly right!"

"I suppose," Libby sighed, "it makes sense. But perspective does naught to relieve the pain from the loss you do suffer."

"Time does," her grandmother said with a loving smile.

Libby wiped at her face one last time and looked at the stack of letters on the table. The stack was much smaller than when she'd first gotten them, for she had used many in her spread.

"I guess I can look at this stack and say, 'Lucky for me my spread is nearly done, for I am running out of letters for my templates.' But what I really feel is a bit sad that I am almost out of letters to read and stories to hear." She took the next letter in the stack and began to turn it over this way and that, examining the handwriting. She did not recognize it as one she had seen before; in fact, everything about this letter was different. There was writing all over the outside of the letter, and as she opened it, she noticed that the author had not only written horizontally across the pages, as was customary in letter writing, but they had also written vertically—right over the top of the horizontal writing. It gave the letter an odd, checkerboard look that left Libby unsure about where to start reading.

Libby was confused as she shuffled the pages and turned them over and over trying to find the starting point. "Here, child, let me have that and I shall show you where to start reading." Mother Morgan reached her hand out for the letter.

Libby put the pages back in the order they were in when she opened it and handed the letter to her grandmother. "Why on earth would someone write like that? Was it meant to confuse the reader, Grandmother? Do you know from whom this letter comes?"

"Yes, I do, Libby. This letter is from your great-grandfather, John Hammond. He has written many a letter to me over my lifetime and his writing style is unique. It can be a bit confusing until you get the hang of reading it. Here . . ." She pointed to the beginning of the letter, and

Libby could see now that the line was indented and had the date and salutation. "See right there, where it says 'Dearest Daughter' and the date is written?" She handed Libby the letter. Libby looked at the writing and tried to relax her eyes and see only the horizontal writing. Lo and behold, the letter began to come into focus, and she could understand what the words were saying. The letter was quite tragic, and as Libby read the words, her heart became very heavy again.

"How sad, Mother Morgan, how terribly sad." Libby looked up from reading the letter with tears clouding her eyes. "I'm so sorry you could not be with your mother when she passed." Libby was overwhelmed at the thought of losing her own mother—particularly if she were not there to hold her hand and comfort her. The upcoming trip to England had caused many new fears to surface in Libby's mind, fears about one or the other of them dying while she was away.

"There, there, child. Do not fret." Mother Morgan patted Libby's hand where it lay clutching the letter on the table. "Mother and I wrote quite often—great, lengthy letters of our days and goings-on. Grandfather Abbott was kind enough to carry our correspondence and packages back and forth when he crossed the Atlantic. You mustn't think we had no contact. I believe, in truth, that we had a closer relationship through our writing than if I had lived next door." She continued to rub Libby's hand as she spoke, "I am sorry I was not there when Mother passed, too, but only because of Father. He must have been so lonely and sad. As I remember, he even wrote that he was anxious to follow her into the arms of Jesus. But they were quite well along in their years, child. God had allowed them a long, lovely life together, and if you read a little further, you will see where Father mentions why he was anxious to leave this world."

Libby picked the letter back up, found her place, and continued to read the scratchy writing on the paper: *"My Savior has given me so many days on this earth. I hope I have lived up to His great expectations and fulfilled*

His purpose in my life. And Margaret, forgive me for saying this, but I pray he lets me follow my beloved Jane Marie home soon, as I have not slept a single night in these past sixty-five years without her. The bed seems so big to me now that she is gone."

"It's just too sad for me to continue reading, Grandmother." Libby handed her grandmother the letter. She could no longer hold her own fear inside and soon found herself speaking the words that troubled her mind. "I'm so afraid to go tomorrow. I'm excited about going, but mostly I'm afraid."

"Afraid of what, dear?" Mother Morgan asked softly.

"I'm afraid I might not get home again. Or that Mother will die while I'm gone. I don't know, I'm just afraid . . . and I can't really explain it." Tears rolled down Libby's face as she tried to describe her jumbled feelings of anticipation, excitement, and fear.

"Those are all justified feelings, Libby. You have every right to feel that way. And honestly, those things are possible." Mother Morgan spoke very matter-of-factly to Libby, and it startled her a bit. She was more accustomed to her mother's usual 'Nonsense child, nothing bad is going to happen' line. But Mother Morgan had just stated that Libby's biggest fears were possible.

"Excuse me for being rude, Grandmother, but this isn't making me feel better." Libby said as she wiped the tears from her cheeks.

"It's not intended to," Mother Morgan said with the same frankness in her tone. "I think it's good that you are considering the possibilities you may encounter on this trip. I think it's important to know the good *and* the bad when considering any situation. But there is something very important that you are not considering. So I'll ask you: Will you allow fear to hold you captive? Will you allow being afraid of what *may happen* or what you *may feel* prevent you from doing something you may enjoy? For if you do, you will most certainly live an unsatisfied life in a self-inflicted stronghold."

Mother Morgan took the letter from Libby, folded it back up, then stood and walked around the table and stopped in front of her. Reaching out her arms, she urged Libby into her embrace and whispered in her ear, "Trust me when I say this, for I know it to be true. I have lived in fear far too long, child. I've forced myself to stay away from England and my family because I was crippled by my fear and sorrow. But tomorrow, I will face my fears head on and get on that ship. Fear will conquer me no more."

Chapter 23

The morning fog was lying heavy on the docks as Libby kissed her mother for a third time. When she had departed for Ashford, saying good-bye to her father hadn't seemed this difficult, and Libby wasn't exactly sure why she was so emotional this time. Her mother's stoic expression gave Libby reason to pause and question the desire for making this journey, and though her mother hadn't shed a tear, Libby felt somehow that her mother's apprehension was founded in fear.

Libby felt the tension in her mother's hug. "Do not fear, Mother," she said, letting go and taking hold of her grandmother's hand. "Mother Morgan will guard me with her life." She winked at her mother and hugged her one last time.

"You are in the most capable of hands, I know this to be true." Her mother smiled bravely and kissed her mother-in-law's cheek, kissed her husband several more times, and gave one last hug to her father. Then she quickly stepped onto the stoop with her back to her family. Libby knew her mother was crying, for she could see her shoulders sink and her hands cover her face. Being the one left behind, Libby thought to herself, was certainly far worse than being the one leaving.

Libby continued to wave good-bye from the coach window as they rolled away from the house, and she was rewarded for her efforts when she saw her mother quickly spin around and wave just as the coach turned the corner out of sight.

As she sat back from the window, Libby was filled with mixed emotions; there was a bit of sadness for leaving her mother behind but also excitement to be starting her new adventure.

The family arrived in New York around four o'clock that afternoon. A quick stop at the grocer near the train depot was necessary to pick up a few food items that would keep them healthy during the transatlantic crossing—food was not the best on the steamships, even in first class. "I'm getting some hard peppermint candies for you ladies," Grandfather said to Libby and Mother Morgan. "The peppermint will sooth the tummy, and the sweet will satisfy the appetite without leaving much to heave up if you are sick."

Following the grocer, they had supper at an inn not far from the docks—it would be the last meal they would have on stable ground for several weeks, and Libby's grandfather insisted it be a good one. After the meal, they headed straight for the docks to board the ship. They were scheduled to depart New York with the morning's outgoing tide, and all passengers had to be boarded no later than ten o'clock that night.

From the time she stepped off the train until she was settled in her cabin on board the ship, Libby felt like she was caught up in a whirlwind of activity. They'd taken a cab from the grocer near the train depot to the noisy, busy inn where they dined. And as the cab was kind enough to deliver their luggage to the docks, they had only the barest of essentials to carry during their walk from the inn to the ship. She found her hand clasped securely by her grandmother as they walked from one place to the next, and it was lucky for her, too, because as she gawked at the many different sights and sounds, she nearly stepped off the dock into the water. Mother Morgan jerked her back on the walkway as her father grabbed Mother Morgan's arm to prevent her from being taken over as well.

"Elizabeth!" her father scolded. "Keep your eyes on the road, child. You nearly took your grandmother for a swim. I know things here are new and exciting, but really, you must pay attention."

Libby blushed and apologized to her grandmother. "Never you mind, dear. Your father did the same thing when he was young. He was forever running into things or people when we would come down to greet a ship or collect your mother on her journeys. He could barely keep himself from falling in on several occasions. It happens to everyone. There is just too much going on, and it's so difficult to watch where you are going and still see all that your eye is drawn to." She gripped Libby's hand tighter and said, "Fret not, child, I won't let you fall in."

The sun was nearly set when the family reached the steamship, and in the dimming light, Libby could see the grand ocean vessel with a massive stovepipe emerging from the center of the deck. The giant paddle wheel was situated just behind the pipe and there was one foremast and two aft-masts hung with all sorts of riggings. The large, dark ship loomed before her in the twilight and she was somewhat daunted by it's enormity. Grandfather patted her back and said, "Not as lovely as my *Ariana*, but a nice looking ship, don't you agree?"

"It is," was all Libby could say, for her eyes were taking in every detail, and the many people and sailors moving about the deck distracted her thoughts. Her father walked closely behind as she crossed the gangplank to board the ship, and she was grateful for his steady hand on her back.

Once aboard, Libby's eyes were wide and her mouth agape as she stared at the unexpected luxury of the steamship. The halls were opulently filled with polished brass and wood, lush carpets, and velvet draperies. The overstuffed furniture resembled that which she had seen at the Masterson house in Hartford, and she was reminded of her mother's words, "Don't touch!"

They walked one deck below the lounges to their cabin, and though she'd thought they would all share a single cabin, to her surprise, Grandfather Abbott had purchased *two* first-class cabins; one for Libby and her grandmother to share and one for Libby's father and himself to share. The rooms were situated right next door to one another, and her father assured her that he would always be just a shout away should she find herself distressed. Libby stood in the doorway of the cabin and asked, "Where are our things, Father?"

Libby's father opened his door and looked inside. "Mine are here, dear; yours should be in your cabin as well." Libby turned around and saw the small trunk she had packed was off in the far corner, and Grandmother's larger trunk was against the far wall.

Mother Morgan said, "I think, Captain, that perhaps we shall not join you for drinks later; I would like to get things settled in the cabin, and Libby and I would both benefit from a good night's sleep." The ship gave a slight dip with the outgoing tide, causing Mother Morgan to waver in the doorway. Grandfather Abbott reached out and steadied the old woman as she regained her composure. "Goodness, it has been so long since I was aboard a ship; I have forgotten how the movement can affect one. I think it may take some time to get my sea legs, Gerald." She gave Captain Abbott a smile and retreated back into the cabin, holding the furniture as she went.

"It has been a long day, Margaret. I think we will all benefit from early retirement. I'm going up to see the ship's captain, and then I shall return for some much-needed rest." He bowed slightly toward Mother Morgan, patted her son on the shoulder, and said, "Would you like to join me?"

He nodded and the men walked down the hall, so Mother Morgan closed the door quietly. Libby was opening and closing every door and drawer in the room, curious as to what she might find. "Finding anything interesting?" Mother Morgan asked just as Libby opened the final drawer below the washbasin.

Libby straightened up quickly and looked at her grandmother with a sheepish grin. "I was just seeing if the last passenger left anything in the cupboards."

"Clever child, I never thought of that. Well? Find anything?"

"No, ma'am," Libby replied a bit disappointedly.

"Well, let's get unpacked, shall we? Then we can think of something interesting that *we* can leave for the next passengers." Libby chuckled at her grandmother's idea.

The room was small but quite nice and clean. Wood panels lined the walls, a throw rug covered most of the floor, and a single stuffed chair sat in one corner of the room. Oil lamps were mounted on the wall next to the chair and near the door, and there was even a looking glass over the basin. The beds were stacked one on top of the other and were made with fine linen sheets, but only a single thin blanket. "I hope it doesn't get too cold," Libby said as she examined the bottom bunk's thin wool blanket. "Would you like the top or the bottom?" she indicated each bed with a joking smile, knowing her grandmother couldn't climb up on the top bunk easily.

"Why, top, please!" Mother Morgan said with a serious tone, and Libby wasn't sure if her grandmother was sincere until she winked. "It would take some of the ship's rigging to get me in that top bed!" They both laughed.

There were two small wooden chairs next to an exceptionally small writing table, which was topped with a tray and a tea service for two. Libby saw her grandmother contemplate the teapot for a moment before turning to unpack her trunk, and it struck a thought in Libby. "Where shall we get our water?"

"Let's worry about that after we unpack," her grandmother replied.

The very small closet was only slightly large enough for Mother Morgan's dresses; Libby left her clothes folded neatly in her travel trunk, thus eliminating the need for her to do much else than change into her bedclothes and tie up her hair. She was sitting on the edge of the bed when she heard a soft rap at the door.

Mother Morgan rose and walked to the door and opened it only far enough to see who was on the other side. Libby heard her grandfather's voice say, "Hot water?" Mother Morgan swung the door wide as Libby's grandfather stepped into the small room carrying a kettle filled with freshly boiled water; he made his way immediately to the table with the small teapot and filled it to the brim then poured the remainder into the pitcher on the wash basin. "Oh, Captain, thank you ever so much!" Mother Morgan patted the man's shoulder and said, "Libby, dear, fetch the red tea safe from my trunk, will you, please?"

Libby went to Mother Morgan's travel trunk and took a small red box from one of the drawers. She handed the box to her grandmother and scrambled back to her place of hiding on the upper bunk.

"Good night, Captain," Mother Morgan said with a sigh, "and thank you for the water; I have been thinking about this cup of tea for the past hour."

"Good night, Margaret. Good night, Libby. Enjoy your rest—our adventure begins at high tide." Grandfather Abbott slipped out the door, but before it closed, Libby's father poked his head inside.

"I came to say good night to my favorite girl."

"Why thank you, Thomas." Mother Morgan smiled and Libby falsely pouted.

"Did I say girl? I meant girlsssss!" He corrected his statement

Libby's father hugged his mother, and she kissed his cheek. "Thank you for coming with us, Mother. It means so very much to me, and Libby, too, I'm sure. Without you, this trip would have been impossible for her."

"Yes, Grandmother, I don't think I've told you how grateful I am that you decided to come along." Libby was indeed grateful. "Thank you so very, very much!" She gave her father a hug and he patted her head.

"You are both very welcome," replied Mother Morgan honestly.

As Libby's father stepped out of the stateroom and quietly closed the door, Mother Morgan placed the tea leaves in the pot and gave it a stir. She replaced the lid and turned to her granddaughter just in time to see Libby's mouth offer a wide, uncovered yawn. "My goodness, Libby, how tired you must be from such an emotional and exciting day. Come, let's get washed for bed."

"Grandmother," Libby said as she scrambled out of the upper bunk, "do you think we will encounter pirates?" Libby's voice was quite serious and her concern showed on her face.

"I think, Libby, we shall have a journey across the Atlantic that you will never forget," she paused and patted Libby's hand and gave a quick wink, "whether or not we encounter pirates."

Chapter 24

*L*ibby did not awaken with a start; she simply came into awareness of her surroundings because she was trying to figure out what that strange banging sound was. It lasted only a short time and then stopped, and a new sound met her ears. There was a sort of rhythm to it, like the "chugga-chugga-chugga" sound of the train she had ridden the day before, and after a few moments, she figured it must be the steam engines or perhaps the paddle wheel, for she felt the motion of the ship begin to change. She rolled over on her side and glanced about the dark room, trying to make out what time of day it might be, but instead of getting up, she stayed put in her bunk and listened to the rhythmic sound of the paddle wheel.

Libby heard Mother Morgan stir in her bed, and her pressing bladder made her whisper, "Grandmother, is it time to get up yet? I need to use the privy."

"I think we have pulled anchor and are moving out of the harbor, dear. You may get up and use the chamber pot, but I'm sure it's still a few hours until breakfast. You will want to try and sleep a bit more, I think." Libby could hear Mother Morgan yawn and roll over in her bed.

She clambered out of her top bunk and found her way to the chamber pot. Her mother had given strict instructions to use the pot in the room unless her grandmother accompanied her. She had been forbidden to wander the halls of the ship alone. When she finished, she made her way back to the bunk and climbed back under the warm covers. Mother Morgan had given her a large wool shawl to use as a second blanket, and it had kept her warm and cozy throughout the chill of the night.

As she lay quietly in her bed, she could feel the gentle rise and fall of the ship; she could hear faint sounds of shouting men and the odd banging about of things above her head. She figured that the deckhands were busy at their tasks for getting the ship underway and out of the harbor. She wished she could be up on deck to see the sunrise as the ship sailed away from New York, but her grandmother's soft rhythmic breathing could be heard quite clearly, she having fallen back to sleep already, so Libby knew there was no hope of waking her in time to catch their departure from New York Harbor. She decided instead to ask God for a safe passage and to keep her family far from any storms or sickness that could be so common aboard a ship. As an afterthought, she mentioned the pirates she had worried over and asked God to keep her far away from them, too.

Having eventually fallen back asleep, Libby began a series of wild dreams about her kitty chasing the ship rats across the deck, and pirates that were standing at the helm drinking ale and singing songs about gold. In her dream, she was frantically searching for her mother and crying out for grandmother to help find her . . . and just as she tripped on a rope and was falling over the side of the ship, she woke suddenly to her grandmother giving her a gentle shake to wake her from her fitful sleep.

"Libby, dear, I'm here!" she said with compassion as she rubbed Libby's arm. "Wake, child. You are having a nightmare."

Libby opened her eyes with a start and grasped her grandmother's hand in terror. "Oh, Grandmother, I was falling off the ship . . . and Princess was eating a rat . . . and there were pirates, and I couldn't find Mother."

"Now, now, girl. It was only a dream. A scary one, to be sure, but just a dream." She reassured Libby as she climbed out of her bunk and hugged her grandmother fiercely.

"I was so afraid . . . and then I was falling . . ." She sobbed a bit into her grandmother's arm and buried her face in the folds of her nightclothes.

"It's going to be just fine," Mother Morgan said as she petted Libby's hair, "I'm sure your nerves are a little raw from such a busy day yesterday, and having to leave your mother behind must have been so difficult. How about we fix you a nice cup of tea and get you all the way woken up? A few lumps of sugar in your tea will surely chase those demons from your mind." Mother Morgan gave her granddaughter a smile and a warm embrace.

Just then, there was a soft rap at the door and a strange man's voice said with a very thick British accent, "Steward Wallingsforth, Madam. Shall I bring you ladies some hot water?"

Mother Morgan made her way to the door, opened it slightly, and replied, "Perfect timing, young man. We would love some."

"Yes, Mum. And breakfast is being served in the first-class dining room in half an hour." He bowed slightly to Mother Morgan and turned to fetch the hot water.

"Elizabeth, dear, let's get dressed for breakfast. And bring along your sewing basket with your blocks. We will spend some time in the Ladies' Lounge this morning working on your patchwork."

"Yes, Grandmother," Libby said, a little downcast.

Mother Morgan examined her granddaughter's expression and then asked, "Was there something else you had in mind?"

"Well, since you asked," Libby said a little sheepishly, "I was hoping we could explore the ship a bit . . . this being my first trip and all."

Mother Morgan replied, "How about if we work on your patchwork first, just after breakfast, and that will give your grandfather time to establish himself with the captain and other crewmen. Then we can ask *him* to take you on an expedition, for I assure you, Grandfather Abbott can take you places on the ship I cannot. You will have a far better time with him than with me. What do you say?"

"That is a great idea, Grandmother. I hope you don't think I don't want to spend the morning with you . . . it's just that the ship is so new and exciting."

"Nonsense! Don't give it another moment's thought. I completely understand your excitement. Now hurry and dress, the steward will be back with our hot water any moment."

Chapter 25

*L*ibby had put on her best blue delaine skirt and jacket, and Mother Morgan was wearing a very fashionable plaid silk dress with a lace collar and pagoda sleeves. The exceptional workmanship of their clothing and their current style made Libby feel like an equal with the other affluent ladies and gentlemen who filled the first-class dining room.

Breakfast wasn't nearly as bad as Libby had expected; Grandfather referred to it as "standard fare" aboard the mail ships and informed her that it was only going to get worse as the trip progressed. Libby ate everything on her plate and barely opened her mouth to talk except to ask for the butter or another biscuit; but her eyes were ever on the move around the dining hall.

As discreetly as possible, for she did not wish to be scolded for staring, she examined all the elegant ladies and gentlemen talking quietly amongst the tables. She scanned the room for any other young girls her age, but to her disappointment, she found none. It seemed a different lifestyle than she was accustomed to—everyone was so proper and well-mannered. Only once did she hear a loud cackle come from an overweight woman sitting at a large table in the corner.

When they had all finished eating and had a second cup of tea, Mother Morgan informed Captain Abbott of her intentions to take Elizabeth to the Ladies' Lounge for a few hours. She suggested that they gather later in the afternoon for a quiet snack in the room, and then perhaps the men could take Libby on an exploration of sorts about the ship. The plans were agreed upon, so Mother Morgan and Libby excused themselves from the table, collected their sewing bags, and traveled through several passageways until they found the Ladies' Lounge just in the place Grandfather Abbott had said it would be located.

As they entered the room through large wooden doors, several ladies looked up from their books or sewing to observe the newcomers. Libby, conscious of the fact that she was the only young girl in the room, walked with her grandmother to a small table that was out of the way of the other ladies and their conversations. They found comfortable chairs and sat down to begin their stitching. Libby again found herself staring at the opulence with which the room was decorated, but upon hearing Mother Morgan quietly clear her throat, she shifted in her seat and regained her composure. She opened her sewing bag and took out several of her beautiful chintz blocks and a small stack of white patches. She threaded her needle and commenced to sewing the white patches around the chintz blocks. Then, remembering that she had not washed her hands after her meal, she set down the patchwork and looked at her hands. Confident that they were not overly dirty, she picked up her work and began to stitch the white pieces to the flower blocks. Mother Morgan took out a very fine piece of lace, nearly as fine as the Chantilly veil she had made for Aunt Ellen's wedding, and began to apply a lovely border to the piece. She wondered why Mother Morgan worked the complicated lace pattern instead of working on the simple patchwork with her.

Libby looked up from her sewing for a moment to see two fancily dressed ladies looking at them from across the room and talking in quiet tones. She continued with her patchwork but quietly said without looking up, "Grandmother, those ladies are looking at us."

"Yes, dear, don't let them distract you from your task." She leaned over and looked at the work Libby was doing and offered a gentle correction, "Keep your stitches small, please, Elizabeth. I want this work to be your best. Do not rush."

Libby looked at her work and her grandmother's and decided to remove her last five stitches. They had gotten rather large and sloppy. As she pulled out the stitches, she wondered why her grandmother had been referring to her as Elizabeth instead of Libby ever since they came aboard the ship. She had the distinct feeling that her grandmother was on her very best behavior, and she wondered why. She knew that manners were important, but she was beginning to feel like they were putting on airs for the other passengers on the ship. She thought to ask, but decided it was a question best saved for later. She looked up from her stitching to see an older woman in a green-striped dress walking toward them, and Libby could see a girl trailing closely behind; the girl did not look up but kept her face downcast. Libby thought she must be shy, but she was excited nonetheless to see another girl about her age.

"Good morning, ladies." The woman offered a warm smile and a slight curtsy.

Mother Morgan looked up from her stitching and smiled back and said, "How do you do?"

"May I present my granddaughter, Miss Gertrude Tredwell. And I am Mrs. Eliza Tredwell. We are traveling to London on holiday."

"How do you do, Mrs. Tredwell? It is a pleasure to make your acquaintance. I am Mrs. Margaret Morgan, and this is my granddaughter, Miss Elizabeth Jane Morgan."

"How do you do?" she said to Mother Morgan and then to Libby in an overly proper tone, "And how do you do, young lady?" She picked up one of Libby's patchwork flowers to examine it. "Your patchwork is quite lovely. And your workmanship is excellent. It is good to see a young lady mastering the finer arts of womanhood. So many of our young girls forgo the gentle crafts for books these days." She gave a look to her granddaughter and Libby noticed the girl cringe ever so slightly.

206

Libby thought to say how she loved to read as well but decided a sincere, "Thank you, ma'am," was a better alternative.

"Gertrude," Mrs. Tredwell said in an irritated tone, "fetch the steward to bring over some chairs please." Libby noticed her look of annoyance and immediately felt sorry for the girl, who continued to stare at the floor. Gertrude curtsied and moved in the direction of the steward by the door.

With chairs in place, the two adults partook in casual conversation about the ship and the Atlantic crossing. Libby continued to work on her patches and tried to ignore the adult conversation while Gertrude simply sat looking at her hands folded in her lap. Once, Gertrude shifted in her chair, and Mrs. Tredwell glanced at the girl and scolded, "Stop fidgeting, Gertrude!" in a rather harsh tone of exasperation, then she went back to her conversation with Mother Morgan. Libby looked up at the young girl to try and catch her eye in an effort to start a conversation, but Gertrude did not budge. She was like a quiet little mouse, with a fearful gaze that seemed to know if she moved even a finger, she would be pounced upon by her ferocious tiger of a grandmother.

Together, they sat for about an hour while Libby and her grandmother worked on their sewing. Gertrude sat in complete silence, and Mrs. Tredwell chattered nonstop about everything under the sun. Libby tried to ignore the situation, but finally she had had enough. She wanted to talk with someone, and so she made up her mind as to how she might bring Gertrude out of her shell. She reached into her sewing bag and pulled out the bag of peppermints that Grandfather had purchased for her trip. She extended the open bag to Gertrude and said quietly, "Would you like a peppermint, Miss Gertrude?"

Gertrude glanced at her grandmother and found that the older woman had scooted her chair closer to Mother Morgan and was now sitting with her back in the direction of her granddaughter. She looked up at Libby, held her finger up to her lips, and silently mouthed, "Sshhh."

She quickly grabbed a peppermint and stuffed it into her mouth then returned to her position of head down and blank expression. Libby put one in her own mouth, quietly put the bag of treats back into her sewing bag, and smiled to herself. "So," she thought, "there is more to this little mouse than meets they eye."

Mother Morgan expressed a desire to excuse herself to the toilet-room, and Mrs. Tredwell said she would join her. "If you don't mind, Grandmother, I will stay here with Miss Gertrude." Mother Morgan gave Libby a knowing smile and said, "That's just fine, dear. Come along, Mrs. Tredwell, I'll let you show me the way," and she gestured for the woman to lead.

With the two women out of the room, Libby felt Gertrude relax a bit, and she thought perhaps this was the best time to get the girl to open up a little. "Miss Gertrude, are you enjoying the ship?" It sounded rather formal, but it was all Libby could think to say.

"Goodness, no!" Gertrude said with a worn-out sigh of relief. "My grandmother is a beast, as I'm sure you can see. She insists upon the most proper of manners, and I'm not allowed to 'gawk' at the other passengers. The only way to make her leave me alone is to just look at the floor or my hands, and to keep my mouth closed at all times. It is *exasperating* being with her!"

"I'm sorry," Libby replied earnestly.

"How old are you?" Gertrude asked Libby with a curious tone.

"Thirteen, how old are you?" Libby replied with an encouraging smile.

"I just turned fourteen. We are going to London for 'the season,' and I'm just fourteen—can you believe it? My grandmother thinks that I need to be settled by sixteen, and she is taking no chance in getting me a husband. My mother said it was really just a 'pre-season' visit, but if I know my grandmother, she will have me married off as soon as possible."

"But you are so young," Libby said, shocked.

"I am the last of seven daughters in my family. My parents have gone broke trying to marry off my sisters. My grandmother is hoping to make a more . . . profitable match for me in London amongst her society friends." Gertrude made this last statement with a flip of her hair and the raising of her nose.

"I'm so sorry." Libby could think of nothing worse than to be "married off."

"I'm all right, I can handle myself. I have no intention of getting married any time soon. I'm going to be a writer and make my own money. That is why Grandmother is annoyed with me. She hates that I like to read and write; if I could, I would read all the time, and it bothers her."

Libby smiled at Gertrude and told her she liked to read, too. Gertrude smiled a wide, toothy smile back at Libby and asked, "Did you happen to bring any books with you? Grandmother has forbidden me from taking any books from the lounge!"

"I have a couple of *Godey's* with me, but I didn't bring any books. You are welcome to borrow them if you like . . . but . . . you don't think she will throw them overboard if she finds them, do you?" Libby was a bit aghast at the thought.

"She just might!" responded Gertrude. "I'm so bored. I'm going crazy with Grandmother. I wish there was something to do that didn't involve her!"

Libby had an idea. "Well, my grandfather is taking me on a tour of the ship this afternoon. Perhaps we can ask if you would like to join us. My grandfather can be very charming; I'm sure he could convince your grandmother to let you go. Would you like to go?"

"Would I? Goodness, yes!" Gertrude jumped up to hug Libby, but the door to the lounge opened and Mother Morgan stepped through. Gertrude quickly sat back down and resumed her demure position.

At first, Libby didn't understand the sudden change in her demeanor, but when she heard the door behind her close, she knew that the grandmothers must have come back into the room. Mother Morgan glided to her place and gracefully sat down in her chair. Gertrude looked up and gave Libby's grandmother a sweet smile then cast her eyes back to her lap, and Libby stifled a giggle. Mrs. Tredwell resumed her position, and the two ladies continued to converse over another cup of tea while Libby worked on her patchwork and Gertrude escaped into the recesses of her own mind for the duration of the morning.

Chapter 26

The Tredwells joined Libby and her family for lunch in the dining room, and at Libby's request, Grandfather Abbott invited Gertrude to join them on the ship tour. Mrs. Tredwell declined the offer, insisting that her granddaughter had already had enough excitement for the day and they were going to retire early, but Libby gave her own grandmother a look that pleaded Gertrude's case.

"But, Mrs. Tredwell, I must insist you join me for a stroll on the deck and allow the girls to join Captain Abbott on his tour. It will be good for me to get some fresh air, and I would enjoy your company. Too many of these younger passengers have fanatical new ideas, and I much prefer your conversation to theirs." Mother Morgan patted Mrs. Tredwell's hand in encouragement, and the old woman blushed with the exaggerated compliment.

"Well . . . if you insist, Mrs. Morgan." Then, looking at her granddaughter, Mrs. Tredwell said in a less than kind voice, "Gertrude! Gertrude! Look at me when I speak to you, child! The good captain is going to take you on his tour, and you are to be on your best behavior, do you hear me? Stay close to Libby and do not gawk at the crew. Are you listening, girl?" Gertrude nodded her head, though her eyes were set on her plate. She did not look at her grandmother.

Mother Morgan and Mrs. Tredwell fetched shawls from their cabins, and Libby's father retired to the Gentlemen's Lounge to read over some legal documents concerning his Glasgow investment venture.

Libby's grandfather, with a girl on each arm, began his tour about the ship. He pointed out all the relevant parts of the first-class deck, making note of the fine works of art that hung in the halls and the ornate craftsmanship that went into the wood rails and paneling that lined the walls.

After they toured the entire first-class deck, Grandfather took them directly down to the boiler room, where the black gang would be shoveling coal into the steam engine. As they snaked their way down some narrow passages, they had to maneuver over tight ladders, and for the girls in their dresses, this was no easy task. They were unable to walk side by side, the halls and ladders being too narrow, so Grandfather lead the way with Gertrude in the middle and Libby bringing up the rear. On several occasions, Gertrude's shoe slipped on the ladder, and she nearly toppled onto Libby, but each time she managed to catch herself. As they emerged into an open area deep in the bowels of the ship, the excessive heat and smell of body odor mixed with fire assaulted Libby's senses.

"Grandfather, what is that awful smell?" She was polite enough to whisper her question as there were seamen about, and she did not wish to offend anyone.

"That, my dear, is the smell of hard work. You will be given just a peek, ladies, so take a good look around this corner."

As the girls peeked around the corner, they could see a dark room with almost no light that was filled with steam, smoke, and fire. Most of the men were shirtless and all were sweating profusely. Libby had also begun to perspire, and she was ready to leave immediately. The smell and the heat were becoming unbearable, but she took a good, hard look at the room and the activities going on. She could see several men shoveling coal from one cart into a wheeled barrow, and others taking the coal and putting it into the mouth of a large fiery machine. Gears and wheels were turning, and men were talking loudly. One man stood near a couple of white-faced gauges that Libby was sure must be important, for the man did not partake in the conversation, and he almost never looked away from the gauges. When the girls had seen enough, Libby's grandfather motioned for them to follow him back up the ladder.

"These men are called the 'black gang,' and why do you suppose that is?" he asked after they had gone up two ladders to a relatively quiet deck.

Gertrude blurted out, "Because they were all covered in the soot and coal."

"Exactly right, young lady! These men have some of the most difficult jobs on the ship, and you should keep them in your prayers, for never a day goes by that someone isn't injured in some capacity. It takes a special skill to maintain the temperature on the steam engines and ensure that the boilers do not overheat. It would be a catastrophe for the ship, the crew, and we passengers were the engines to become too hot."

Libby noted Gertrude's enthusiasm on the tour and knew it was because they were away from Mrs. Tredwell. She thought of how Gertrude wanted to be a writer, and she was glad that Grandfather could provide her with some fuel for her stories. What providence it was for Gertrude to see the hardworking men and smell the stench of the boiler room—she was sure her new friend was making mental notes with every step in order to remember all the details. "Marriage!" thought Libby. "How could she ever marry so young and miss out on so much of life?"

After the boiler room, Libby and Gertrude followed Grandfather through the storerooms where the food and water supplies were kept, and the mailroom where the international mail was stored. They found themselves on the deck where the steerage passengers were lodged, and Libby was shocked at their quarters. She recognized the stench of close confines with too many people, and as she walked past an open door, she caught the eye of a little girl sitting on her mother's lap in the corner of a compartment filled to nearly overflowing with people who had similar features to the little girl. Holding a small rag doll and sucking her thumb, the child's gaunt face and sad eyes reminded Libby of the children she would see from time to time on the streets of Boston. It tugged at her heart, and she wanted to give the little girl her bag of candy; she had even made up her mind to do just that when she was called by her grandfather. "Come away, Libby, we are off to the galley." The image of the gaunt little girl with the dirty face stuck with her.

The galley deck was a bustle of activity. Stewards and crewmen were running to and fro gathering food or putting away dishes or cleaning up after the cooks. Grandfather motioned for the girls to stay back out of the way of the busy men, and just as he was about to say something, the second mate from the bridge, who was conversing with the head cook, saw him and motioned for him to come over. Grandfather Abbott asked the girls to step into the passageway and out of the galley for a moment.

Libby and Gertrude stepped into the quiet passageway and closed the door of the galley. They stood for a moment, and before either one could say a word, a boy ducked out of one of the cupboards that lined the walls of the passageway. He turned around to see the two girls looking at him and froze in his tracks like a deer. Libby thought for sure the boy was up to something judging from the guilty look on his face, but Gertrude smiled and said, "Hi . . . who are you?"

Libby could tell he was frightened, and she didn't want to scare him further, so she said in her kindest voice, "Are you lost?"

The boy stood stock-still and didn't respond. Having spent the summer with her cantankerous cousins, Libby could see he was formulating a plan of escape and half expected him to bolt away. When he did not, she asked again, "Are you lost?"

He relaxed his posture and said, "Yes . . . um . . . I am lost."

Libby was sure now that something was amiss. "What deck is this?" the boy asked, scratching his head and trying to look confused.

"This is the galley deck," Gertrude replied in her innocence. "Are you looking for the steerage deck?"

"Yes, that's it . . . the steerage deck. I thought this was the steerage deck." Libby knew the boy was lying because he would not make eye contact.

"Steerage is two decks below," she said, trying to remain as kind as possible in her tone. Though she suspected something about this boy, she didn't want to be rude if she was wrong.

"Thanks . . . um . . . I'll just be going then . . . bye," he said then bobbed his head, turned, and rushed out of the passageway and around a corner.

"That was odd," Gertrude said with a perplexed look.

"Rather," Libby agreed, and then she had a thought. She walked quickly down the corridor to the door from which the boy had emerged. She tested the handle and found that it turned, so she opened the door a crack and peeked inside. It was just a storage closet, with various boxes and sacks of food stacked along the walls—nothing out of the ordinary. Then something caught Libby's eye in the far back corner behind a large box that seemed out of place. There was a corner of a wool blanket sticking out from behind the box, so Libby swung open the door to let in some light and stepped into the cupboard to investigate.

Behind the box, Libby found a small nest of sorts made of a wool blanket and a small sack. She picked up the sack and found it contained some clothes with something heavy tucked into a pocket. It was a painted miniature portrait of a stately looking young man. She returned the items to its place and placed the sack back on the blanket. If her suspicions were correct, the boy was hiding. "I think he must be a stowaway," Libby said over her shoulder to Gertrude, who was standing in the doorway. She quickly retreated out of the cupboard and closed the door just as her grandfather and the second mate came out of the galley. They had not seen her exit the cupboard. "Shall we continue our tour?" Grandfather asked as he passed the girls in the hall.

Gertrude gave Libby a sheepish grin and held her finger up to her lips and motioned, "Sshhh," just as she had done in the Ladies' Lounge earlier that morning. Libby clutched her new friend's hands and offered a big grin and a wink, indicating she understood the secret they now shared.

The rest of the tour paled in comparison to the excitement of the storage cupboard and the stowaway boy they had seen on the galley deck. Libby longed to talk with Gertrude about their new secret, but they were kept busy with Grandfather, discussing the details of the ship. When the tour was over and Grandfather and Libby were walking Gertrude back to her cabin, Libby asked if Gertrude and Mrs. Tredwell could join them for supper. Grandfather said yes, and when Mrs. Tredwell opened the cabin door, he extended the invitation for her to join them at supper.

"Oh, why thank you, Captain Abbott. But I will have to ask that we join you another night. I fear the walk on deck gave me a chill; we will be dining in tonight." Libby thought Mrs. Tredwell did look a bit weathered from her walk on deck.

"Perhaps you wouldn't mind if Miss Gertrude joined us so that you can rest quietly?" Libby asked with sincerity. It was a bit rude to address the woman directly—Libby being a child—but she really wanted to have more time alone with Gertrude, so she took the chance of getting a scolding.

"It would be rude of me to turn down such an offer from our new friends, Grandmother," Gertrude said sweetly. "And with me out from underfoot, you can relax and enjoy a quiet meal. I am feeling quite full of energy after our excursion. I don't see how I can settle down so early." Libby began to see that Gertrude could be quite the manipulator.

Gertrude began to tap her foot and fidget more than normal, and Libby was sure this maneuver was simply to encourage her grandmother's decision in her favor. She watched Mrs. Tredwell's expression change from her usual look of annoyance to one that appeared too tired to argue with the girl. "I think that would be fine. Yes, you may join your friends for dinner. But you must come in now and rest a bit before you go. And get cleaned up. For heaven's sake, Captain, where did you take these girls that they smell so?" She wrinkled up her nose as Gertrude walked past her and into the room.

As Mrs. Tredwell turned around to close the door, Gertrude looked over her shoulder and gave Libby a quick wink.

Chapter 27

*D*inner that evening was exciting for Libby and Gertrude. Grandfather arranged for them to sit at the end of the long table so they could be close to one another and chat. They were mostly excluded from the adults' conversation except to say please and thank you when offered something to eat or drink.

The girls quietly speculated about the boy. "Do you think he is running away to become a pirate?" Gertrude asked. "Or maybe he was kidnapped and is trying to get home."

"We don't even know for sure he is a stowaway," reminded the more practical Libby. "Perhaps he is just a boy from steerage that didn't like the multitudes of people in his cabin and went to find a quieter place to sleep." Libby thought Gertrude had a wild imagination—perfect for someone who wanted to be a writer.

"Maybe if we can slip away from the adults, we can go see him . . . take him some food or something. He looked rather thin, don't you think? Do you want to come with me?" Libby listened as Gertrude formulated a plan to sneak out from her room in the middle of the night and go to the galley deck. She, on the other hand, was wondering if they should tell her grandfather about the boy. Certainly, he had dealt with this sort of thing before, and he would know what to do.

"Mother Morgan would never allow me to wander the ship with just you," whispered Libby. "She promised my mother I would never be left alone. And trust me, if there is one thing you can be certain of, it's the promises my grandmother makes. So I don't see how it would be possible to escape her watchful eye."

"Unless you weren't with *your* grandmother," Gertrude said with a conniving smile, "but with *mine*."

"What are you suggesting?" asked Libby, more than a little curious.

"Well, I don't exactly know the whens and hows just yet, but I will give the matter some serious thought tonight, and we can talk more about it tomorrow. You think about it, too, and try to figure out what we can do to get you alone with me and my grandmother. Because I can assure you, my grandmother isn't the most intelligent person when it comes to children. Especially girls!" Gertrude made a funny face at Libby, and the two girls fell into laughter.

After dinner, when they had walked Gertrude back to her room and said good night, Libby and her family walked back down the hall to their own cabins. Libby was thinking about the boy and wondered what would happen to him if he really was a stowaway and were to get caught. She decided her question would be safe enough if she didn't reveal all the information, so she asked, "Grandfather, I was thinking after our tour today . . . there are so many places to hide on board . . . have you ever had a stowaway on one of your ships?"

Grandfather answered, "Yes, Libby, I had a stowaway once. It was quite an unpleasant trip for me. He was a young lad, well seventeen and nearly a man, but quite innocent of the world. He was trying to make his way to the Americas because he was running away from the London police. They said he had stolen something of value from his employer; I don't really know the details of the situation, just that he was caught with the missing object. The police were going to transport the lad to Australia as a criminal . . . a terrible situation, to be sure . . . but somehow the boy was able to escape from the officers on his way to the ship. He hid himself in a box that was being put onto my cargo ship, and we were long out to sea before we found him. When we reached

New York, I had to turn the boy over to the authorities, and I regretted every minute of it. I wish now that I could have done more for the lad, for I believe he was innocent of the crime."

"That's awful, Grandfather. Why did you have to give him over to the police?"

"Too many of the ship's crew knew of his existence and the charges against him. If I had shown leniency, I would have lost the respect of the crew. That, dear Libby, is the worst thing that can happen to a captain. Most of my crewmen were roughnecks who had been in trouble at one time or another, but all of them understood authority and respected it. I did what I thought was best for everyone in that situation, Libby, not just what was best for the lad."

Libby thought a lot about what her grandfather had said that night. As she lay in her bunk, feeling the rise and fall of the ocean, she asked the Lord above to keep the boy hidden and safe from being caught. She figured he wasn't much older than herself or Gertrude; he was only slightly taller than them but still thin and scraggly looking. She did not want him given over to the authorities, or worse. Who knew what a captain might do with a stowaway; her mind envisioned him being pitched overboard and sinking into the black recesses of the ocean. She clutched her blankets close around her as thoughts of the cold, dark sea swallowing the blond-haired lad filled her mind. She shook her head a bit and rolled over in her bunk, thinking that her imagination was becoming as wild as Gertrude's. She drifted off to sleep, trying to figure out whether or not she and her new friend *should* sneak down to the cupboard to talk with the boy and hear his story.

Chapter 28

*B*y early the next morning, the seas had become considerably rougher than any time since their departure, and Libby's grandmother was feeling ill. Grandfather was sure it was just a mild case of seasickness but wanted to err on the side of caution, so he suggested that they take the day's meals in their cabin. Libby was a little disappointed because she would not get to see Gertrude, but she was also relieved that she would not have to make a decision about sneaking out to see the boy.

Mother Morgan sat in the overstuffed chair next to the small table and sipped a cup of peppermint tea. Libby sat on her grandmother's bed and stitched on her quilt top. She had put together enough of the flower units and white hexagons to create a large shape about twenty-five inches long, and after she had put in a lovely yellow-and-blue block, she held the top up to admire it. With each block she sewed into the top, she took special care not to put two flower units of similar color near one another, especially when it came to any of the Prussian blue or steam-green prints. The vibrant colors were so strong they needed to be scattered about the quilt top so that the eye could travel and not be focused on a single point. Libby was surprised at how quickly the quilt top was coming together.

Feeling the need to take a break from her stitching, Libby took off her thimble and carefully put it back in her huswif. She did not want to lose the special silver tool, particularly since it had belonged to Mother

Morgan as a child. She was thinking how lovely it would be to have something from her grandmother to pass along to her own granddaughter some day, and that led her mind down the path of having children. She was not averse to marriage—not like Gertrude—but she did not wish to marry too young. She wanted to have a little time to grow up and enjoy being an adult before the burden of a husband and children came along.

"Poor Gertrude!" she thought to herself. "How awful to be carted off to London by her grandmother in order to hunt down a rich husband." She thought about being married at such a young age and wondered if it was scary to a young girl. Then she remembered that Mother Morgan hadn't been much older than Gertrude was now when she married her Grandfather Edward.

"Grandmother, may I ask you a question?" Libby asked tentatively.

She could tell that Mother Morgan was lost in her thoughts, holding tiny pieces of fabric and stroking them with her fingers as she stared off at nothing in particular. Her question seemed to snap her grandmother out of the trance; she placed the pieces of fabric back into a small box on the table then turned to Libby and gave her a small smile. "What is it, dear?"

"Gertrude told me that she was going to London so her grandmother could find her a 'profitable match.' But she said she didn't want to get married," Libby said, lowering her voice.

"And?" Mother Morgan questioned.

"Don't you think she is too young to get married?" Libby asked.

"Yes, I do. Why do you ask?"

"Well, it's just that I think she is far too young. I mean, when you get married you have to have children, and she is still just a child herself. She told me something that scared me a little." Libby paused for a long moment then looked at her grandmother, who sat quite still and did not speak. As their eyes met, Libby sensed her grandmother offering her encouragement to continue, her face calm and her eyes inviting. Libby continued in a concerned and serious voice, "She said she wasn't going to get married, no matter what her grandmother did. She said she was going to be a writer, and if she had to run away to do it, then she would. I think she's serious."

"Well, child, she may very well be serious. I think she is far too young to be married. Especially to someone she doesn't know. I'm not sure what we can do about it, but I will certainly speak with her grandmother. Mrs. Tredwell does have a rather high opinion of her own agenda, but she can be quite companionable when you break through her tough exterior. We had a lovely stroll on the deck and nice conversations about the old London."

"I don't think you should do that, Grandmother," said Libby in a bit of a panic.

"But I thought you were worried, child?" returned her grandmother.

"I am . . . but if you say something to Mrs. Tredwell, then Gertrude will know I told her secret. I didn't mean to betray her; I was just worried that she might do something silly. Please don't tell her grandmother," Libby begged.

"All right, all right now, no need to get upset. I won't say anything about Gertrude's secret. I will be very tactful in my questioning, I assure you. Mrs. Tredwell will not know about Gertrude's plans."

Libby was reassured by her grandmother's comments and breathed a sigh of relief. She felt a strong friendship bond with her grandmother and trusted that her comments would not be betrayed. She spied the little box sitting on the table in front of her grandmother and wondered why she had not noticed it before. It was such a pretty little box, with two hearts painted on the top. "What's in the box?" she asked curiously.

"What box?" Mother Morgan asked. "Oh, of course, that box. How silly of me. Seems you had completely taken my mind off of that for a moment." Mother Morgan took the small box from the table and opened it, took out the contents, and laid two pieces of fabric on the table in front of Libby.

"What are those?" Libby asked, wide-eyed with wonder.

"Well . . ." Mother Morgan began in a tentative voice, "these are the two pieces of fabric from my first babes. This one is the piece given to me by the washer woman who took them away to the Foundling Hospital," she pointed to a dirty piece of pink fabric, "and this one is the piece they gave me at the hospital when I went to collect my daughters." She pointed at the other piece of cotton that looked like a cleaner version of the first.

Libby looked at her grandmother and then at the pieces of fabric. She remembered the story told about the babies being taken and how Mother Morgan needed the piece of fabric to claim them. She was astonished that her grandmother had kept these bits of fabric, and as she thought more, she was saddened to think this was all that was left of her twins. Libby felt a strong tugging in her chest and knew the feeling to be compassion for another she loved dearly. She started to reach for the pieces of fabric, then, thinking otherwise, she looked up at her grandmother. "It's fine, child, you may," Mother Morgan said, motioning for her to take the fabrics. So Libby reached across the table and took the two pieces gently into her hands.

"Seems so strange, even now after all these years, to think that I had two little girls who never grew up. And poor Edward . . ." Mother Morgan looked so forlorn as Libby looked up from the fabric to see her expression, "he grieved for his daughters for many years. It wasn't until your father was born that he really stopped being sad. It gave him new hope when I told him I was with child. I remember how his face lit up so!" Her spirits seemed to lighten a bit.

Libby listened as her grandmother talked on about having her next two children and how with each one she felt her spirit renewed; but there was always the pretty little box with the swatches of fabric that could quickly bring her mind back to the little girls and their deaths. While she talked on about her feelings, Libby examined the two pieces of printed cotton.

The design on the fabric was of tiny flower buds with lots of vines and leaves that made up the background. The fabric had a lighter pink background with a darker pink printed design of leaves and flowers and buds. As she examined the cleaner piece of cotton, she could clearly see that the leaf next to the bud had three parts to it: a larger center leaf and two smaller side leaves. She then picked up the dirty piece of cotton and looked closely at the design. At first, she thought she was seeing things, so she blinked and rubbed her eyes. She set the dirty piece of fabric on top of the clean one and compared the pieces again, side by side. "No, they *are* different," she thought to herself. Her mind began to race. The fabrics were different. She was sure of it. But what could it mean? Did it mean something? Perhaps her grandmother knew the fabrics were not the same. She looked at the pieces again for a moment and then asked in a very quiet and solemn voice, "Grandmother?"

"Yes, dear?"

"Can you tell me again about the babies . . . about what they looked like? You don't have to . . . if it hurts your heart too much. I was just wondering how you were sure they were your girls."

"Well . . ." Mother Morgan paused then said, "I'm not sure what you mean, Libby." She began to recount that day, "When I got to the hospital I could barely talk. I tried to explain about my girls, that they were twins about a month old, and I gave the nurse that piece of fabric that Dwyn had given me." She motioned to the dirty piece of pink cotton. "The nurse looked at me and then at Edward. Then she motioned for us to follow her, and together we walked through the halls of the hospital until we reached a back room. I remember there were shelves along both walls filled with ledger books and a large desk in the center of the room. She only asked me one question, 'How long has it been?' and through my tears I muttered that it had been almost a week." Mother Morgan got a little choked up so she paused and took a sip of her tea.

"The nurse opened the ledger book that was on the big desk and flipped back a few pages, then she compared the swatch of fabric in her hand to the one in the book. That was how it worked, you know, at the Foundling Hospital. You needed to have a piece of the fabric or part of the little token that had been left with the child in order to claim them." Libby thought that was a silly method to claim back a child. She furrowed her brow and continued to look at the two pieces of cotton while her grandmother talked. "The nurse cut the majority of the piece of fabric out from the book and left only a small piece still pinned to the page. She handed me the fabric and told Edward and I to follow her. Inside a small room were some chairs, and the nurse motioned for us to sit down, so we sat, holding hands, terrified of what was to come."

Mother Morgan paused and took another sip of her tea; she took a deep breath and continued, "The nurse came into the room carrying one of my babes. There was another woman behind her, and as the nurse handed me the babe, the other woman spoke with Edward quietly. I held the tiny girl in my arms and looked at her face through my tears. She was so tiny, so very tiny, and her breathing was much labored. Then I heard Edward say, 'No!' It startled me because it was said in such anguish." Mother Morgan's voice was almost trance-like in her storytelling, and Libby found that she couldn't take her eyes off the woman.

"Edward came to me, looked at his daughter and then at me, and said, 'She is gone, she has died and they buried her this morning.'" Libby had to look away; she could no longer look at her grandmother's face for fear she would break into tears. There was such sorrow in telling of the deaths. "The nurse quietly explained that the girls had been ill and that the child in my arms would not make it through the night;

she offered Edward and me a quiet room to be with the babe in her last hours." Here Mother Morgan paused a long quiet moment, and then she said, "She was right. We buried her the next morning."

Libby held the two pieces of cotton in her hands and didn't know what to do. If she were wrong about the fabrics and their differences it would most certainly be hurtful to say anything. But what if she were right? Oh, if she were right, what could that mean? She felt in her gut she must say something—felt that she must take a chance at being wrong and show Mother Morgan the differences in the fabric pieces. She steadied her nerve, took a deep breath, and said as kindly as she knew how, "Grandmother, I think you should look at this," as she held out the two pieces of printed cotton.

"Look at what, dear?" her grandmother asked, confused.

Mother Morgan leaned into the table as Libby laid one piece atop the other and pointed to the details in the fabrics. "See here, see how this piece has the vines and leaves and bud? But if you look at this one, there is the vine and the bud and the leaves, but only two leaves, not three like the other piece. Did you know that the fabrics were different?"

Mother Morgan still looked a little confused, and she scooted closer to the table and adjusted her glasses to look again at the swatches. She picked up the pieces and examined them closely. Then she laid them back on the table and put one piece atop the other. She looked at the swatches for a very long time then sat back and said in a voice that scared Libby, for she had never heard her grandmother sound so serious, "Libby, fetch your grandfather, please." Mother Morgan sat stock-still in her chair and looked across the room with an expression that was void of emotion. Libby felt sure she was going to get into trouble, but she jumped from her seat and ran to the door. She flung it open and dashed into the hall, stopped in front of her grandfather's door, and began banging on it. "Grandfather, Father, come quickly, it's Grandmother! Please, come quickly!"

The door sprung open, and Libby's father was standing there scratching his head and trying to focus on her. "What is it, Libby, what's the matter?"

"It's Grandmother, please get Grandfather and come quickly." She turned and ran back to her room. No sooner had she entered the room than her father and grandfather were right behind.

"MOTHER . . . MOTHER . . . what's the matter?" her son begged.

"Margaret, what is it? Are you feeling worse?"

When the two men saw Mother Morgan sitting in her chair sipping her tea they each looked at Libby with stern expressions, and Libby's father let out a sigh and said, "Goodness gracious, child! Why did you make it sound so urgent?" Both men looked irritated.

"Gerald, Thomas, come here . . . I need you to look at something Libby has noticed and tell me what you think." She motioned for the men to come closer to the table, and she pointed at the two pieces of fabric.

"What is it, Mother?" her son asked, looking between her and Libby.

As the men hovered over the table, she again gestured to the two pieces of fabric. "Look at these two pieces of cotton and tell me what you see."

Libby's father picked up the two pieces and held them up to examine them. Grandfather Abbott looked over his shoulder at the pieces and said, "Looks like two pieces of pink printed cotton to me. One is dirty, but they appear to be of the same design."

"One would think so," Mother Morgan said with a very serious voice, "but look closer, if you please."

"Look at the leaves," chimed in Libby.

"I see . . . yes, they are different, though only slightly," Libby's father replied in a curious tone. "What is the significance of these pieces of cotton, Mother?"

Grandfather was scratching his head. "Margaret, are you sure these are both the right pieces?" Libby could tell that her grandfather knew where the bits of cotton had come from. "You haven't by chance mixed them up with some other pieces you may have had?"

"No, Gerald, I have kept them these many years in this little box my mother gave me when we came home from the hospital the day we buried our daughter. The fabrics are the ones that were given to me by Dwyn and the nurse at the hospital." She looked at Grandfather Abbott with a pleading expression and said, "Do you think it possible, Gerald?"

"Think what is possible, Mother?" Libby's father asked. She knew exactly what Mother Morgan was thinking, but could tell that her father did not.

"Father, the fabrics are different . . . clearly they are different! It has to mean that the babies at the Foundling Hospital were not Mother Morgan's children! That is what you are thinking, isn't it, Grandmother?"

"Yes, Libby, that is what I was thinking. And so I ask you again, Gerald, do you think it possible? Could my babes have been confused with another set of twins?"

Libby looked eagerly at Grandfather Abbott. He scratched his head and took a deep breath and looked at Mother Morgan. "I don't know, Margaret." He shook his head. "I don't mean to sound skeptical, but two sets of twin girls both brought to the hospital in the same week? The odds are not in your favor." He looked at Libby's father then at Mother Morgan again. "I wouldn't get my hopes up if I were you." Then he quickly added, "But we should investigate. Most certainly we should investigate as soon as we reach London."

Libby went over and stood next to her grandmother. She gently placed her hand upon the her shoulder and said in a sweet voice, "Grandmother, I shall pray . . . I shall pray good and hard."

Mother Morgan reached around her granddaughter's waist, gave her an affectionate hug, and replied, "I will pray as well, Libby, and we shall see. I won't get my hopes up, but I think it curious that the two fabrics *are* different. Do you think so, Gerald?"

"It is rather odd that they would be different. Thomas, look at those pieces again. My eyes are not what they once were. Look at them and tell me, does it look as if the third leaf may have just faded from the print?"

He again examined the fabric swatches closely. He went and stood next to the lamp for better lighting, and then he said, "They are different. There is no doubt. To the untrained eye, one would not notice that the prints were not the same, but when examined closely side by side, the differences can be seen clearly."

"I think, Gerald, I would very much like to take a stroll on deck and look at the ocean." Mother Morgan rose from her chair and collected her shawl. "Libby, would you mind staying with your father for a while?"

"Of course, Grandmother. I will work on my patchwork." Libby hugged her grandmother again, kissed her cheek, and patted her hand reassuringly. Mother Morgan walked through the door, and Libby looked up at her grandfather and offered him a large toothy grin. He smiled at his granddaughter and said, "Quite the little detective, you are!" and affectionately patted her head as he turned to follow Mother Morgan out the door.

Chapter 29

*L*ibby's head was swimming with possibilities about the Foundling Hospital mix-up, and she tried to imagine where Mother Morgan's girls might be so many years later. She had made up her mind not to mention the situation to Gertrude; really, she didn't know the girl all that well and didn't want her to share the secret with her grandmother for fear something may be said to Mother Morgan. She thought it best to leave the subject alone despite the fact that she was so very excited.

Over the course of the next week on the ship, Libby and her grandmother spent most days sitting and chatting in the Ladies' Lounge with the Tredwells while Grandfather Abbott and her father busied themselves with the other gentlemen on the ship. Gertrude had come out of her shell a bit in front of the grandmothers, and the two girls often sat at a separate table talking quietly and pretending to work on Libby's patchwork. Gertrude proved herself competent with the needle, so Libby allowed her to sew in a few of the blocks.

Mother Morgan and Mrs. Tredwell conversed about the *old* London but Libby noticed that Mrs. Tredwell immediately became the authority on any subject and monopolized the conversation. She felt certain her grandmother didn't mind just listening to the chatter—likely it gave her time to think about what was to come in London.

One quiet afternoon, Libby and Gertrude were sitting together talking about nothing in particular when Libby noticed that the grandmothers were getting up from their table. She nudged Gertrude and gestured in their direction.

"Libby, dear," Mother Morgan stopped by the table, "we will be right back, we are going to fetch one of the oranges from the cabin and get Mrs. Tredwell's shawl."

Once the older women exited the lounge, Gertrude immediately swung into action. "Now is our chance! Hurry up—let's go!"

"Go where?" Libby asked with a shocked look on her face.

"To see Finn," Gertrude said as if she were talking to an imbecile.

"What? Wait, what do you mean? And who is Finn?" Gertrude had not mentioned the boy since the first encounter, and Libby had left the subject alone. She did not wish to bring any trouble upon herself by wandering the ship without an adult, and yet here she was doing just that.

Gertrude whispered in an exasperated tone, "They will take more than a few minutes, and if they come back while we are gone, it won't be long before we get back. We can just say we went to the toilet. Come on, I need to bring Finn something to eat. I haven't seen him since yesterday morning."

Libby's head was reeling with questions, but rather than ask, she found herself setting down the patchwork and trying to look inconspicuous to the other occupants of the lounge as they hurried out the door. Gertrude stopped just outside the door, looked down the hall, then quickly turned and headed to the nearest ladder down to the galley deck. Libby was scared of getting caught, but being perfectly honest with herself, she was also a bit excited. She was not the type of girl to do anything that would get her into trouble, and though she was precocious, she was not much of a risk taker. And this situation felt very wrong, but for reasons she could not explain, she continued to go along with Gertrude.

They quickly made their way down the ladders until they reached the galley deck. Gertrude peeked around a corner and down the hallway where the boy's cupboard was located, and Libby recognized the place immediately. Gertrude quickly opened the cupboard and motioned for Libby to follow. Once inside with the door closed, both girls sighed with relief and the blond-haired boy slid out from behind the box. "What's she doing here?" he asked Gertrude.

"Don't worry about her," Gertrude reassured him and then said, "here, I brought you something to eat." Libby looked confused so Gertrude added, "Finn, this is Libby. Libby, meet Finnian."

The boy took the food and gobbled it up in several bites then replied with his mouth full, "Fpleased ta meecha." He swallowed and looked eagerly at Libby and Gertrude. "Do you have anything else?"

"No, that was all I could sneak off the table. I'm sorry it took me so long to get it to you. My grandmother was watching every move I made. I think she may suspect that I'm sneaking out."

"How long have you been coming here?" Libby asked Gertrude in amazement.

"Since the first day after we saw him."

"And you have been bringing him food?"

"Yes, he's hungry. I was right you know—he is a stowaway. He is going to Glasgow to find his father."

"Hey, why are you telling her everything?" Finn said angrily.

"I told you, she's fine. She won't tell anyone, will you, Libby?"

"Goodness, no!" was all Libby could say as she shook her head.

"You don't have any more food?" he asked Gertrude again with a hungry expression.

Libby remembered the candies in her pocket and reached in to get them. "Here," she offered. "It's not much, but it might stave off the hunger until we can get you something else to eat."

Finn took the small paper bag and opened it. His eyes lit up like it was Christmas. "I can have this?" he asked Libby.

"Of course. I wish I had more to give you, but that is all I have in my pockets. I'll bring you some of our apples next time." She was concerned that Finn hadn't been eating much, but more than that, she was concerned he would be found out and thrown overboard, or worse, transported to Australia.

Gertrude tugged on Libby's arm and said, "We better go, they are probably back already and wondering where we are."

Libby smiled at Finn and said, "Don't worry; your secret is safe with me."

Finn smiled back at Libby and his blue eyes met hers. Her tummy did a flip-flop and it caused her to stumble back a step . . . but then she realized it was really Gertrude tugging at her sleeve.

The girls left the close confines of the closet as quietly and as quickly as possible. Sure that they had not been seen, they made their way back to the ladders and headed up to the first-class deck. They stopped outside the lounge doors, and Gertrude told Libby to take a big breath in and let it out. She did the same herself. "Now, act natural," said Gertrude as she opened the door and sauntered into the lounge. Libby followed behind as nonchalantly as possible, but she didn't feel as convincing as Gertrude.

"Where have you been, girl?" Mrs. Tredwell snapped at Gertrude. Libby couldn't make eye contact with her grandmother—her guilt in lying was overwhelming.

"We needed to use the toilet. Why, Grandmother? Is something amiss?" Libby was amazed at how convincing an actress Gertrude was.

"Is everything all right, Libby?" Mother Morgan asked.

"Yes, Grandmother, everything is fine." Libby didn't sound very convincing and still couldn't lift her eyes to meet her grandmother's.

"Libby needed to use the toilet, and I knew she shouldn't be going down the halls alone, so I went with her. It took longer than expected," Gertrude said in an overly loud voice then rolled her eyes when she looked at Libby.

"Gertrude Mayflower Tredwell!" Mrs. Tredwell said in a hushed voice. "That is quite enough. You know better than to speak of such things." Libby watched as Mrs. Tredwell looked around the room to see who may have overheard her granddaughter. "Go back to your table and tidy up, please. We need to retire and rest before dinner."

As the young girls headed back to their private little table, Libby felt certain Mother Morgan was on to them because she could feel the woman's eyes boring through her back as she walked away.

They all left the Ladies' Lounge and made their way down the passageway to their own rooms. As Libby and Gertrude parted company, Gertrude gave her a hug so she could quietly whisper, "Try to gather some leftover food in your pockets for Finn. He is awful hungry, and I can't get enough to keep him fed." Then she stepped back, checked to see that the adults were not looking, and gave Libby her signature silent "Sshh" with her finger held up to her mouth. Libby winked back at her friend and nodded her head to indicate she would keep the secret.

Once inside her cabin, Libby waited impatiently to be asked about the incident in the lounge, but Mother Morgan kept quiet about it. Unnerved that her grandmother was acting out of the ordinary, Libby silently slipped out of her dress and into a robe then sat on the edge of her bed and watched as her grandmother did the same.

"I think a nice nap will be good before our big evening, don't you Libby?" Her grandmother knew, Libby was sure, but she did not let on for reasons Libby could not surmise.

235

"Yes, I think so. Who did you say would be joining us with the captain this evening?" She tried to sound normal, but forcing normal only made Libby sound more nervous.

Grandfather Abbott had arranged for them to dine with the ship's captain and several other special passengers. "A famous opera singer and her husband, I believe." Mother Morgan looked at Libby and with a smile and quick wink added, "Rest now, child. You have had an exciting morning." And she patted Libby's leg as she crawled into the bed below her granddaughter.

Chapter 30

*A*fter a few hours rest, freshly washed face and hands, a clean dress, and a quick use of the necessary, Libby was ready to meet the captain of the ship. She was very excited because they would be dining in the captain's private quarters with only her family and two other passengers: the famous opera singer, Jenny Lind-Goldschmidt, and her husband, Otto, would be joining them for dinner. Mother Morgan had explained to Libby the importance of being on her best manners and not speaking unless spoken to.

"Grandmother, who is Mrs. Goldschmidt? I mean, I understand why we are dining with the ship's captain, Grandfather also being a ship captain and all, but who are these other passengers, and why are they so special?" Libby asked curiously.

"Jenny Lind-Goldschmidt is a very famous opera singer, Libby. She is best known under the name Jenny Lind, and I will tell you she is regarded as the most wonderful soprano. I never had the opportunity to hear her sing firsthand, but I do recall reading about her grand tour of America. She was in all the papers, and many people paid to see her sing. It's quite an honor to dine with these people, dear. I hope you can appreciate the significance of it one day."

Libby did not fully understand the importance of spending an evening with the famous Jenny Lind, but she was certain her grandmother did, for she wore her excitement clearly on her face, and Libby was glad for the distraction.

She had watched Mother Morgan spend the better part of the week in quiet contemplation since they had found the differences in the fabric pieces. She was worried that her discovery had brought about memories and questions that were difficult for her grandmother. And she worried that perhaps her grandmother felt guilty for not noticing the differences before now.

There was a knock at the door, and it brought Libby out of her daydream. "That will be your grandfather, Libby. Are you ready to go?"

"Almost," Libby said looking through her trunk of clothes. "I was just looking for a small bag to carry so I look proper." She was lying again, but this time the lie came out of her mouth easier than before.

"You may carry something of mine, if you like," said Mother Morgan.

"Here, I can take this, don't you think?" Libby said, holding up the rather large bag she used to carry some of her sewing things.

"Heavens no, child, that is far too big. Here," she said, handing Libby a crocheted reticule with a drawstring, "this will do, I think."

Libby took the bag and examined it on her way out the door. It was smaller than the one she had tried to bring, but it would do the trick. She just needed something to sit on her lap that she could sneak food into for Finn.

Libby and her family made their way to the captain's cabin and were invited in by a young steward who was wearing a formal uniform. His manners were impeccable and he bowed as Libby and her grandmother walked past. The singer and her husband were already chatting with the captain, and as they approached, he excused himself and came to greet his newly arrived guests. "Ah, Captain Abbott, how kind of you to join us." He extended his hand to shake with Grandfather Abbott. "And this must be your family." The captain shook hands with Libby's father, bowed ever so formally to Mother Morgan and kissed the back of her hand, then stood in front of Libby and said, "And who is this lovely young lady?"

"Captain MacMartin, may I present my granddaughter, Elizabeth Jane Morgan." With the mention of her name, Libby gave the captain her best curtsy. The captain bowed in reply. "How are you enjoying your voyage, young lady?" the captain asked.

"It is a lovely ship, to be sure, Captain MacMartin. The food is even better than expected," Libby said honestly. Her comment gave her father and Grandfather Abbott cause to cringe a bit, but Captain MacMartin threw his head back and laughed loudly.

"Excellent," he chortled, "she reminds me of you, Gerald!" the captain said then motioned toward the other couple in the room and said, "Come this way . . . I would like you to meet my other guests."

Following introductions, the party sat down to dine. Wine was poured around the table, and even Libby was offered a small glass of the red liquid. She gave her father a sheepish grin, but he simply indicated for her to try it. When she did, she wrinkled her nose and set the glass down and didn't drink any more. It was definitely not to her liking.

As the adults talked with one another, Libby tried inconspicuously to drop pieces of her meal into her lap. Once she placed her napkin next to her plate and put a piece of bread atop it, then she quietly covered the bread with her hand and moved both the bread and the napkin to her lap. It was a big piece, and she wasn't sure it would fit into the bag Mother Morgan had given her, but she stuffed it in nonetheless.

The dinner party was nearly over, the food had been eaten and the table cleared, and after dinner liqueurs had been poured, at the suggestion of her husband, Jenny Lind agreed to sing "By the Sad Sea Waves" a capella, and Libby could see that Mother Morgan was quite beside herself.

The lovely young opera singer had just finished her song and the party was offering a warm applause when there was a loud knock at the door. Libby saw Captain MacMartin give the young steward an annoyed look and indicate for him to get the door, then he finished giving his guest the attention her song deserved. Libby watched as the steward opened the door, and there was the first mate Libby had seen when touring the ship with Grandfather. He stepped into the doorway, and hanging from his outstretched arm was a young lad being held by his ear. Libby immediately recognized Finn, though his face was contorted from the pain he must have felt by being lifted nearly off the ground by his ear. Her heart began to race, and her shock emerged in the form of a gasp. Mother Morgan and her father turned to see who was at the door.

"What is this all about?" Captain MacMartin said as he walked toward the door. "I told you I was not to be disturbed this evening unless it was urgent."

"I'm sorry, Captain, but one of the cooks found a young stowaway in a galley cupboard, and I thought perhaps you should know."

The first mate began to tug on Finn's ear until he was standing on his tiptoes, and Fin began to yell, "Let me go, you're hurting me!" Then he kicked the man in the shins and was immediately let go, but by then the captain was standing in front of him and grabbing him by his shirtfront.

"What is your name, lad?" Captain MacMartin demanded. "Tell me the truth, or surely I will toss you overboard." Libby gasped at the statement, and Mother Morgan put her hand on her granddaughter's arm for reassurance.

"I'll not tell you my name. I'll not tell you anything until you take your hands from my shirtfront, sir." Finn was trying to pull away from the captain but he was unsuccessful.

"How do you know the lad is a stowaway?" the captain asked the first mate as he released the boy's shirt.

"There was a young girl with him, a first-class passenger who was smuggling him food. I returned her to her grandmother's custody but explained to the woman that you might want to interview her. The boy buttoned up his lip the moment he was caught, and the girl wouldn't say anything except that he was a friend and she was bringing him something to eat. We've checked the steerage passengers, and no one knows anything about the lad." The first mate looked at the boy and said, "The only thing we found on him was a small sack with a change of clothes and this." He handed the captain the miniature portrait of the fine-looking gentleman.

"Who is this?" the captain asked and showed the tiny portrait to the boy.

Finn did not speak.

The first mate smacked Finn on the back of the head and Libby cringed. "Answer the captain, you little rat."

"Let me say this just once, boy," the captain said harshly, "you will tell me who you are and why you are on my ship or I shall pitch you over the side. No one on the ship claims you, and you don't have any papers indicating that you purchased your passage. You will most certainly NOT be missed! So speak up!"

Libby could no longer stand the torture of knowing Finn and saying nothing, so she jumped from her place at the table and said, "Stop it! Please, stop!" She turned to her grandfather and begged, "Grandfather, make them stop. Finn hasn't done anything wrong. He hasn't stolen any food, he hasn't stolen anything." She looked at her grandfather and pleaded Finn's case, "Grandfather! Please, ask the captain for mercy!" Libby was tugging on her grandfather's sleeve and looking between him and Fin frantically.

Finn stood looking at his shoes and did not look up. "Mr. Turnbow," Captain MacMartin said to the first mate, "lock him in the brig. I shall deal with him on the morrow."

"Grandfather," Libby tugged on her grandfather's sleeve, "can't you do something? Please?"

Her father got up from his chair and walked to Libby. "That is enough, Elizabeth." He reached out and took her arm, maneuvering her by his side. He tried to comfort Libby, but she continued to beg for Finn's release.

"Elizabeth," Mother Morgan's voice was stern, and it made Libby stop short. "Explain how you know this boy."

"Gertrude and I saw him on the day Grandfather gave us a tour of the ship. Gertrude has been bringing him food, and just today I saw him again . . ." Libby looked at her grandmother apologetically because she knew her lie was now out in the open. "Look, see here," she held open her bag of food, "I was bringing him food, too. He is not stealing. Please don't throw him off the ship . . . please . . . don't lock him up." Libby was so distraught she began to cry. "Grandfather, please help him," she said through her sobs, remembering the story her grandfather had told about the young stowaway on his own ship.

Libby's eyes pleaded with her grandfather and he looked questioningly at her. "Is he the reason you asked me about stowaways and what happens to them when they are found?"

Libby nodded.

"Captain," Grandfather Abbott sighed and addressed Captain McMartin, "may I speak with you privately . . . as one captain to another?"

"Of course, sir," said Captain MacMartin. "Wait in the passageway!" he said to the first mate. "And don't let that little rat get away." He begged pardon from his guests and motioned for Grandfather Abbott to follow him into a small private room off the main stateroom.

Libby sat in her chair wringing her hands as the Goldschmidts conversed quietly with each other. Her father looked at her then at his mother, and with an expression of shock, he asked, "Did you know she was feeding this boy?"

"No, Thomas, I did not know about the boy. Something did happen today with Libby and Gertrude that required my attention, and I was going to ask about it, but I was waiting for Libby to come to me with the truth. And I believe she would have . . . eventually."

"I'm sorry I lied to you, Grandmother. I'm so very sorry." Libby began to weep. She was feeling guilty about her lies, but her tears were for Fin. She was praying that her grandfather could do something to stop Finn from being locked up, or worse!

The door to the private room opened, and Grandfather Abbott stood in the doorway. "Thomas, can you join us for a moment, please?"

"Excuse me." Libby's father bowed to the Goldschmidts and stepped into the private room.

A few moments passed in silence as they waited for the men to emerge. When they finally did, all were in good spirits. Libby was confused and relieved, though she did not know exactly why.

"Elizabeth," her father said, "please say good night to the captain and his guests, it's time you went to bed. I think this evening has been overly exciting for you."

"But what about Finn?" Libby asked with desperation in her voice.

"I'll explain later, Elizabeth." Her father gave her a reassuring look. "Mother, would you mind taking Elizabeth back to her room and putting her to bed? I do think she has had enough excitement for one day."

"Not at all, Thomas. Elizabeth and I have a lot to talk about, don't we dear?" Mother Morgan looked at Libby with her blue eyes and Libby felt the steel of them pierce her. She was a bit frightened about the conversation to come because she knew that discipline was not something Mother Morgan played at, and Libby felt sure her lies warranted severe discipline.

"Captain MacMartin, I would like to sincerely thank you for your hospitality. Mr. and Mrs. Goldschmidt, the pleasure of your company was a delight this evening, and I shall always remember your lovely song. Thank you ever so much." Mother Morgan curtsied to the couple and Libby did the same, though she kept her eyes downcast in shame at her outburst before strangers.

It was a quiet walk back, and Libby was trying to formulate excuses in her head. By the time they reached the cabin, she had decided that no excuse was worthy enough to be used. She had made a rather large mistake by lying, and perhaps if she had not, Finn would not have been caught. Perhaps if they had told her grandfather instead of keeping it a secret, he could have helped the boy somehow. But that was all moot now. There was nothing left to do but take her punishment—she deserved it, and that was that.

"Get into your bedclothes, please. I shall make us some tea, and we shall have a few words together before bed." Libby thought Mother Morgan's voice was overly stern.

"Yes, ma'am," she replied ashamedly.

As she was finishing buttoning up her nightdress, there was a soft rap on the door. Mother Morgan opened it, and there stood Father with Finn by his side.

"Thomas, what is this all about?" she asked as she looked the boy over.

"Mother, may we come in please?"

Mother Morgan pulled open the door and said, "Yes, dear. Do come in."

Libby's father walked in first, and Finn hung back in the hall, but Libby's father looked back at the boy and said, "Please come in, Finnian. We must explain our new circumstances to the ladies."

Finn entered the room and stood near the door, keeping his eyes downcast. Libby's father looked at his daughter and then at the boy. "I assume you two already know one another, so introductions are not necessary. Mother, may I introduce to you Master Finnian MacAlister, lately of New York. I learned that he has met with a recent tragedy, the death of his dearly loved mother, and he is now en route to Glasgow to find his father, Mr. Arthur MacAlister."

Libby hung back, watching the exchange between Finn and Mother Morgan. She saw how her grandmother reached out her hand to shake the boy's hand and how they looked one another in the eyes. "I'm very pleased to make your acquaintance, Mrs. Morgan." He was obviously brought up with manners, Libby thought.

"Mother, Elizabeth, your grandfather has offered to take Finnian on as his ward for the duration of our passage. If, when we reach Liverpool, Finn would like to continue with me on to Glasgow, he is much welcome. He will be staying in our cabin next door, and as Grandfather's ward he will be allowed access to the dining hall with us. I hope that you ladies will make him feel welcome." Libby's father kissed her on the cheek and said, "You and I will have a conversation on the morrow. For now, get some rest."

"Yes, Father." Libby looked guiltily down at her bare feet. "Good night."

"Good night, ladies," her father said as he headed out the door.

As Finn followed, he glanced back at Libby and smiled. She returned his smile, and again she felt the flip-flop in her tummy. Blushing, she turned to see her grandmother watching the exchange, and when their eyes met, somehow Libby knew her grandmother sensed the connection between she and Finn—a connection she was only beginning to be aware of herself.

Chapter 31

The remainder of the journey to Liverpool was over before Libby knew it, and she was saying a tearful farewell to her new friend, Gertrude. She had never expected to find such companionship on her Atlantic crossing, and now that her time with Gertrude was coming to an end, she found her heart breaking. Gertrude promised to write often, and Libby assured her she would do the same. It was only in remembering that her own parents had formed a lifelong love through correspondence that Libby was able to say good-bye confidently, knowing that she would write to her friend and that they would see one another again. Libby promised to send along all the details regarding Finnian because she knew Gertrude had likely made him the main character in one of her many stories.

Libby, her family, and their new charge left the ship and made it just in time to catch the last train leaving for London. As she stood on the platform waiting to board, Libby felt quite wobbly in her legs, as if the earth was still moving like the ship she had just left. "Grandfather," Libby said as she steadied herself by grabbing her father's arm, "why do I feel like I'm still floating on the ocean? My legs feel wobbly."

"Yes, dear, you will feel that way for a day or two. We sailors call it 'getting your land legs back.'" Grandfather Abbott chuckled.

Throughout the train ride, Libby would look up to find Finn staring at her. When their eyes met, he quickly looked away. She took each opportunity to observe his features, thin though they were, and thought him a handsome boy. His blond hair was thick and straight, ending just below his ears in a crooked line. Clearly he had cut his own hair. Father had provided Finn with some new clothes— a clean white shirt, vest and jacket—and though they mostly hung on his thin build, they certainly changed his look from that of "stow-away boy" to "clean young man." Libby liked his eyes most of all, blue with flecks of green that seemed to sparkle when they looked at her. His face was still boyish, but his facial structure was beginning to fill out like a man. She wondered at his age. There was never much opportunity to talk with Finn during the remains of the trip; she was never left alone with the boy, and her grandmother was at her side constantly.

After an uneventful trip by train to London and a coach ride to a large house on a quiet street in Chelsea, Libby found herself being passed around the room for hugs and kisses by her Grandmother Abbott, her Aunt Angelina, and all her cousins. She and Mother Morgan were shown to a large and lovely suite of rooms they would share; each room had an oversized canopy bed, a desk and chair by the window, and a lounging settee in the corner of the room near the wardrobe. The two rooms were joined by a walk-through vanity area with a looking glass and dressing table, plus a private indoor privy for the two ladies to share. The room was more opulent than Libby had imagined or expected.

It was late in the evening when they had arrived, so Libby went straightaway to bed. She did not know what happened to Finn; he had been swept away shortly after their arrival, and though she was worried about his whereabouts, she was far too tired to investigate.

When she woke the next morning, it was very late. Her room was empty, and she wondered where her grandmother had gotten to, so she hurried to wash, dress, and attend to her hair; then she made her way out the door and down the large staircase, all the while looking about for any form of life. Grandfather's house was much larger than Libby had expected—it was even larger than the Masterson house in Hartford. On her way down the stairs, a young girl in a tidy maid's uniform with a clean, starched apron and stiff white hat greeted Libby. The girl wasn't much older than Libby, and her face was screwed up in an expression of annoyance. "Morning, Miss," she said and gave a slight bob. "I see you've dressed yourself!" Her eyes inspected Libby from head to toe, then she stepped behind Libby and began to re-pin the back of Libby's hair.

"Good morning," Libby returned, trying to ignore the servant's annoyed look and fumbling hands. "I'm looking for my grandparents; can you please tell me where I may find them?"

The servant reappeared in front of Libby and bobbed again but didn't offer any words; she simply turned and led Libby down the stairs and to the dining room where the family was partaking in a late morning meal. "Here she is," said Grandmother Abbott, seeing Libby coming through the door. "Good morning, Elizabeth. Did you sleep well, dear?" Here again she was inspected from head to toe, but this time it was by the lady of the house.

"Yes, thank you, ma'am," Libby replied in a formal manner and gave a slight curtsy. She found her place at the table—the only unoccupied chair was next to Mother Morgan, for which she was grateful, and before she had a chance to place her napkin in her lap, she was being served her breakfast. Hungrier than she thought, Libby began to gobble up her meal, but with a look from Mother Morgan, she slowed her pace and lowered her fork between bites. She did not gulp her food, she remembered to use her napkin occasionally, and she did not clink her silverware on the dishes or her teeth—all the things she had been taught by her mother to show the Abbotts she had not been raised as a savage in the New World.

Libby looked around the table, but did not see Finn.

"We shall be meeting with the solicitors today, Mother," Libby's father said.

"Yes, dear. I am aware," Mother Morgan replied quietly. Libby thought her grandmother's mood overly dark this morning and noticed she was a bit withdrawn as she sipped her tea.

"I have retained us good legal counsel, and we shall be meeting with the Montclief solicitors at eleven," Grandfather Abbott added to the conversation. "I expect the meeting won't take long." He looked at Mother Morgan plainly. "Margaret, would you like to go to the hospital after our meeting, or shall we save it for another day?"

Libby watched the interplay between friends. Mother Morgan shot her grandfather a sharp look but replied in her sweetest voice, "I think that we should attend to the hospital matters as soon as we are able, Gerald. They are more important to me than the solicitors, as I am sure you can imagine." Thinking her smile a bit overly sweet and noticing her eyes were shooting daggers, Libby contemplated how her grandfather had quite the ability to prod Mother Morgan along in a direction *he* chose for her to go. By the expression Libby noted on her grandmother's face, she presumed it to be very irritating to the woman.

"I thought as much," Grandfather Abbott replied with a smug expression, "so I have arranged for us to take a meal after the meeting with the solicitors, and then we can be on to the hospital straightaway. It is only a few short blocks from Gray's Inn Square."

Libby was still distracted by the lack of Finn's presence at the table, and she could no longer stand not knowing his whereabouts. It was odd how this boy was always in the forefront of her mind. When the others seemed engaged in conversation, she leaned over and whispered to her grandmother, "Mother Morgan, where is Finnian this morning?"

"Why, Libby, dear, I do not know." She was not quiet in her response. A wicked grin appeared on her face as she looked at Grandfather Abbott. "Gerald, what have you done with your new charge?" As she spoke the words, she looked at his wife to see her reaction. By the puzzled expression that appeared on Grandmother Abbott's face, it was clear to Libby that she had not been told about Finnian.

Grandfather Abbott replied, "I have given him his bed and breakfast in the kitchen and put him promptly to work this morning. He needs to repay his passage." Libby could see his annoyance with the question.

"Charge? What charge, Gerald?" Grandmother Abbott looked confused.

"A young lad, Caroline, it's nothing." Grandfather Abbott dismissed the question with a wave of his hand.

Libby thought that perhaps Grandfather Abbott was trying to keep Finn a secret from his wife, but she needed to know his whereabouts, so she innocently asked, "Grandfather, will Finnian be coming with us today?"

"Yes, Gerald, will he?" Mother Morgan grinned again. "I would very much like Elizabeth to join me at the hospital today; will you be bringing your new lad along as well?" She offered an innocent smile, but her eyes twinkled with mischief.

"I had not planned on taking either of the children, Margaret, but if you would like Elizabeth to join us, then she may. Finnian has a great deal of work to do."

"Gerald, who is this Finnian?" Grandmother Abbott was getting irritated—Libby could hear it in her voice.

Grandfather Abbott shifted uncomfortably in his chair and cleared his throat several times, but before he could answer his wife, Mother Morgan indicated to Libby it was time to leave. "If you will excuse us, we must attend to some matters before we leave. Come, Elizabeth, let us get ready."

Libby excused herself politely and rose from her place at the table. Just as she was stepping away, she saw Mother Morgan look at her grandfather and wink. The exchange between her grandparents very much reminded her of how Albert and James would try to get one another in trouble. She realized her cousins certainly came by their mischievousness naturally!

Chapter 32

*M*other Morgan and Libby were ready in a flash and waiting in the front parlor for Libby's father and Grandfather Abbott. Libby was excited to see the streets of London; it had been dark when they had arrived the night before, and though she had been positioned next to the window in the cab from the station, they had kept the curtain pulled during the ride. She had only glimpsed the street before she was hurried into the house to greet her Grandmother Abbott, Aunt Angelina, and her many cousins.

Mother Morgan paced back and forth in the room between the front window and the chaise, all the while wringing her hands and clutching her small bag. Libby felt her anxiety and knew she was nervous about going today—but not to the solicitors', she was sure it was the thought of the Foundling Hospital that was making her nerves so raw. She had watched her grandmother put the small box, which held the fabrics into her reticule, and it frightened Libby to see how badly her grandmother's hands shook as she did it. She prayed that Mother Morgan would find the answer she was looking for today, answers that would indeed break her heart with either possible outcome, but at least she would know for sure. The likelihood of finding her twin daughters alive was so miniscule it was almost not worth hoping for, but still, Libby prayed.

The door to the parlor opened and Libby's father stepped in. "Are you ladies ready?"

"Yes, Father, we are," Libby replied with a smile. Mother Morgan only nodded.

As she was getting into the coach that was waiting in front of the house, Libby spied Finnian heading around the corner at the end of the block. "Father, look, there goes Finn. Where is he going?" She pointed in the direction the boy had gone, and her concern showed in her eyes and in her voice. She wondered if he was running away from the house.

"Fear not, Elizabeth, he's not running away; he has gone on some errands for me," her grandfather said reassuringly. "He will be back before we return. Speaking of Finn, Margaret, I wondered how you would feel if he were to sup with the family? The boy has potential, and I would like to see his manners refined a bit. I have spoken with Caroline and she has indicated that it would be insulting to our guests were we to allow an orphan boy at our table, but I assured her you and Thomas would not mind. Was I being presumptuous?"

"Not at all, Gerald. I don't mind a bit. I think Libby would welcome the lad, too. She seems to worry after him, and it may ease her mind to have him dine with us. I think she feels responsible for him to some degree," she looked at Libby, "am I right, dear?"

"I do feel a bit responsible for him," Libby replied shyly. "It was Gertrude and I that caused his capture. I'm sure if we hadn't been feeding him, he could have gone unnoticed for the duration of the trip."

"That is not likely, Elizabeth. It is not often a stowaway lad goes unnoticed on a ship, even a large ship such as the one we were on. They are eventually found out and dealt with . . . usually in much harsher ways than Finn experienced. He was fortunate to have you as an advocate. I can assure you, most captains would have simply tossed the boy overboard or pressed him into service." Grandfather Abbott sounded more callous than Libby knew him to be, and she believed it was *his* intervention that kept Finn from being pitched into the sea. For that, she would be eternally grateful to her grandfather.

Libby had deliberately positioned herself near the window in the coach and looked out as they made their way to the solicitors' office. It wasn't a long ride from her grandfather's home in the borough of Chelsea to the legal offices on Gray's Inn Road, and as she observed the busy streets of London, she felt the same affinity she had for her own Boston. The people looked the same to her, busy folks with carts or goods of all sorts hurrying to their destinations. She remembered how her mother had explained that all cities had the same feel about them; many were even planned out with the same grid-like layout to the city center. Libby found that she very much liked the city of London, even though it was a bit dirtier than Boston, and the streets were a bit narrower. She liked the ornamentations found at the top of most buildings and the green trees that lined the streets—they contrasted quite nicely with the red brick used in the buildings, brick so similar to that found in her own hometown. And because it was so similar to Boston, she almost forgot she was an ocean away from her cozy home and her loving mother. Almost!

The coach arrived in front of the solicitors' office, and Libby looked out the window at the looming building before her. When she looked at her father, she saw how he fiddled with his wedding ring and constantly glanced at his mother as if looking for support, but Libby could see that Mother Morgan was lost in her own thoughts. Grandfather Abbott patted her father's leg as he exited the coach and said, "Come on, lad, let's see what they have to say!"

Libby could not remember seeing her father so disquieted before, and she did not fully understand what it was they were doing at a legal office, but since she was not asked to wait in the coach, she presumed she would find out soon enough.

The room where the family was asked to wait was rather gloomy and dank, with stained, dark paneling, wooden floors that were highly polished, and floor-to-ceiling bookshelves that lined most of the walls.

There were three large windows that allowed some natural light in, but mostly the room was lit by oil lamps that were placed on the tiny strips of open wall between several of the bookcases. The shelves were filled with massive volumes of books in every size and color and were so crowded that some shelves were two or three rows deep. Though they were crammed into the bookcases, there was a feel of strict organization to the placement of the volumes of books and manuscripts. As Libby gazed around the room, she tried to remember to keep her mouth closed, though from time to time it fell agape with the awe of the sheer quantity of books. "Grandfather," Libby whispered, "do you suppose someone has read all these books?"

"I don't think so, I would imagine that these are reference books to past cases, and when the solicitor has a particular legal matter to argue, he will look up the important information that came from a prior case and use it to help make his point. I do not think anyone has read all these books, dear," Grandfather Abbott said as he looked around at the enormity of books on the shelves.

Just then, the door opened and three gentlemen came into the room. It was clear to Libby that the first two stuffier-looking men were the lawyers for the case; the last man was a more nervous sort, much younger than the first two, and he was carrying a large folder with many, many papers inside. Libby presumed he was a clerk of some sort. The men made their way to the large table at the center of the room, the younger man placed the folder down and began shuffling through as if looking for something, and the oldest-looking gentleman looked at Grandfather Abbott and said, "You must be Captain Abbott?"

"I am, sir, and may I introduce Mr. Thomas Morgan, my son-in-law." The men shook hands. "May I also introduce Mrs. Margaret Morgan, widow to the late Sir Edward Alexander Montclief Morgan, and this is her granddaughter, Miss Elizabeth Morgan. Our counsel should be joining us shortly, gentlemen, and I would like to hold any discussion of the case until their arrival."

"Of course, Captain Abbott, of course." The elder gentleman was clearly leading the group. "I have asked my clerk to bring them back directly upon their arrival."

It didn't take more than a few minutes before the solicitors hired by Grandfather Abbott arrived, and they all settled down to the matter at hand.

"As I am sure you are all aware, Thomas Morgan is the only living male heir to the Montclief estate. Many years ago, papers were drawn up to ensure that the estate remained in the Montclief family and could not be passed outside the direct line of Montclief men. Baron Montclief's father put this entail into effect when he knew his son intended to marry the late Baroness. As it stood then, there were no stipulations on the entail; however, prior to his death, the Baron Montclief attached several provisions of which you may or may not be familiar.

"The first was that the estate could not be passed on to Thomas or any other heir until the death of Baroness Montclief, which happened just recently after many years of her infirmity. This paper describes in detail the amount of monies she drew on the estate since the death of her husband. He left specific instructions that she not be allowed to sell any part of the estate, and in turn he provided her a small personal allowance—not including the cost of household staff and provisions—that was not to exceed thirty-five pounds per year. Since he did not know how long she would remain after his own death, there was a substantial sum set aside for her care, as you can see here." The solicitor pointed to the figures on the paper. "But now that she is no longer with us, God rest her soul, the remainder of her accounts will revert back to the general estate funds." The elder solicitor took off his glasses. "Are there any questions thus far?" He looked around the table.

Grandfather Abbott's lawyers took a moment to examine the document that contained the information about Baroness Montclief's allowance. One whispered to the other and was met with a nod, and then they both looked at the elder solicitor and shook their heads. They both looked at Libby's grandfather and again shook their heads. They had no questions; everything seemed to be in order.

One of the solicitors for the estate looked earnestly at Mother Morgan. "Mrs. Morgan," he began tentatively, "the Baron knew well that Edward's son was American-born and raised. It was painful for him to think of his beloved estate passing to a non-Englishman, notwithstanding the family connection. He also knew that the fortune would be passed on with the Baroness's death, and at that point, the estate could be sold or kept at the whim the heir. Baron Montclief's father . . ." Libby watched the man search for the right words, ". . . disliked his son's wife and wanted to be sure she would never acquire control of the estate, nor would she ever be able to pass it on to her own family. It seems his son was in concurrence, so he did not argue the matter of the entail. And it appears," the solicitor turned to Libby's father at this point, "that he had even more concerns."

He paused and turned the page of the document he was reading. "Your great uncle, the late Baron Montclief, felt strongly that whoever was to inherit the estate needed to have ample opportunity to fully experience its wonders and beauty before given access to change or otherwise sell the estate. The provision he placed upon the inheritance is this, and I quote, 'An heir to the Montclief Estate must take residence and remain upon the Estate of Braidsmuir for a period of five consecutive years, leaving the estate for no more than seven days at any time. During said five years, all monies and properties, including household staff, will be managed in trust. A personal allowance will be given in the sum of one hundred pounds per year to the resident heir. Under no circumstance, giving exception to general maintenance and estate upkeep, is the resident heir allowed to make changes to the estate during the five-year period of occupation. On the three hundred and sixty-fifth day of the fifth year, all lands, structures, titles, monies, and associated property shall become the legal property of the heir to the Montclief Estates and said heir may dispose of these properties as they see fit.'"

The young man paused and looked at Libby's father then continued reading rather quickly, "'If an heir is unwilling to follow through with this provision and refuses to reside on the estate for a period of five years, then the estate and all its holdings will be liquidated and the sum total of the estate holdings shall be given in donation to the Foundling Hospital in memory of my granddaughters, Franchesca Jane and Louisa May Morgan.' The rest goes on to explain how the hospital is to use the money to build a new infant wing for sickly children. I can read it if you like."

Libby's father slumped back in his chair and looked at his mother. Libby had been watching Mother Morgan during the reading and saw how she flinched at the mention of her daughters. Her grandmother had cast her eyes onto the table, trying to remain as expressionless as possible, and Libby looked between her father and grandfather, confused about what had been said. Her father brought her suspicions to the surface when he asked his own legal counsel, "Does this mean that I am to live at Braidsmuir for a period of five years in order to inherit the estate?"

His solicitor extended a hand to the estate lawyer and asked to read the document for himself. The papers were handed over, and the two lawyers scrutinized the documents for a long, silent moment. "It appears . . . that is exactly what it means, Mr. Morgan."

Libby was wringing her hands in her lap. She wanted to speak up but knew that in the presence of this many adults, it was best she kept quiet. Her mind was reeling with the thought of having to move, permanently, to London for the next five years of her life. What about their shop? What about her cozy home and familiar streets? What of her family she loved so in Connecticut, and what of her cat, Princess? Would Princess be allowed to cross the Atlantic and come to London? She did not think so. She did not understand all the implications of the provision, but she knew, based on her father's expression, that it was not something anyone had expected to hear. And as he shook his head, she could tell it was not what he wished to do.

"I don't know," he said, still shaking his head. "I just don't know. I can't make this decision without consulting Mary." He looked at his mother, but she kept her face turned down toward the table, expressionless.

"There is no rush, son." Grandfather Abbott had gotten up from his chair and was standing behind Libby's father, patting his shoulder. "We can take a few days. Let's finish your business in Glasgow and allow our counsel to look the papers over thoroughly. We don't have to decide today."

Libby's father covered his eyes with his hands and rubbed his temples. Libby felt overwhelmed by all she had heard and could only imagine her father's feelings.

"I'm afraid, sir, that your decision must be reached quickly." A lawyer hired by Captain Abbott spoke up. "There is more here, at the end. It seems His Lordship didn't wish to allow you much time to make your decision. He stipulates that if a decision is not made within a fortnight of the formal reading of this document, the estate is to be sold and the monies transferred to the Foundling Hospital. It seems he did not wish for you to think much on the matter but to make a decision to accept the provision or to let the estate go."

"Fourteen days?" Libby saw her father was shocked even further by this new disclosure. "That isn't even enough time to get a letter home to Mary!" He stood from his place at the table and walked over to the window. He stood with his back to the group, and Libby could see the tension building in his broad shoulders. He just continued to shake his head. Her heart was beating fast, and she knew this was a tense moment for everyone.

"Is there anything else?" Grandfather Abbott asked of the solicitors.

The man looked at the documents, turned the papers over, and finished reading them completely. "No, sir. Nothing else."

"Right, then," Grandfather Abbott said as he crossed the room to Libby's father and put his hand on the young man's back, "we shall excuse ourselves for now and reconvene at another date. Come, Thomas, you have some thinking to do, and I'm sure we could all benefit from a strong pint."

Libby's father walked over to his mother. There she remained, still looking at the table, expressionless. He gently reached down and touched her arm. "Mother, dear, come along. I fear this has been overly taxing on your emotions. Let's go home to Captain Abbott's."

Libby looked about the room at its occupants. The lawyers were re-examining the documents, Libby's father and Grandfather were collecting their hats, and Mother Morgan was still sitting quietly looking at her hands folded in her lap. "What about the Foundling Hospital?" Libby directed her question at her grandmother, and as she spoke, she noticed how her small voiced echoed in the library.

"Margaret, I really think we should go home. There is much to discuss and decisions to be made." Libby's grandfather did not acknowledge her question but simply made a statement that Libby did not agree with.

"Nonsense!" Mother Morgan replied, seemingly recovered. "We have a plan for this day, and we are going to follow through, isn't that right, Elizabeth?" She stood and motioned for Libby to accompany her. "Come along, child. We have a mystery to solve."

Libby looked at her grandfather then at her father. She could see they were not going to argue with Mother Morgan, so she stood and took her grandmother's hand and offered her a reassuring smile. Grandfather put on his hat and bowed to the solicitors. "Gentlemen," he said, then he headed toward the door. Libby looked at him with a half smile as she and Mother Morgan made their way to the door "After you, ladies!" he said in his most formal voice, and he looked Libby solidly in the eyes as they passed. She wondered for a moment if perhaps he was angry with her for mentioning the Foundling Hospital but decided if he was or not didn't matter much. She wanted the mystery solved sooner than later so that her grandmother's babies could finally be laid to rest, or as she hoped, resurrected. She decided to push the estate matters out of her mind and focus on the mystery at hand.

Chapter 33

*L*unch was delicious. Grandfather took the family to a delightful French restaurant that was just off Gray's Inn Road—it was a personal favorite of his. They were seated in a large booth in a back corner, away from the main tables so that their conversation could be kept private. Libby enjoyed her meal enormously and wanted a second helping, but she knew that when dining out, it wasn't customary to have more food than was brought to the table. She was feeling only partially satisfied by the meal when the dessert trays came. "I've asked the chef for a special dessert in honor of your first visit to England, Libby." Grandfather smiled at her.

Two waiters had arrived at their table with large platters of French pastries in every shape and size. "Indulge yourself!" her grandfather added with a wink as the trays were set before her. "But if you get sick on the ride home, it's not my fault!"

Libby looked to her father for guidance, but he had already delved into the platter of pastries, so she followed suit. "Mother Morgan, which one would you like?" Libby asked just before taking a bite of a tiny fruit tart.

"Mmm, cream puff, if you please." She smiled at Libby as she was handed a chocolate-topped, cream-filled pastry. "The first time I ever had one of these was with your father," she said to her son. "Eating this makes me miss him more, if that's possible."

"Are you certain you want to go over to the Foundling Hospital, Mother?"

"Yes, dear, I do. I most certainly do. Don't you, Libby?" She redirected the conversation to her granddaughter in an attempt to change the topic.

"Yes, I do, Mother Morgan. I want to know the truth about the fabric swatches and see what is written in the books. I do hope beyond hope that we find out the truth." Libby had her eye on another tiny fruit tart that had strawberries, and Mother Morgan picked up the pastry and placed it upon Libby's plate and said, "Well, eat up, then, and we shall be on our way."

The meal was finished, the bill paid, and the coach was brought to the front. As the family climbed in for the very short trip to the hospital, the sky that had threatened rain all day began to drizzle. Libby thought it fitting for Mother Nature to weep over her grandmother's broken heart. She was, herself, crying inside.

The rain had caused most people to take shelter in nearby businesses, so the streets along Gray's Inn Road were nearly empty as the coach made its way to the hospital. Libby kept a close watch on her grandmother's expression and could see the wounds of long ago being chiseled open with every *clop, clop, clop* of the horses' hooves that drew them closer to the front gates of the children's resting place. She wanted desperately to turn around and go home, to keep her grandmother as far from those tiny graves as possible, but her desire for the truth was stronger than her need to run. She knew her grandmother needed to know who lay buried in that ground.

The family was greeted in a large open courtyard by one of the many nurses who worked at the hospital. As Libby looked around the outer courtyard, she could see many children, mostly younger than herself, standing in groups or walking around, some even playing with toys. They all looked quite solemn and were all dressed in exactly the same black-and-white clothes. Her heart felt heavy for these youngsters, much the same way she had felt when she was in the steerage part of the steamship. She wanted to give them things—food, anything that might make them happy.

As they stood in the open courtyard, Libby watched Mother Morgan steady herself with her son's arm and look around as though trying to gain her perspective. She was looking for the chapel, Libby thought, because there was the cemetery and the two tiny graves of her daughters.

"Good afternoon," came a lovely voice, and Libby turned to see a beautifully dressed young woman walking toward them. "I am Mrs. Hamilton. Nurse Moony informed me that you have some very important questions you need answered." Mrs. Hamilton smiled politely to the family, and Libby saw Mother Morgan's expression of fear and hope all mixed together with terrible memories. She felt certain her grandmother needed to sit down. Then the woman added, "How about if we take our meeting inside? I'm sure I can find us a more comfortable place for this conversation," and Libby thought Mrs. Hamilton could perhaps read her mind.

The family followed Mrs. Hamilton down a few paneled corridors and found themselves in a smallish room with a table and a few chairs. She took Mother Morgan by the hand and led her to a seat, then turned and asked, "Now, what is this all about?"

"Well, I'm not sure where to begin," said Grandfather Abbott, looking at Mother Morgan. "Our story goes back some thirty-eight years, back when Mrs. Morgan's babes had been stolen from her and brought here to the hospital." As Grandfather Abbott retold the sad tale, Mother Morgan reached into her bag and brought out the small wooden box that contained the two pieces of fabric. She used her handkerchief to wipe away a tear that had escaped her eye and then held up the fabrics for Mrs. Hamilton to see. "If you will please look at these pieces of fabric, you will understand why we came." She handed Mrs. Hamilton the pieces and Libby wanted to blurt out her findings, but she wanted first to see if the woman would notice that the fabrics were not the same.

Mrs. Hamilton looked at the clean piece of pink cotton fabric and then at the dirty piece. "So very tragic indeed! And how may I be of assistance to you these many years later?"

"Please look closely at the fabrics, ma'am. You will see that they are not the same." Her father spoke kindly.

Mrs. Hamilton looked at the pieces again. She went over to the window and stood in the better light to examine them closer. "My heavens . . . they are not the same. Oh . . . my!" Libby saw her face and knew she understood the implications being presented. "How long ago did you say this was?"

Mother Morgan looked at Mrs. Hamilton and said sorrowfully, "Thirty-eight years."

"We were wondering if it would be possible to look through the records for the time when the babes would have been brought here. Our hope is that there was another set of twins brought in about the same time . . ." Grandfather Abbott dropped off the rest of his comment because Mrs. Hamilton was bustling into action. She turned from her place at the window and walked over to Mother Morgan, bent down, took the older woman by the hands, and said, "Dear woman, please do come with me. We have many ledgers to examine. In fact," she said to the rest of the family, "all of you come with me. It will take all of our eyes to solve this mystery."

Chapter 34

*M*rs. Hamilton led the family to a large room that contained several tables and chairs and invited the family to sit while she fetched the ledgers. Mother Morgan was immediately taken back to the night she had come for her babes. Though this was not the same room, it had the same feel, and the coldness crept into her bones and made her shudder.

Feeling the need to move, perhaps to remind herself that she was not waiting for them to bring her the sickly child as they had done so many years ago, Mother Morgan rose from her chair and walked around, looking at the lovely paintings and expensive furniture that clothed the room in which they were waiting. It was obvious that the hospital had many benefactors with deep pockets in order to purchase and maintain what she had seen on this visit. Then she thought again about Baron Monclief and his decision to leave his entire fortune to this hospital charity in memory of his grandchildren.

A feeling of condemnation came flooding in and she wondered how she could have been so hard on the man all these years. Why had she not seen this part of him? Why had she not seen beyond her own grief to notice how he, and others, may have been hurting at the loss of the twins—hurt that wasn't much different from her own pain. In fact, she had turned her grief into hatred for the Montcliefs and their money and high-society lifestyle. But she was sorry, now, that she had not tried harder to forgive them and to encourage Edward to put right his relationship with his uncle; perhaps if she had had a softer heart, Edward and his uncle may have seen one another before the Baron died. And perhaps then her Edward could have passed on without the regret he felt over never reconciling with the man he thought of as a father and friend.

She let out a long sigh. So many regrets! But all that was water under the bridge now, and it could not be changed. The Baron and his wife were dead. Edward was gone. She wanted to stop feeling guilty and just forgive the Baron for his shortcomings. Even though he was gone, it was clear from his will that he did care about the children, and there was never any doubt he cared for Edward. She could see his repentance in his final actions. And then it dawned on her—it wasn't forgiving him that she struggled with; he was easy to absolve—especially now that she knew his true heart. It was the Baroness for whom she had no compassion—not even in the woman's painful, drawn-out death did she feel sorry for her. She believed the Baroness to be wicked to the core, and it made her ill to think about feeling anything other than contempt for such a person.

And now, sitting here, in this opulently decorated room, Mother Morgan realized what was really troubling her heart. She knew she must forgive the unforgivable Baroness if she were ever to find peace in this life. It wasn't for the benefit of the Baroness, especially since the woman was dead, but Mother Morgan knew peace could not exist where hatred dwelled. She had to find a way to rid herself of the resentment she felt for the wretched woman from whom she would never hear an apology.

Her grandmother's troubled expression gave Libby cause to cross the room and stand next to her. "Mother Morgan," she patted her grandmother's hand, "this must be so hard for you. Please, come and sit, rest awhile . . ." she paused then added, "I think this is going to take longer than we expected." She noticed Mrs. Hamilton and two other women coming back into the room with armloads of ledger books.

Mrs. Hamilton made it to the table just as she was about to drop some of the books, but the other woman was not so fortunate. Luckily, Libby's father reached her just as two of the books fell from her arms. He caught them and then took the remaining books from her and placed them on the table.

"I have pulled all of the ledgers from the year in question," Mrs. Hamilton said, "and I'm certain we will find what we are looking for in these. We can eliminate some of the books if you know the month you were here." She looked at Mother Morgan sitting at the table.

"It was June," Mother Morgan said forlornly as she clutched her granddaughter's hand for comfort.

"Well, good! That will make our job a little easier," Mrs. Hamilton said with an encouraging smile. She found the books she was looking for from May, June, and July—eight ledgers in all for the family to look through.

"I think we can speed the process up a bit if we each take a book and start looking. And remember, we are looking for twins, so that should make it a little easier."

Libby and her grandmother sat on one side of a table with a book between them, and Mother Morgan's head shook with every page Libby turned. No twins in this book.

Grandfather had a book in front of him, and as he turned page after page, he too shook his head. He found no twins.

"Here!" Libby's father yelled. "Here are twins, in early June!"

Her father's shout contrasted greatly with the quiet page-turning that had been the only sound in the room. Mother Morgan startled in her seat, and Libby almost jumped out of her shoes. Everyone dashed to her father's table and stood crowded round to look at the entry.

"See . . . here . . ." her father pointed, "see the fabric . . . it's the same! But which one does it match?" he asked, reaching for the pieces of cotton held protectively by Mother Morgan.

She handed her son the two pieces of printed cotton, and Libby crossed her fingers in anticipation of the answers.

"The entry in the book matches the clean piece of cotton . . . the one that was given to Mother Morgan by the nurse when she came for the children." Libby's comment was made with a very downcast tone, for it was not the match she had hoped for. But then she remembered they were really looking for two entries, so their task was only half-completed. She burst forth, "Now we must find the second entry, the one that matches the piece given by the washer woman who took Mother Morgan's girls." She tried to sound more encouraging. "Come on, everyone, let's continue looking, we mustn't give up now . . . we are only half-finished."

For the next half hour, the party finished looking through the books that Mrs. Hamilton had said were from the months in question. As each family member drew near the end of the book they were scanning, their moods sank even further into despair. Libby looked over the final page in the last book, and when she did not find another entry for twins, Mother Morgan let out a loud sigh.

The room fell silent for an awkwardly long moment, and no one had anything encouraging to say.

"I'm sorry, Mother. Really, I am," Libby's father said with a gentle touch to Mother Morgan's shoulder.

"Perhaps Dwyn mixed up the piece of fabric she was given with something in her scrap bag?" Grandfather Abbott offered.

"NO!" shouted Libby. "It must be here . . . it simply must!" Her tone was desperate, for she could see a cloud of sadness engulfing her grandmother, and in that moment, she made up her mind she would continue looking . . . even if she had to look in every ledger book she found in the building, she was not going to give up the search. "Give me those books." Libby frantically reached for the books from the months before and after the times they had already searched, "we mustn't stop looking." Tears had begun to run down Libby's face, and she wiped them away as she turned the pages in the August ledger. "So many entries," she said. "So many babies left here!" Her tears fell onto the pages of the ledger.

Mother Morgan sat quietly wringing her handkerchief as her son rubbed her shoulders. Grandfather Abbott turned and walked quietly to the window, his eyes downcast with defeat. Only Libby's occasional sniff and the frantic turning of the ledger pages broke the shroud of silence that enveloped the room.

"It must be here," she mumbled between sniffles, "it simply must be here!" Over and over, she repeated the phrase as she turned the pages.

Then Libby was silent.

Mother Morgan sat crying softly, with only the comfort of her son's hand on her back. "I'm so very sorry, Mother. Really I am!" her son repeated as he patted and rubbed her back as if she were his child and not the other way round.

Libby stood staring at the book she had been frantically searching, wiping her eyes and looking over the page repeatedly. She didn't move for a few moments, and then she looked at Mrs. Hamilton and motioned for the woman to come look. The date at the top of the page was mid-August.

Libby looked up at Mrs. Hamilton and then back at the page, pointing to the place where two names were written—twins!

Neither spoke.

Libby and Mrs. Hamilton looked at the entry carefully. Libby touched the fabric glued in the book and was heartened to see that it was exactly like the other piece of fabric; it was even soiled.

"Mrs. Morgan," began Mrs. Hamilton, "are you quite certain of the date that you came to the Foundling Hospital in search of your daughters?"

"Quite certain. Why do you ask?" She looked past Mrs. Hamilton to her granddaughter, and Libby offered her the biggest smile she could muster.

"They are here," Libby mouthed, and then unable to contain herself, she yelled out as if she couldn't believe it either, "THEY *ARE* HERE!" She was pointing at the entry in the August ledger book.

Grandfather Abbott turned around when he heard his granddaughter and rushed to the table. He placed his spectacles back on and examined the book closely. He asked for the fabric swatches and compared the pieces of cotton and began nodding his head in concurrence. "Yes, Margaret, it's true, these pieces are the same."

The entry for the twins covered two full pages, and Mrs. Hamilton read each and every word. Libby could tell that she was looking for something specific, so she asked, "What is it? What are you looking for?"

"I'm trying to find out which nurse made the entry. They always sign their names, but I don't see any signature here . . ." She scanned the page with her finger several times, reading and re-reading each line.

Libby looked on inquisitively and then asked, "Perhaps it's on the next page?"

Mrs. Hamilton turned the page, and sure enough, there was a signature at the very top of the page just before the next entry. It looked to Libby as though the signer was in a rush, and she listened as Mrs. Hamilton struggled to sound out the name, "Ehh ehhd . . ."

"It says, "Edwards," I think," said Libby.

"I think you're right, child," responded Mrs. Hamilton. "Hmm! I just wonder? If you all will excuse me . . . I need to find someone!" She looked at Mother Morgan and said kindly, "I'll be back, I promise!" She curtsied to the gentlemen and turned to rush out the door.

Mother Morgan sat looking at the ledger book her granddaughter had placed in her hands. "See here, Grandmother. The fabrics are an exact match . . . even down to the dirt." Libby pointed at the soiled pink fabric. "But why would it be logged in the August ledger book? I don't understand. Didn't you say you were here in June?" Libby's inquisitive mind was exploring all the possibilities.

"It was June. I remember quite well. It was June, wasn't it, Captain?" Mother Morgan asked.

"Yes, Margaret, it was June. You remember correctly," he reassured her.

Libby was quite pleased with herself and sat down in a stuffed chair next to her grandmother. Her father looked at her and said, "Elizabeth, you are quite a bird dog! You managed to find the needle in the haystack that none of us ever noticed, and today your perseverance has outshined us all. I had given up . . . in fact, I think we all had," he looked around the room at the others nodding their heads, "but not you! You never gave up hope. I'm very proud of you, Elizabeth!"

"Yes indeed, I am proud of you too, child. And grateful. I don't know what any of this means, and it may mean nothing at all, but right now, I am so very proud of your tenacity." Mother Morgan patted Libby on the hand and smiled at her.

Mrs. Hamilton had been gone for well over half an hour, and the occupants of the room were becoming restless. "Where can she have gotten to?" asked Mother Morgan. Libby was just about ready to go find the woman when the door opened.

Mrs. Hamilton, with an elderly woman scurrying closely behind, scooted into the room. "I do beg your pardon for taking such an inordinate amount of time on my task." She walked over to Mother Morgan and curtsied then said, "Mrs. Morgan, I would like to introduce you to Miss Seren Edwards. She has been a nurse and wonderful companion to the children of the Foundling Hospital for some forty years."

Miss Edwards curtsied to Mother Morgan. Libby was examining Miss Edwards and could see how uncomfortable she was to have everyone staring at her. She saw how the old woman shifted from foot to foot, like a child caught doing something naughty, and it made Libby wonder if Miss Edwards was just overly shy or if she was perhaps not right in the head. "Miss Edwards has dedicated her life to the children of our establishment, and we are so very grateful for her service." Mrs. Hamilton took Miss Edwards's hand and patted it gently, and it solidified Libby's thought that Miss Edwards was, in fact, mentally infirm. She wondered if the other family members noticed, too.

"When I saw that the signature on the ledger entry was that of a 'Miss Edwards,' I thought how coincidental it was that I knew of a 'Miss Edwards' to be employed at the hospital this very day. I needed first to find her and explain these rather strange circumstances and then ask her some very important questions before I could be sure of my suppositions. As it turns out, Mrs. Morgan, our very own Miss Edwards was at the hospital the night your daughters were brought in by the abductor."

With this statement, Libby let out a gasp, and Mother Morgan quickly looked at Grandfather Abbott and then back at Miss Edwards. She took hold of the woman's hands and begged, "You were here? Do you remember my girls?"

Libby watched as Miss Edwards pulled her hands back uncomfortably from Mother Morgan's grasp and wiped them on her dress front as she looked back at Mrs. Hamilton. Libby saw Miss Hamilton nod, and Miss Edwards began, "I remember your girls quite vividly." As she spoke, Libby was amazed at how childlike the old woman sounded. "It was so strange that we would have been brought a set of twin girls so soon after the last twin girls had been left with us. Less than a week, I think, since the last twins came . . . but these new babes were different . . . so much healthier than the first two. And I remember the woman who brought them. She was so scared . . . not sad, like most mothers. She kept looking back over her shoulder whenever there were any sounds. I took the children from her and asked if she had any token to identify the babes should her circumstances change and she wished to collect the children. I did the right thing, just like I had been instructed."

The old woman looked at Mrs. Hamilton, who again nodded and reassured her that she had done nothing wrong. She continued. "I remember she took a very long time to answer me, not like the other mothers who already have something for the book; she just tore off a piece of her apron, handed it to me, then rushed out the door. Most mothers sit for a while and say good-bye to their babes, but not this woman. I remember thinking how sad it was that she showed no love for her little ones."

Mother Morgan had tears running down her face, and Miss Edwards looked between her and Mrs. Hamilton with a nervous expression. "It's all right, Seren, you are not the reason for Mrs. Morgan's tears. Please, tell the rest of the story you told me. Explain why the twins were logged in the August ledger instead of in June when they arrived," Mrs. Hamilton encouraged with a warm smile.

Seren looked down at the floor and again Libby thought she looked like a child being scolded. "I'm not supposed to take in the children without one of the other nurses or the doctor with me . . . on account of . . . sometimes . . . I forget things." She looked back at Mrs. Hamilton, who offered another smile. "But there was no one at the gate that night, and Doctor Manfrenson was attending to the sick children in the south wing. All the other nurses were so busy with so many sick children, so when the bell rang . . . I went out. Was that all right, Mrs. Hamilton? Did I do all right?"

Mrs. Hamilton patted her arm. "Yes, dear, you did just fine. You did exactly as you should have done answering the bell. Now tell Mrs. Morgan the part about the ledger."

"I had the two babes and only two arms," Seren began again tentatively, "so when she tried to hand me the torn piece from her dress, I couldn't take it from her, and it fell onto the floor. When the nurse came to help me with the babes, I picked up the cloth and put it into my apron pocket. I . . . I . . . well . . . I forgot about the piece of fabric, you see . . . because . . ." she drew out her statement and looked at Mrs. Hamilton.

"Mrs. Morgan, the year your daughters were brought to our hospital was a dark time for our establishment. We had such severe cases of cholera, and so many of the children were . . . lost." Mrs. Hamilton chose her words carefully. "We were trying hard to save those children who were brought to us healthy, so as soon as possible, we sent them out of the hospital until they were old enough to go to school. Apparently, your daughters were sent to the country the very day they were brought to us." She was looking at the August ledger. "By the entry in our ledger, I can see that the girls were baptized the very morning they came in and then were given to a nurse mother who lived near Surrey. See, here in the ledger, the *actual* date the girls were brought to us is mentioned here," she pointed to the date and note written in the margin of the ledger. "It seems Seren forgot about the fabric in her apron pocket and no one checked to see if the children had been logged before they were sent away. But when Seren found the fabric, she remembered they had not been logged, so she made the entry for the girls correctly, provided the fabric, and the margin note with the actual date the girls came to us. She has an *excellent* memory . . . when she does remember." Mrs. Hamilton looked apologetically at Mother Morgan. "It is an unfortunate turn of fate that her log entry was made *after* you had come to collect your girls. Apparently, the nurse who helped you when you came did not know that a second set of twins had been brought in and sent straightaway to Surrey. Nor did she look very closely at the piece of cotton fabric to be sure it matched the one you had provided."

"Grandmother," Libby began tentatively, "do you think this new information is good news? I mean . . . it is good to know that the children who died were not your daughters . . . isn't it?" Her question brought with it an awkward silence to the room.

"Margaret, I am so very sorry, and yet . . . this news brings new hope." Grandfather Abbott turned to Mrs. Hamilton. "Is there some way for us to know what happened to the children? Is it possible to find out which of the nurse mothers took the children and where they would have been taken, exactly? Perhaps there is an entry when the children came back to be educated at school?"

"Why yes, Mr. Abbott, all that information should be available in our records." Mrs. Hamilton looked over the entry made so many years ago. "Here we can see the names given to the girls at their baptism," she pointed to the names written in the ledger, "Rosemary and Ruth Cavendish. We should be able to track them through the letters written by the Inspectress of Nurse Mothers. She would have communicated to the hospital when the children were vaccinated, as well as any time there were health problems or other difficulties with the babes. And then again, we should find them when they returned to the hospital to be schooled. I daresay, Mr. Abbott, this is a great task and it will take some time. I do not think it is something we can accomplish at this late hour of the day."

Grandfather Abbott looked at Mother Morgan and asked, "Margaret, I think it best we act on this information as soon as possible. I would like your permission to hire a gentleman detective to continue searching for the girls and to uncover what has happened to them. I believe I may have a contact through my club for just such a person."

Mother Morgan was staring at the two pieces of fabric sitting on the ledger book. She picked up the clean piece and held it as a single tear fell slowly down her cheek; she used the fabric to wipe the tear away. "Those poor girls . . . those poor, poor girls . . . to have grown up thinking that their mother could just give them away . . . they must hate me." She was shaking her head and wiping more tears as they fell from her eyes.

"Grandmother," Libby began as she tenderly stroked Mother Morgan's arm, "we mustn't focus on that now, we mustn't. We need to see the good in this, remember, like you told me about perspective. There is so much of what we have learned that is good. Please, let's focus on the good just like you taught me."

"Yes, Mother." Libby's father came quickly and knelt beside his mother's chair. "Think on the comfort you provided that poor dying orphan child, whose real mother could not be with her. She did not die alone. And we have such hope for finding my sisters, hope we did not have before today. Please, Mother, let us look at the good that is to come from this new discovery and move quickly to find the girls."

Mother Morgan reached up and stroked her son's head. "I am so blessed to have you as my son . . . so very blessed." She turned her eyes on Libby and smiled. "And you, my tenacious young girl, have never let me give up hoping for the impossible." She then turned to Grandfather Abbott and said, "Gerald, do what is necessary to find the girls. The cost is irrelevant, hire ten investigators if you must, just find them . . . I must know what has become of my daughters."

Chapter 35

*I*n the days after the Foundling Hospital visit, Libby's father and Finnian took the train to Glasgow with strict instructions that Finn was to stay with and obey Mr. Morgan, and under no circumstances was he to depart from his ward or explore Glasgow on his own. When Mr. Morgan's business was concluded, he would assist Finn in finding his father. Grandfather Abbott gave Libby's father the name of a contact in Glasgow as well as a letter that would open doors to establishments that were normally closed to Americans.

The household was fairly quiet with Libby's grandfather gone most of the day, coming home very late in the evenings and departing early in the mornings. He had important business to take care of at his company headquarters, and aboard his new ship, the *Argile*.

Knowing Mother Morgan had experienced quite a shock finding out her daughters were quite possibly alive, Libby was not surprised when her grandmother took to her bedchamber and rested quietly with only her Bible. Libby had tried to get her grandmother to join the rest of the women in the parlor, but Mother Morgan explained how all the new information swimming around in her head easily led her to tears, and so she wished to remain in her chambers should she feel the need to cry. Libby understood and did not press the situation further.

Left to spend her days sitting in on her younger cousins' school lessons or putting the finishing seams into her mosaic quilt top did not distract Libby from speculating about her missing aunts, and so she spent several hours writing to Gertrude about the situation. She had yet to receive word from her new friend as to her own predicament regarding marriage and anxiously awaited the mail each day.

She sewed diligently when not otherwise engaged with her cousins. Libby finished putting all the pieces into her spread, and she was finally ready to layer and quilt the top, so she went to her Grandmother Abbott and asked, "Grandmama? Grandfather said I should tell you when I'm in need of the backing and wadding to finish my garden spread. I brought it along so you can see . . ." Libby had begun to open the folded quilt top when her grandmother said, "Wait, child. Not in here. Bring it along to my sewing parlor where we shall have more room."

Grandmother Abbott rose from her chair and glided out the door. Libby noticed how lovely she moved, slipping gracefully along like a beautiful swan. No wonder her own mother was so graceful; she must have learned from Grandmother Abbott how to walk like a lady. Libby tried to emulate the older lady's grace, but failed miserably when her toe caught the edge of the carpet and she went careening into a chair. Fortunately, Grandmother Abbott was already out of the room and didn't notice her faux pas.

When they reached the sewing parlor, Grandmother Abbott found a seat and asked Libby to show her the bed covering. As she opened her spread, Grandmother Abbott exclaimed, "Oh, my heavens! Bring it here, dear, and let me look at your workmanship." She held out her hands for Libby to bring the quilt closer.

"My goodness, child, you have a lovely hand. Your stitches are so even and small. Mother Morgan has taught you well, and you are obviously a good student." Grandmother Abbott turned the quilt this way and that to look over all the blocks. "Your choice of fabric combinations is exceptional. If I didn't know better, I would say this was the work of a much more experienced seamstress. Well done, my dear, well done."

Libby stood taller for the compliments. "Some of the blocks were done by Mother Morgan and a few by my mother, Aunt Ellen, and even my cousin James. He likes to sew, you know. But most were my own hand."

"And so you would like some fabric for the backing? Hmm, let us just see how much you shall need." Grandmother Abbott measured all four sides of the quilt with a yardstick and added up the numbers she had jotted down on a piece of paper. Libby watched as she made a few mathematical calculations and came up with a number then sat looking at a door on the other side of the room as if pondering something important. "Since your quilt is not so very big, I think we can get away with three widths of fabric. Each width will need to measure two meters long. See here, where I have calculated it." Libby looked at the figures on the page and nodded, though she wasn't exactly sure where her grandmother came up with her numbers. "We will sew the three widths together to make a single wide piece that will be your backing. Now, let's just see which of my fabrics I have in six-meter lengths." Her grandmother got up, and carrying Libby's quilt top, walked toward the back of the room and stood before the door she had gazed upon. "Come along, child. Let's find a piece of chintz that you would like to put on the back."

She followed, and as her grandmother slipped into the small room on the other side, Libby froze in the doorway and gazed at what the room contained. It was all she had imagined and more. Here was the room filled with nothing but fabric, just as she had once envisioned. Some of the pieces were rolled up and standing in the corners, but most of the fabric was stacked on shelves that lined the walls. Her eyes were wide and her mouth had fallen open, and as her grandmother walked past, she pushed Libby's chin up and said, "It's not polite to gawk, child." She winked and smiled as Libby caught her eye.

Libby scanned the room and tried to imagine why anyone would need so much fabric—unless, of course, you owned a mercantile store and were selling it to other people. She thought to ask but decided against it; her relationship with Grandmother Abbott was not the same as what she shared with Mother Morgan. But like a mind reader, Libby heard her Grandmother Abbott say, "You are probably wondering why I need so much fabric, aren't you?"

Before Libby could answer, her grandmother continued, "Well, I don't *need* it! But I do *like* it, and I do *want* it." Her tone was teetering on the defensive. "Let me tell you a little secret, Elizabeth," she leaned closer to Libby, "I simply love fabric . . ." she smiled warmly at her granddaughter and walked over to a shelf that was stuffed to overflowing with smaller pieces of printed silks and cottons, ". . . and your grandfather knows it!" She grinned widely. "He often brings me fabrics from his trips," she pointed to the overflowing shelves, "and I bring some home from my trips to Europe. They really do make the loveliest chintz in France." She pointed to a different shelf of larger cuts of fabric that were neatly folded and stacked according to overall color.

"May I ask," Libby began tentatively, "what is it you *do* with all your fabric?"

"*Do?*" her grandmother looked perplexed. "Well . . . nothing, I guess, but I do so love to collect it! Oh," she said as an afterthought, "and I let my girls and my granddaughters use what they like for their projects, provided they don't use all of a particular piece—especially ones that I cannot replace."

Libby walked over to a shelf and began to examine some of the pieces. She let her hand glide across the pieces, and she noticed that many were glazed and slick, just like some of the pieces she had received from her grandfather.

"Can you imagine, Elizabeth, this is only a very small sampling of the number of fabrics that are in the world, and every day there are more and more printed." Her eyes sparkled when she spoke of fabric, and her smile was glazed over like her chintz. "I don't know what it is about it, and I know I have more than I will use in three lifetimes . . . but I just love it!" She picked up a piece of vibrant blue chintz and brought it over to Libby. "Isn't it lovely, dear? See the glaze, how it shines? I love to compare pieces and see how some design elements are used and re-used in other fabrics."

This last statement made Libby think about Mother Morgan and the two pieces of pink cotton that were almost identical except for a few little leaves.

"Your grandfather took me to Marseille in France one year not long after we were married. I was able to see how the fabrics were dyed and printed. Textile printing can be a very simple process *or* it can be extremely complicated; did you know some colors take weeks to produce? I find the whole thing very interesting, and I hope some day you will be able to see how it is achieved. I believe one cannot truly appreciate a piece of cloth, be it silk or cotton, wool or linen, until one understands the manufacturing and printing processes of that cloth." She held up a chintz piece so Libby could see all the detailing of the design—the picotage and vibrant colors, the fineness of the cotton, and the sheen of the glaze applied to the finished goods. "It really is incredibly beautiful!" thought Libby to herself.

"Now, let me see . . ." Grandmother Abbott was looking at the quilt top Libby had draped across the table and glancing at several of the fabric-filled shelves. "Did you have a particular color in mind?"

"Yes, ma'am, I do. I'm quite partial to red. The quilt Mother made for me is blue, and I do love it, but red is my favorite . . . and I think it would be lovely with all the blocks in my new quilt. What do you think?"

"I think," she paused a moment then winked at Libby, "that you are a child who knows her own mind. I like that about you! Red it is.

Now the question at hand is which of the red colors do you like? There are so many varieties and styles." She walked over to the shelf that held many yards of red fabrics. As she scanned the shelf looking for her bigger pieces, she said, "Are you partial to the madder reds," she indicated one shelf, "or the Turkey reds you see on this shelf?" She held up a piece of vibrant, almost glowing, deep red cloth with a stylized fleur de lis design in bright yellow and blue. Then, she reached over and grabbed a madder red fabric and held up a piece with an all over brownish-red background with a design of vines and flowers in blue, green, and dark brown. "Do you see the differences in color?" she asked Libby.

"I do." Libby said with a smile. She was drawn to the more vibrant Turkey red, so she reached out and took the piece from her grandmother. She let her hand glide across the top of the folded piece of fabric.

Her grandmother said, "It was printed in Glasgow, you know, at the very mill your father is visiting."

Libby glanced up at her grandmother and said, "Thornliebank?"

"Yes, see here," she turned back the first fold and showed Libby the stamp on the back of the red fabric, "most manufacturers and print works will label their goods with a stamp or paper label."

Libby continued to examine the red fabric she held, and her grandmother continued, "Well, now," she selected several more of her larger cuts of Turkey red, "let's take them out into better light and see which one is your favorite."

The two fabric connoisseurs walked to the table and laid out all the pieces. Then her grandmother draped Libby's quilt across the reds without covering them all the way. This allowed Libby to see her quilt next to each of the prints on the table.

Her eye was caught by one of the Turkey reds with a medium-scale trailing vine print in dark browns, bright yellows, and greens, with rich blue flowers. Libby pulled the piece of fabric out and opened it up to see more of the print. "I think this one, please." She smiled at her grandmother. "I think it is the best one for such a large area as the back. I like the . . ." she searched for the right word, "movement, I guess is the word. The design seems to flow, don't you think?"

"It is exactly the one I would have chosen. And the benefit of this piece is that when it is stitched together, the seams will be not be noticeable, unlike this stripe, or this one with the half-drop repeat in the design."

Libby was nodding her head. "Let's measure, shall we, and see if we have enough." Grandmother Abbott opened up the folded fabric, and holding one end out the full stretch of her left arm, she held up the middle of the fabric to her nose. "This is just about one meter," she told Libby, then, repeatedly moving her left hand to the place she touched to her nose, and holding the right side of the fabric up to her nose again, she quickly measured out the length of the red fabric.

"Unfortunately, we are just short with this piece. But, this fabric is so similar," she pointed to another piece of red fabric on the table, "I think we can add this on a corner and it won't be too noticeable. What do you think?"

"Yes, I think you're right, Grandmama. It will blend in just fine."

"Wonderful," her grandmother said. "I shall send Peggy to fetch the wadding this afternoon, and we can get the top into the frame for quilting by tomorrow." Her grandmother folded up the pieces of red fabric they would use for the backing and handed them to Libby, who had just neatly folded the quilt top. "Now run along, dear, and show Mother Morgan your choice. Perhaps it will brighten her spirits." She gathered up the remaining fabrics from the table and took them back to her hidey-hole. Libby watched her grandmother slip through the door into the small room packed with the many different fabrics, and the thought that crossed her mind was, "Just like a little squirrel—stashing her treasure away for another day."

Chapter 36

Several days were spent around the quilting frame with Grandmother Abbott, Mother Morgan, Aunt Angelina, and all the children. Libby was quite heartened to have Mother Morgan emerge from her room and participate in the quilting of her spread. She thought the color was returning to her grandmother's complexion, and it made her happy. The older children did some quilting as well, while the younger ones sat around the suspended quilt frame and fetched items for the quilters when needed. Libby laughed repeatedly as Baby Grace, her youngest cousin, sat on the floor beneath the quilt, giggling and squealing with excitement every time her older brother played peek-a-boo from behind a chair.

Libby was sure her cousins were quite glad of a quilt in the frame because it meant a break from their regular schooling. Grandmother Abbott enlisted all capable hands; even the smallest fingers could be used to thread needles for those doing all the sewing. Grandmother wanted to be sure Libby took home a finished project to show her mother how productively she spent her time in London.

Quilting instructions were a bit more challenging for Libby than the piecing of the blocks had been. Mother Morgan showed her the importance of loading her needle with as many stitches as she could so as to reveal a nice even line of tiny stitches. It proved more difficult than Libby expected, and she found she was only able to rock her needle a few times before she had to pull through. Aunt Angelina used an entirely different stitching method, and Libby was amazed at how quickly she could stab her needle into the fabric, draw it down, and then back up with the hand on the bottom. Her stitches were exceedingly accurate for such a procedure, and Libby noticed she hardly looked at her hands when she sewed. And then there was Grandmother Abbott. Libby watched her intently from time to time and noticed that she really didn't sew many stitches. She spent a great deal of time chatting about the current gossip or offering advice to her granddaughters and less time actually quilting. Libby wondered if she even liked to sew, and the more she thought about it, the more she decided that while Grandmother Abbott really loved fabric, she didn't seem to love quilting as much.

Each day, as they sat around the quilt frame, Libby asked when her father would return, but neither of her grandmothers knew the answer. She was curious as to the outcome of Finnian's quest and wondered if they had found his father. If they did, would he return or stay in Glasgow? Then, early one afternoon, Libby heard some commotion downstairs in the front foyer. She dashed to the top of the stairs hoping that it was her father and was excited to see him standing in the hall calling her name. She dashed down the stairs and found herself engulfed in his arms. "I missed you, Elizabeth!" he said as he hugged her and kissed the top of her head.

"I missed you, too, Father!" she said, but when her eyes fell upon Finn, her excitement waned. His face was downcast, and his eyes were locked on the floor. She knew immediately that he had not found his father. "And Finn," she said as she let go of her father and stood before the boy, "how was your trip?"

Finn did not speak; he looked at Libby's father and then back at the floor. Libby's father responded to the question. "We did not get to meet Finnian's father. It seems he relocated to Australia some years ago, and so I have brought Finn back with me in the hopes of securing him a position with your grandfather." He patted Finn on the shoulder, and Finn looked up at him with a half smile. "Don't worry, son, you shall find him yet," Libby's father reassured the boy.

"I'm sorry, Finn," Libby put her hand on the boy's arm and continued, "I just know my grandfather will find you a position. You will not be turned out, I promise." She was so glad to see the boy again. Her heart skipped a beat as she touched his arm. A feeling of guilt welled up in her for being glad he had not found his father, for it had brought him back to her. She tried to look sad for his circumstance, but inside, she was quite happy to see him standing next to her father.

"It's all right; it's not as if I even knew him," Finn replied disappointedly.

Libby could see that the boy needed a distraction, so she asked him if he wanted to read the letter she had recently received from Gertrude. "Sure," he replied. "I just need to put this away." He motioned to his very small case on the floor next to his feet.

"Take it to your room, lad, and then meet us in the front parlor, and we shall have a bite to eat. Libby, while I put my case away as well, how about you run to the kitchen and see if you can convince the cook to provide an early lunch. We missed our breakfast this morning and are famished." Her father smiled at her and gave her another hug before he turned to head up the stairs. Finn took his case and headed toward the back part of the house where the servants' quarters were located. Libby headed off to the kitchen and then to fetch Gertrude's letter. She was excited to have Finn back but didn't want to show it as she knew he was so disappointed. She knew she would need to curb her enthusiasm for a bit until he had come to terms with his disappointment.

Mother Morgan and Grandmother Abbott joined the three in the front parlor, and they all partook in an early lunch. Aunt Angelina had an afternoon engagement, so the children were sent back to school and the quilting postponed for another day.

Following their meal, Libby and Finn chatted quietly in the corner as they read over Gertrude's letter. Libby had brought with her a piece of paper, a pen, and ink to write back to Gertrude, and while she did, she asked Finn what he would like to say to their friend.

Libby's father was explaining to his mother and mother-in-law that his trip to Glasgow had turned into quite a good business venture. He was now going to be importing to Boston last season's shirting and suiting goods from the Thornliebank Mills at a significantly reduced rate since they would no longer be saleable in England. A newly established shirt factory in Boston would use the goods to manufacture ready-to-wear shirts and suits for the booming economy out west. "You see, Mrs. Abbott, the gold rush in California has proved to me that the ready-wear clothing industry is where my business is heading. A tailor's hand will always be desired by the wealthy of this world, and there is good money to be made if your work is of the highest quality and your clients recommend you, but I believe there is a fortune to be made in this budding new industry. Most men have a desire to dress well, just like the wealthy. And I think we can make clothing for the common man that is fashionable *and* affordable!"

"Well, dear, you do seem quite passionate about this new venture. And that leads me to my next question. Have you made any decisions about your inheritance? Will you accept the terms of the Baron's will, do you think, and stay in England for the next five years?"

Before he could answer this last question, there was a commotion at the front of the house. Grandfather Abbott had thrown open the door and was shouting, "Margaret! Margaret! Where are you?"

Everyone jumped to their feet as he burst open the parlor door and rushed in shouting, "They are alive! They are alive! Your daughters are alive!"

Libby turned quickly to see Mother Morgan fall back into her chair and cover her face with her handkerchief. The words had barely escaped Grandfather's mouth before she began to cry. It was as if she had been anticipating this moment for the past few days, knowing it could happen at any second, and when it did finally happen, she was totally overcome. Grandmother Abbott saw Mother Morgan's swoon and rushed to her side.

Libby and Finn looked at each other and then at Grandfather Abbott, who had stopped short when he saw his son-in-law staring at him from across the room. "Thomas! Good Lord—when did you return?"

"Late this morning," Libby's father replied anxiously. "Do tell, what is the news?"

Grandfather Abbott crossed the room and knelt next to the chair where Mother Morgan still sat with her face covered by her handkerchief. He gently placed his hand on her arm and nudged her hands down so he could look into her eyes. "Please, Margaret, forgive me. I was overcome with excitement and didn't take your feelings into consideration. The investigator brought me news just this hour, and I rushed home to tell you."

Mother Morgan sniffled again and dried her eyes. She looked up at her lifelong friend and gave him her best smile. "What news, Gerald?" she whispered.

"The girls are alive, Margaret." His manner was gentler now and his excitement toned down. "The investigator found that girls have been alive these many years and living not far from here."

Libby was shocked by the news and excitedly hugged Finn, then, realizing what she had done, she sat back in her chair and blushed a deep crimson. Finn just gave an awkward grin and blushed himself.

"I don't know what to say!" Libby turned her attention to the words Mother Morgan spoke. "Thirty-eight years have come and gone, and my daughters have lived all this time without knowing me." She paused and said as a tear rolled down her face, "Gerald, what they must think of me?" She shook her head in disgust and covered her face once again.

"Whatever do you mean, Margaret?" Grandfather Abbott was confused.

"They were left at the Foundling Hospital, Gerald. Abandoned! They were given new names and grew up thinking that their mother gave them up . . . that *I* gave them up!" She pounded on her chest with this last statement as she grew angrier with each word she spoke. "Perhaps the best thing to do is leave them alone. To let them live out their lives and not know me."

"Mother Morgan, please," Libby interrupted from across the room. "Don't be afraid that they will hate you. How can they hate you? It wasn't your fault. They were taken from you, and in a strange twist of fate, they were kept from you for so long. But they are alive and we have found them." Her words begged her grandmother's fear to abate. "Surely they have a right to know the truth about their lives."

She got up and moved next to her father; as she looked up at him, he offered her a comforting smile, reached down, and took hold of her hand as if to reassure her.

The emotion in the room was thick like London morning fog, and it lay heavily upon the occupants. Finally, Finn's words cut the silence like a knife as he spoke to Mother Morgan, "Excuse me, ma'am, but I would have to agree with Libby."

Libby looked quickly at Finn to see him glance in her direction, and when he smiled at her, she encouraged his words with a smile in return.

Finn walked over to Mother Morgan and knelt before her chair. "I am sorry for your pain, truly I am. But you should know that I would give anything to know the truth about my father, to know where he is and why he sent my mother away to America." Libby could tell that the boy was trying very hard to hold back his tears. "To be able to ask him why he never visited, never sent money. Nothing, for fifteen years, not a single word from him." He paused and looked deeper into the Mother Morgan's eyes. "But no matter the reason, I know I will find it in me to forgive him and make room in my heart to love him, if only he were to ask it of me. And I can assure you," his voice cracked and a tear fell, "I will be tortured to my bone if I have to live the rest of my life *not* knowing the truth about how I came to be in this world!" He paused then added, "Do not give up hope of reconciliation."

Libby held on to her father as Mother Morgan looked at the boy and was quiet for a long time, gazing into his young blue eyes. It seemed to give Finn a moment to recover his emotion. Libby found she was glad for him to have shared something so personal with her family and took it to mean he was comfortable with them. That made her happy.

When Mother Morgan looked back at Grandfather Abbott and asked quietly, "Will *you* come with me to meet them? I don't think I can do this without you," Libby almost burst with joy.

"Of course I will. It would be my honor to introduce you to your daughters." Grandfather patted her hand.

"And you," Mother Morgan looked back at Finn pointed her finger at him, "you are wise beyond your years, young man. And you have given me much to think on. So here is something for you to think on." She looked him square in the eyes and said, "I have seen your character come through on more than one occasion since we first met. You are honest and forthright. You are a lad with a long fuse and a quick wit. I like you! Yes, I do. And I pray you will consider yourself an orphan no more. You are invited to be a part of my family, lad. One way or another, you belong with us. And if you do not desire to stay in England, then you are invited to come home with me, back to my farm in Connecticut."

Libby was overwhelmed at her grandmother's generosity, and she could tell that Finn was, too. "You are most generous, Mrs. Morgan. Thank you."

"Don't feel as though you need to decide now, Finn," Libby's father spoke up, "there is still much to be done to find your father. After we have exhausted all our resources, then you may decide what your future will hold and where you would like to live."

It was Libby's turn to speak. She had held her comments and questions while Mother Morgan recovered from the news of her daughters, but seeing her improved, Libby asked, "Grandfather, when may we meet my aunties?"

Grandfather Abbott looked at Libby. "That is not my decision to make." He turned to Mother Morgan and asked, "Margaret, when would you like to meet them?"

"Do they know about me?" she asked tentatively.

"I gave explicit instructions to the investigator that he was to remain anonymous and that my identity was *not* to be exposed under any circumstances. He assured me of the utmost anonymity. No, they do not know about you, or me, or even that they were being investigated, for that matter." He tried to put this last part as tenderly as possible. "The decision is only yours to make, Margaret. These are your daughters and I will honor your choice."

Libby could feel the fog of sadness beginning to lift as Mother Morgan sat looking at her family and friends. Her expressions suggested an internal debate that was trying to resolve itself before she spoke, and when she finally did break the silence, Libby was relieved. "Well, my friend," she looked at Grandfather Abbott, "God has answered my prayers this day. So long I have asked Him for my girls back . . . asked that they had not died and that I would wake from my nightmare to be united with them once again. So many times I asked my Father in heaven to change the past and give me back my daughters. And when I had finally given them up to Him, finally let their memory rest in the arms of my Savior and resolved myself to my mother's words, that we would all 'be reunited in heaven,' this happens." She threw up her arms and let out a long sigh. "God gave me what I have asked of Him, Gerald, and so I must accept it *despite* my fears of rejection." She took a long pause then added, "Make whatever appointments are necessary . . . and the sooner the better."

Libby was elated with Mother Morgan's decision, but she held back her excitement, for she knew the time for celebration had not yet arrived. She looked up at her father and saw his countenance had shifted a bit into quiet contemplation. Grandfather, on the other hand, looked excited and ready to make a move. He grabbed the hat he had thrown onto the table when he rushed into the room, turned to Grandmother Abbott, and said with a grin, "There is much to be done, Caroline. I fear I shall be late this evening." He kissed her cheek and placed his hat upon his head, but before he dashed out of the room, he turned to his son-in-law and said, "Thomas, before I go, I need a private word with you in the hall, please." So Libby's father joined Grandfather Abbott and left the room.

Grandmother Abbott looked at Mother Morgan and said softly, "Margaret, dear, I'm going to make you some chamomile tea." She patted her friend's hand and then rose from her seat as Mother Morgan said with a smile, "Thank you, Caroline, that so is very kind. If you don't mind, I think I shall take it in my chambers," and she rose to leave as well.

Libby and Finn were left alone in the room, and the silence was awkward, so she looked at Finn and said matter-of-factly, "Let's finish our letter, shall we? We have much to tell Miss Gertrude!"

Chapter 37

*I*n the cigar lounge, Thomas and Captain Abbott talked quietly. "First, let me ask, how goes Glasgow? You are home much sooner than I had expected." Captain Abbott walked over to the bar and poured them both a glass of whiskey.

Thomas sat himself down in a comfortable chair and accepted the drink Captain Abbott offered. "Perfectly, sir. In fact, I couldn't have hoped for a better outcome. We shall have ready-made clothing heading to California by this time next year."

"Outstanding news, Thomas. Now I have some news for you, though I'm not sure if you will view it as good or bad." Captain Abbott sat himself down and sipped from his glass. "As you know, I've had our solicitors combing through the will, looking for anything that would allow you to inherit the estate without having to abide by the mandate of living at Braidsmuir." Thomas sat quietly in his chair, sipping his drink.

"It seems, Son, that our solicitors found what one may call . . . a loophole, as it were. The stipulation states that 'an heir' to the estate must reside at Braidsmuir for the duration of five years in order for 'the heir' to inherit. The lawyers argue that 'an heir' and 'the heir' do not necessarily have to be one in the same. The verbiage is tricky, but it can be interpreted that the person living on the estate is 'an heir' to the Montclief fortune, but not 'the heir' who is to inherit the estate.

"In other words, it may be possible to have your sister, Ellen, live at the estate for the required five years. She is now considered an heir to the estate since the Baroness is deceased and the entail has been dissolved. The lawyers say the term 'heir' must only be someone of the Montclief bloodline, but it no longer must be a male heir. So I had considered sending word to Ellen asking her and her new family to come to England for the next five years. I thought perhaps the schools would be good for the boys, and they could make some new business connections for young Mr. Masterson. But I knew we would not be able to get word back to her and have her arrive before the fourteen days expire. I had all but given up hope of a solution that would allow you to return home to America and still inherit the estate, but now, finding out that your sisters are alive changes our circumstances considerably. If—and I do mean *if*—one of your newly found sisters is willing to live at Braidsmuir for the duration of the stipulation, then according to our lawyers, they can go to court to petition the case, and likely you will inherit the estate and all its fortune."

"What do you know of the girls, Captain? What of their upbringing and their lifestyle?"

"My investigator has discovered a great deal. They went straight-away to Surrey and lived with a nurse mother as babes . . . a Mrs. Callingham, I believe . . . who took in and reared many young children over the years. It seems she was one of the more reputable nurse mothers and held to strict moral practices, so the girls were well cared for early on. As we were told at the hospital, cholera was epidemic and many of the children died. It was a tragic time for England. So many were lost. You know, my brothers sent their wives and children out of the city for a time so that they would be far removed from the illness." Captain Abbott shook his head sadly. "The investigator said that Mrs. Callingham lost many of the children in her charge," Thomas looked up in alarm at this comment, "but not your sisters.

"Now, normally, the children would have returned to the Foundling Hospital at about age five to attend school and then be apprenticed at age fifteen based upon their skill set. But when Mrs. Callingham also lost her husband in a farming accident, and only your sisters and one other child were still in her charge, she asked for the hospital's permission to legally adopt the three girls. She was granted permanent guardianship of all three and shortly after sold her farm and moved into town with her mother and two sisters. The girls *were* educated, but minimally so, and they were apprenticed to Mrs. Grayson, a milliner with a shop on Regent Street." Captain Abbott sighed and looked at Thomas. "Mrs. Grayson died ten or so years ago, and the girls, grown into young ladies, took ownership of the shop." Captain Abbott smiled at Thomas and added, "Apparently, they were quite skilled in their trade; the shop is very popular with many of the affluent families of London. Not surprising they would be skilled in a trade that involves sewing, don't you think?"

Thomas nodded at Captain Abbott and asked, "Have the girls married? Are there any children?"

"Apparently, they have not. It seems they are spinsters who have stayed single these many years, living together above their shop." Captain Abbott took a long slow sip of his drink, and the room fell quiet for a moment. "My plan," Captain Abbott began again, "is to speak with them on the morrow. I would like to break the news about Mother Morgan and the unfortunate twist of fate that took them from their real family without having your mother present. I think the emotion of it all would be overtaxing on her right now. It will be hard enough for her to meet the women for the first time. But I would like another to help judge their character, and I was wondering, would you like to come with me?"

"I would be happy to accompany you, Captain. Do the women know anything about us?" Thomas asked.

"As I told your mother, they do not. My investigator was very discreet."

"I imagine this will come as a great shock to them, don't you think?" Thomas paused and then added, "And what of the inheritance? Are *they* not the legal heirs to the Montclief fortune? I mean, technically, they are the firstborn, are they not?"

"Technically, yes, but the legality of it is tangled up in their adoption; one could argue that they are no longer legal heirs. I have our solicitors working on that problem as we speak. But I think that we will have to see about their character before we know how things will play out. Their reaction to the revelation of finding out they are not orphans after all and their reaction to you and to Mother Morgan will tell us how to proceed. Perhaps if they are willing, we could offer them a buyout from the family fortune and the responsibilities of the estate—it is a lot for an uneducated woman to handle alone . . ."

Thomas interrupted Captain Abbott. "I wouldn't put too much hope in that thought. My own mother was not overly educated, but she is sharp as a tack when it comes to money and estate management—you should know that by now. If they are even remotely like her, or my father, you can rest assured they will not settle for a buyout. And, it seems they know enough to manage a successful business of their own. But I think you are right, we will just have to wait and see about their character. Do you know anything of their reputation?"

"The investigator suggested that they are well liked by their patrons, but nothing further."

"Well, I guess we shall see tomorrow." Thomas set his empty glass down on a nearby table, as did Captain Abbott, and the men rose to leave. "Do you think, Captain, that my mother will recover from this?" Thomas's face was cast in a shadow. "She seems to have aged this past week, and I fear the stress of it all may be too much for her nerves."

297

"Pah!" Captain Abbott spit the word out of his mouth. "The day something is *too much* for Margaret is the day the earth stops spinning. She is the strongest woman I know, Thomas, tougher than you and I combined. Mark my words, son, she will get through this and be stronger for it."

Chapter 38

Mother Morgan was relaxing on the settee when Libby softly rapped upon the half-opened door. She poked her head into the room and said, "Mother Morgan, may I come in?"

"Yes, dear, do come in."

"Father asked me to let you know dinner would be served at seven. Are you feeling well enough to join us today?" It had been nearly two days since finding out her daughters were alive, and in that time, Mother Morgan had remained confined to her chambers. She had taken her meals alone in her room and hadn't even joined the other women around Libby's quilt. Worried that her grandmother was taking the news far worse than expected, Libby decided that she would see if she could brighten her grandmother's mood.

"Oh my, is it that late already?" Her grandmother looked up from her Bible and glanced at the window.

"No, it's not for a few hours yet, I just wanted to let you know well in advance of the time so you could prepare if you wanted to take supper with the family." Libby was trying to be kind and not push, but she missed her grandmother during meals. Dining was far too formal with the Abbotts, and Mother Morgan brought Libby reassurance when she was beside her at the table. "We have nearly finished the quilting, you know. It goes so fast when there are so many hands doing the work. I will need your assistance finishing the edges tomorrow, I think. Do you suppose you would like to help me select a fabric for the edging?"

Libby thought Mother Morgan's countenance seemed improved, though she was not fully returned to her normal self.

"I have been giving that some thought, Libby," Mother Morgan said with a half smile. She folded her Bible closed and set it upon the table then patted the open seat on the settee next to her. "As I remember, your Grandmother Abbott has a rather large spool of woven tape on a shelf in her closet. It is something she paid one of her staff to weave. They both agreed upon a price per meter, and within the week the girl brought her the spool. Imagine your Grandmother Abbott's surprise when the girl showed up with one hundred meters of twill tape! It seems they had agreed upon a price, but not an amount. But Caroline is a woman of her word, so she paid the girl and thanked her immensely for such fine workmanship. I remember now the letter she wrote telling me about the twill tape and how angry your grandfather was for having to pay for such an expense. I asked her the other day if she had any of that famous twill tape left, and she giggled and showed it to me. When I saw it, I thought immediately that it would be a lovely edge treatment for your quilt. The mix of colors will accent the edge of your quilt nicely, and I think it much simpler to finish than to turn the edges in on themselves."

"Perhaps tonight at dinner you can suggest to Grandmama that I use the tape for my quilt." Libby thought herself very clever in suggesting Mother Morgan make the request at dinner.

"Cheeky girl . . . I haven't said yet that I was coming down for dinner, have I?" She looked at her granddaughter and winked then added, "But since you seem overly concerned, I *will* join you all this evening. I would hate to think my condition has caused any distress. Besides, I think I've found what I was looking for, and it has eased my mind considerably."

300

"What do you mean? What were you looking for?" Libby wondered what Mother Morgan could possibly have found—she hadn't left her room in days.

"Ammunition, child, simple ammunition to help me get through this ordeal."

"I don't understand, Grandmother."

"When I am confused, Libby, when I am unsure or otherwise frightened about what to do, I generally do nothing for a day or so. I spend some quiet time reflecting on the circumstances and try to look at the situation from all angles. This is a solitary process for me, and it often involves long hours of forming questions, and then many more hours in consultation looking for answers to those questions." Mother Morgan paused.

"Whom do you consult?" Libby was perplexed, for she knew her grandmother had been alone and without visitors these past few days.

"That, my dear, is the tricky part, and why sometimes it takes longer than others. I do not consult a single person. I consult my Lord and Savior!" She paused again then added, "And since I am neither prophetess nor seer, it often takes time to figure out the answer. But eventually, the Lord reveals Himself, and I know what I am to do. My Bible plays an important role in the process. Just reading His word can calm my spirit; so often the problems which affect my life are similar to those in the Bible stories. So I read . . . and I read . . . and I pray . . . and eventually, my heart is calmed, and I feel like I can make a move in a direction that I know is right for me. It helps me to feel empowered. Do you understand?"

Libby looked up at her grandmother's tired eyes and asked softly, "And what has the Lord revealed to you this day, Grandmother?"

"Faith, child . . . He has reminded me that I must carry a shield of faith to guard against the arrows of the evil one, arrows of lies that seek to plant fear in my heart. He tells me to have faith which believes that even the dead can be resurrected if it be His will!"

Chapter 39

$\mathcal{A}$s their coach pulled up in front of the millinery shop, Libby watched as Mother Morgan tried to calm her shaking hands by grasping her handkerchief. She knew her grandmother's fear of rejection was mingling with the anticipation of seeing the daughters she'd thought long dead. Libby hoped their conversation about faith the night before would give her the resolve she needed to get out of the coach and walk through the shop door. Libby was herself quite anxious, and as she looked at the other occupants in the coach, she surmised that everyone was of the same mind.

Grandfather Abbott and Libby's father had been to the shop the day before and spoken with the two women, both of who were shocked and overcome to the point of closing their business for the remainder of the day. When Libby's father asked if they may return on the morrow with their mother, both women broke down and sobbed into their handkerchiefs inconsolably. They did, however, agree it best to meet her as soon as possible, and so encouraged the men to return.

As the family opened the shop door, a tinkling bell rang out, and Libby noticed that the sign in the window indicated the shop was closed. She caught a glimpse of a fluffy gray-and-white cat slinking off into the back of the shop, and she thought it wonderful that her new-found aunties were also fond of kitties—that was something they all had in common.

The two sisters stepped into the shop from the back room, and Libby was taken aback by their appearance. The women were identical in feature, and were it not for the difference in their dress color, Libby was sure she would not be able to tell them apart. Libby thought their hair color, full lips, and front teeth resembled her Aunt Ellen's. Even the way they carried their hands as they walked reminded her of her aunt back home in America.

Upon seeing them again, Grandfather Abbott offered his warmest smile as they joined the family in the main part of the store. "Good afternoon, ladies. It is a pleasure to see you again." He bowed more formally than normal and said, "It is my sincerest pleasure to introduce to you Mrs. Margaret Jane Morgan, lately of America." He turned and gestured to Mother Morgan and then said, "Margaret, I would like to introduce you to Miss Ruth Callingham and," he gestured to the other sister, "Miss Rosemary Callingham."

The sisters both bobbed at nearly the same time, and Libby marveled again at their exactness. She wondered how her grandfather knew which sister was which. Mother Morgan stepped closer and extended her hand. Rosemary also stepped forward and took her hand, and the two women stood for a moment holding on to one another. "I have prayed so long for this day to come," Mother Morgan squeaked out the words, "and now that it has, I hardly know what to say."

"Words cannot express how we feel, Mrs. Morgan." Rosemary clutched Mother Morgan with one hand and then reached for her sister with her other. Ruth took her sister's hand and reached for Mother Morgan, and the three stood in a circle holding on to one another. Finally, persuaded by the awkward silence, they released hands, and Ruth gestured for Mother Morgan to take a seat in a nearby chair. Rosemary looked at Libby's father and smiled. "It is good to see you again so soon, Thomas." She looked earnestly at Libby and said, "And this must be Elizabeth." She extended her hand and Libby accepted it and then found herself pulled into Rosemary's arms in a tender embrace.

A tear ran down Rosemary's cheek as she stood back from Libby, took her hands again, and said, "I have no words to say . . . what you have given back to Ruth and I . . . the joy you have brought to us. Your grandfather explained that it was you we have to thank, but saying thank you does not seem to be enough."

Rosemary's hands were gloved in lace, but even shrouded as they were, Libby could tell that they were larger than normal and slightly gnarled and rough. They reminded Libby of Mother Morgan's hands— strong and aged from overwork.

"I'm very pleased to meet you, Miss Callingham." Libby curtsied slowly, as though greeting royalty. Ruth stepped up, and Libby and was again embraced for a tender moment and kissed upon the top of her head, then she was released to find her seat with the others.

The two sisters were in chairs nearest Mother Morgan, and Libby watched as they sat together quietly looking into one another's eyes. Rosemary could no longer contain her emotion; she threw herself onto the floor at Mother Morgan's feet, laid her head in the woman's lap, and wept inconsolably. She occasionally tried to talk but was unable to form words that did not involve snuffles and snorts. Ruth sat in her chair, quietly weeping into her hands, so Mother Morgan extended her arm, inviting the woman to join them again. Ruth quickly dropped to the floor, embraced her sister, and laid her own head onto her newfound mother's lap.

Libby watched the tender scene play out as Mother Morgan stroked the two women's hair while murmuring comforting words as only a mother knows how. Libby's father came and stood behind his mother and placed his hand upon her shoulder. He bent down and embraced all three women as a tear rolled down his cheek.

Libby was feeling a little uncomfortable because she was actually grinning from ear to ear instead of crying like the rest of the occupants in the shop, so she looked up at Grandfather Abbott to see his reaction to the reunion. He, too, was smiling broadly. She caught his eye, and he waved for her to join him, so she went and stood next to his char. "Well done, Libby, dear," he said as he patted her on the back. "Well done! We all have you to thank for this glorious day of reunion."

Epilogue

$\mathcal{L}$ ibby was surprised to see her mother's condition as she stepped out of the coach in front of their tiny row house in Boston. There she was, standing on the porch with her arms outstretched, waiting for her family. James ran to his wife, threw his arms around her waist, and lifted her from the ground as he buried his face in her neck. He spun around then gently placed her feet back on the ground and stepped backward, leaving his hands on her swelling belly.

Libby could see his surprised expression and hear her mother's laugh. Thinking of the child to come, she was glad her father had decided not to stay at Braidsmuir after all. Crossing the Atlantic was perilous enough for anyone, but imagining her mother doing it alone and with child was unthinkable. She clutched a large package to her chest as she walked toward her mother; her heart bittersweet in the knowledge she would have to share about Mother Morgan.

The lawyers had declared Libby's father legal heir to the Montclief Estate, and because Ruth and Rosemary were also considered heirs to the estate, the sisters were able to fulfill the stipulation of 'an heir' living at Braidsmuir so that 'the heir' could inherit the property. One tiny little two-letter word mistakenly written into the will had allowed Libby's father to return home to America and still be found the legal heir to an English nobleman's estate.

The sisters had graciously accepted their newfound family, happy for the opportunity to sell their shop and live at Braidsmuir with a generous allowance. Rosemary had longed for a better education; the minimal amount of schooling she had received left her hungry for more, but the need for self-sufficiency had kept her desires at bay. Freed now from the chains of labor, and with money at her disposal, Rosemary was excited to pursue her new life, learning from hired tutors and the opportunities that come from wealth beyond necessity.

Ruth, the more tenderhearted of the two, though less ambitious of any formal education, was no less fruitful in her enterprise. She had decided that her hours free from the labors of the shop would now be spent in fulfilling some of the Baron's desires—she would volunteer much of her time and significant sums of money at the Foundling Hospital, helping to educate the children in the industry of sewing.

As she walked toward the house, Libby could see her mother looking toward the coach, and her heart sank a bit knowing she was looking for Grandmother. "Where is Mother Morgan?" she asked.

"We have much to tell you, Mary," Libby's father said with wide eyes and a glowing smile. "Come inside and we shall reveal all."

But she ignored her husband as she opened her arms to Libby. "My sweet girl, how I have longed to hold you in my arms. I've missed you so these past months. My goodness, you look so mature in that dress—is it new? And look, you must have grown a foot since last we were together." She hugged her daughter again and again.

Libby looked at her mother's growing belly and said with a smile, "It seems you are growing as well!"

"It is grand, isn't it, dear?" Libby's mother rubbed her belly and said, "I so wanted to tell you," she grabbed her husband's arm, "but I knew if I wrote you about it, you would want to come home immediately and perhaps leave your business unfinished. Besides, the easy part was early on, it's now that I am in need of the help." She led her small family back inside their cozy home.

"Ah," Libby's father sighed as he crossed into the parlor and spied his favorite chair, "it is so good to be home."

The family sat together as Libby explained all. Her mother's shocked expression caused Libby to tear up just a bit as he told of the reunion between Mother Morgan and her daughters. When she told of how Mother Morgan had decided to stay in England, to stay with her girls and live at Braidsmuir for at least the next five years, Libby's mother cried tears of joy for Mother Morgan's newfound happiness. "I wondered how it was going to be for her now that Ellen is married. They'll be doing a good bit of traveling with John's business ventures, and I daresay once the boys are in school, Mother Morgan would have felt like a bit of a third wheel. I am so glad she has found her daughters, and gladder still that they want her with them. It must have taken great courage to meet them—especially after so many years of them thinking she had left them as orphans, and her thinking they were dead."

"They are quite lovely women, don't you agree, Libby?" her father asked.

"Yes, they are. It is uncanny how similar they looked to each other. I still don't know how Grandfather could tell them apart." Libby sipped the tea her mother had waiting for them and continued to tell her mother all about her passage to England and her new friends, Gertrude and Finnian. She told of the dinner with the ship's captain and the famous opera singer, and how Finn had been discovered that night, and how Grandfather had come to his aid. She went on to explain how Father had been unable to find the boy's family in Glasgow, and how Grandfather had taken Finn on as apprentice and cabin boy. "Grandfather promised Finn he would dispatch an investigator to Australia in order to locate Mr. McAlister. Isn't that kind of him, Mother?"

"Your grandfather is a generous man, Libby. Now, tell me, what is in the wrapper?" she asked curiously, motioning toward the package Libby had brought home.

"Ah, I almost forgot!" Libby jumped from her seat and grabbed the large package and opened it carefully. It was her finished quilt. She spread it open for her mother to see. They all stood around the quilt, and her mother praised Libby's fine workmanship. "I especially love the Turkey red backing fabric and the twill tape edging."

Libby smiled at the compliments her mother showered on her. She ran her hand over the quilt and thought about the many hours she had invested making it. It gave her a feeling of accomplishment to know that her hand had worked the fabrics to create something so lovely. She thought about all the help she had received; her mother, aunts, grandmothers, and cousins had all participated in making her quilt, and knowing that the stories from so many letters had been stitched into the layers of her bedcovering made Libby feel special.

"What is that, just there?" her mother asked, pointing at a corner of the quilt.

"What?" Libby answered and pulled up the corner where her mother had pointed.

To her surprise, appliquéd onto the back of her quilt, she found two tiny, pink hearts, one dirtier than the other, and each cross-stitched with a tiny letter "R."

She thought for a moment about the hearts. "R" for Ruth and "R" for Rosemary. She touched the pink fabric and knew in her heart that Mother Morgan had stitched them there. But it wasn't just for the names of her newfound daughters that Mother Morgan had stitched the letter "R." Libby knew it was meant to serve as a reminder of the Resurrection, and of the Reunion of hearts that would never be parted again.

Glossary of Textile Terms

*T*he following textile and quilting terms are found throughout the story. Their definitions are provided here:

Applique – A needlework technique in which patterns or representation scenes are created by applying smaller pieces of fabric onto a larger, contrasting piece.

Block Printed – A hand printing technique where dyestuff and mordant are transferred to fabric by means of hand carved wood blocks. This process of printing was eventually replaced by plate, cylinder or screen-printing.

Blocks (or Patches) – The smaller, sub-units that make up a spread or quilt. Can be comprised of simple or very complicated geometric shapes. Sometimes comprised of shapes cut from other fabric and applied (appliqued) onto a ground fabric. Blocks can come in a wide variety of shapes and sizes.

Blue Resist – An 18th and 19th century method of indigo printing in which a resist paste inhibits the dye from getting on the fabric during the dye bath.

Chintz – A glazed cotton cloth of plain weave. Block printed in the 18th and early 19th century. First manufactured in India, then imitated elsewhere. Printed designs usually have at least five colors and are frequently large-scale floral patterns.

Chintz Cut-Out – Also known as 'broderie purse' - French for 'Persian embroidery' is a style of appliqué embroidery which uses printed elements to create a scene on the background fabric.

Counterpane – Can be a blanket, quilt or woven coverlet, hemmed or fringed piece of cloth, lined or unlined - used to conceal the undermost bedclothes. Today we refer to them as bed spreads.

Delaine – A lightweight, finely combed wool dress fabric made in a variety of colors and prints: sometimes from the Delaine Marino breed of sheep, but not always.

Glazed – Used with the term Chintz (glazed chintz) - A piece of chintz having a smooth and lustrous surface on the exposed, or right, side only. Cotton fabrics may be glazed with starch, glue, paraffin or shellac and polished with a hot roller; these finishes do not survive washing.

Godey's Lady's Book – An American magazine published from 1830 through 1877 focused on women's interests such as music, fashion and literature.

Huswif – Also called 'housewife' or 'sewing roll-up' - a small and portable rolled sewing tool kit holding the necessary items for sewing. Most often made from small pieces of fabric (cotton, linen or wool) and sometimes tied closed with woven tape.

Indigo – A plant based material in use for many centuries to dye fabric blue.

Lapis Blue – A color combination print style where indigo blue was printed adjacent to madder red without a white or black outline. Prior to 1808 this printing technique did not exist.

Madder – Plant based dyestuff - Eurasian herb used in dyeing to produce a moderate to strong red color or shades of purple, brown and pink depending upon the mordant used. The term 'madder' is often used to describe the color - e.g., madder red.

Mosaic – The art of creating images using small pieces of material such as fabric, glass or stone. Quilts comprised of many small hexagons are sometimes referred to as mosaic quilts

Ombre Print – Also known as Rainbow - a textile printing technique in which color or color value blends from one to the next without separation. Popular in America textiles in the 1830s

Palampore – A cotton bed covering from India, usually printed or painted with large-scale, highly naturalistic designs, often of tree of life.

Picotage – Design or area formed of tiny specks or dots were used to provide shadowing or accent to a printed design on cloth. Sometimes used as the ground design of a printed textile.

Prussian Blue – A greenish-blue mineral dye with a more vibrant blue tone than indigo. This dye was popular with textile printers in the United States from about the 1830s up to before the Civil War.

Spread – Unquilted bed covering with finished edges. Sometimes used interchangeably with 'counterpane' or 'summer spread.'

Toile de Jouy – Sometimes referred to as just Toile - generally refers to a copperplate-printed fabric in monochromatic colors with multiple scenes depicting a variety of subjects. Historically popular as a furnishing fabric, though has been found occasionally in costumes.

Turkey Red – An extremely bright, clear and colorfast red dye derived from an ancient, multistep dye process involving oils.

Twill Tape – Also known as 'woven tape' or 'tape' - Woven narrow strips, plain or striped, used to bind raw edges of fabric, cover seams and accent the outline of upholstery goods of all sorts. Often made at home on small looms.

Wadding – Also known as 'batting' - large sheets of carded fibers that are used for interlinings in quilts, comforters and some clothing. Historically cotton or wool has been used, but sometimes worn quilts, blankets or thin sheets will be seen. The term 'wadding' is more commonly used when referring to a thicker interlining.